The
Excalibur
Parchment

The Excalibur Parchment

To Bev + Alvin Morgan

Enjoy

Barrie Doyle

Barrie Doyle

Book One - The Oak Grove Conspiracies

THE EXCALIBUR PARCHMENT
Copyright © 2014 by Barrie Doyle

All rights reserved. Neither this publication nor any part of this publication may be reproduced or transmitted in any form or by any means, electronic or mechanical, including photocopying, recording or any information storage and retrieval system, without permission in writing from the author.

This is a work of fiction. Names, characters, places and incidents either are the product of the author's imagination or are used fictitiously, and any resemblance to actual persons, living or dead, businesses, companies, events, or locales is entirely coincidental.

Printed in Canada

ISBN: 978-1-4866-0616-0

Word Alive Press
131 Cordite Road, Winnipeg, MB R3W 1S1
www.wordalivepress.ca

Cataloguing in Publication may be obtained through Library and Archives Canada

For Kathryn, Karen and Laurie, who encouraged me and kept me pressing on through this whole crazy ride and whose unwavering support was incredible.

Alone with none but thee, my God,
I journey on my way.
What need I fear,
when thou art near O king of night and day?
More safe am I within thy hand
Than if a host did round me stand

—Prayer of St. Columba

Pronunciation Guide

B

Bach	as in the composer; a term of friendship and endearment; meaning small, or little one
Banwen	"*ban-wen*"; high, bleak upland moors
Bedwyr	"*bed-oor*"; companion to King Arthur, one of the Knights of the Round Table
Belenos	"*bell-en-os*"; Celtic god of shining light; Celtic honor name given to Ogmios agent
Bryn	"*brin*"; hill, small mountain
Bryn Penbarryn	"*brin Pen-bar-rin*"; fictional mountain in south Wales

C

Cymllyn Abbey	"*Coom - th -line*"; fictional abbey in South Wales
Coity	"*Coy-tee*"; castle located north east of Bridgend, in South Wales

D

Da	as it looks; Welsh diminutive for Father
Dyfrig	"*Dif-rig*"; early Welsh Christian saint

E-G

Gwynfi	"*gwin-vee*"

H-L

Huw	*Hugh*
Llanmerdynn	"*thlan-mer-th-inn*"; Sons of Lleu compound near Carmarthen, Wales; "th" soft as in 'thin';
LLanffyron	"*thlan–vi–ron*"; church named after St. Byron, squire to Bedwyr. Welsh language often interchanges letters,

	looking more to sound rather than letters. Thus "ff" is pronounced as "v"
Lleu	"thl-ew"; Celtic god; name of the Welsh Druidic movement led by Rhiannon

M-N

Maesgwynfi	"Ma-yes G-win-vee"; fictional village located near Bridgend, S. Wales
Maes Haberth	"Ma-yes Ha-berth; means fields of sacrifice
Merdynn	"mer-th-inn"; hard 'th' as in "the", not soft as in "thin"
Mynydd	"min-ith"; mountain; hard 'th' as in "the"

O-P

Pen-y-Bont	"Pen-ee-bont" Welsh name for Bridgend, market town located 20 miles west of Cardif

R-S

Rhiannon	"Ree-ann-on"; leader of Sons of Lleu and overall leader of the Druids

T-Z

Taranis	As it sounds; Celtic god of thunder and war
Tir Iarll	"tear – ee—arl; The "Earl's land"; a portion of Glamorgan north of Bridgend and west of Cardiff, encompassing several valleys, open moors, mountains, and streams. Taken from the Welsh inhabitants by Norman conquerors
Tuatha	"Too-a-tha"; Celtic/Druidic movement in Ireland named after the Tuatha De Danann, a Irish/Celt mythical people derived from the old Celtic gods
Yns Mons	"inn-iss Mons"; Druids' holy island; modern day Anglesey in North Wales

Barrie Doyle

List of Characters

United States

Stone Wallace	American Journalist
Pierre Aubin	1st Secretary, French Embassy, Washington
Chad Lawson	DC Police Detective and SID agent
Greg Michaels	charter boat operator, upstate New York
Liam Murphy	Senator, Presidential candidate

London and Wales

Huw Griffiths	Welsh historian and professor
Myfanwy (Mandy) Griffiths	Huw Griffith's daughter; historian, university professor
Rhiannon	Dragon Master
Damien Wyndham	Business mogul; Second-in-command to Dragon Master
Colin Maddox	Crown agent
Freddy Garret	Crown agent
Sir Giles Broadbent	Crown chief
Will Hamilton	Crown agent
Keith Rumford	Crown agent
John Fowler	Crown agent
Will Hamilton	Crown agent
Keith Rumford	Crown agent
John Fowler	Crown agent
Carys Bromley	Druid agent
Charlotte Thackery	Crown agent

Wales, 1300's

Thomas of Gwent	Welsh monk, 1300's
Godfrey of Ashforth	Abbot of Cwmllyn Abbey, Wales 1301
Gethin of Yns Mons	Sacrist of Cwmllyn Abbey; Druid leader
Brother Emlyn	Sub-sacrist of Cwmllyn Abbey; Druid

The Excalibur Parchment

Brother Owain	monk of Cwmllyn Abbey
Prior Edwin	Prior of Cwmllyn Abbey,
Sir Bedwyr	Companion of King Arthur, circa 490 AD
Byron	Squire to Sir Bedwyr; priest St. Dyffrig's (near Cwmllyn)
Alys	Village girl, betrothed to Owain
Lord Payne de Tuberville	Lord of Glamorgan, 1301

Brittany, France

Andre Tonnerre (Le Patron)	Breton; leader of Taranis faction
Jean-Marc Hebert	Tonnerre assistant
"Belenos"/Louis Carveau	Tonnerre's security chief

Venice, Italy

Giovanni Bertucci	Venetian bookseller
Mario Bertucci	cousin to Giovanni
Father Joseph Panterra	Vatican medieval historian

Places

Beauvais	Village in Brittany, France
Bridgend	Market town in South Wales
Broceliande Forest	Brittany, west of Rennes
Bryn Penbarryn	Fictional mountain in South Wales
Budleigh Hampton	Fictional village in Buckinghamshire, near London
Caernarfon	Town in North Wales
Cardiff	Capital city of Wales
Careg Cennan	Castle ruins near Carmarthen, West Wales
Carmarthen	Market town, West Wales
Castell y Gwinfi	Ruins of castle near Bridgend, Wales
Chantilly	Virginia suburb of Washington, DC
Coity Castle	Castle near Bridgend, Wales
Cymllyn	Fictional village and abbey in South Wales
Euston Station	Main line railway station in London, England
Glamorgan	Old name for county and Norman holdings in South Wales
Helsinki	Capital city of Finland
Llanffyron	Fictional village near Bridgend, Wales
Llanmerddyn	Fictional Druid compound near Carmarthen, West Wales
London	Capital city of United Kingdom
Maesgwinfi	Fictional village near Bridgend, Wales
Maes Haberth	Fictional Druid grove and sacrificial ground, near Bridgend, Wales
Mynydd Margam	Mountain near Margam, South Wales
New Forest	old forest located south and west of Southampton, England
Paimpont	Small town in Brittany, France
Rennes	City in Brittany, France
St. Brigitte	Fictional Druid compound, Brittany, France
St. David's	Cathedral town in West Wales
Tir Iarll	Moors and mountain uplands, north and west of Bridgend Wales

Venice — Italian city
Washington DC — Capital city, United States

Celtic Gods

Arawn	King of the Otherworld; ruler of the old gods
Cerunnos	God of the underworld; the 'horned one'
Belenos	God of fire; God of the Sun
Brigitte	Goddess of fire and water; one of key Celtic goddesses
Lleu	Welsh god; "the shadowy one"; also known as Lugh (Ireland)
Danu	Goddess of creation; the universal mother
Ogmios	God of oratory and eloquence

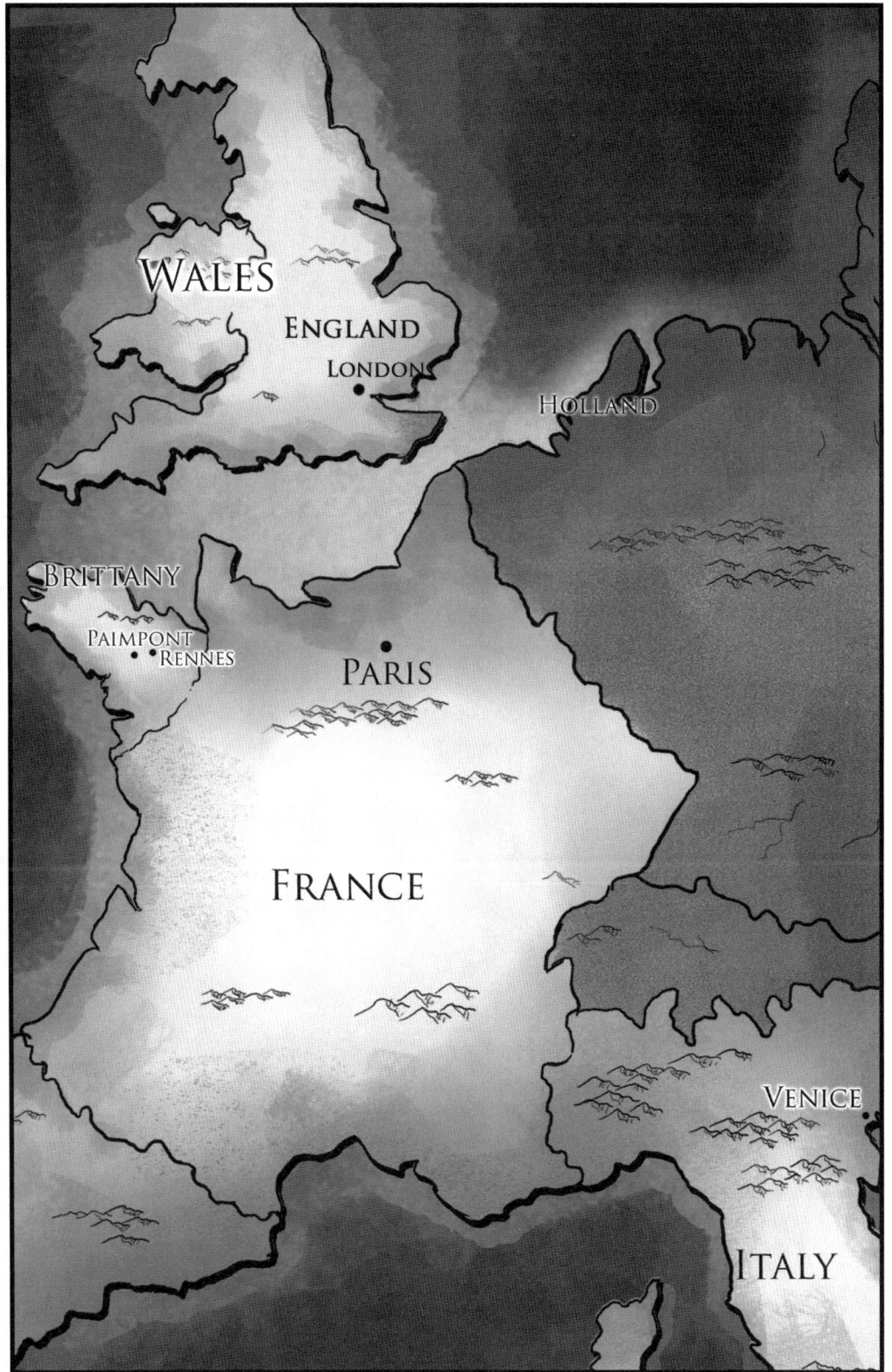

WALES

- Yns Mons (Anglesey)
- Irish Sea
- St David's
- Carmarthen
- Careg Cennan
- Swansea
- Cymllyn Abbey
- Margam Abbey
- Maesgwinfi
- Coity Castle
- Caerleon
- Newport
- Cardiff
- Bristol Channel

Prologue

Wales, Spring 1345 • Llanffyron Church

I alone survive who knows the secret of Excalibur.

I sat still, reveling yet again in the beauty of the sparkling sunset. Fingers of grey-pink cloud spread across the entire valley, sprinkled with the oranges, fire reds, merry yellows as well as the grey-whites of the topmost clouds. All painted against the glowing sunlight and the dark greens of the valleys. God himself was illuminating his own manuscript. And I was humbled yet again thinking of my own puny efforts of illuminating when I was in the Abbey Scriptorium.

I was perched on a moss covered rock peering down on the valley and tiny village of Maesgwynfi. The rock was an unpleasant place to sit. Its sharp, dagger-like edges poked and prodded my old body in places and ways that ever reminded me of my physical and spiritual mortality. But it was my special place of prayer and penitence. A place where I could look out over the village I served and also the secret I was sworn to protect.

The blackness which still inhabited my soul, the doubts and fears, come back too often for all that I hear that men call me a good and kindly brother. God knows differently. He knows how much and how many times I fail him.

Behind me I sensed the strength of the solid grey stones of the church—my church! It was not a sense of pride—God forbid—that embraced my thoughts that morning. It was a recognition of truth. Llanffyron. A place of God dedicated to St. Byron, squire to Sir Bedwyr; he who served King Arthur. The church I built to remember the sacrifices of those who died to protect the secret.

I have so often pleaded with God to release me from my vow of silence about Excalibur. I have argued with him that the story must be told. I begged for someone I could confess to that God would let me share my story with others around me.

I swore before God to Abbot Godfrey that I would not reveal the mystery of the sword and I had kept my promise. But the situation changed I told God, and therefore I should not be held to my earlier pledge. Generations of holy, sainted abbots preserved it for seven hundred years in the shielding, cloistered confines of our lonely, unimposing Cwmllyn Abbey. But now, of all the monks at Cwmllyn, of all the monks in Britain, of all the monks in Christendom, I was the only one who knew about Excalibur.

It was not fair, I rebuked God. I had been condemned to pain, sacrifice, and suffering, battling wickedness at its most terrible yet condemned to do it in silence. It was not just, I repeated to Him over and over and was He not the God of justice? I wrestled mightily with Him, much as did Jacob in the Holy Scriptures.

But I battled with myself as well as God; such was the conflict in my soul. For if I was to tell, then my hearer would be open to the assails of hell, an embattlement of evils they could not even begin to fathom. For as surely as the grass is green and the sky blue, anyone I shared the tale with would suffer the assault of powers beyond this earth. Could I lay such heaviness on the soul and mind of any of my fellow men? And even if I could choose someone, who would I sacrifice—for sacrifice it would indeed be—burdening him with a knowledge that could likely mean his death and probably countless others as well. The power of the pagan Druids would be unleashed against a defenceless man. Could I, before God, condemn him in such a way as I felt condemned? Every time I came to this clear thought, I fell to my knees in grateful humbleness and adoration that God had protected me and preserved my life, unworthy though it was.

In the cool, dark nights over the past weeks, I sensed God speak to me. His soft whisper penetrated my mind and then pierced my heavy heart. Keep the story for others yet to come, his soft voice said. Speak to no one yet living, but take up a quill and record the story for those who will need to fight this evil, generations after you have gone. My dreams and visions became stronger and more vivid. Write, he said. Write. I asked him who I should reveal the writing to. The answer came in the rippling wind that he would choose the one to read at a time and place of his choosing. My only task was to set the story down.

As the sun so gloriously set that evening, I dropped to my knees and surrendered my will to him yet again. I continued to kneel in prayer for some time. The lingering warmth of the sun transformed itself into the warmth of God penetrating my soul; the sunset's luminous brilliance reflected the new understanding of my heart. Below me, the green trees and meadows, the glistening water of the river and the muted sounds of wood chopping, cattle lowing and horses whinnying reminded me of the newness and freshness of life renewed. I poured out my thanksgiving to God. The decision made, I felt a lightness of spirit for the first time in many months, nay years.

The old moss covered rock serves me well as a penitent place these days but it is still sharp, hard and unyielding to my old body. I tire so easily. My chest heaves and wheezes and my joints ache. I struggled to regain my feet, my knees protesting in agony as I pulled myself up to stand renewed.

A stiff cool breeze swirled around my habit. Along with darkening clouds it was a portent of rains to come tonight. I did not mind. While some men cursed the rain for the miserable cold it often brought, I saw the coldest soaking rains as a friend; a God-sent friend. So many times those rains had protected me in times of dire circumstance when my life was nearly forfeit. Those following after Noah had the rainbow to remind them of his protection and presence. I had the icy, soaking Welsh rains.

This evening, I finished prayers at Compline and heard confession as I always do. But I grow weary. My memory acts passing strange these days. Truly, I remember things from many years past as vivid as the day they happened. Yet I confess I struggle to recollect those that happened last week or last month.

I lit the taper and sat at the table and pulled a parchment towards me. It was time. As the blessed Saint Paul said, I have fought the good fight. I see that I am now finishing my course.

If I am to tell my story in truth, I must begin at the beginning. I swear before God Almighty that the words that follow are the truth.

Chapter One

Washington D.C.; May

If the human body could radiate the heat of anger, the man sitting opposite Stone Wallace would have fried to a crisp ten minutes ago.

Stone sat at the restaurant table pushing his knife and fork angrily around the food, playing with it rather than enjoying it. He clenched his utensils so tightly they almost bent under the stress. For the past five minutes he'd been on the receiving end of a vitriolic verbal assault. Time now to end this charade, he thought, painfully aware he'd made a mistake in agreeing to the lunch. It was intriguing too, since he thought the French embassy surely had more critical things to think about after the French President's horrific assassination two days previously. Images of the bloodied bodies and burned out cars around the Elysee Palace dominated newscasts while pundits in print and on the air pontificated on the identity of the unknown killers. With the French President, his wife and four bodyguards dead and up to a dozen wounded, the French nation was tottering on the edge of chaos while Paris was a city in lockdown. Why should an American article on a bunch of religious nuts in Brittany warrant this kind of Embassy attention, he wondered?

Stone's verbal assailant, bald head bobbing up and down as he shoveled food into his mouth, continued speaking, aware of the tense body across from him but determined to force this American trifle to submit.

"Simply put, M'sieur Wallace, my government cannot allow these lies to remain unanswered. The story must be retracted and you must apologize. The honor of the French people demands it!" Pierre Aubin, the thin-faced, sharp-jawed First Secretary of the French Embassy, jabbed his knife at Stone to emphasize his demand.

"The Taranis movement in Paimpont are a good, devout people bringing increased tourism to the region. You assaulted a religion as well as the innocent people of Brittany when you wrote that story." He sniffed as if the air around him had an unpleasant odor and glared at Stone, daring him to respond.

Stone's recent series of articles in the *Washington Herald* had loosed a furious response from the French embassy, a response he found initially amusing, then puzzling, then aggravating. The stories documented a rapidly growing, aggressive group in Brittany called Taranis who exemplified a startling revival of ancient pagan rituals cloaked under a Druid banner, The cult was based near the small Breton village of Paimpont and their military-like security, excessive hostility and sometimes brutal treatment of non-Taranians, had split opinion in Brittany. Many hated the thought of what one local official had called "a poison in our presence", while others enjoyed the new-found tourist money and interest. Stone was proud of the stories, reckoning they elevated him above the usual travel pieces that highlighted only foods, sights, drinks and accommodations. He penetrated the generally unseen unique aspects of a place.

An angry war of words between Stone, the newspaper and the Embassy culminated in Aubin's demand for a formal lunch 'to clarify our position'.

Wallace glared at the pompous Frenchman, not allowing emotions to show on his face. He suddenly slammed his knife onto the table in front of him. Simmering, he forced his words between strained lips, his six foot frame tensed and rigid.

"For the past ten minutes, M. Aubin, all you've done is spew accusations about my work, challenged my integrity as a journalist and insulted me personally. Not once have you offered a shred of evidence to back up your claims." Stone held his hand up in front of the Frenchman to stop an interruption. "As your government's representative, I get that your job is to protect French interests in this country. But I did my job too. And it was accurate."

Stone white-knuckled the table and leaned across. His icy tone spit out the words, his steel blue eyes glaring intently at his target. "Every word I wrote is true. You have a nest of vipers—Druid vipers and religious nuts—in Brittany and your government is doing nothing about it. You asked for this meeting, but unless you have some facts—facts mind you, not opinion or propaganda—this lunch is over!" Stone threw some bills onto the table. "My share" he barked and stalked out, leaving a slack-jawed Aubin staring at his retreating back.

Outside, Stone allowed himself a brief cheerless smile. If Aubin thought the *Herald* article was a problem, wait till he caught the piece he'd produced for the Independent News Network's weekly public affairs show. He gave a quick snort and without a backwards glance headed toward his office. The strong warm breeze played across his neck as his wiry frame strode determinedly down the sidewalk, grim-faced and barely concealing his still boiling internal fury.

Traffic blared and rushed by. As he stormed along even the passersby added to his frustration. First a woman stopped suddenly in the middle of the sidewalk causing Stone and another woman to bump into her. Then at the stop light a student more intent on his iPod than other pedestrians, swung a backpack into him. Everyone in Washington, it seemed, was in hurry. Lobbyists, staffers and hangers-on crowded the streets and office buildings of the capital eagerly swapping any particle of gossip or information, angling always to better themselves or their clientele. Surely the remaining crowds—the non-political ones—could at least slow down and follow a more languid lifestyle, Stone muttered to himself. But no. This was Washington and everyone and everything was important—self delusional or not—and all had to be done at double speed. Such was life in what some called the center of the universe.

The lights changed and Stone crossed the 14th Street and G intersection quickly, snaked through the crowds and ducked into the lobby of his office building. The elevator stopped at the tenth floor and he stalked rapidly down the hall and into the cramped office he shared with four other freelancers.

Piccadilly Street, London

Colin Maddox slammed the cab door shut and stormed towards the hotel entrance. Worry and frustration were etched on his face. He ignored the revolving door, flinging open a side door in aggravation instead. He strode in, rushing through the sedate chandeliered foyer, a leather underarm briefcase jammed against his body as he muscled his way through more doors into the refined, quiet atmosphere of the restaurant. Only the subdued chatter of the patrons, the quiet clinking of tea cups and the sedate melodies of a harpist broke the silence.

Halfway up the room he smiled as he saw an impeccably dressed man sitting at a table that backed against the restaurant wall, his blue pinstriped suit, white shirt and conservative striped red and blue tie contrasting with a tee-shirted, slightly overweight camera-clad tourist at the next table beyond him.

Maddox slid into a velvet covered chair opposite. Before he could speak, the man nodded. "The Guvnor will meet with us momentarily, Colin. We have much to discuss." He signaled to a hovering waiter.

"Tea? As the waiter poured, Maddox anxiously drummed his fingers on the table. The ritual complete, the waiter left.

"Freddy, you're sure Sir Giles is aware of the need for action as quickly as possible?" Maddox eyed the always sartorial elegance of his boss' deputy.

"That's why he pushed his schedule to meet you here and asked me to attend. He doesn't normally mix business with pleasure at his favorite lunch spot unless he's convinced it's vital."

Lifting his teacup to his mouth, Freddy was about to say more when he suddenly nodded his head towards the rear of the room. Maddox twisted in place and saw Sir Giles Broadbent, director of the Crown Security Branch breezing his way through the lounge towards them.

"Fred, Colin." Sir Giles nodded at each and eased his huge bulk into a chair beside them, waving Fred down and keeping Maddox seated. "Sorry I'm late. Meeting with the Prime Minister. Foul mood. Some cock up in the Foreign Office."

Sir Giles' tendency to speak in short almost ungrammatical bursts mirrored his mind, factoring out all the unimportant matter and focusing only on the vital.

"Read the report. Tragic. Losing Harry Lange that way. No joy from the PM either." Sir Giles shook his head in resignation. "Spoke to the Americans. No idea what happened. No leads. Nobody saw the killer." He paused and added quietly, "Tragic. Already been down to see Harry's widow."

Maddox swallowed his impatience to ask for immediate action. He knew Sir Giles cared deeply that his special projects team had lost a man—a good man. Harry Lange's bloody, throat slashed body was found two days ago crumpled behind bushes on a grassy verge near a Congressional office building in Washington.

"Sir Giles, we had a very definite lead that Harry was following up. We know that his last report very carefully built up the case against the American Senator Murphy. We have to follow up. We must get a man into Washington as quickly as possible. I'd like to go myself. I know Harry's work and I was his controller." He quickly reviewed Lange's evidence for the great man and then waited for Sir Giles to respond.

Freddy seemed uninterested in the conversation. As Sir Giles and Maddox talked quietly, his eyes constantly scanned the room carefully sizing up each and every person entering or leaving. He even kept his eyes on the busy waiters and waitresses bustling in and out, serving up the afternoon tea to their well-to-do business and tourist customers.

For all the bluster and stodgy image he fostered, Sir Giles was a brilliant analytical individual. Since his days as a young, enthusiastic and dedicated MI 6 operative, he'd built a solid reputation. He'd risen rapidly in the intelligence services, scoring his biggest successes in Northern Ireland during the IRA crisis. Time and again his quick mind identified potential threats, spotted flaws in their own operational strategies and swiftly yet precisely analyzed situations to determine the most favorable outcomes. Now he controlled the Crown Security Branch of British intelligence.

The small but highly efficient branch was formed in 1850 following several attempts on Queen Victoria's life. It had served the government and, in particular, the monarch, ever since. Sir Giles was merely the latest of the invisible men who'd covertly protected the crown. He was virtually unknown outside the intelligence community but was a legend inside the service. To the few who might be interested he was Sir Giles Broadbent, just another civil servant among the masses but his nondescript service title belied the power his office really wielded. To his staff he was simply "the Guvnor"—the boss; to the Prime Minister and the Queen he was the supreme authority on security matters.

He fixed his eyes on Maddox. "All we've got?"

"No sir." Maddox pulled a small file from his underarm case. "We've traced Murphy's movements in the past few months as they impact us. Apart from his normal senate duties and speaking at various fundraisers in and around his state, he's had some unexplained disappearances."

Sir Giles raised his eyebrow but said nothing. Maddox continued. "They were listed on his schedule as private time, vacation and so on. As far his staff was concerned he was at his mountain retreat in Virginia." Maddox paused. "In fact, he was in Wales most times he disappeared. Other times he went to Brittany and Ireland."

Sir Giles' other eyebrow rose.

"I wish I could say it was brilliant field work on our part but actually it was good old fashioned luck. One of our team, John Broderick, was at Cardiff airport arriving home on holidays."

"Cardiff? Not Heathrow?"

"Our question exactly, sir. John recognized him and tried to follow discreetly but lost him as he rushed through the airport. John lost him as he hopped in a car that was obviously waiting. Fortunately, he managed to get the number plate and it came back registered to a Dr. William Merlin in Swansea. No such person. No such address."

He paused. "We checked passport control; nobody by the name of Murphy entered the country. There were no American passports listed that day either. Since there were no North American flights scheduled that day, he had to come either by private aircraft or from somewhere other than the United States. And there were no private aircraft movements that day either.

"But, we did find that a single Canadian male, Robert Wilson from Toronto, entered the country off a flight from Amsterdam. He registered his destination as a bed and breakfast outside Cardiff. Again no such establishment. Then we ran Wilson through our own immigration controls as well as that of other EU countries. Mr. Wilson it seems also visited Ireland and France several times in the past two years."

Maddox pushed his advantage and refreshed the guvnor's memory about Murphy's career from his time in Massachusetts politics and his unexpected appointment to the Senate after a private air crash that killed the incumbent Senator.

"There was a lot of controversy about that appointment. The crash spawned all kinds of rumors especially when the investigation proved inconclusive. Conspiracy theorists had a field day. There were rumors that Murphy might have engineered the crash but they were quashed by investigators and the Justice department. However there are still those in New England as well as Washington, who harbour suspicions."

Maddox paused while Sir Giles absorbed the information. At a nod, he continued. In the Senate Murphy's no-nonsense style and brusque manner merged with a winsome charm that won over many. The source of his bottomless well of money was unknown but, Maddox pointed out, suited the very expensive American political campaign system. His campaign financial records show no massive injections of funds from political action groups or even individual donors, yet he lacked for nothing.

"His fundraising engagements did more for fellow politicians and the party than himself. He has popularity inside and outside the party and next week it seems inevitable he'll be his party's presidential nominee this year." Maddox hesitated dramatically. "Sir, the next President of the United States could be tied tightly to the resurgent and dangerous Druid movements."

"An enigma potentially President of the United States? Why should Crown Security be concerned?" Sir Giles posed the question bluntly to Maddox.

"His association with, and overt support for, the radical wing of the IRA plus, more importantly right now, his evident support for the Druids," Maddox responded quickly, knowing the Guvnor's hot button. "He's hosted fundraisers in Boston for Irish republicans and Sinn Fein leaders have been his guests on their visits to the United States. I believe the Druids are just as threatening to us here as anything the IRA could throw at us. To have someone with those connections heading our greatest ally..." Maddox's voice tailed off, letting Sir Giles contemplate the thought.

The Guvnor nodded thoughtfully as Maddox passionately urged him to authorize further action.

A flicker of movement caught both their eyes. As they looked up, Freddy suddenly threw himself on top of Sir Giles. Soft pops of gunfire erupted from a seating area across the room. Blood spurted from a waiter's white jacket as he toppled into a cream tea display, a Walther PPK half drawn in his hand. At the table next to them, the tee-shirted tourist calmly held a gun he'd just fired and nodded at Freddy while another of Sir Giles' bodyguards across the room jumped up, weapon raised, surveying the panicked crowd for other potential killers.

As restaurant patrons and staff ducked or scrambled screaming for the doors, upsetting trays, tables and chairs, Sir Giles, Freddy and Maddox jumped up almost simultaneously. Sir Giles stared at the waiter, brushed his impeccable Savile Row suit and nodded across to his still seated bodyguard. "Damned good." He glanced down at the body sprawled over the display. "Pity we couldn't question him."

Maddox knelt by the body and pulled the dead man's sleeve up. He peered at a tattoo on the man's forearm. "Black dragon. The mark of the Druids. They know we're closing in on them, Sir Giles. First Harry, now this!" He stood up, eyes locked with Sir Giles'.

Sir Giles gave a quick nod at Maddox. "Priority for you Maddox. Whatever it takes. Do it." Within moments he was hustled quickly out of the restaurant by his agents.

Freddy thrust a hotel key card into Maddox's hand. "Room 428. Wait for me there." He brusquely turned aside to deal with the shambles. Maddox left.

Throughout the entire brief interlude only the harpist remained in place, immobilized with a stunned look on her face.

Chapter Two

Washington D.C., October

Stone's career had stalled. At the wrong time. All thanks to that miserable Frenchman and those damned Druids. Six weeks had passed since the last assignment came his way. The Embassy's quiet campaign against him was taking effect all too well.

He cleared a pile of old newspapers off the chair in his cluttered office, slumped down and stared out the window. Running a hand through his carefully groomed reddish brown hair, he docked his iPod into the speaker, sifted through his eclectic mix of classical and jazz and selected a piece. Soon the soothing tones of Pachelbel's *Canon* infiltrated the office.

He wasn't used to prolonged inactivity and the newspaper boycott against him rankled. Since his first hard-hitting exposes of European low cost airlines, his reputation as a travel journalist had soared, with assignments from prestigious magazines and newspapers quickly adding up. His strapping frame, mid-America boyish charm and warm, friendly nature led to appearances on *Today* that in turn led to a standing gig as INN's travel expert on weekend news shows. His cheery face and jovial nature was now a fixture on many TV talk shows, sprinkling travel insights with political and historical details. It helped that his photographic memory—he never forgot a face once he'd seen it—meant he always remembered bellhops, museum guides, local officials and the like. And they in turn felt like Stone's personal friends, even if they'd only met once before.

But his drive for success had cost him more than one relationship. It also slyly eroded his ability to recharge his batteries regularly. He was more familiar with the lounge at Dulles airport than his own Georgetown living room. Laptops and smart phones were his constant and dependable companions instead of people. Maybe, he thought, the dry spell was a blessing in disguise.

He needed a break. But just as quickly as the thought crossed his mind, he dismissed it.

As Pachelbel ended and one of Bach's Brandenburg Concertos began filling the room, the jarring ring of the phone interrupted. Stone briefly contemplated letting it go to voicemail but, programmed as he was to respond promptly, he groaned, leaned forward and lifted the receiver.

"Bradstone, my boy! How are you?"

Stone's strained face cracked immediately into a smile at the lilting musical voice on the other end of the line. There was only one person who used his full name. As a kid he'd hated his given name, an affectation by his upwardly mobile father. To his parents he'd been Brad and to everyone else he was Stone. But he was Bradstone to one person and one person only.

"Huw! It's been too long. Sorry I haven't been to see you in Wales recently. Where have you been and where are you now?"

The soft accent instantly brought feelings of peace and rest as he reveled in the call from his friend and, more recently, mentor. "Where I've been is on a long, interesting and most illuminating hunt. Where I am now, boyo is in your own backyard." The warm voice brought back memories of fascinating discussions with a man recognized by many as one of Britain's foremost historians or, as Professor Huw Griffiths himself preferred, "historical theologian".

"I need to see you Bradstone. This afternoon if possible." Huw's tone took on a serious demeanor. "It is rather urgent."

Stone didn't hesitate. "Anything for you Huw, you know that. Do you want to come here?"

"No!" The professor's sharp response oozed anxiety and nervousness. "Can you come to Fairfax? I'm at George Mason University, but I'd prefer a quiet location near here."

Stone thought for a moment. "There's a British pub not far from you. It's the Fox and Fiddle on Braddock Road just off the Beltway going towards Annandale. Is thirty minutes OK?"

The call was completely out of character. What in the world has the old professor's shirt in a knot he wondered? The phone was silent.

"Huw? Are you still there?"

More moments passed, and then the familiar voice came back on the line. "Sorry Bradstone. I thought someone was at my office door. I cannot take chances on someone listening in. It's too risky."

"Risky?" Stone bolted upright in his chair. "What risk? What are you talking about?"

Huw paused again. "No worries boyo. I will tell all when I see you. Just think on this. What do you know about Arthur? Well, cheerio then. See you in a bit." The professor hung up abruptly, leaving Stone gripping the handset, as if trying to squeeze an explanation from it.

As he drove out of the District and into Virginia, Stone remembered his first encounter with Huw at a tourism conference in Frankfurt, Germany. A seminar curiously titled *"Jesus' footprints through Europe"* was led by a greying 60ish professor at Glamorgan Vale University in Wales who also, it turned out, was a former church minister and rugby player par excellence. The unusual title and bio combination intrigued Stone, so he sat in on Huw's skilled presentation that pulled together seemingly unconnected facts and drew unconventional but intriguing conclusions. A long post-seminar discussion followed by dinner then lunch the next day sealed the unusual friendship. It also left Stone with the basis of a series of unique articles. Since then, Stone had called on Huw many times; at first just for information, but lately just for the comfortable rapport and camaraderie.

Last year, while visiting Huw in London, Stone met Huw's daughter Myfanwy, "That name is too easily botched," she'd laughingly introduced herself, "so call me Mandy," He remembered a stunning beauty with a soft easy grin and penetrating grey-green eyes topped by an always unruly mane of burnished mahogany. Despite her own career as a history lecturer at the University of Caernarfon in North Wales, she still helped her father in what she lovingly but somewhat dismissingly called "his eclectic and obscure research."

There was no doubt, Stone admitted to himself, that he relished any time spent with Huw because Huw was now the closest he now had to a parent. His prosperous but demanding businessman father died in a plane crash when Stone was only thirteen and his mother of cancer just eight years later.

Huw was probably the person who knew and understood him best, even better than himself, Stone admitted. Long hours of unburdening himself in Huw's welcoming and non-judgmental presence had sealed that relationship. Stone's mind drifted as he followed the familiar route toward Virginia, recalling the times he'd debated with Huw over issues of life and its meaning. The professor's interesting and varied career and stable life was suddenly marred by the death of his wife five years ago. Stone marvelled that Huw's grief was tempered by a strong faith, something Stone could never get his head around.

It was easy for Huw, Stone supposed. For some, faith and conviction came easily and helped ease pain. But for him, death and loss were open wounds. Discussing them—as Huw tried to do often—merely ripped the scabs off those wounds. God, death, and the role of faith were areas the pair danced gently around. They were always present in conversations like lingering shadows, but only addressed in a vague philosophical context. He could handle it no other way.

He manoeuvred his car easily down the busy Shirley Highway and past the Pentagon. The breathtaking view of the pristine white structure still impressed him despite the many hundreds of times he'd driven past. Stone wrestled with worry over the uncharacteristic communication. Normally, after the booming "Bradstone, my boy", Huw would make some erudite statement on the world's current state of affairs followed immediately by a terrible pun or corny joke. Today's call was altogether too abrupt and mysterious.

It still nagged at his mind as he finally pulled into the pub's gravelly parking lot. Inside he saw Huw sitting in a booth at the back, looking anxiously at him and around him. Stone weaved his way around tables and wait staff, and swung himself into the booth with a quick grin and hearty handshake.

"Huw, it is so good to see you again," A grin the size of a sunny Caribbean vista stretched across his face then faded into a puzzled frown. "But what's with all the mystery and cloak and dagger secrecy?"

The professor's short cut silvery grey hair framed a ruddy face that was all smiles.

"In a moment, boyo. All will be revealed." Even as he beamed and spoke, Huw's eyes darted past Stone and around the room, his unruly bushy black eyebrows flexing with each eye movement. Stone watched him intently. Huw stiffened as two men entered the pub, and then relaxed as they joined three other businessmen sitting at a large table near the front.

"I told Mandy I would meet with you but she objected to involving you in this." Huw paused. "But I must. I need your help".

"Of course, Huw. You know you can count on me."

Huw nodded as if he expected nothing more. "What do you know about Arthur?"

The question was sharp. Huw's eyes fixed grimly on Stone. There was none of the normal chitchat or small talk. The unexpected and sudden transformation from geniality to severity was disconcerting.

"Arthur who? A colleague of yours? Or some new Brit celebrity I never heard of?" Stone smiled to cover the sting he felt by the abrupt question.

Huw exhaled slowly, his head shaking. "I'm sorry Bradstone my boy, truly sorry. Most rude of me and quite unwarranted. Please forgive me. Too much strain these days." Huw's contrition was sincere, his words dropping away to silence.

Stone waved off the apology with a hearty "no apology necessary" and, elbows firmly on the table, leaned forward eager to hear more.

"Seriously, Bradstone, what do you know about King Arthur?" One of Huw's uncontrolled bushy eyebrows was raised in his old professorial query style. Stone thought for a moment as Huw stared intently, waiting for his response. This was no quickie 'Huw version' of Trivial Pursuit.

"Not a lot. A Legend. Knights of the Round Table and all that sort of thing. Camelot, Merlin, Excalibur, Lancelot," He rhymed the list off lightly, pausing before adding "plus towns all over Britain and even in France that claim connections to Arthur all of whom have tourist traps to fleece the unsuspecting and unknowing vacationer. There's even a pub in Tintagel named 'Excali Bar' simply because the town claims that it's Arthur's birthplace!"

"What else?" The university lecturer posed the question as if to an unruly and flippant student. There was no crinkle of a smile around Huw's lips. The upraised eyebrow remained firmly in place.

This time Stone adopted the serious mien of his mentor. "Apparently a great king who united Britain. Legends place him in the medieval period with knights in shining armor and all that kind of stuff, but most probably the stories are extensions of myths about a leader who lived in the Dark Ages."

Under Huw's silent gaze, Stone dredged as much as he could from his memory. "My guess is that some characters like Lancelot and Guinevere were add-ons to embellish the story as the legends grew, I think they were actually composed by a writer in the middle ages as allegorical tales identifying the ideal society.

Huw drummed his fingers on the table. Again he shot a quick look at the door as a bulky bearded man entered and headed to the bar with only the briefest look towards the back. He stayed silent while a bouncy but very non-British waitress took their orders in her Virginia drawl and hustled off. "Carry on." Huw gave no hint of his thoughts.

"I also remember something about Arthur or Merlin—I can't remember which—lying asleep…It must have been Arthur…whereupon he would somehow come back to life and save England again." Stone finished and looked pointedly as Huw shook his head sadly and absentmindedly brushed his hand through his hair.

"Not bad as far as it goes. Totally wrong, of course, but not bad." Huw looked up with the slight hint of a smile curling at his lips. "By the way Bradstone, that last bit about returning to save England? The legend says he will come back to save Britain. Please remember dear boy that there is more to Britain than England. As a Welshman I am offended and so too would the Scots and even the Irish; well, those from Ulster anyway."

He pursed his lips and framed his fingers in front of them in a prayer-like posture.

"Suppose I told you Arthur was real? Very real. And that his legacy still exists today and might have the power to either save or destroy Britain and possibly Europe or even the world. What would you say then?"

"You're kidding right?" Stone stared intently at the professor to see if he was pulling one of his frequent pranks, but one glance at Huw's solemn visage cut that idea in mid thought. "If it's true, and you can prove it, you're onto one of the biggest historical finds and news stories of the past few centuries."

He waited quietly while the waitress placed two pints of cider on the table in front of them. "You said on the phone you were onto a big hunt. Is this what you meant?"

Huw ignored his friend's amazed face as he penetrated Stone's question with yet another of his own. "You mentioned Excalibur. What do you know about Excalibur?"

There was a longer pause this time as Stone marshaled his thoughts. Huw was deadly serious about this line of questioning. It neither a joke nor a test. Stone wracked his brain to scour his mind for flimsy strings of long forgotten childhood books and movies.

"A sword. Arthur's sword. He pulled it from a stone and then when he died one of his knights threw it into a lake or pond or something. I think it was the sword that made him the king, wasn't it?"

"There's dim you are, boy!" Huw snorted. "All kinds of conjecture multiplied with half-remembered bits of childhood stories and legends. Hardly a shred of truth or knowledge in any of your statements, my boy. You disappoint me. You who have traveled and written about so much in this tired world and traveled through the old kingdoms of Europe so that your countrymen would become informed and travel to these magnificent places."

For the first time Stone saw a wisp of a smile as Huw shook his head in mock sadness.

"Bradstone, my boy, you are so sadly lacking in knowledge of this one particular king of Britain. Disappointed in you I am."

Stone smiled. This was more like the Huw he knew, questioning and thrusting with the best; demanding precise knowledge and lightheartedly deriding when you fell short of the target.

"Okay, professor. I didn't study for this test and I bow to your superior knowledge on King Arthur, Excalibur and whatever else is on your mind today. But for the life of me, I don't understand." Stone looked squarely at Huw. "And this nonsense about not wanting people to listen into you on the phone. Since when have you never wanted people to listen to you?"

"Bradstone, if my information falls into the wrong hands, it could have disastrous consequences for my country and possibly yours as well." Huw looked keenly at Stone, anticipating a pooh-poohing of this statement. "It is not an exaggeration when I say this, dear boy. Lives could be at stake. Mine and Mandy's included! And if you become involved, possibly yours as well!"

Gaping, Stone waited for the explanation,

"Arthur *was* indeed the High King of Britain! He was a very real person." Huw emphasised the point tapping his finger firmly against the table on each of the last three words. "He lived a full life, as dramatic and heroic as any of the legends, though none of them come close to the truth. He *did* forge a unity between the Celts and the remaining Romano-British people to fight Saxon invaders after the legions abandoned them. And he *did* foster the spread of Christianity across Britain." Huw carefully and quietly emphasized each key word with his finger again.

He leaned forward intently, one hand curled around his glass, the other poised in a lecturing fashion, elbow on the table and finger jabbing the air. "Make no mistake. He was real enough and his sword is a very real and very priceless icon. There are many who would pay much—and take whatever steps necessary—in order to possess it."

He stopped momentarily while some patrons brushed by. "You had lunch some time ago with a Frenchman, did you not? The abrupt change of topic floored Stone. "He was upset about an article?"

Stone nodded; convinced his jaw had dropped three feet. "Yeah, but what's this got to do with Arthur?"

"His objection was to your article on the Taranis Movement in France was it not? You ruffled some elevated feathers with that one, my boy. I even heard about it at the university. But you missed the most important part of the story." The lecturer in Huw was never far below the surface.

"Mandy's a historian too, you know. A good one," he said nonchalantly but with obvious pride. "Her work on pre-Christian religion in Britain has filled in many missing pieces in my own studies." Abrupt changes of topic were a frustrating aspect of dealing with Huw, but Stone knew that eventually all the obscure ends were always tied up neatly. He waited.

"Her studies of the Taranis group show a close connection with some other similar bodies, birthed by a group of Druids in Wales. Taranis is named after an old Celt god worshiped in Brittany and old Gaul; the god of thunder and of war!"

Huw shifted closer and dropped his voice to a whisper. "They want to change our world and force us to return to what they see as the power and wonder of the old gods

"All of these Druidic camps, all of them," he waved his hand around as if to encompass them, "want to bring back the power of the Druids, the power of the old religion, around the world. In Ireland they are known as Tuatha de Danaan, the Children of Danu. In Wales they are known as the Sons of Lleu." He pronounced it the Welsh way 'Thchlew' sounding to Stone almost like he was clearing his throat ready to spit. Huw slapped the table quietly but forcefully with each name.

"Each is named after a Celt god or goddess. They are tapping into the Celtic revival happening around the world and wrapping their own distorted evil beliefs around it. They organize themselves much like the old Celtic tribes. Each group is responsible for its own fiefdom but they are united and cooperating in the overall goal. More importantly, they believe the old powers of the ancient Druids."

"So what *is* the overall goal of these groups?" Stone looked intently at Huw.

"Groups," Huw snorted, "that makes them sound like some kind of club. No, rather you should use the term 'gangs' or probably more accurately 'clans'. What's their goal? Very simply put, power; the destruction of Christianity and any other solidly held faiths leading to domination of Europe and therefore a major role in world affairs."

A short sharp laugh burst from Stone's lips. Huw had always been fond of little jokes and it seemed likely this was another such made even more delicious by the involvement for whatever reason of his daughter.

"Oh come on, Huw, pull the other one while you're at it. Old gods? Druids? Destroy the church? Political upheaval? Are you feeling okay? Man, I thought I needed a rest, but it sounds like you need one worse than I do."

"You think it's a joke? That we're making up some ridiculous story for our own amusement." He scowled, his frown deepening. Huw's eyes flashed in irritation.

"I called you because I thought I could trust you to believe me. I called you because you've already done research on the Taranis movement. Your attitude disappoints me, boy."

Stone recalled his attempts to interview the Taranis leader, Andre Tonnerre that were rebuffed repeatedly. To Stone they seemed nothing more than a cult attracting unsuspecting but gullible Bretons to menial work supporting the lavish lifestyle of Tonnerre much as Jim Jones' followers had done decades earlier in Guyana. But he'd also described Tonnerre's henchmen as thugs, noting their brutal reputation in the region. That, as much as anything it seemed, led to Aubin's reaction. It was not good for tourism to report that a vicious force held sway in a particularly beautiful and popular area.

Stone leaned back as Huw frowned at him over the table. Whatever Stone might think, Huw was deadly serious. He stared at Huw trying to read this face to see if there was yet a glimmer of a smile. But the stern, worried visage of his mentor convinced him that from Huw's perspective it was not a tall tale. Whatever it was, Huw believed it. Deeply. Huw had never lied to him or led his astray before. He wiped his mouth with a napkin.

"OK. You've got my attention. I believe you. What have you got about Arthur, these Druids and their ambitions?"

Huw shifted in his seat, took a deep swig of his cider. "There's a lot you need to know. We can't do much more in terms of research, let alone stopping these fanatics. We know that Arthur lived and that Excalibur exists and is probably hidden away somewhere today. I'm not sure I even totally understand it myself, but Mandy and I believe this sword could be the key to their power. Maybe it's real power, or maybe it's symbolic. Either way, those Druids want it. They want Excalibur. I also know they want a medieval manuscript I found. It shows that Arthur and Excalibur existed and the Druids will stop at nothing to get either or preferably both."

Stone suddenly realized Huw was wound up tighter than a drum. His tension radiated out at Stone. Huw pulled some bills out of his pocket and put them down on the table beside the empty glasses. "Come with me, my boy. I want you to see something."

With a youthful stride, Huw led the way out of the pub. Unnoticed, the tall man at the bar waited till after they'd passed and followed. As the two friends walked across the parking lot towards Huw's car, the man briefly raised his hand in signal.

Stone's head wrenched round as he suddenly heard the screeching roar. In the blink of an eye, a black Ford raced towards them. Reacting without thought he pushed Huw out of the vehicle's path as he himself jumped the other direction. Stone heard the shots and felt the exploding glass shards as the windshield of Huw's vehicle disintegrated. He was sure he felt the Ford's fenders brush his trouser leg as it sped away.

He turned quickly to see the car stop at the pub's entrance, door flung open as the stranger from the bar jumped in, wildly firing two more shots as the vehicle skidded onto the road and raced away towards the Beltway interchange.

Stone scrambled up and ran over to Huw's form lying face down between two parked cars. Other patrons began running towards them. He saw Huw roll over and struggle slowly to his feet, dusting himself off as he did so.

"Thank God, you're alright."

Huw stood shakily still brushing dirt off his trousers and shirt sleeves. He peered owlishly at Stone, smiled knowingly and winked.

"I told you. They will stop at nothing."

Chapter Three

St. Brigitte's, Paimpont, France

"I realize it was a grave error Rhiannon. But even now it can be salvaged. My men are on the job as we speak. I will ensure their success this time."

Andre Tonnerre, self-proclaimed Chief Druid, or *Le Patron*, of the Taranis compound shifted his razor thin tall, balding body in his chair, condescending to the angry woman on the phone. Beyond the window he could see followers working and beyond them the Broceliande forest which acted as a thick natural barrier that complemented the technological security for his complex. He switched the phone receiver to his other hand, listening intently, but playing unconsciously with a small grotesque bearded pewter figure dangling from his pendant.

The fury in the woman's voice was palpable. "It is crucial that we get that manuscript away from Huw Griffiths. It holds the key to where we can find Excalibur. There can be no more mistakes, no more foul ups. You were given a job. Do it!"

Tonnerre recoiled at the cold voice, angry that this…this woman…had the temerity to lecture him like a wayward child. He was Andre Tonnerre, by the gods, leader of her para-military arm. It mattered not that she was the Dragon Master. He rolled the pendant figure back and forth in his hand as he listened, beads of perspiration breaking out on his forehead. His other hand rubbed his protruding jaw feverishly.

Exasperated, he interrupted. "If Griffiths knows anything at all, he would have moved by now. I think he's trying to recruit Wallace into helping him." Tonnerre's English was flawless but he was finding it difficult to keep the disdain out of his voice.

"Just get it done Andre. No more excuses. No more mistakes."

The line went dead. Tonnerre slammed the phone down and pushed a button on his desk. Moments later, his office door opened silently. His aide Jean-Marc Hebert walked cat-like towards him, soundless on the deep black carpet. Apart from the sculpture of a wizened man on the wall above the desk and symbolic icons woven into the carpet, the room was empty of all except the gigantic desk and chair. The aide opened his mouth to speak, but shut it rapidly as Tonnerre shook his head. He stood waiting.

The Druid leader pushed a second button. Rhiannon insisted that the movement organize into monastery-like complexes so they fit in with twenty first century ideas and concepts of new age type spirituality. In her calculating mind, there was something 'safe' about a phrase like monastery in society's collective mind.

The austere office suited that image but did not ignore technology. Silently from the ceiling above the right wall, a massive plasma screen lowered. As soon as it reached its full extent, Tonnerre leaned over slightly and spoke. Within moments he could connect with his followers anywhere in the world. Daily security sweeps and encrypted phones protected them from the prying, listening eyes and ears of satellites and electronic eavesdropping from governments and agencies curious about the burgeoning Druidic establishments around Europe.

Switching smoothly to the old Breton tongue, Tonnerre barked into a concealed microphone. "Personnel positions; North America." The screen instantly flashed a detailed map of the continent. Yellow LED lights popped up, particularly along the eastern seaboard from Massachusetts to Nova Scotia. "Security only." Yellow lights blinked out and red flashed on. "Washington D.C" he demanded.

He watched as the screen quickly zoomed in on the American capital city. Google Earth has nothing on our system, he thought. Five red lights blinked. "Belenos." The screen went dark briefly, then filled with the face of the husky man from the Fox and Fiddle.

"*Patron?*" He pronounced it the French way, emphasizing the "on".

"You failed me, Belenos."

"Wallace moved too fast. He pushed Griffiths out of the way. Others were running over. We had no time to go back and finish the job."

"Nevertheless, you failed. Where are they now?"

He listened intently as his security team leader explained their flight from the restaurant leaving behind a third member of the team to follow Wallace and Griffiths.

"They spent a lot of time with the police, stopped at Wallace's office then headed towards Georgetown. My man is following them."

"I want someone into his office tonight. Search his files. See what he has. Stay with Wallace but whatever you do, don't lose either one of them." He glared at the screen knowing that his security leader could see the displeasure on his face. "If you can separate them, bring Griffiths back to me."

Belenos nodded. "And if Wallace is involved and helping the professor?"

Tonnerre hesitated momentarily then answered coldly. "Dispose of him. But it must not be traceable. And tell our embassy contact to get in touch immediately." His hand dropped to the button and cut the video link as he turned slowly to his assistant.

"The Dragon Master was not happy."

Tonnerre sat on the end of his desk incessantly fingering his pendant. "She is convinced that Griffiths knows where or how to find Excalibur." He stood and leaned forward towering over his short, stocky assistant. "With Excalibur, and its power in our grasp, nothing can stop us from reclaiming our past glory and bringing this world under our leadership." His voice rose with fanatical passion.

"Think of it, Jean-Marc. The world is ready for us. For centuries they have tried to eliminate us and our gods. But now the world is ready for us; open to the truths of our way." Elation filled his face as he raised his arms and looked skyward.

Jean-Marc waited. Once Le Patron was in this state of self-congratulatory ecstasy, it could be a while before the realities of day-to-day hit him again. But he feared his master enough not to move. The rage and punishment he would face was not worth the inconvenience of waiting.

The minutes passed. Muted sounds from outside were the only noise that penetrated the stillness. Finally, Tonnerre turned slowly and faced Jean-Marc.

"Our god Taranis has spoken," he murmured, fingering the pendant lovingly. "He has promised that we will lay hands on Excalibur. We will succeed and destroy those who oppose us."

Hatred of all things Christian drove every fiber of his being. Already in France, Christianity—particularly Roman Catholicism—was now more a cultural rather than a faith thing. Indeed, Muslims were already bragging that theirs would be the majority faith in France by 2020. But their faith would be destroyed as easily and summarily as the Christians, Tonnerre sneered. That he could promise them.

Rhiannon was right. The key was Excalibur. The story of its mystical creation by the first Dragon Master Merddyn or Merlin, and then its disappearance, was rooted in Druid history. She'd showed all the leaders ancient records that proved its supernatural powers.

In Brittany, Tonnerre's followers were well aware of the alliances and kingdoms that connected them to Merlin and Arthur in particular. He never let them forget; reminding them constantly that Merlin himself forged Excalibur and filled it with supernatural powers for the use of the High King Arthur. Then Arthur betrayed them all, embracing the Christian beliefs that were wiping out Druid power and influence. The sword was lost, supposedly thrown into a lake by one of Arthur's men as the king lay dying. But Merlin himself rejected the implausible Bedwyr story. No, he knew that Excalibur survived but was hidden from his second sight.

Tonnerre strode over to the window and glowered out at the compound. Excitement tempered with frustration and impatience swept over him. For him, the reality that Excalibur might soon be in their grasp brought the day of the Druids tantalizingly close. Across Britain and France the Celtic people were rising and with them, the Druid faith. Even in North America the Irish, Scottish, and Welsh immigrant successors would welcome the new Celtic nation demanding that their own dissolute and self-indulgent political leaders join with them. Then, then the power of the old gods would destroy that most Christian of nations, the United States, Tonnerre raged inside himself. Those weak and vulnerable sheep that followed the Christ would soon be fodder for the gods. Already, a solid core group of several thousand led by the American Presidential candidate Murphy himself, was setting the stage. Judiciously sprinkled in major power positions in Congress, in business, in the military and the media, they were quietly working to prepare the way for the new era.

Excalibur. It all hinged on Excalibur.

Washington D.C., late afternoon

Stone opened the door to his townhouse on a quiet street not far from the famed gothic buildings of Georgetown University. Ushering Huw in, he quickly locked the door and waved him into the study.

Newspapers, books, magazines and files overflowed every surface. Stone cleared a spot on the black leather couch for the professor and pulled up a chair. Before sitting, he slipped up to the window and peered carefully out at the street.

"Don't look now Huw," he spoke lightly but seriously "we've been followed!"

He was sure the dark blue SUV parked at the end of his street was the same one that followed them out of the restaurant and again through the city to the house.

Stone pulled out his cell phone and punched some numbers. "Chad, I need a favor real bad."

Since his early days as a rookie reporter, Stone had maintained a close friendship with an old police contact and close friend, Detective Chad Lawson of the DC Police force. He quickly explained his request but left out the attempted hit and run, fearing he might seem paranoid and hoping the Virginia police had not forwarded details to their DC colleagues. Plus he wanted Huw's full explanation of the bizarre day before embroiling anyone else.

"Yeah, you're probably right. It could be someone my writing has annoyed." As Lawson spoke Stone listened then hung up. He remained to the side of the window confident that he was in shadow in the setting sun and therefore invisible to the watcher.

Within five minutes a police car swung around the corner and a cop approached the SUV. A minute later the SUV moved off, patrol car following.

Huw remained silent through the whole exercise until Stone moved away from the window, closed the shades and took his place in the chair. Huw's eyebrows rose quizzically but he said nothing, content, after his brush with near disaster, to let Stone take the lead.

Stone stared at Huw for a moment. "OK. You got my attention. Big time. Now tell me who they were and what's going on. No lecture. No questions. Just tell me what you're into." He settled back.

Huw's eyes glistened with excitement and not a little alarm. He ran a hand through his hair again and began. "As I was researching British life after the Roman Legions left I kept coming across references to the mighty war leader, Artos--our Arthur--but I also began to discover suggestions that there was a deeper, darker story. Naturally, I had to find out more."

As he'd delved deeper, he found a puzzling series of references to a Druid leader named Merddyn. "Of course, any Welshman worth his salt knows immediately that this was the character we've come to know as Merlin. The town of Carmarthen is, in fact, named after him—Caer Merddyn—Merlin's castle."

But the Merddyn, Huw discovered was not the wise, benevolent counselor of legend. "I discovered a man leading pagan Druidic practices and beliefs and consumed with hatred for Christianity. The Merddyn I found was a sly, manipulative and powerful man intent on destroying this new religion.

"The legends we have of Arthur—the ones you quoted to me at the pub—were the compilation of rewritten stories by a somewhat discredited author, Geoffrey of Monmouth. He wrote *Historia Regum Britanniae* or a History of the Kings of Britain around the year 1136.

Except that it was not much of a history, and his 'kings' were more than a little suspect."

Stone nodded, as much to speed up the explanation as to signify agreement. "No lectures, okay! So how do you know Arthur was real and how does it all fit in with your comments about the Celtic movements? More importantly, why were we attacked and then followed?"

Huw continued as if he's not been interrupted.

"Whatever Geoffrey of Monmouth might have done to muddy the waters with his embroidered stories, there is already too much circumstantial evidence suggesting Arthur was real. We have written references from early writers like Henry of Huntingdon, William of Malmesbury, Gerald of Wales and others. In Wales we have stories and literature like *The Mabigoni* and *The Black Book of Carmarthen*. No my boy, there is too much material for us to consider that Arthur was just some fairy tale.

Stone stood exasperated at the pedantic way the professor was spinning the story. "Huw! No lectures. Get to the point. What's going on?"

Huw huffed. "There's impatient you are bach." But he bowed to the demand.

Softly he explained that as he'd pored over the details of his research, he'd become more and more agitated at what it revealed. As he spoke his soft Welsh accent became even more pronounced.

"Very well, bach. In short, I found a substantial portion of a manuscript written by a Welsh monk at the beginning of the fourteenth century. He writes of another letter by an early saint of the sixth century that tells the story of Arthur's last battle and death and proves beyond a shadow of a doubt that Arthur lived and ruled a huge swathe of Britain! So whatever we may think of Geoffrey's scholarship and veracity as a historian, he may indeed have been working from hard factual knowledge of King Arthur even if he embellished liberally.

"Stunning it was when I found it. Stunning!" He paused to peer intently at Stone. "You must understand, Bradstone. This is a hugely significant find. Everything we have in our libraries, museums and archives dates from the Middle Ages. Everything we think we know about Arthur comes from this conjecture and mythology. They in turn sparked Sir Thomas Mallory and ""*Le Morte D'Arthur.*" Then there was Alfred Lord Tennyson and T.H. White's *Sword in the Stone* that contributed to the mythical balderdash.

"But this writing is the first and so far as I know, only authentic documentation we have. It is contemporary, don't you see? With solid irrefutable proof that Arthur existed and was a powerful king and warlord as well, it would give the Celtic movements across Europe new impetus; it would fire up their ambitions and give them legitimacy. More followers, including the rich and powerful would be tempted to join them. Arthur would be their beacon.

He shifted forward on the couch then spit out "and Merlin would rise with them to bring back his black, occult beliefs."

"What makes you say occult, Huw?"

"The monk makes it clear that Excalibur was given supernatural powers by its maker, Merddyn or Merlin, and that even back in the 1300's the Druids were desperate to obtain it."

Stone interrupted. "You have this manuscript?"

"Yes." Huw hesitated. "And no."

"I discovered it in the archives of the University, buried in an old trunk load of materials salvaged from an old church before it was torn down. But it is not the complete parchment."

"So where is it now, then? Have you got it with you?"

"It was destroyed, supposedly." Huw looked sheepishly at Stone.

"I was so excited that I mentioned my find to some of my colleagues. Evan Evans, our Dean of history found out and called me in demanding more information. I should have been more careful because Evans is a very strong supporter of the Druid revival." he said ruefully.

Stone tried to follow the bewildering story, but in spite of himself couldn't help chuckling out loud at the Welsh propensity to use the same name for given and surnames; Evan Evans, Thomas Thomas, William Williams…only the Welsh.

"I know. It was stupid," Huw flared, misunderstanding Stone's laugh.

"Anyway, Evans didn't believe me until I showed him a small part of the parchment. He asked me to keep quiet about it, that we would do some more research and see if we could find more. Then we could make a major announcement. But then I had no choice, so I agreed."

Huw shrugged in embarrassed recognition of his own folly.

"Evans took the fragment to his office, 'for safekeeping' he told me and swore me to silence. I thought it was so he could wait and manipulate an announcement to glorify himself and snag major research funding.

"I was stunned the next morning to find police and fire crawling over our faculty offices because there had been a 'fire' in Evans's office. Supposedly his bloody pipe ashes had set fire to some papers on his desk. Much of the clutter on his desk and some of his books were consumed before he was able to put it out. He told me that the manuscript portion I gave him was one of those burned."

"You believed him?"

Huw, exasperated, shook his head firmly. "Not at all. It was so transparently obvious. That evening he rang me warning me to keep my mouth shut, demanding I turn over everything to him and forget it ever existed."

Huw sniffed. "Do they think I was born yesterday? Or living in some trashy American detective novel?! I refused, of course, and left the university immediately. Mandy, bless her heart, put me up at her flat. Now she's helping me."

Stone was frustrated by the twists and turns of Huw's convoluted account.

"So you found this thing that proves Arthur lived and it got destroyed or stolen? If you think it gave you a clue to the original document, what's keeping Evans from doing the same and then finding it?"

"Bradstone, my boy," Huw looked sheepish. "I may be old and I may be too academic and pedantic for the likes of many, but I did not fall off the back of the turnip lorry yesterday. I know that Evans—despite all his faults—would never willingly destroy such a valuable document. No, he has it safe somewhere and is trying to decipher it and find the rest of the document. Of that I am sure."

His lips curled into a secret smile. "I said I only gave Evans part of the document. The piece that gives me real information…I held it back."

Stone gawped at Huw. The roller coaster story had taken yet another dip. "You kept it? You have it now?"

"Oh give me some credit boy! No. It's safe. For all our sakes, I cannot divulge where. But, I do have a photocopy of it my boy. And I brought the copy with me here to America. Furthermore, I believe—no, I know—that the rest of parchment tells us where we can find the Excalibur."

Stone jumped up, threw his arms in the air in annoyance and began pacing. Huw had surprised him many times with information pulled out of a seemingly invisible hat, but this was a story for the ages. Before he could think through his next question clearly, the insistent ringing of his phone interrupted.

"What the devil are you up to Stone?" Lawson's harsh Midwestern twang barked through the phone. "We got your guy out of there, ran his plates and they're clean. Next thing I know, I get the Captain on my case because your boy is connected with the French embassy and my bosses don't like us hassling people with diplomatic status. No matter what we want or think. Fortunately, we've had a rash of break-ins in Georgetown. He thinks I had a tip and just stepped up vigilance, so he calmed down. But, Stone, if those guys are trailing you pal, I can't cover you officially. You're on your own."

He waited a moment and said more calmly,

"So why is a Frenchie following you across the District?"

"Don't know, Chad. Can't figure it out myself."

He hated misleading his old friend but he wanted to let fanciful story percolate before he could talk about it.

"Why don't I believe you?" Chad let the question hang for a moment. "Listen, you know how to reach me. My guys said this French dude was a real nasty looking piece of work, a sort of prissy bouncer in a thousand dollar suit." His tone softened slightly. "Watch yourself, okay? I'll keep the patrol stepped up in your neighborhood."

He rang off and Stone turned to Huw.

"OK Huw, continue. Explain to me why were we nearly killed over this Excalibur?"

French Embassy, Washington D.C., late

Tonnerre's voice ripped over the phone. He was obviously not happy with any of them.

Aubin listened, his dapper figure hunched over the papers on his desk. He hated being dressed down like an errant school boy. He was Pierre Aubin, First Secretary of the French Embassy, by the gods, not some lackey to be ordered around like a servant. Nevertheless, he held himself in check. He easily slipped into the Breton tongue.

"Yes *Patron*. I warned Wallace months ago about his article. I have also expressed the embassy's displeasure to his editors at the Herald."

He listened with growing but silent frustration. It was no use reminding Tonnerre that he was not a field man; that he was a high level political attribute not an errand boy. The Druid was an impatient man at the best of times, and today was obviously not a good day.

"Oui, Patron. A bientot."

Aubin hung up the phone and almost immediately picked it up again a, summoning his assistant. *"Le chef de securite. Maintenant!"*

There was no getting around it. Today was a fiasco. First his men or rather, Tonnerre's bungled their mission to kidnap Griffiths, trying instead to kill him! Worse, Griffiths was now with that reporter. *Merde!* They couldn't even move in on the pair because his men were now being harassed by the local police. Wallace. His blood still boiled after that aborted lunch. Aubin's musings were cut short when the door opened and in strode the embassy's security chief.

"You sent for me Pierre?" said the man known to Tonnerre as Belenos.

Aubin's frustrations boiled over.

"I am the First Secretary of the French Embassy here in Washington D.C.," he snarled. "In my presence you will address me by my title and never my first name. Your insolence is intolerable. Do I make myself clear?"

Belenos smirked and planted himself forcefully on the office sofa and put his legs up on the classic Louis Quinze coffee table.

"In this office, when it's just the two of us I will call you what I like. Remember who you work for—who we both work for—and who has charge of this mission!"

He swept his feet down and leaned towards Aubin.

"This office is secure. We do a security sweep four times daily. In here, alone, I am in charge. YOUR insolence is intolerable. Do I make *myself* clear?"

Aubin's head jerked back as if hit by Belenos' massive fist. He glared defiantly and was about to speak, but the diplomat in him decided to avoid a major confrontation. Belenos' muscle was need right now, far more than a turf war.

"*Le Patron* has given orders. Griffiths is to be neutralized and taken to the Dragon Master. How you do it is up to you. My orders are to cover your backside. I've already had to call the Washington police and stop them harassing your men outside Wallace's townhouse. But I cannot protect you from your own bumbling and stupidity."

Aubin blanched as Belenos launched himself at the diplomat, holding back his fury at the last second. Fists planted firmly on the desk, Belenos spat out French and Breton oaths, questioning Aubin's own manhood and parentage. Then he subsided and glared at the diplomat.

"And Wallace?"

"You have the authority to take whatever steps you need regarding Wallace." Aubin saw the cruel desire on his face. He shuddered involuntarily, aware he'd just authorized the writer's execution.

Without another word, Belenos rose and headed for the office door.

"*Merci*, Pierre" he sneered.

Chapter Four

Georgetown, late evening

Huw's story captivated Stone. As he followed the professor's thinking and decision-making though, he seized on a flaw. "This parchment was supposedly written in the early 1300's. What makes this any more believable than, say, Geoffrey of Monmouth's writings?"

"I've already explained that Bradstone," Huw sighed. "It shows there is contemporary proof. The portion I have gave me three clues. First, the monk—his name was Thomas—states very clearly that he copied material written by a man who served Arthur. The monk takes pains to ensure that his readers understand the genuineness of what he was copying.

"Second, the Abbot at the monastery apparently added a note swearing before God that this was indeed a true copy of a real document. Those two were apparently destined personally for Pope Boniface VIII in Rome.

"Finally, the monk also wrote a journal—that's what I have a portion of—telling the story of Excalibur. Fascinating, it is boy. Fascinating. I've already translated much of it from the Latin myself but still have more to do."

He paused and peered intently at Stone. "Do you Understand, Bradstone? The monk's whole package was to be sent to the Pope in Rome."

"You mean this copy and the letter is in the Vatican right now?" Stone felt like his mouth dropped open another few yards.

Huw raised his hand to forestall further questions. "I believe it is entirely possible, so until we learn to the contrary, yes. And before you ask, that crucial bit of information was not on the material I handed to Evans."

Huw leaned forward and took a sip of the water Stone offered.

"A very close colleague of mine, a church history expert, is searching for it at the Vatican." He paused. "I haven't heard from him for a couple of weeks which is worrying. Father Joseph is usually meticulous in communication."

Huw shook his head slightly and fiddled briefly with his hands.

"This is where I need your journalist's investigative skills, my boy. I want you to help me find Excalibur."

Wallace got up and paced the room. His head was swimming with the incredible story and an equally incredible number of questions. But there was no doubt. He was hooked. The tale was too intriguing and challenging to ignore. He finished pacing and sat down once again.

"Where and when do we begin?"

Chuckling with delight and excitement, the old professor bent forward over the coffee table. "Tomorrow! They already tried to get me and now your life is in danger as well. So we must begin immediately." He paused. "I have a confession. I was so sure you'd agree, I couriered one of those memory sticks with my copy of Thomas' journal on it, to this address." He smiled cheekily. "You should get it before 10 a.m. tomorrow if their advertising is accurate! I didn't want to take the chance that I might…well, let us say, might be intercepted with it on my person. I had to get it to you."

Stone was incredulous. "Does Mandy have a copy as well?"

Huw shook his head. "She knows that the manuscript exists, but I did not give it to her for her own safety."

Stone felt like a leaf spinning and bobbing along a spring melt stream with no sense of control or direction. It was an uncomfortable feeling for him who valued, indeed celebrated, the ability to simultaneously control many things with equanimity.

"You'll have to stay here Huw. It's not safe at your hotel. The police are keeping an eye on this place and you can borrow my car tomorrow and get your things. But now we have to sit down and work on a plan of action."

"Thank you Bradstone. I knew I could count on you."

"Right, then. Let's get started the proper Welsh way! You put the tea on and I'll scramble some food together. Then we'll figure out something." Stone headed to the kitchen, pausing only to put the thumping strains of Beethoven's Fifth Symphony onto his player.

As they worked through a late supper, Huw detailed his research and brought Stone up to date on the way the new Druids had spread their tentacles into Europe and North America, becoming a small but powerful group. Stone spread maps of Europe and North America on the coffee table.

"Each has a level of independence and autonomy, but all are tied to the movement's headquarters in South Wales. There are two other key compounds." He looked up at Stone. "You're already familiar with one of them," he said, pointing at Paimpont in western France. "There's another near Tara in Ireland, north of Dublin."

On the map, Huw rapidly identified other key locations then paused over South Wales, jabbing at a point northeast of the town of Carmarthen.

"Down by here. That's the epicenter of the evil web. The leader is someone called Y Feistar or, the Master but nobody has any idea of who that is. The 'face' for the movement is a woman, Rhiannon. They call her the Dragon Master. She was a renowned academic and lecturer at the University of Wales. She's erudite and charismatic and founded Sons of Lleu about twenty years ago. Now, her vision of Druidic restoration is coming to fruition."

He continued his dissertation, happily noting the fascination in Stones' face. "The Taranis are the most reclusive and brutal faction. Ah, indeed and to goodness you stirred a hornet's nest when you wrote that story," he chuckled.

Ancient Druids, he explained, were not only religious leaders but also their society's historians, diplomats, and revered wise ones. They worshiped a pantheon of gods including the sun, earth, water and war. Primarily, however, they worshiped the gods of the underworld.

"It is satanic, pure and simple," Huw continued, "especially when you consider their hatred of the church. The Druids' power was absolute and unassailable. The community obeyed them totally."

Likewise, Huw explained, each of today's Druid compounds have a specific role and demand absolute obedience from its followers. Huw stood, stretched his arms and began to pace to room as if back in the classroom.

"Rhiannon and the Sons of Lleu lead. The Irish Tuatha provides cultural resonance and mysticism. They connect with those who embrace the popular Celtic music and symbolic artwork, thus providing a publicly acceptable face."

He stopped, hands on hips and faced Stone. "I'm not talking about the so-called 'Druids' who mess about with poetry and music at our Welsh Eisteddfods. That's a sham based on a charade formulated by a Welshman in the 1700's!

"No. Our Druids are a hate-filled nasty lot, not like those who play at it." He picked up a pen and circled the Taranis compound in Brittany.

"Andre Tonnerre is a vicious thug. He's feared, even in the Druid community, as their equivalent to the Nazi SS and Gestapo. Taranis is the god of thunder, and Tonnerre certainly personifies that with his violent temper and incomparable arrogance." Huw suddenly stopped short. "I'm lecturing again aren't I?" Stone smiled, nodding.

"Alright Huw, but you said they could impact the world. How?"

"They're wealthy. They may be relatively few in number but they have legions of followers, a multitude of apologists and sympathizers, excellent, successful PR and marketing. They are powerful politically as well as economically and see themselves as a new world order, willing to rid society of what they consider decadence and corruption. In particular they're determined to rid the world of Christianity which they blame for many of the world's troubles."

"They won't find an argument there from a lot of people, me included. Look at the wars and horrors inflicted in the name of Christ over the centuries."

Huw glowered and argued that Christianity had also brought education, health care, love, justice and compassion to the world.

"If you are going to be a good, honest journalist my boy, open your mind. Even that classical music you enjoy so much was written by men who followed Christ. Bach himself dedicated every piece to 'the glory of God'. So without Christianity, you wouldn't even have your favorite music!"

He waved his finger back and forth in front of Stone's face.

"I know, I know. You blame God for the early deaths of your parents. But you need to get beyond that childlike response. People die. Sometimes unexpectedly and tragically and, in our minds, too early. To blame God for all the bad things in life is too simplistic a response. I expect better of you, my boy."

Huw peered intently at Stone. "You would do well to open your mind to love and faith rather than keep it locked with the iron keys of doubt and anger." He pointed at Stone. "God has a purpose for you in his kingdom."

"I'm not in his kingdom, Huw. You know that."

"Ah, but you are. I know it, and more importantly, God knows it. You just don't realize it…yet."

Stone shrugged uncomfortably but said nothing in response. They were getting into dangerous territory again. He picked up the map. Huw took the hint and continued his dissertation.

"To most people, Rhiannon, Tonnerre and the others are like the hobbyists that play at history, much the same as your own Civil War re-enactors. To others, they are either misguided nuts or irrelevant. And it's that dismissal of them that makes them all the more dangerous! Very few people understand the depth of their hatred of the church and determination to force their beliefs and way of life on others. It's a black, malevolent force that pre-dates the time of Christ. That's why we must expose them. That's why we must find Excalibur first!"

A strong silence hung over the room. Stone's gaze returned to the map. "Where was the church that was torn down and had the manuscript?" Huw's finger moved unhesitatingly to a spot in the South Wales valleys. "Down by here. St. Dyfrig's near the ruins of Cwmllyn Abbey".

Llanmerddyn near Carmarthen, South Wales

Rhiannon, a short and somewhat stout woman with a shock of white slashing through her thick long black head of hair, adjusted her long black featureless dress as she settled in her chair. Behind her, a window covered most of the wall, affording an unparalleled view of the imposing stone ruins of Careg Cennan castle high atop the crest of a limestone ridge some six miles distant. It was a view that never ceased to inspire her. The broodingly silent ruins dominated the green valley below. She looked out on a landscape that could not have been more typically Welsh with its verdant green meadows and hills cluttered by hundreds of distant white clumps that were some of the three million plus sheep that populated the country.

From its position in the virtually people-empty valley, Llanmerddyn was just as much a fortress as Careg Cennan. It too was situated on a hill with only one way in, a narrow laneway, traipsing lazily more than a mile to the main buildings. Not far away was the main road that led to the junction with the main route into mid Wales.

An innocuous cattle guard at the beginning of the laneway was in fact, a sophisticated monitoring device recording the speed, weight and classification of each vehicle entering the road. Unauthorized vehicles could be electronically disabled before they went more than a few yards. In the trees, camouflaged cameras and motion sensors scrutinized movement along the length of the road. Armed guards disguised as workers patrolled the grounds regularly.

Hidden away from view behind towering oaks and yews at the top of the hill was a Disney-esque version of dark ages village around a large common. Sitting apart and slightly above, was a larger T-shaped structure featuring massive gold-gilt doors fronting the laneway and opening into a sizeable meeting hall. Across the top of the T, one wing contained a well-stocked library and classrooms that would put many a university to shame. The other wing held Rhiannon's living quarters overlooking the valley. Immediately below her apartment was a sophisticated control center that monitored each aspect of the community's activities and was the heart of her communications web.

Rhiannon was protected. This was her spiritual center and stronghold. For twenty years she'd constructed her empire. First recruiting amongst like-minded academics and then building contacts with other burgeoning Celtic groups and movements. Her cajoling brought in money and followers; first a trickle, then a flood. Her vibrant passion was enflamed by her belief that she was a descendant of the Arch Druid Merlin and it was for him she named her stronghold.

She had to think. Tonnerre's precipitous action against Huw Griffiths infuriated her by undermining her careful plans to ensnare the professor. Lleu, she was angry! Her ebullient mood of earlier that day was dissipated

Griffiths was a scholar she respected highly. His parchment discovery gave her the chance to offer him power and prestige inside the movement. But first the fool Evans drove Griffiths away and Tonnerre had now compounded things with his ham-handed attack. She clenched her fist into her thigh. Her chance to seize Excalibur quietly and peacefully had evaporated. Obtaining Excalibur would be much more problematic now.

It came at the worst possible time, since the world situation was setting the stage unknowingly for the Druid revival. In France, the Bretons celebrated their Celtic forebears. In Wales, Welsh language schools proliferated, Welsh radio and television infiltrated the airwaves and Welsh signage now dotted the roads and motorways. Ireland was the same. So was Scotland. An explosion of other tribal and linguistic groups demanding independence and recognition as nations was igniting the world. From the Quebecois in Canada to the Kurds in the Middle East and tribal groups across Africa and Asia, demands for nationalism were growing.

Rhiannon had quickly realized this was her golden opportunity and moved to seize it. The Celts—led by the Druids—would create their own nation and a new Europe. Yes, the movement was close to its goals.

But Tonnerre had exposed one of the problems of the structure she'd insisted on. She might be Dragon Master but each leader had a huge measure of autonomy. Sometimes, like today, she fumed, they made short-term decisions which had negative long term ramifications. Tonnerre's violent approach to every problem created a mess. The old Celtic problem of shifting tribal allegiances and alliances was again rearing its ugly head.

It had to stop. Now!

Instinctively she stroked her personal talisman, a bronze representation of the god Lleu that hung around her neck. Her other hand reached forward and pushed a button that would connect her with the control centre three floors below. In seconds she was in visual and audio contact with her powerful second-in-command, Sir Damien Wyndham at his Boston office.

The ruddy-faced trans-Atlantic billionaire was one of Rhiannon's former lovers as well as strongest supporter and funder. He'd launched several major international enterprises including a global airline *Air Celtica* and was creeping higher on *Fortune 500*'s wealthiest people list every year. Ten years earlier he'd moved many of his operations to the United States as part of the plan to lay the groundwork and fund the Druids in America, though he maintained homes on both sides of the Atlantic. Briefly Rhiannon explained the predicament.

"I can be in Washington first thing tomorrow," Wyndham said, adjusting his schedule on his Blackberry. His manicured mid-Atlantic accent still held a trace of the Welsh valley intonations of his youth.

Rhiannon's stern face cracked into a slight smile. Whatever his faults, she knew she could count on both his reliability and his ruthlessness. "Tell Griffiths you will fund his research or whatever he wants to hear. He must be brought in." Rhiannon's brows furrowed. "Wallace though is another problem. He's to be neutralized, not killed. Not yet, anyway. As long as he's alive Griffith will be more malleable. Do I make myself clear?"

Wyndham scoffed. "He's a journalist. Just present him with a hot story and he'll drop the good professor like a poisonous snake." He thought for a moment. "We're introducing a luxury stretch version of our A380 jumbo jet in a few weeks. I'll offer him an exclusive on the inaugural flight from Los Angeles to Heathrow. He'll jump at it."

French embassy, midnight

The persistent ringing drew Aubin back to his office. He'd spent hours working on the French cultural festival scheduled for the Kennedy Centre. Now he merely wanted his bed.

"*Oui*, hello?" he barked into the phone.

"*C'est moi*, Belenos. Things are taken care of. After tomorrow Wallace will be out of the picture. We will pick Griffiths up, but you must expedite his removal to France."

"What are you planning?"

"You don't need to know that nor will you hear from me again. My replacement is on his way to Washington. The Embassy files need to show that I was reassigned to Paris two weeks ago."

Aubin agreed and hung up. Quickly he fired up his computer and worked swiftly and silently to expunge all traces of Belenos from the embassy's records. Relieved that the menacing bulk could no longer intimidate him, he allowed himself a quiet smile as he worked.

Thirty minutes later, humming a tune to himself, he left the embassy in his chauffeur driven limousine.

Georgetown, midnight

As the patrol car turned onto the dimly lit street, the officer in the passenger seat looked at the house they were ordered to watch. "I think that guy just stopped in front of the house."

The patrol car slowed to a crawl. As he watched the shadowy figure beside by a car disappeared from view. Before the officers could react, he popped up again and walked swiftly towards the corner.

"Must have dropped his keys or something."

The patrol car driver yawned and nodded agreement.

"Think we should call it in?"

"And report what? That a guy dropped his keys in front of the subject house?"

He took one more glance at the rapidly disappearing figure and looked again at Wallace's house, noted that the ground floor lights were still on. The patrol car drove on.

Chapter Five

Georgetown, morning

The insistent pounding on the door brought Stone back to reality. Harried dreams populated by ancient warriors, swordplay and sorcerers trying to break down his castle gates melded into a bleary recognition that someone was indeed banging on his door. Still in his rumpled shirt and slacks from last night, he peered through the security peephole, opened the door, groggily signed and accepted the proffered package stepped back inside.

"I guess it's come" he yelled, recognizing that Huw was probably just as fuzzy as him this morning. They'd talked and critiqued each other's half-shaped plans until only a couple of hours ago. The dreariness of the heavy morning rains mirrored Stone's own feelings.

"Remember, Huw. Make whatever excuse you need to your colleagues by phone but pick up your luggage from your hotel. You're staying here from now on." Stone tossed his keys to Huw. "When you get back, we'll do some digging and find where your Father Joseph is."

Stone dropped the package on the kitchen counter and pulled instant coffee off the shelf. He looked back over his shoulder as Huw disappeared out the front door. "Take a coat with you, it's raining," he shouted,

The explosion a minute later shattered the windows. He saw a fireball as he raced through the door screaming Huw's name. Outside, people were running up the street and pouring out of neighboring townhouses. Through the rain he could see Huw's bleeding figure staggering away from the destroyed car. Stone reached him as he collapsed. A policeman ran over from a nearby parked cruiser. Already he could hear the sirens of emergency vehicles.

Gently but forcefully the officer pried him away from Huw, and laid the professor on the sidewalk, shouting urgently for blankets, coats, umbrellas—anything to keep the drizzly rains off the victim. In what seemed seconds, a crowd gathered around while the newly arrived paramedics treated Huw and firefighters worked to douse the burning vehicle.

A paramedic looked up at Stone. "He's alive. Looks bad, but your friend may have been lucky." He pointed into the crowd. "That lady over there says he got into the car, started it and was getting out again for some reason. He was almost totally out of the car already when she blew. Probably forgot something and was going back."

Stone looked frantically around. A neighbor ran over and called "I'll look after the house. You go with the ambulance."

With a nod, Stone took a last look at the burnt out mess on the street and accepted the police offer of a ride to the hospital.

St. Brigitte's, Paimpont, France

"Fool. Imbecile. Cretin!" Tonnerre's screams of rage blasted the video image of Belenos.

"How were we to know that Griffiths would take Wallace's car?" The terrified man wiped sweat from his blanched brow and whined his excuses to Tonnerre.

"Think! The gods surely gave you a brain to go along with that brawn?" Tonnerre let his fury fly, pounding his fist repeatedly against the desktop in his tantrum. More invective flew across the ether until he was exhausted. He gripped the edge of the desk, breathed deeply then looked up and snarled new orders to return to Paimpont the fastest way possible.

Tonnerre flicked his hand towards Jean-Marc who silently reached over and cut the connection.

He slumped into his chair, hands shaking with anger and his own apprehension. Now he had to tell Rhiannon that the man she wanted alive was probably dead and the man she wanted neutralized was in fact very much alive. Gods alone knew how she would react, but it would not be pleasant.

Then too he had to consider how that stuffed prig Sir Damien would react. His jealousy of the businessman was barely concealed at the best of times. Wyndham was too rich and too tightly tied to Rhiannon. Gods, he would love to diminish Wyndham's power and ego. Instead now he would be the target of Wyndham's derision and wrath. He had to move fast and minimize the damage.

"Jean-Marc, convene the leadership for Belenos' arrival. This must be dealt with swiftly before Rhiannon can intervene. Belenos has failed again. There are no excuses, no escapes. He must pay." He knitted his fingers together, using them as a chin rest while he considered his options.

"*Patron*," Jean-Marc's harsh nasal voice betrayed his Marseilles accent. "Do you want me to connect you with Rhiannon?" He waited.

After a long pause, Tonnerre slowly lowered his hands.

"No. Not yet. Let me think."

Silently, Jean-Marc left the office. Tonnerre moved in front of the desk, knelt and fumbled under his robes for his effigy of Taranis. He stared at the deformed face that represented his god, placed it reverently on the floor and prostrated himself. He prayed also to Ogmios, the god of eloquence as he had never prayed before. He would need all of that gods' help to explain this.

George Washington University Hospital, Emergency Room

Stone slumped wearily against the wall in the crowded waiting room, eyes closed.

"You look like hell warmed over. Ever thought of becoming a botanist? It would be a more peaceful lifestyle!"

Stone' eyes opened to see Chad's familiar craggy unshaven face leaning against the same wall. A lock of wavy blonde hair stood in unruly singular protest at the back of Chad's otherwise obedient head of hair and his warm brown eyes were riveted on the wall-pressing writer. Stone straightened himself and smoothed his coat quickly. The detective nodded and jerked his head behind the nursing station.

"Come on. I got permission to go behind the firewall and I've arranged police protection till we figure out what's what." He led Wallace past a glaring, officious nurse and into the corridor. "Your friend is still alive, but it was a lucky escape."

Together they slipped past the nursing station. Outside one room a policeman nodded at Chad and opened the door for him.

Stone was unnerved seeing Huw hooked up with more wires and tubes than should be allowed to exist. Above and beside him, various screens beeped and squawked as multi-colored lines blipped up and down in constantly changing patterns. Huw weakly moved his hand acknowledging Stone.

"Call Mandy. Tell her." Huw's eyes squeezed together in pain. "St. David's… lives there now…for her safety."

Stone opened his mouth to speak but the young-looking doctor beside the bed shook his head, stepped forward, and led Stone into the corridor. Chad followed.

"I take it from the detective here you're his friend and that he's a Brit." Stone nodded. "He's in shock and a lot of pain; burns on his arms and legs and multiple fractures to his right leg. There may also be head and internal injuries. We won't know for sure until we send him for tests. I take it he was asking you to call someone?"

"His daughter." Stone looked at the doctor. "What should I tell her? What are his chances?

"You can tell her the prognosis is guarded. He's critical and we don't know about long term damage. He looked at Stone for a few moments. "Can you act for him until she gets here?"

Once Stone had signed the necessary forms, the doctor turned back into the room. In the nearly empty corridor Chad turned to his friend.

"Want to tell me what's up now? In a few short hours I've got a 'being followed' complaint and I've been hassled by the French embassy. That was followed by a car bombing—your car—and, by the way, a break-in at your offices. Funny how everything revolves around you, Stone." Stone opened his mouth but before he could speak Lawson told him that a suspicious janitor saw people leaving his office at two in the morning and called police.

"I just happened to see the B&E report minutes before we got the call about the explosion."

Stone's shoulders slumped in resignation and anxiety. He grabbed Chad by the arm and pulled him further down the hall away from the officer outside Huw's door. Swiftly in a half whisper he filled the detective in on the events of the past day and a half.

"You mean these guys are chasing after some old sword thinking it's going to give them some kind of magical power?" Stone shushed him, look quickly around to see if anyone heard, then smiled for the first time that morning

"That was exactly my reaction when Huw met with me yesterday." He jerked suddenly. "The package! It was delivered just before the bomb went off. I can't do anything here for a few hours. How fast can you get me back to the house?"

Llanmerddyn

She shook with doubled and redoubled rage. The one confirmed means of finding Excalibur was dead, killed by the stupidity and impatience of Tonnerre's warriors. It beggared belief.

Rhiannon locked her door and walked to the bookshelf, grasped a miniature statue of Lleu and spoke one word quietly. Silently a hidden door opened beside the shelves. She slipped through into the darkness and the door hissed shut behind her. Carefully, she descended the circular steel steps to the bottom and made her way along a tunnel. As she proceeded, motion sensitive lights flicked on, marking her path until it opened into an ancient grotto, carved into the hillside. The cave's crystal formations reflected and danced around the walls dazzling and enthralling her every time she saw it. Only Rhiannon and a few key associates knew that the Crystal Cave, long demoted to the realm of folk lore, was actually very real.

But she and she alone knew its deeper secret.

She glided into the heart of the cave, knowing the route by heart. At the far end, she crouched slightly and pushed through a fissure into an even larger crystal cave that danced and sparkled though even she had never discovered its light source. She peered into a dark recess at the back of the glittering grotto. Grasping her talisman, she dropped to one knee, eyes fixed straight ahead into the gloom.

"Master."

Wyndham Building, Washington D.C.

Wyndham strode purposefully across his main offices overlooking K Street. His short, stocky frame trailed staff behind him as he swept into his inner sanctum. Aides, briefed by a call from his private jet, began firing their findings at him as he sat down. Griffiths was still alive at GWU Hospital. Wyndham allowed himself the first smile since receiving Rhiannon's urgent call in flight. So there was still a chance. His mind worked feverishly to find a way to capitalize on the latest turn of events.

That gods-cursed fool, Tonnerre had really opened a Pandora's Box. Now, in the post-September 11 environment, the scrutiny would be intense. It would not stop with the DC police, but absorb the FBI, the CIA, Homeland Security and the gods knew how many other acronymed agencies the general public had never heard of. Tonnerre had become a massive liability. As soon as this situation stabilized, he had to be eliminated.

In quick order, he placed successive calls to contacts in the FBI, and various security agencies to try and derail the investigation. From others he sought as much information on the incident as he could get. He would not make Tonnerre's mistake. He would gather all the facts and options before he called Rhiannon.

Subconsciously, he rubbed his right eyebrow as he always did when thinking and planning. He'd come too far to give up. Rhiannon may think this was about the sword—a magical icon to fire up the Celtic peoples and lead them to a new and glorious future—but to him this was about nothing more than pure power. If it meant momentarily playing the loyal subordinate, so be it. Let her play her mystical games in the oak grove at Llanmerddyn. He understood and embraced the real, untapped power of the old faith. It was he, not Rhiannon, who should and would rule.

Above all, he considered himself a realist. He believed in the gods, but knew that real power ultimately came from earthly action. It was simple really. Call on the gods, and then seize power. He'd prayed to his favorite god Cerunnos, the horned one, to bless him with absolute earthly power. Cerunnos would not fail him.

Leadership demanded action, regardless of the bleating of the media; regardless of the fallout. The whole concept of modern democracy stunk in Wyndham's nostrils. One leader must rule and one only. The rest must follow.

That's the way he built his business empire. Wyndham did not suffer fools gladly. He confronted those whom he wished destroyed and by the time he was done, they were either locked in his embrace or dropped on the garbage dump of life; it was no matter to him which result as long as he got what he wanted.

His face darkened. Tonnerre's impulsive actions had potentially screwed up the ultimate plan. Wyndham had already selected his launching pad. In a fit of theatrical energy he'd codenamed it "Operation Crowning Glory". One massive demonstration of power to destabilize Britain and create a new government based on Druidic laws and culture. Shortly after, the Taranis would seize power in France, pointing to the power and success of the new Britain. Ireland would follow as would North America. Already the Canadian Prime Minister and the next President of the United States, Liam Murphy, were sworn followers beholden to him politically as well as financially. They in turn evolved their own cadre of followers and minions. Yes, North America would fall into line and be a supporting entity to his ambitions. No doubt about it. The rest of the western world would then buckle.

Rhiannon and Tonnerre were mere stepping stones. They would be used and then given a choice: accept Wyndham as ultimate leader or be discarded. Pawns had no rights. They could only move forward or back or else they were removed.

Crowning Glory even fit perfectly with the fast approaching Samhein, the celebration of the Druidic New Year that this time would truly usher in a new year.

Georgetown

Thanks to good neighbors and excellent insurance adjustors—helped by prodding from the police, Chad reminded him—Stone was surprised at how much had been cleaned up at the house in the past few hours. In the kitchen he ripped open the courier package. A memory stick slipped into his hand. Nothing else.

Chad roamed the living room picking up the maps and papers strewn around from the late night planning session. Apart from glaziers, who were still working on the upper floors, the officer on duty reported nobody had entered the house.

Stone walked into the room holding the tiny blue thumb sized unit in his hand.

"That's it? That's what was in the package?"

"Yeah." Stone placed it gently on the coffee table as if afraid it would either break it or blow up in his hands.

"I'd better call Huw's daughter before I look at it though. I don't even have her phone number."

He moved through a second doorway into his study-cum-office, booted up his computer and was soon online with the British Telecom Directory. He began shaking. "What am I going to tell her?" That her father was blown up in my car at my house? It's my fault. I brought him back here and I let him go out alone to take a car that was booby-trapped!"

Chad calmed him down, recognizing delayed shock. "Tell her he was hurt in a terrorist bombing. Get her to focus on him and finding a quick flight over here. You can tell her the rest when she arrives."

Stone turned to the computer. He could not shake the waves of guilt flowing over him. He forced himself to enter her last name into an online British phone directory, only to find there were more than one hundred 'Griffiths' in that tiny community. He tightened the search, adding her first name, winding up with ten listings.

Wyndham Building, Washington D.C.

"We've done a check on the professor. He has one unmarried daughter last reported living in a place called Bontnewydd near Caernarvon in Wales." An assistant put the sheet of information in front of Wyndham.

"Track her down. I want someone ready to visit her personally and offer our fullest assistance including funds if necessary."

Already, a plan was forming in his mind that would convince the girl he had her and her father's best interests at heart. The daughter might just prove the means towards the end. With her in his pocket, the professor would be putty. And with both of them in his control, Rhiannon would not be a problem.

He placed a call to a follower at the British Embassy.

Georgetown

On the seventh try, Stone connected with Mandy and broke the news. He assured her that Huw was being looked after by the finest medical staff in Washington and that he would stay connected with the hospital until she arrived.

It was evening in Wales, too late for a flight that day. She agreed to make her own arrangements and within twenty minutes emailed Stone with her flight information for the next afternoon, arriving at Dulles airport.

Stone burrowed his head into his hands. If he was honest, Huw was all he had left and today he'd almost lost him. Guilt clung stubbornly, despite Chad's reassurances. If only he hadn't offered Huw the keys to the car. But, his alter ego argued, if he'd gone with Huw one or both of them might now be dead. Huw's last minute decision to return for his coat had saved him. Be grateful for that, he scolded himself.

He stared at the tiny memory drive. Stone knew that once he read the contents, he was truly committed. He could walk away now and leave matters in the hands of Chad and the police. Or he could insert the drive and let the world evolve as it would.

The one thing he would not do he told himself, was pray. God had not answered his prayers about his parents so why would he answer on Huw. If indeed he even existed.

On a whim, Stone Googled the Sons of Lleu. You're putting it off, he chided himself. As the website appeared, he noted a striking woman staring out at him. Rhiannon, he breathed. Swiftly he read the movement's material, printing off each page as he needed. Staring at the woman's picture and reading the site he made his decision.

Chad wandered back into the study, two glasses of wine in hand, peering over Stone's shoulder. "Sons of Lleu? More like sons of bitches," he grunted.

"I don't think they're the ones who planted the bomb. "I'll bet it was the Taranis faction. Remember, the guys who followed us were French, connected to the embassy." Stone concentrated on the website in front of him.

Chad settled on a stool beside Stone. "Well? Are you going to read this almighty secret letter or not?"

Stone fingered the drive in his hand then leaned forward and inserted it into the USB port. He opened the document and began to read.

Chapter Six

Wales, 1301 • Cwmllyn Abbey

My name is Thomas of Gwent, a brother at Cwmllyn Abbey since I was but a lad of ten. In that time I faithfully kept the offices, obeyed my superiors and settled my heart joyfully on any task set before me. It was therefore strange that our Prior, Brother Edwin, told me after Compline one night to present myself before our Lord Abbot the next morn.

Cwmllyn is nestled beside a river in one of many valleys in this part of South Wales. The forested hills and the bare mountain tops only lead to more valleys, rivers, moors and mountains. At the top of the valley it widens into green meadows where our Abbey was built. It was already near one hundred years since brothers from Tintern Abbey first chose this spot. Our Abbey is a quiet place set deep in a beautiful wooded valley. It is built on the site of a much older church, that has been a place of worship since the time after the Roman Legions left and near to the village church, St. Dyfrig's.

Cwmllyn has always been a place of solitude and peace. The growing village was slowly surrounding our Abbey which had its own infirmary, mill, orchards, cowsheds, and river access. The lay brothers worked hard daily to glean the grains, bake the loaves and do the many tasks that keep this holy place going. The brothers and I gathered for the holy offices each day where we worshiped. I still love the grandeur of the abbey church and the peacefulness of the cloisters where I enjoyed many days hidden in a corner where I could read, contemplate and pray.

Cwmllyn has never been a rich or famous abbey, like some others. Our Cistercian rules demand poverty of course, but many abbeys owned rich farmlands as part of their estates. Cwmllyn had nothing such. No, it was a small, calm place far off the beaten path that quite suited me for I had no real taste for travel and adventure other than to complete a pilgrimage. I wanted, nay yearned, for a quiet life where I could pray and read and learn.

Abbot Godfrey's summons caught me by surprise. I thought I must have sinned somehow, somewhere, else why would he want to see me, a lowly brother? I trembled in my heart and pleaded before God that I might know the sin I had committed. I reasoned that if I confessed beforehand, I could assure Abbot Godfrey that I was clean and sinless in Christ.

I presented myself after Lauds, trembling as I knelt in obeisance before him. I was surprised therefore when he gently raised me and warmed my heart with a smile. To my further surprise, he held my shoulder with one hand, dismissing the Prior with the other. I gainsay that Prior Edwin was annoyed at being sent away plagued him by curiosity. No less than it plagued me.

The Abbot's warm voice was kind and soft that day. I have oft heard it bellow in anger and many times fill the Choir and Chapter meetings with inspiration, but never have I heard it so gentle.

"Brother Thomas. I have noted your faithful obedience in all matters. I have a task for you that will test your obedience and discretion, I warrant, but one I am confident you will complete."

The Abbot's white coarse wool robe swished as he led me to a table on which stood a quill and pot of ink as well as many parchments. He was a smallish man. I myself was his equal in height (though not, I assure you, in holiness). But his sturdy body belied his thinning tonsured white head. Never in the years I'd known him had he looked so strong in health.

Beside the table was a weathered old overlong wooden chest. Its clasps and locks seemed ancient and worn but as I looked closely I saw that in truth they were well oiled. He noted my interest in the chest, eyes dancing with a secret amusement.

"Patience, Brother Thomas, Patience," he said, still not unkindly.

As he beckoned to me to a chair he put more logs on the fire. It was early spring and a cold damp pervaded all our quarters, including those of Abbot Godfrey. He handed me a mug of excellent tasting wine, much better than the mead we brothers normally drank. My mind was confused. Never had the Abbot treated me this way nor, to my knowledge, any of the other brothers either.

Abbot Godfrey pulled up a stool and sat beside me, earnestly studying my face. "Thomas. Each Abbot before me since this Abbey was founded has carried a secret burden. It is a parchment and a relic that came into the protection of the Holy Church long before it was given to this Abbey for security. Every Abbot of Cwmllyn has taken this responsibility seriously and passed it along in a letter of instruction, one Abbot to the next. Each Abbot vowed to safeguard these items and also to keep silent on the matter. It is a solemn trust laid upon us."

I could barely breathe as he spoke the next words.

"I have decided after much prayer and much time on my knees before God, to break that vow." He looked intently at me. "And you are the only person other than His Holiness Pope Boniface himself to know this."

He beckoned me to the chest and opened it. Inside I saw the hilt of a sword, sparkling even in that musty box. Its shaft was covered in purple cloth such as would enrobe a king. Abbot Godfrey ignored the sword but reached down beside it and drew out a thick oiled leather pouch. He drew out a sheaf of parchment and laid it on the table before him.

I felt in that moment that time itself stood still. The sounds of daily life—the mill wheels creaking, the shuffle of brothers working, the lowing and bleating of animals—all disappeared. He closed his eyes as if in prayer and his quiet contributed to the deafening stillness around me. I remember only once hearing the fire crackle. I know not how many seconds or minutes passed. I said naught for fear of breaking the hush.

Abbot Godfrey looked up. "You know that I have just returned from Rome?"

Indeed, the Abbot's return from pilgrimage was one of great rejoicing within the community. I nodded to my Lord Abbot in response to his question. Until now I had remained in utter silence.

"Good brother," he laughed, "you are allowed to speak. Be not silent."

Abbot Godfrey's smile warmed my heart. I gulped and gazed into his face. "My Lord, I along with the other brothers here at Cwmllyn rejoice in your safe return. We did miss you."

He laughed again, lighter this time. "Lord bless you, Thomas! And did you miss my remonstrations and lessons?" This he asked waving his hand to prevent an answer. "Nay, do not answer my son. T'was in jest."

He drew his stool closer but told of his journey and his discussions with Pope Boniface, revealing only that which he deemed critical to my knowledge I now realize. How I wish we had spoken further on this matter in the few weeks we had left.

"I decided that I would speak personally to the Pope about this matter. I told him what is in the chest and the parchment. We are agreed that this knowledge is too great a burden for one man or one community to bear any longer. The church has protected this secret for more than seven hundred years since our Abbey was founded. It comes from the original priest at St. Dyfrig's and we have protected it. But now I fear for the future. There are dark days coming and I am afraid that the days I and my successors can protect this chest are ending.

"His Holiness instructed me to find a faithful monk with a good hand, to copy the parchment and its information. He told me to choose one whose ability to keep confidence is beyond reproach and one to whom I could entrust this solemn and holy duty. They will be for our records. The original parchment and the relic will be sent to Rome for protection." His eyes bored into my soul. "I have chosen you Thomas."

I dropped to my knees in surprise and supplication. "Pray God, I will of course obey. But surely my Lord, there are others more worthy in this community?"

He lifted me up and bade me sit. "I have prayed much about this. God has shown me who will carry out this great task." He smiled again. "He showed me you."

My eyes must have been as big as two trenchers. I am sure that my jaw gaped open. Abbot Godfrey reached behind him and picked up the parchment. It was old and wrapped in cloth, I could see, bound by a simple purple ribbon that matched the one covering the sword. He gently and reverently laid it in my hands. His kindly voice grew solemn and his body seemed to grow in stature as he spoke.

"I charge you Thomas of Gwent, Brother in this Abbey at Cwmllyn, to prepare faithfully two copies of this parchment. You will do this carefully and diligently so that your hand can be read by future generations. I will adjoin a letter in my own hand confirming the truth of your manuscript. Both will then be sent to His Holiness." The solemnity dropped slightly out of his voice and in an almost wistful way he added, "And His Holiness will then carry its burden."

In the meantime, he told me, my regular duties would be assigned to another Brother while I worked in a small cell adjoining the Abbot's quarters. There, except for celebrating the Offices and sleep, I would stay and copy the parchment. My hands began to tremble with awe and fear that I would not be up to this task laid upon me. He gently took the parchment from my hands.

"Go now, my son. It will soon be Prime. You will need this day for prayer that God will grant you both wisdom and strength of soul to finish this undertaking. You will begin on the morrow. And remember, Thomas, long after this task is done and even after I have departed this earth, you must remain silent. This matter is to remain between you and God to the end of your days. Speak of it to none."

I stayed my voice for a moment. I needed to fully understand and convince myself that I was up to the responsibilities laid upon me. "My Lord, does no one in the community know of this task? Not even the Prior?"

"No my son. None."

Abbot Godfrey now led me to the door swiftly but courteously. He opened the door, turned and smiled at me once more. "Only His Holiness, Pope Boniface, myself and you. For a Brother in Cwmllyn, Thomas, you keep high company." He ushered me out as the bell rang for Prime.

I hastened towards the Choir, picking up the hem of my robe as I ran. As I did, I saw the short bearded figure of Brother Gethin of Yns Mons, the Sacrist, staring up towards me with a strange angered look on his face. Prior Edwin was walking away from him towards the chancel, but Gethin looked my way unmoving.

I confess that I never liked Brother Gethin from the moment he arrived three years past. His cruel, harsh demeanor, especially with the novices, was well known. His fist as much as his voice was used against those who displeased him. He glared as I ran past, but I did not stop. I wanted a time of private prayer in the chancel before we celebrated the Office of Prime.

In the Choir stalls, my heart stopped pounding and I tried to take my place as quietly and reverently as I could. I could not help but notice though, that as I arrived a whisper of gossip ran back and forth through the brothers. Several of them gestured or pointed in my direction but before anyone close to me could speak, the Precentor began chanting the first psalm of Prime. I joined in but I confess my mind strayed constantly, swirling with thoughts about my new task. I knew the other brothers were curious beyond themselves, yet I could say nothing. Only the strict rules we live by save me from relentless questions and comments during Prime.

I was in the refectorium at mid-day when Brother Owain tried to speak with me. Owain was my very real friend. He'd lived in a small village over the mountains several valleys from the Abbey. He was a year younger than I, which is to say nineteen, and together we had shared many days of quiet companionship since his arrival two years earlier. Owain had a startlingly unkempt mane of straw colored hair that could not even be controlled by his regular tonsure. His penetrating eyes always seemed full of mischief and his fun loving ways often got him, and sometimes me, into trouble.

Our rules, as in all Cistercian monasteries and abbeys, require silence as we eat and listen to the reading of Holy Scripture. Only the Brother reading may speak. The rest reflect silently on God's goodness through the bread before us and the Bread of Life we hear read to us. Nevertheless, if one finds a place at a table separated from the more strict brothers, it is sometimes possible to have quiet whispered words. The tables stretched around the room and Brother Wilfrid was reading from the raised pulpit along the long side of the room.

"Is all well Thomas?" Owain whispered.

I bobbed my head in acknowledgement. The sonorous monotone voice of Brother Wilfrid droned on, reading through the sixteenth psalm. I looked up to the High Table and noted the Abbot watching me carefully. I felt myself turn red as I felt his gaze. Owain hissed at me again. Underneath the table I kicked him hard to warn him off. It was just as well I did. Behind us I heard a shuffle of feet and Brother Gethin appeared.

His icy black eyes framed by a hook nose and bushy black eyebrows bored into me. Gethin never smiled, never showed expression of peace or joy. Rather, his visage was always fixed with a permanent rage flaming out at those unfortunate enough to be near him. He placed his hand roughly on my shoulder and bent down to my ear. "I must speak with you following Sext." Nothing more. His grip tightened harder to cause pain and he then released me and walked off. My redness of face was replaced with a whiteness of fear.

The Sacrist never spoke with the brothers individually except there was trouble and invariably it would end in a beating administered with the help of his equally hate-filled Sub-sacrist, Brother Emlyn. I myself often suffered unjust punishments and beatings for minor sins such as being late for Chapter or nodding off during Vespers or Vigil. In truth, Gethin and Emlyn administered punishments with undue haste and enjoyment.

I fixed my eyes ahead and finished my beans and bread then drank my mead all the while praying, for I dared not look up into another questioning face. After the meal, I lined up for our ritual hand washing. In Chapter each morning, our daily tasks were set out. My work for this day was already set by Abbot Godfrey; to pray and prepare myself for the service ahead of me. As the other brothers left to take up their various jobs, I simply pulled my cowl over my head—a sign that I wished to be alone—and walked slowly but determinedly towards the north cloister. I had a book with me on the life of St. Herbert but it was difficult to concentrate as I sat there in the warming sun of the afternoon. I read and prayed, prayed and read.

The hours passed quickly. I must have nodded off because next I heard the bell for Sext. I hurried to the Choir, chagrined at my failure. Abbot Godfrey had instructed me to spend the day in prayer and I had already failed him. I was not worthy of the great work he had set before me. Humbled, I worshipped and chanted as we observed Sext. As the brothers dispersed, Brother Gethin waved me to follow him into the sacristy, closing the door behind us.

"Brother Thomas, my Lord Abbot has given instruction that you are to be provided with table, quills, inks and parchment in the alcove just inside the Abbot's quarters. He also told me that you are to be excused from daily functions until this work he has assigned is complete." Gethin peered at me through grey-black slitted eyes. "Regrettably, he neglected to tell me the nature of your task and why you need separation from the brothers while you do. As Sacrist, it is my responsibility to ensure the smooth functioning of this Abbey."

He leaned in at me. "So naturally I want to provide all the assistance and materials you will need. Tell me, what are you to do and why must it be done only in the Abbot's rooms."

I said nothing.

"Come, come Brother Thomas. You have permission to speak. There is no punishment here. I merely seek to help you." He loomed over me, his hand once again gripping my shoulder tightly. "I do, however, insist on obedience. Answer my questions. What task has the Abbot set you to?"

The pain in my shoulder was increasing for Brother Gethin grasped me in such a way that I was beginning to lose feeling in my left arm. I winced and he released his hold, waiting for my response.

"I cannot tell you much that you do not already know. Abbot Godfrey instructed me to make copies of some Abbey documents because I have a fair hand and he believes I will do a better job if I am allowed quietness and separation from the others. As to the rest I know not."

I could see the angry flush rising in his eyes. Before he could speak however, the Sacristy door swung open and Prior Edwin stepped in.

"Ah, Brother Gethin, Brother Thomas, just the two I was looking for. Brother Gethin I have assigned two novices to help prepare the alcove for Brother Thomas's work. They are on their way to you now."

He turned to me. "Brother Thomas, pray come walk with me. My Lord Abbot has instructed me to move your bed into the alcove outside his quarters. We can do this right away if you please."

Dear loveable Prior Edwin. If ever there were a more kindly yet totally unaware monk in all Christendom I would very much love to meet him! As I turned to leave, Gethin seized my arm and twirled me around. "We will speak again. I demand an answer," he hissed at me quietly.

Life in our Abbey is very much the same day in and day out. Such is the existence St. Benedict outlined for us—prayer and worship seven times a day that we called the Offices, private prayer, simple meals and sleep. In between we worked on tasks inside and outside the abbey according to our skills and assignments. These rules bring such peace and order to our daily lives that it truly allows each of us to concentrate on our prime purpose in life; to devote ourselves fully to God and worship him to our highest ability.

Normally I would have run into Brother Gethin several times a day, but Brother Edwin arranged for me to eat with the cooks and other laborers rather than the brothers and also allowed me to miss Chapter meetings. Thus I was able to avoid Brother Gethin

I began my work the next day. As time wore on, I was stunned by what I read. It intrigued me and thrilled me. I could not long put it down before I wanted to be back copying. I found myself struggling not to read ahead. I had to force myself to ignore the story and simply copy letter by letter, word by word, and line by line.

In truth my mind was controlled by the parchment. I drifted from the study of Holy Scripture and I ignored the daily life and gossip of the community. The days became even simpler than before. I slept, ate as little as possible and wrote—all separated only by corporate prayer that we could not, should not, avoid. Abbot Godfrey visited often, observing my work and commenting upon it. Each time I left the cell, every trace of my work and all that I had accomplished that day was locked in the chest. Abbot Godfrey alone had the key, though he showed me where it was kept should I need it.

As I copied, I realized the parchment's importance and I understood why Abbot Godfrey was burdened. It was written by the blessed Saint Byron himself. Long had our stories told that Byron was a brother of King Glywys of Morganwyg (which we now call Glamorgan) and that he served with King Arthur. Astounding though it was to actually hold such a document in my hands, it was the content that that truly moved my mind and heart.

Byron told of his days as squire to Bedwyr, one of King Arthur's companions. It was the story of a sword forged by the Arch Druid Merddyn himself and empowered with unworldly forces. Merddyn fought the Christian faith, turning against the King when Arthur embraced it, and swore to extinguish Christianity. As the King lay dying Byron and Sir Bedwyr agreed to keep the King's presence alive even though his mortal body was gone. After giving the King a warrior's cremation, they kept Excalibur as a symbol of Arthur's continuing presence, but knowing that the Merddyn would seek it for his own evil purposes.

The Blessed Byron turned to God and became a priest in his later years, leaving his war-filled blood-strewn life for the sanctity of holy orders. He hid the sword at St. Dyfrig's, his last church, committing his successors to secrecy in order to protect it. It meant the sword wrapped so carefully in the chest was indeed King Arthur's own sword, the magical Excalibur! And I had laid my eyes upon its hilt!

I began to wonder if it was wise to involve the Pope in a British matter! Can you imagine? I, Brother Thomas, questioning the wisdom and decision of both Abbot Godfrey and His Holiness?

That last week was particularly difficult. I was almost finished my work yet despite my best efforts to keep out of sight, Gethin waylaid me several times, demanding information and threatening me. One time his fist was thrown in anger at me and struck my chest. I am sure he would have beaten me then and there except that once again our Lord showed mercy for by a miracle, Abbot Godfrey rounded the corner. Gethin growled at me to keep quiet and walked swiftly away.

Some two days later, or was it three? I cannot recall. Abbot Godfrey found me in the warming room just after Vespers and beckoned me to follow him. Gethin started towards me until he saw that I was following the Abbot. In my haste to obey him and get away from Gethin I am afraid that I must not have latched the door securely behind me, for it was still slightly open later when I left. As we entered his rooms, Abbot Godfrey spoke.

"Brother Gethin is not happy with your work for me?"

My shyness and silence in his presence was gone. I freely spoke to him. "He asks questions constantly, about you and my work. He is also more than passing interested in the chest."

"You told him nothing?"

"No. I have no knowledge of how he even knows about the chest."

He stared at me a long time then sighed. "Brother Gethin is not to be trusted. I am afraid that he has been corrupted by a desire for power." I drew my breath in shock. Before I could respond, Abbot Godfrey wagged his finger at me. "I will appoint a new Sacrist and Sub-sacrist as soon as possible. So be patient and forebear, Brother Thomas, for this too shall pass." He smiled at me kindly. "You are finished the copies?"

"Yes My Lord Abbot." I reached to my own table and handed my finished second copy and St. Byron's original parchment to him. I confess I was reluctant to do so. My magical, wonderful time with the King, his sword and his saints was over. On the morrow I would renew my normal Abbey duties knowing that I was forever changed and yet still unable to tell anyone.

Abbot Godfrey smiled gently at me, knowing I suppose, the feelings I had. He picked up a document from his desk. "This is a copy of my statement to His Holiness, Thomas. It commends you for a fine job. I have already sent this to the Holy Father along with the first copy of Byron's tale." He held up his hand against my protestations and asked me to put the copy and parchment in the chest with the copy and the sword. "These we will keep for our own Abbey records. The sword will be prepared for the journey to Rome. I thank you Thomas for your faithful service." He then dismissed me.

As I left his rooms I heard swishing as if cloth was brushed against stone, but I saw nothing in the halls as I went. Not an hour or two later, Brother Owain found me in a small alcove abutting the north cloister. It was my secret place where I went when I had much to think and pray about. Darkness was settling around in part because of the time and in part because of the heavy clouds.

"Thomas, don't speak. Just stay in the shadows," he whispered. He stood with his back to me looking down the cloister halls. I heard much shouting in the background through the Abbey and suddenly the bell began to ring sonorously.

"They found Abbot Godfrey dead. Murdered. A dagger through his heart."

I gasped aloud. Abbot Godfrey dead? How could that be? I had grown to love him in the weeks I worked closely with him. Not an hour ago he was in the prime of health.

"Brother Gethin is accusing you, Thomas. He says it was your dagger and you were the last to see him. Brother Edwin is protesting and arguing with him".

My mind swirled. How could he accuse me? I was innocent. I had done nothing. Then I remembered that unlatched door and the sound of cloth against stone. My mind wrestled with the news but one thought stood out above the others. Gethin must not get the chest or its contents. Abbot Godfrey was convinced of Gethin's treachery. Therefore I had to obey Abbot Godfrey's last wishes and protect the sword. I pulled my cowl tighter over my head.

"Get me to the Abbot's quarters. There is a window along the wall just past the infirmary hidden by some bushes. I can hide there."

Quickly yet as unobtrusively as possible, we took a different route to the infirmary. Noise and shouting abounded. The bell rang constantly. Most of the brothers ran directly towards Abbot Godfrey's rooms. None glanced in our direction. There were no sick in the infirmary this day so nobody saw us as we scurried by. The infirmary is located beside the Abbot's residence and therefore separated from much of the hustle and bustle of normal Abbey life. From there, I just might be able to get in to his rooms. If Prior Edwin followed tradition as he should, the door to the Abbot's quarters would be sealed and guarded. No one would be allowed in until his body could be dressed and prepared for burial. With luck I would climb unseen into my alcove cell from that window near the infirmary.

At the bushes I thanked Owain for warning me. I repeated on Christ's blood that I was innocent and feared Gethin. I bade him Godspeed back to the cloisters. He did not move.

"Do you think I would abandon you at this hour, my friend?" He put his face close to mine. "Hide behind this bush and wait. I will try to misdirect the brothers as they search, so do nothing until then." He spun and ran off.

I heard the shouts and cries and saw the flames rising from lit torches as the brothers searched for me. To my relief they headed out across the orchards and past the mill. Somehow Owain had convinced them I had left the Abbey that way.

Several hours passed. Clouds darkened the moon and rain began to fall. I pulled my robe tightly around me as the cold damp wind began to howl. I shivered and scrunched down hard against the stone wall, shielded from view at least by the corner of the wall and by the shrubbery.

At one point, I was sure I was found. I heard voices rounding the corner. My heart stood still. I forced myself deeper into my hiding spot. There was no mistaking Gethin's harsh voice.

"Now that Edwin has sealed the doors, we cannot get the chest. We'll have to wait until the Justicar has come and certified death. Keep a close watch on the door to see that no one else enters and removes it."

I shook with terror when I heard Gethin's next words. 'Whatever you do, ensure that Thomas dies. There is no telling what he knows and does not know so I cannot take chances. See to it."

The bell pealed mournfully in tribute to the slain Abbot. I could hear the brothers chanting as they prayed for his soul. As they did the skies opened up and the rain began to pour down as if they too cried for Abbot Godfrey. Thunder crashed and lightning creased the clouds.

"Thomas. Come." The cry was so soft I scarce heard it at first. The bush parted and Owain's rain-soaked face appeared.

I scrambled out, surprised to see him dressed in a short tunic and hose. He thrust a sack at me. "Change into these. I took them from the lay brother's storage hut."

I changed quickly, grateful for warm dry coverings and looked up at the window opening. Owain followed my glance. "Quick. Let me boost you up."

He cupped his hands around my feet and lifted me. This was a new confident leader-like Owain unlike the studious yet fun-loving one I had known. I clambered through the opening and into the chambers above. Even though it was pitch black, I knew my way around. Just then a flash of lightning lit the room briefly and I saw Abbot Godfrey lying on his bed seemingly at sleep. I murmured a quick prayer whilst I fumbled for the chest key

I knew I could not take the chest but I silently promised Abbot Godfrey that Gethin would not have the contents. My vow of obedience would see it done. It opened silently. I reached in and removed the great sword. Even in those moments of stress and fear, I was in awe that I, a lowly monk, held Excalibur in my hands. In the darkness I felt the parchments, carefully opened the oiled package and thrust them in. I pushed the bulky parcel into my tunic and crept back to the window. I leaned out and handed the sword to Owain then dropped down beside him.

Never did he ask about the weapon I handed him. I took it back once I was on firm ground, and used my robe as a belt to tie the sword onto my back, for I wanted my hands free. Owain crouched and began creeping towards the Abbey walls. I followed. We stayed in shadow until we came to the millrace.

"Can you swim?" I nodded and without hesitating he slid into the frigid water. Together we quietly swam and floated down the millrace into the river.

I remember the icy soul-numbing cold of both rain and river. The river ranged from neck deep in places to waist deep in others. The sword was a tremendous burden and at times I feared it would take me down. At one point

Owain caught hold of some floating branches and together we lay half dead across them as we drifted slowly but relentlessly downstream banging into half submerged rocks and boulders. Later I saw my legs bleeding and scraped but that night my numbed body felt nothing. I heard the Abbey bells distantly tolling when Owain pushed our branches towards shore. We scrambled up a small pebbly bank as he urged me to quickly follow him.

This was certainly a different Owain. He knew that the river led to this place and knew his way in the woods, striding knowingly across a barely discernible path until we came upon a small shelter. We scrambled in and Owain knelt to light a small fire. "It won't be seen" he said without turning his head, "this is too deep in the woods."

I huddled around the warming flames. "You amaze me Brother." They were my first real words since our flight had begun.

His shoulders moved up and down as he chuckled. "Not every night do I spend in prayers Thomas." As the small fire crackled he wistfully told me that for the past year he'd regretted his decision to take holy orders. On one of his outside trips to deal with traders he'd come to a village and met a girl.

"We fell in love and meet at this hut whenever possible. Alys is a lovely girl, beautiful and wonderful." As the fire began to warm the hut and our bodies, he softly continued and his face told me he was thinking of her and not our situation. "I told Abbot Godfrey about her. He asked me to wait and pray six more months. If I was in the same mind, he would release me from my vows. I agreed but I know I cannot live without Alys. Next month he would have let me leave."

He fell silent. Flames and shadows danced on our faces as we removed our soaked tunics, tying to dry them and our bodies. After several minutes he stood and pointed to what I assumed was east. "We must head back over those mountains. If we can get to my village we can hide. I doubt anyone would look for you there. Gethin will assume I ran away by myself. He knew I was unhappy."

As we lay down to rest Owain finally asked the questions I knew had been burning in his heart all night. "Why was Abbot Godfrey murdered and why were you blamed? And what marvel of a weapon is this that you removed it from the Abbot's chamber?" He posed the questions quietly, without accusation or rancor. "I cast my lot with you because you are my friend. If you care to say nothing, I will still help you."

I could not begrudge him. No matter how much he hoped, I knew that his disappearance would be linked with mine. It was only right that he should understand.

And so I began to tell my tale.

Chapter Seven

Wyndham Building, Washington D.C.

Wyndham did not handle frustration well at the best of times. He picked up the reports from his various operatives a third time, scanned them and threw them down in disgust once again because the facts didn't change. Huw Griffiths' daughter had disappeared. His operatives traced her from the university in Caernarfon to a tidy little village, Bontnewydd, a few miles from the castle town. But there her trail went cold. She'd left her rented flat three months ago the day after she resigned from the university, leaving no forwarding address or contacts.

Wyndham spun his chair to look out the window. Unlike most Washington views, all he saw was uninspiring, noisy K Street and its non-descript buildings. He glowered out at the street. Nobody vanishes that easily, he raged. Gods alive! He slammed his fist on the desk. Did he have to do everything? Was he the only one who could think? He shouted for his assistant. A bubbly blonde flew into the room immediately, smile pasted on her face, her zeal to impress and satisfy him easily read.

He barely looked up. Information was knowledge and knowledge was power. His methodology demanded that he know everything about his adversaries. To their chagrin, erstwhile business partners and opponents knew that reality all too well. Wyndham knew them better than they knew themselves before he ever engaged them in conversation or negotiations. He knew their needs and their weaknesses. It was how he'd built his empire. It was how he would build his new world order.

He began firing a series of commands. His London office had to make the girl a priority, authorizing any and all means at whatever cost to find her. In Washington, Stone Wallace was the target. By this time tomorrow he would know everything from the size and state of Wallace' bank balance to the date and time of his first baby burp. Lastly, his personal jet parked at Reagan National Airport was to be fueled and a tentative flight plan set for his private airport in Wales immediately. By Lleu he was thankful he'd bought that redundant Second World War airfield north of Carmarthen those many years ago. He'd paid the government peanuts, because they were so anxious to rid themselves of redundant properties in the face of severe armed forces cutbacks. The cost of upgrading hadn't mattered because it gave him a convenient base only thirty miles from Llanmerddyn and away from prying eyes.

Armed with his orders the girl left. He thought a moment longer then called one of his plants at the British embassy. In short order he outlined his needs, instructing the functionary to meet him at a coffee shop in nearby Chevy Chase with the required documents in less than two hours. The girl was called back in and told to find a qualified doctor and medical personnel capable of handling severely injured patients on a long journey all within the same time frame. Time, not expense, was the determining factor.

He stood and bundled the reports and papers on Griffiths into his laptop case and stalked into the main office. Nervous staffers kept their heads down working while trying to see their powerful leader out of one eye. His stern demeanor swept a chill through the room anytime he visited, but today's brief stopover had been punctuated with frenzied comings and goings out of his office. Tension pervaded the entire space. Sir Damien was either on the warpath or he was in the midst of a major crisis. You could always tell.

With little more than a glance at his comely assistant, she got the message and scurried into his inner office to retrieve his suitcase. As she did, Wyndham thrust his laptop at her to carry as well. With no acknowledgement of their presence he strode towards the door, aides trailing behind him, looking for all the world like a giant aircraft carrier leaving harbor trailed by its escort vessels.

Dulles Airport, Washington, D.C.

Stone and Chad stopped at the hospital briefly in the morning, pleased there'd been no change in Huw's condition, and then headed to Dulles Airport to meet Mandy's early afternoon flight.

Eventually he spotted her. She wore her rich mahogany hair bundled into a ponytail, framing the hazel green eyes and the spray of freckles perched on her nose and under the eyes. As always she had a book in hand as she struggled to juggle her wheeled suitcase, passport and purse while frantically looking over the crowd. He moved toward her just as she saw him and briefly flashed her sparkling grin in recognition. As she got within shouting distance she blurted "How's Da?"

"Better today, but still sedated." Stone reached down to take her bag and introduced Chad. She nodded a quick hello. As the three headed towards the hospital Stone filled her in on the events of the past few days, He'd thought long and hard about how much to tell her, finally deciding to gently find out what she really knew of Huw's investigations before revealing all. His wonderings were cut short.

"It was those damn Druids wasn't it?" she demanded as the car sped towards the city. "I warned him they would try to hijack his research. You know him; nothing deters him once he's got the bit between his teeth." She sighed and stared out the car windows oblivious to her surroundings. "He told me he'd found something critical—a document of some kind—and that he sent it to me. But it hadn't arrived before…this. And I told him not to involve you in this Stone."

Before Stone could respond fully, they pulled up outside the hospital's emergency entrance. Quickly they made their way to intensive care and asked the formidable nurse on duty for access to the professor's room.

She stared blankly. "He's gone. He was taken not more than an hour ago."

In shock, the trio gaped at her. Mandy gripped Stone's arm. Ever the cop, Chad barged past the nurse flashing his badge and disappeared behind the door. The nurse spun to halt him, only to be stopped in turn by Stone's loud and angry shouts.

"Wait a minute. This is Professor Griffiths' daughter. Until she arrived from the UK, I was responsible for any decisions regarding his care. Nobody informed me of any changes in his situation. You had my contact info. Why wasn't I called?"

The nurse wagged her hands trying to shush him. Calm and quiet was the order of her world and she would have it or else. "The gentleman from the embassy and that businessman Sir Damien. They had papers authorizing it." Before she could continue, Chad burst back through the door, ear glued to his cell and speaking forcefully. She was about to protest when Stone interjected with more questions.

"What embassy authorization are you talking about and who the hell is Sir Damien?" He leaned forward on the wooden counter and put his face as close as he dared to the woman. Jaw tight with anger he quietly hissed at her. "Get that doctor out here now."

"My guys were pulled off protection when the Brits arrived," Chad reported after ending the call in anger. "They were given a written order signed by the watch commander." As he spoke, the door swung open and the doctor strode through, his beaming face throwing wide smiles at Stone and Chad. "Well I must say I'm impressed with the care and concern of the British government for one of its citizens." Without waiting for a response he carried on, oblivious to the tension.

"I admit I was concerned about his care but when I found out that Dr. Horvath was taking over the case, well…I mean he was the one I would have summoned anyway. You know he really is the finest neurosurgeon in the city. Professor Griffiths is lucky to have him as the doctor in charge." He stopped and gawped at the upset and angry trio before him. "Is something wrong?"

Stone and Chad began shouting simultaneously. The nurse cringed behind her counter but stood her ground, perplexed as the rest.

Mandy stepped up to the doctor and introduced herself. "Where is my father, doctor?" she asked quietly. Stone and Chad fell silent.

Frazzled, the doctor hurriedly explained that less than an hour before, a group had showed up armed with letters and documents authorizing him to take Professor Griffiths to Britain immediately.

"It was Sir Damien Wyndham, the billionaire with a gentleman from the Embassy. Showed his credentials and all. Plus, of course, Dr. Horvath and a private nurse."

"He was my father, doctor. You had no right to discharge him to total strangers," Mandy said, thrusting her passport at the doctor.

Chad demanded copies of the documentation and as the nurse scurried off to bring the papers, the doctor dropped into a defensive mode. "The papers seemed legitimate plus I had no qualms when I met with Dr. Horvath and realized he'd be travelling with the professor to ensure his safety and care."

He'd gone over all the charts and reports with both Dr. Horvath and his nurse, looking at treatment and in-flight needs. "I was satisfied the patient would be given a high degree of personalized and professional care.

And the aircraft is often used as a fully equipped medevac craft when not needed by Sir Damien himself. There seemed no credible reason, medical or otherwise, to refuse."

"Exactly where did they take him?" a seething Stone asked.

Both doctor and nurse were adamant. They'd simply been told they were flying back to Britain. Other than that they knew nothing.

Defeated, the three returned to the car. Once inside, Chad used his cell again and briefly explained his need to trace Wyndham's aircraft. At the same time Stone was on his own cell hunting down Wyndham's office number.

Angrily, Mandy grabbed Stone's arm before he could make another call. What now?" she demanded.

Stone sagged back in his seat then looked at Chad.

"I've got people trying to trace his plane," Chad said. "It could be at any one of a number of airports. If it's trans-ocean capable then it must be fairly big. Even so, it could be at Reagan, Dulles or even Baltimore-Washington. Without some kind of lead though, it will be like looking for a needle in a haystack." He spun his cruiser out of the hospital lot and headed towards the Beltway that surrounds Washington. "I can get to any of those airports easier from the Beltway than I can from in town," he shrugged, "and anything's better than sitting in this parking lot.

Reagan National Airport, Washington, D.C.

Ground crew bustled around the Airbus A319CJ corporate jet that dwarfed most of the Embraers, Gulfstreams and Beechcraft parked on the general aviation ramp. For the past fifteen minutes a constant stream of workers had hustled up the stairs into the aircraft's interior lugging boxes and supplies. Other ground crew loaded baggage and other supplies into the hold. As they did, a fuel truck finished pumping into the plane's thirsty tanks.

The pilots walked across the tarmac from the VIP terminal office and mounted the steps prepared for their long flight. Inside, the two flight attendants finished sprucing the cabin, arranging a quiet location aft where the patient could be made comfortable en route.

Sirens blaring, an ambulance roared onto the apron and came to a halt by the stairs leading into the big jet. As the paramedics jumped out, a black stretch limousine pulled up beside it. In short order, the stretchered and sedated patient was lifted gently aboard.

Wyndham and his limo passenger spoke quietly away from the bustle. "Remember, if the ambassador asks questions, refer him to me. You were helping a British citizen in need and I offered my assistance. Other than that, you know nothing. Understood?" Wyndham reached into his jacket and pulled out a neatly bound bundle of hundred dollar bills. "This is to thank you for your help." The fair-haired young man gratefully took it. Without a further word Wyndham bounded up the stairs and into the aircraft.

The young trade officer jumped into the back of the limo and closed the door. With this kind of quick cash he really did not care what Sir Malcolm Huddley, Her Majesty's high and mighty Ambassador said or thought. He could count on Wyndham for protection and was sure he'd impressed Sir Damien that he was a man ready to do any job requiring knowledgeable and discreet employees—particularly if they didn't mind bending the rules a bit.

Quickly, the ground crew rolled back the stairs and unseen hands inside the aircraft closed the jet's door. As the two vehicles rounded the corner, the jet's engines began turning over and slowly but obviously, the luxurious craft moved sedately towards the taxiway.

At VIP terminal window, a sturdy figure kept one hand in his dark grey suit pocket while the other adjusted his glasses. He watched the activities with great interest, staring intently as the aircraft began rolling towards the active runway.

Across the many taxiways and parking stands, he finally glimpsed the jet as it took its place in the takeoff lineup. Even at this distance he saw the giant Air Celtica dragon logo prominent on the tail as it sped down the runway and gently lifted off. He watched it begin a hard climbing left turn to avoid the Washington's sensitive airspace. He stood watching until it disappeared, then walked purposefully out of the terminal to his car. He negotiated the complex roadways around the airport onto US 1, turning north towards the Pentagon and Arlington National Cemetery. By the time he passed the 14th Street Bridge and the Merchant Marine memorial he was delivering his report curtly by cell phone and receiving orders. Abruptly, he acknowledged and scurried to Dulles to catch an immediate flight to London.

He didn't notice the speeding unmarked police cruiser, lights flashing, dashing south towards the airport.

Georgetown

Exhausted, frustrated and shaken, Stone and Mandy entered the townhouse while Chad parked. Silently Stone waved her towards the sofa as Chad banged into the hallway with Mandy's luggage. For the past hour they'd driven the crowded Beltway, finally rushing to National airport on a tip, only to miss the plane's takeoff by minutes.

"Can we get them to turn back somehow? Mandy asked.

Chad shook his head. "No. It would take too long to get authorization to order the plane's recall, even if we had valid security reasons. By the time we could get anything, they'd already be over the Atlantic and out of American airspace."

Throughout the trip from the airport to Georgetown, Stone tried and repeatedly failed to get his phone calls past an officious assistant in Wyndham's office. All she would repeat is that his message would be conveyed to Sir Damien as soon as possible. Threats and pleadings could not sway her.

The normally effervescent Mandy had mostly been silent since the hospital fiasco, responding to questions and comments in brief monotones. Eyes reddened from quiet tears, she asked for and disappeared into the washroom.

Stone slumped into the nearest chair. He looked up as Mandy returned. "Chad has taken your bags upstairs. You can stay here in the guest bedroom if you want," he said lamely.

"Don't!" She glared at him

"Don't what?"

"Don't do that. Don't look at me with that 'poor puppy dog' look, Stone." Her eyes blazed as she looked straight at him. "I am exhausted, I have jet lag, I am worried sick about my father, I am angry at him, at you and Wyndham for creating this mess and mostly I am bloody fed up with traipsing around this city with no idea of how to get my father back and taken care of. So don't give me that solicitous, poor baby look. As we say back home, this has been a right cock up!"

She turned and headed up the stairs, passing Chad on the way up. The detective crumpled his bulk into a nearby arm chair. "She's right, you know. We've bungled this mess badly. Me primarily. I thought police protection would be enough. I certainly didn't count on someone like Wyndham moving so quickly and scooping the professor like that.

"Listen, I called some people I know in intelligence. We'll find out where that plane is going and how Wyndham and the embassy got involved. In the meantime, I have some other things I need to do, people I need to talk to. I'll still have my guys watching this place in case you need us. You and Mandy going to be OK? Uncle Chad says both of you need to try and get some sleep."

Sleep, though, was the last thing Stone could think of. His mind raced, grappling with the enormity of the past few days. Until now the whole Excalibur thing had been a bit of an adventure, an almost theoretical intellectual lark. The bomb and now Huw's 'kidnapping' changed everything. He cradled his face in his hands, exhausted and baffled. I can't handle this, he said to himself. I'm a reporter not some kind of super robocop."

For hours he paced the floor, made numerous cups of coffee, looked over the notes he'd made with Huw and reviewed the maps yet again, all the time wracking his brain for plausible reasons and concrete solutions for their circumstances. Nothing came to him.

Finally, with sleep still eluding him and no answers evident, he switched the computer on and turned again to Brother Thomas's journal.

Chapter Eight

𝔚𝔞𝔩𝔢𝔰, 1301 • 𝔅𝔯𝔶𝔫 𝔉𝔬𝔯𝔢𝔰𝔱

Morning broke bright and clear. I have no idea how long I slept except that, praise God, it was a blessed black hole of darkness, free of dreams and nightmare. I sensed immediately that I was alone. I lurched out of the hut into the sunlight flickering through the branches and leaves of that deep forest glade. Nowhere could I see Owain. Concerned I ran back into the hut. Thankfully, the sword was where I left it, still wrapped and beside it the comforting bulk of the packet. I stepped back outside, circling the hut searching for any sign of Owain and perhaps some water while my stomach rumbled with hunger.

I took myself off to a fallen tree trunk and sat down to contemplate my situation. As the minutes passed I became more and more anxious, so it was with a comforted heart I first heard, and then saw Owain running up the path. Breathless he stopped in front of me, gasping.

"Quick. Brother Gethin pursues us still. He is coming."

Owain grabbed my arm. I shrugged him off and dashed into the hut, grabbing Excalibur and the pouch. He pulled me off the path and together we plunged deeper into the woods. As we ran, fighting loose branches and tripping over roots and stones, Owain gasped out the account of his morning. While I slept he'd crept out, to the village to see Alys and get food and clothing.

"I also wanted to get weapons for our protection but when I got there I saw armed men moving from cottage to cottage, waking people and forcing them to gather on the green. Brother Gethin stood there, shouting that the village give up Owain and Thomas." Owain's white face and labored breathing made the story painful to hear.

"I have no shame in telling you cold fear gripped my heart," he wheezed as we ran. "I had to come and warn you. It won't take long before Gethin finds a villager who'll remember Alys and me going up that path. Then they'll remember the huntsman's hut. Gethin and his henchmen will be behind us soon."

As we ran and stumbled we slowed. Finally, unable to take another step, my side stabbing in pain, I halted. We bent over double, gasping for breath. Whatever St. Benedict's rules did to improve our souls, they had done little for our bodies. I was used to physical labor such as hoeing in the gardens and lifting heavy burdens, but not this demanding race for life. As we slowly gained our breath, I put my finger up to shush Owain. Together we listened painstakingly, fearing to hear noises that would alert us to Gethin's coming.

Instead there was only the silence of the woods, broken by birds singing and the whisper of wind in the trees. Confident now that we could slow down and think, we began walking deeper into the forest.

We talked more about the past two days. I was in a weary state of confusion and could not think straight. We needed to rest. We needed to eat. But at the same time we needed to keep moving. I thought about how to carry out the Abbot's commands knowing I had already broken my vow of obedience by telling Owain some of the story. Yet I must also prevent Gethin—I could no longer think of him as 'Brother'—from finding out about Excalibur and the documents I bore. My mind battled itself. I could not even pray because I knew not what to say.

As we walked we came to the end of the forest. Before us lay the mountains with lots of scrub and gorse but precious little cover. They looked as black as a raven's head that day and the blackness of my despair. I feared for my life. I feared for Owain's life. I feared for Alys. I feared for the church and for Britain. And Gethin filled me with a new dread. This was not the bullying Sacrist and novice master. No, this was a new and terrifying Gethin, representing power and destruction for Holy Church as well as me. What hope was there?

We stayed among the trees and sat down to contemplate our next move. Owain was all for heading out immediately across the mountain. "That is Bryn Penbarryn. We must climb it, then work our way through Tir Iarll towards Mynydd Margam. There, in Margam's shadows, we will hide while we decide what path to take."

I argued we should hold back. It was daylight. The late winter- early spring sun beat down on us, warming us physically if not spiritually. Clouds rolled towards us out of the west, but for now the day was clear. If indeed Gethin followed us, he would easily see us picking our way up the mountain, I reasoned, for Owain admitted that it would take several hours before we could disappear over its top. Also, Gethin had armed men with him, not Brothers from the Abbey. How he came by them and who they were I knew not, but he certainly had men beholden to him. That much was obvious.

"I would not put it past him to have men riding across country and around the entire area looking for us. I do not want to be caught out in the open."

Owain finally agreed. We turned back into the forest a ways. Beside a small brook, he pulled out a loaf of bread he collected as he ran from the village. We lay down and drank our fill, sharing the meagre loaf.

I wondered about going back for Alys, but Owain assured me she could care for herself and knew the way to Owain's village. She would join us there. Silence fell between us. I fiddled with a stalk of grass. Owain closed his eyes and closed his eyes, head back and his hands behind.

"I know a small cave not far from here. We could hide there for this day." He turned to look at me, the slight smile ever present on his face no matter what the trials or tribulations. "I found it one day while wandering the woods with Alys." He blushed but gave no further explanation.

We agreed to hide there for the remainder of the day. As we trudged along I suddenly realized two things. Deep amongst the trees and without Abbey bells and the discipline of The Rule, I had not one idea of what time of day it was. Second, I had gone through several Offices this day without once spending time in prayer. May God forgive me at the time of Judgment! Oh,

Abbot Godfrey, I prayed silently, why did you select one so unspiritual and so unworthy as I?

The cave was ideally situated part way up a small hill and well hidden by bushes. As we circled around the cave to determine its ability to hide and protect us, I noticed a beautiful grove of oak trees not more than one hundred yards away. Between the grove and our cave, the same brook babbled and bubbled. The clear and fresh waters slaked our thirst once more and we rested just inside the cave. It was barely big enough for us both, but was dry and smelled fresh. No animals had made it their lair, thankfully.

We slept through the day, one sleeping while the other watched. I felt safe for now in this idyllic setting although I was only too aware of Gethin's shadow that towered over me like a dark demonic cloud, blacker than night and cold with the chill of fear. Involuntarily I shuddered as I watched, despite the warmth of the day.

It was early evening and the sun's warmth began to fade along with the light. Gloom sifted through the trees as it sifted through my heart. I did not see how I could bear this burden. Indeed, I did not even know my next step. At the Abbey, once the wonderful words were finished my task would have been over. Abbot Godfrey would have sent everything to Rome and I would have returned to my daily routines. But this was not to be. Abbot Godfrey was dead and I was hunted by one who knew how to hate and inflict pain.

I carried Excalibur and the parchment, but what was I to do with them? I had no one in whom to confide. From Abbot Godfrey's last words to me I also knew that there were those who sought to bring destruction on our land. What I now carried had the potential to be part of that destruction. Jesu, my mind swirled with thoughts and fears, hopes and grief.

For the first time that day I began to pray. If I could not be at the Abbey at least I would maintain the Offices. In my mind I began to chant the psalms until Owain poked me hard in the back. "Fool. Someone might hear you."

Only then did I realize that I had actually chanted aloud. Chagrined, I drew back into myself and Owain went back on watch.

Darkness falls swiftly in the forest, particularly in early spring. One moment all is light. Then suddenly all is inky black. It was, I thought, a replica of my past day; light and life one instant and then a stubborn, unyielding darkness.

I stirred my body and stretched as Owain did the same. He parted the bushes that concealed the entrance and was just about to emerge when he stopped and slowly, stealthily withdrew. Even in the dimness of our shelter I could see his white face. He put his hands to my lips to stop my words blurting out. "Someone comes," he whispered.

I squeezed up beside him. Panic and fear invaded my very being. If we were found now, we were trapped. There was no escape. Our only hope was that it was Alys come to find us and succor us with food, for indeed even in that fearful moment my empty stomach made a gurgling sound that would have alerted armed hordes from Caerleon to St. David's. I clutched my stomach as if by sheer force I could keep it silent.

Together we watched. At first it was only a shadow. Then a white figure moved towards the grove of oaks followed moments later by still more white shadows. My first thought of an evil spirit disappeared as I soon recognized flesh and blood, though in the quickly disappearing light I could not see their faces. In all, about a dozen arrived and stood amongst the trees. Silence deepened such that I could even hear them breathing heavily after their walk. The figure leading held a lit torch flickering in the growing darkness. As one, they all stopped to light their own torches from his. Their robes held no resemblance at all to those we'd worn at Cwmllyn with a shinier countenance rather than the coarse wool of our monkly robes.

They stood soundless in a circle. Each, it seemed, with his back to one of those great oaks, themselves also, I suddenly realized, in a large circle. We watched as yet another appeared, striding with authority to the centre. A great golden chain necklace glimmered in the torch light. It was then we noticed a garland of leaves around his head and that he held a long staff topped with a gold carving.

"My companions. My brothers!" he cried out.

We both gasped silently as we recognized the harsh and all too well-known voice. It was Gethin.

I peered intently through the bush, staring at my nemesis. Had he been swarming through the forest with an army of men, searching for us, I would not have been as surprised. But to see him thus, robed but not from the abbey and surrounded by unfamiliar people…well it beggared the imagination.

He was not rushed. Both his hands were raised, ordering silence in a group already silent. In his left hand the staff's carving flashed as torch flames caught it.

"*Ta muid anse. Na deithe a dhruadh*. We are here to honor the gods. O gods whose power gives life to everything that lives, be you here with us."

My eyes closed tightly and I began to pray silently and fervently to our Lord Jesus Christ and to God the father. Now I understood Abbot Godfrey's fears and his oblique warning. As I prayed I heard the unholy chanting rise from the assembled fiends. Owain and I were unwilling witnesses to a Druidic ceremony. The traitor Gethin was one of the old religion, sent as a poisonous, treacherous turncoat to sow dissent in our Abbey, to dissuade brothers from their faith by violence and most importantly to seize Excalibur.

My anger began to seethe and boil inside me. I must have lurched forward, for Owain gripped me tightly and held me down, shaking his head vigorously at me, saying naught but pleading with his eyes. I subsided. We watched.

Hands still in the air, Gethin moved around the grove, tapping each tree and the ground with his staff. The others followed his lead. Soon all were chanting and swaying as they walked around the grove. Gethin glided to the center and fell silent as he raised his staff towards the darkening sky.

"Earth. Water. Air. Fire. Spirits all. We invite you to come upon us all. Bring us your power O gods. Guardians of our faith. We call upon you to give us your power."

The other Druids chanted "bring us the power. Give us your power."

As they intoned their cries to their gods, a darkening sky suddenly lit with lightning cracking from one side of the sky to the other. I felt the thunder shake our shelter. My prayers became more sustained and more fervent.

"My brothers," Gethin cried out. "Let us worship the gods of our ancestors, Arawn, lord of the underworld and Taranis, god of war, who have led us thus far. Let us worship the gods of our ancestors who call upon us to cleanse this land of the Christian plague." His voice grew sharper. "We worship you Arawn and Taranis." The shout of approval came from the assembled Druids. Gethin waited before speaking again.

"The god Arawn calls for a sacrifice before he answers. The god of the underworld calls one of his own. We will not see success until it is done."

He stopped suddenly. Silence enclosed the grove as rain beat down. Slowly he circled the assembled Druids, pausing in front of each one before moving on. Once he had completed the circle he returned to the centre and looked skyward again. Still looking up, he suddenly dropped the arm holding the hazel staff and spun around, leaving the staff pointing directly at one of the Druids. A sigh went up from the rest.

Together, in a sonorous monotone they chanted.

> WE ALL COME FROM THE GODDESS.
> TO HER WE HAVE RETURNED.
> AS OUR ANCESTORS WORSHIPPED HER.
> AIR, EARTH AND WATER.
> HOOF AND HORN.
> HOOF AND HORN.
> ALL THAT DIES SHALL BE REBORN.
> CORN AND GRAIN, CORN AND GRAIN.
> ALL THAT FALLS WILL RISE AGAIN.

The singled out Druid moved slowly to the center of the circle, coming to a stop in front of Gethin. He raised his head, looking up into the skies. Silence oozed through the awful scene. Gethin reached inside his robe and drew out a short sword. Without pausing, he reached up and in one motion swept the weapon across the Druid's throat. Even in the dark I could see the spurts of blood explode out as Gethin stepped back and allowed the body to drop to the ground.

> Hoof and horn, hoof and horn.
> All that dies shall be reborn."
> "Corn and grain, corn and grain.
> All that falls will rise again.

Gethin's harsh guttural voice intoned the chant alone.

He ignored the crumpled body at his feet. "Our brother's sacrifice will ensure our ultimate success. The gods have spoken. We need have no fear, no hesitation as we work to our final goal. We are close my brothers. Within the day, we will have those cursed monks in our hands. They will die and we will have Excalibur."

His voice increased in volume. "With the power of the sword we will sweep the Christians into the seas, away from our shores. We will destroy their god and banish the name of Jesus Christ from the memories of our beloved land.

"Now my brothers, now is the time for action. Return to the village. Destroy it in the name of Arawn. Kill all who stand in your way. And bring out the hounds to track down Thomas and Owain."

Without another word, he strode onto the very path we had stumbled along in our flight to the cave. Still in silence the other Druids fell into line behind him and they disappeared into the gloom of the dark dank forest.

We waited for near one hour as far as we could tell before we moved. In that time we looked at each other, afraid even to whisper in case one of Gethin's underlings might yet be lingering nearby either to trap us, if they knew we were there, or perhaps recover the body that still lay unmoving in the glade.

Owain, I knew, feared for Alys and her family. He wanted to rush out of the cave and race to the village to warn them and protect them, but knew he could not. He burned with anxiety, guilt and frustration. But after what we had seen in the oak grove, we knew that for the good of the faith we had to sacrifice our own desires. God calls on his followers to give much because he has given much. He gave his life for us. Could we not give up our own?

Quietly we crept out of the cave, listening intently for any sign that our enemies were near. Hearing and seeing nothing, we stepped across the brook and into the grove. The Druid's body remained untouched in the center of the grove. Owain, the braver of us, reached down and turned the body over. We gasped and stared into the sightless eyes of our former Sub-sacrist, Brother Emlyn. Blood made watery in the rains, smeared his white robe and soaked into the earth.

"It is clear that nobody stands in Gethin's way. He demands obedience even to the point of death from even his friends."

"If indeed he has friends!"

My fear was that the hounds Gethin mentioned would track us to our deaths. We had to throw them off and lay a false trail. So we walked around the grove twice then headed back towards the village. When the track crossed the brook we stepped into the icy cold water and reversed direction, this time heading back towards the deadly grove. Without a word or a glance at Emlyn's body we trudged along the river bed, our numbing feet trying to pick our way over the rocks and branches lying in the stream. For the second night in a row I found myself soaked in icy cold water. And for the second night in a row the rains came. Although they added to our misery, I also welcomed them. Last night the torrents no doubt shortened the search for us. The clouds had blocked the moonlight, so that I remained hidden. Tonight they would wash out traces of our rampage through the woods, God willing, and clean away our smells so the hounds could not follow. When we felt we had followed the stream sufficiently long we looked carefully until at last we saw what we wanted.

A large rock jutted into the river. Tired, strength waning, we forced ourselves upon onto the rock. It was bare of earth for a distance into the woods. The marks of our leaving the stream would be unseen to anyone searching.

As we began our climb up Bryn Penbarryn I looked back and saw a red glow across the woods. It was the village, put to the torch by Gethin's orders. Owain noticed and stopped. He stared a while into the darkness then groaned and resolutely turned to continue the climb. As we struggled the rain stopped as suddenly as it began. Perhaps, I thought, the rain truly was sent to preserve us and now God knew it was no longer needed. Comforted by that thought, I struggled to keep climbing. My feet soon began to regain their feeling; and the feeling was pain as sharp stones and rocks cut through the thin leather of my footwear.

With nothing other than brief glimpses of moonlight we trudged through gorse and small bushes, stumbling, sweating our way onwards. As we clambered ever upwards I again felt the burden of the sword. I do not mean that it was heavy—though indeed it was—rather, I mean the burden of the knowledge of the sword. Already, many had died; Abbot Godfrey of a certainty, and how many villagers? All were now a burden on my soul. My life, turned upside down the past few weeks, was now forfeit unless I could protect Excalibur.

To this point we had climbed in silence. I could bear it no longer. "I am so sorry Owain. If I could rewrite yesterday I swear before God I would have refused your help. I would not have wished this upon you my very real friend."

"I chose this path for myself, Thomas because I know you are honest and trustworthy and you were my only friend. Except for Alys, that is." He gave me a quick glance and by the light of the moon I could see a brief smile light his face.

"God is faithful and just, my friend." I told him with a confidence I myself did not really feel at that moment. "He will protect Alys. You will see."

I hitched the sword higher on my shoulder. It was time to tell Owain everything else that I had not told him last night.

In particular, he needed to know that I carried Excalibur.

Chapter Nine

Georgetown

The demanding ring interrupted Stone's unsettled sleep. He staggered from the couch where he'd fallen asleep and fumbled for the phone. He glanced at his watch. Just past one in the morning; only forty minutes since he'd dozed off.

"Mr. Wallace? Damien Wyndham here. You were trying to reach me?"

Shocked, Stone shook himself awake and, controlling his anger with difficulty, demanded explanations as forcefully as he could.

"My dear fellow, I simply felt that one of Britain's foremost scholars deserved the finest possible medical assistance. The embassy insisted that I step in to take care of the situation. Rather than let him be treated in America we felt it better that he be home and so with embassy permission I took the necessary steps. Fortunately, my aircraft was available and I was able to bring in highly competent medical people. So the decision was made to retrieve him from hospital and bring him home again."

Wyndham's smooth honeyed voice sounded like he was just next door.

"I had no idea that you had a vested interest or, my assistants now tell me, some ill-defined medical guardianship of the professor."

As Wyndham spoke, Stone noticed a slightly disheveled Mandy slip quietly down the stairs, concern on her face. He mimed for her to quietly pick up the extension and maintain silence.

"…fact of the matter is, only Professor Griffiths' family has the real right to decide medical issues, Mr. Wallace. And, in the absence of any family members on site so to speak, the embassy felt constrained to repatriate him to where the family could indeed make any necessary decisions about his care."

"And did you contact the family, Mr. Wyndham?"

"Unfortunately no. At this point the embassy has not yet reached the professor's relations. But speed was of the essence, so we acted in Professor Griffiths' best interests."

"Exactly where are you, Mr. Wyndham and where are you taking Huw?"

"Exactly? At this point we are exactly out over the Atlantic Ocean east of Nova Scotia. Where we are taking him really is none of your business. But out of courtesy I can tell you that we are at this point heading for Wales. Don't worry Mr. Wallace. The professor is doing as well as can be expected according to our doctor on board and he will soon have the benefit of the finest medical help possible." Without waiting for a response, Wyndham hung up.

"At least Huw is OK at this point," Stone smiled wanly, trying to reassure her. She nodded silently, tears trickling down her face.

"Mandy, we have to strategize. You need to know some things about your father and why Wyndham took him out of the hospital."

She sat down. "I know some of it. He was looking into the Druids and digging into Arthurian legends. I helped him with some of that. But he said the less I knew at this point, the safer I was." Her soft Welsh lilt betrayed her uneasy state. "I knew he wanted to talk to you so he used a speaking engagement over here to see you personally." She looked at Stone, her eyes glaring.

"I was dead set against it. You are not trained as a historian. You may be a good reporter but it needs more than that. Much more. Da ignored my advice. I was furious with him when he insisted on getting you involved. This requires serious study not some ego-tripping piece of fluff for a newspaper or television broadcast." Her voice trailed off and she looked away.

The tension mounted as Stone tried to control his own temper.

"Look. You may not like it that I'm involved, but I am. Huw felt my skills as an investigative reporter would be useful. He also knew I had some familiarity with the Druids because of the Taranis pieces." He stood up and began pacing the room. "I didn't ask to get involved and I'm still having a hard time coming to grips with what he told me. But here's the reality Mandy. I AM involved. It was my car that was demolished by a bomb. It was my friend who was injured. I was the target of bullets and an attempted hit and run. So whether you like it or not, I'm in. So either deal with it or go back home."

She continued to glare at him without response as he told her everything from Huw's enigmatic phone call to her own arrival. Finally he led her into the study so she could read the manuscript as he had. Stone watched her reactions carefully. Her face was animated as she read Brother Thomas's journal. Shock, wonder, anger and fear flashed across her features. Almost to herself she muttered "so this is what Da was doing?" She looked up at Stone.

"What were you planning to do before…before it happened? Why did he come to you?"

"Believe it or not, I do have a knack for getting information. Plus, he trusted me and felt that because I was an outsider I could poke around where he could not. Your father sent some of this information to a friend of his, Father Joe at the Vatican to see if he could find anything but it troubled him that he'd heard nothing back. So our first thought was to track down Father Joe then, pending what he said, either fly to Rome or Wales and hunt for Excalibur ourselves."

He paused, willing her to believe his next statement. "Your father believes that the sword exists and has some kind of supernatural power that's indispensable to the Druids. He believes—and convinced me—that the movement is a threat. More than that, they are a deadly organization on a par with Al Qaeda or the Taliban. They must be stopped."

"Da was always a bit over dramatic, but I think this time he's underplaying it." She crinkled her freckled nose. "I left the university—pressured to leave—by some of these madmen. They wanted me to swallow their mystical Druid mumbo jumbo and teach it in the classroom. No academic freedom. No disagreement with the mantra of the day." Her bitterness was evident. "I refused to go along with their agenda. I had no choice. So I left."

Stone rubbed his hands over his face wearily. "It seems that more and more arrows are pointing at Wales." He gestured at the maps he and Huw had pored over. "Now with Wyndham heading that way, maybe we should go there ourselves."

"Sorry. What?" Lost in thought, Mandy flipped loose hair out of her face and stopped staring at Thomas' journal.

"I said we should fly to Wales. That's where they're taking Huw." She nodded slowly in agreement and sighed, brushing more stray hairs from her face.

"How soon could we get a flight? Tomorrow?"

As Stone nodded and started to rise she suddenly held up her hand to stop him. "You said Da lost contact with Father Joe??"

"You know him too? Huw tried to contact him at the Vatican apparently, but no joy."

"That's because he's not in Rome." She dug into her purse.

"I got this email just the day before you called about Da. Father Joe sent it." She handed him a crumpled fold of paper.

"He's been assigned to Venice? The monastery of San Bernardo?" He shook his head in disbelief. "But he's supposed to be a renowned historian working in the Vatican archives"

Mandy nodded agreement. "He is, but I wonder if this isn't some kind of punishment for burrowing into files he shouldn't have"

"You're joking? You're suggesting that the Druids might even have people infiltrating the Vatican?"

"Why not? According to Thomas they infiltrated Cwmllyn Abbey didn't they? They're penetrating governments, universities and international corporations across the US and UK. Why not the Vatican as well?

She was silent for a few moments, thinking through the implications. "Maybe Father Joe isn't important enough to dispose of. This is simply getting him out of the way. It's a cloistered monastery where they follow a vow of silence. I called a friend of mine in the Church when I got the email. The monastery's on an island in the Venetian lagoon. Obviously a good place to isolate troublesome priests as well."

St. Brigitte's, Paimpont, France

Tonnerre paced his office. Things had gone from bad to worse. First that fool Belenos, then he was the butt of a diatribe from Rhiannon that called into question not only his ability to lead but his devotion to the gods. Making matters worse he'd received an enigmatic call from Wyndham. No doubt that meddler was told about the mess by Rhiannon. *Merde!* He, the great *Patron* called to account by a woman and her stooge and all because of that cretin Belenos. *Merde!* By the gods he would pay!

East of Canadian coast, 25,000 feet

In the dimly lit cockpit the copilot acknowledged Gander Oceanic Air Control Center and accepted a flight level of 35,000 feet on Track W across the Atlantic. As they began a slow climb, the Captain concentrated on the information he held in his lap.

"This weather report is worrying. Shanwick Atlantic air traffic control says heavy turbulence on all tracks due to a Force 12 gale. It'll stick with us all the way." He looked at his First Officer. "Carmarthen is a tough place to put this bird down at the best of times, but a major gale blowing in from the Irish Sea will make it near impossible to set down with a critical patient like ours."

"You going to be the one to tell Sir Richard we might not put down in Carmarthen?"

"No. We have no certainty yet. Let's just monitor for now." He wagged his head at the copilot. "Buzz the galley and see if we can get some brew up here. I'll bother the boss later if it's necessary."

Its climb completed, the craft turned smoothly into its assigned track across the North Atlantic. Darkness enveloped the plane.

Georgetown

The smell of sizzling bacon penetrated Stone's mind as he rolled over and checked the bedside clock. Seven thirty in the morning and already Mandy must be awake. He jumped up, showered quickly, dressed and headed downstairs. In the kitchen, Mandy had made herself at home.

"Morning! Can't provide a full Welsh breakfast I'm afraid. No tomatoes and beans that I can find. But we'll have bacon and eggs."

She pushed a plate across to Stone and added an aromatic cup of coffee in the bargain smiling slightly, refreshed by the sleep, but still worried. Wyndham's enigmatic call and their subsequent discussion had weighed on both their minds. Neither had slept well. Stone surprised himself with his appetite, wolfing down his food. Mandy too, ate heartily.

"So, do we buy tickets for Wales?" Stone pushed the empty plate away. The question hung in the air. His normal decisiveness had fallen apart. He still couldn't fully wrap his mind around everything and now he was dealing with an angry, determined and intelligent woman who also happened to be a daughter who clearly loved her father. It seemed best to defer to her on this one.

Mandy put her knife and fork down. "The heart says yes, the mind says no. Yes, I want to go to Wales, find Da and make sure he's OK. But I'm not sure that's the right thing to do. Oh, it's the compassionate daughter thing yes, but the correct and wise decision? I'm not sure." She paused. "Whatever we may think of Wyndham and the Druids, look you, it's obvious they want Da alive. They've hired the best medical help for him. No he'll be kept alive so he can tell them what he knows."

She scoffed. "It won't work though, because he's a stubborn old sod. They won't get anything of substance from him he'll just dribble bits of useless information to stall them. That gives us time." Mandy took a sip of the strong black coffee. "Practically speaking, we must go to Venice, find Father Joe and talk to him. Maybe he has the documents as well." She shrugged. "If it doesn't work out, well then, we can then go to Wales. Above all, we've got to find the truth behind this Excalibur parchment and put an end to this nonsense." She looked at him smiling fully for the first time.

"You and Da agreed your first step was to find Father Joe, right? I think that's what he'd tell us to do now if he was here."

The bang of the front door followed by Chad's shout interrupted them.

"In the kitchen, Chad."

"Stone, you've got get out. Now!" He waved down Stone's protestations, as he blasted into the room. "Police and FBI will be here shortly. They want to take you in for questioning about the bomb. You're the main suspect."

An explosive "what?" from both Stone and Mandy interrupted his breathless explanation. "I shouldn't be here and shouldn't be warning you. Look, my car's parked in the next street. Grab your things quickly and we'll go out the back garden and down the alley.'

His "just do it!" galvanized them into action.

Within minutes Mandy repacked the few items she'd taken out. Stone grabbed a suitcase kept permanently packed for his frequent sojourns along with his laptop and the flash drive. They hurried across the tiny back yard to a gate and into the alley. Seconds later they jumped into Chad's vehicle.

As they pulled out, Stone crumpled down in the passenger seat. A police car, lights flashing but no siren followed by a dark blue Malibu spun around the corner headed towards Stone's townhouse.

"You've got to get away from here. This is going higher and getting messier. I got a heads up less than thirty minutes ago. The orders to pick you up came from Justice; someone high up in Homeland Security." Chad stopped for a red light and turned quickly to face Stone.

"You've been named as a 'person of interest' in Huw's attack. He nodded at Stone's expletive.

"I know, I know, it makes no sense." He accelerated as the light changed and turned south onto 29th Street.

"Thing is, there are people who want your skin plus you're an easy and highly visible target. My guys think there are strings being pulled somewhere. Whoever it is, he wants Stone Wallace taken right out of the picture."

"You think it's something to do with Excalibur?"

"That would be my guess." Chad slowed for lights then turned east on Pennsylvania Avenue towards Washington Circle. "Anyway, not everyone agrees. You do have friends."

Stone looked up. "You said 'my guys' a second ago. Yesterday and just now you spoke of 'friends'. What's going on Chad?"

A quick grin crossed Chad's face. "Not just another pretty face, you know. Let's just say I moonlight with one of our intelligence services. Done it for seven years."

Surprise and shock crossed Stone's face. In the rear, Mandy leaned forward. The practical side of her took over. "Does that mean the CIA believes that someone else did the bombing? That they know Stone's innocent?"

"Not CIA Mandy. That's not my outfit. Let's just say my team is a small offshoot of the government's security setup." With a twist of the wheel, he steered the car around Washington Circle, slowed for the heavy traffic, then reached into a pocket and handed a package to Stone.

"Here's a cell phone. It's not registered in your name or mine. Use this, not your own. It would be too easy to trace you. If you need to reach me just push star one and you'll be connected immediately."

"I'm going to drop you at the Foggy Bottom Metro station. Take the Orange Line train west to Vienna at end of the line. Get off and head to the car park. Here's a set of keys. Once you've left the car park cross over Virginia Centre Boulevard. On the northwest corner you'll see an office building. There's a green Ford Fusion parked facing the boulevard. Take it and head west on I 66. I'll call you in two hours. By then you should be close to Winchester. Pull over somewhere and wait for my call."

They pulled up at the Metro station. As she looked around, Mandy recognized George Washington Hospital across the street. Shuddering, she quickly followed Stone into the station.

As they made their way through the crowds past the fare barrier, Stone noticed a burly uniformed policeman standing discreetly to the side. He was watching them intently. Stone and Mandy kept pace with the crowds flocking toward the escalator. Suddenly the cop approached them, reached out and grasped Stone's arm.

"Stone Wallace?" The officer said brusquely.

Before he could stop himself, Stone blurted "Yes".

"I thought I recognized you. Hope you don't mind, but my wife and I really appreciate your travel shows on TV. Heading to Dulles airport are you? I don't want to stop you, but do you think you could quickly give me an autograph. For the wife, of course."

Shaking slightly, Stone breathed deeply and nodded, put his bags down, took a pen and signed the officer's note pad. Waving away his thanks and leaving the policeman with a big grin, Stone and Mandy proceeded deeper into the station.

In a daze they stepped onto the westbound train.

Atlantic Ocean, 35,000 feet

Wyndham barged into the cockpit, slamming the door on his way in. "What do you mean abort Carmarthen?"

Swiftly the pilot explained the weather problems facing them. "The field is barely capable of accepting this aircraft in good weather, but in full gale conditions, it's pushing the safety envelope to put down there. The field has little or no margin of error on runway length and few emergency capabilities. This storm is a big one. We've diverted well north of Scotland. Our new flight plan will actually bring us over mid Norway before we swing back west to the UK. We think that will minimize turbulence on the flight." He twisted around to look at Wyndham. "I presume you don't want your passenger bumped around unnecessarily, sir."

"Options?"

"We could return to a Canadian airport and wait it out. Or, we could go around the storm and land at a European field and wait there."

Wyndham stared into the darkness rubbing his eyebrow unconsciously.

"Where in Europe? Would we be enough around the storm that we could land in France?" Already his mind was percolating with an idea.

The pilot checked and looked up. "It'll be close. We have to swing further north and east to avoid the worst of the storm. Our best bet frankly is to swing wider into Northern Europe. Norway, Sweden or Finland would be better and wait it out there."

Dealing with Tonnerre had often meant flying to Breton airports near Paimpont. Wyndham thought for a moment. "Can we make Rennes or Nantes?"

"It might be possible but that storm is rushing towards Ireland then across Wales and within hours it will be threatening France. Nantes and Rennes are both in Brittany, near the coast."

"Dammit, I know where they are. But if we abort Carmarthen I want France."

"As it is, sir, we're adding several hours to our flight time. The storm will probably envelop Brittany before we can land."

Wyndham punched the cockpit door in frustration. "Get as close to France as possible before you have to land. Then Rennes. Let me know immediately you have a confirmed flight plan."

Wyndham disappeared aft, stopping at the galley to get his favorite drink, Chivas Regal Royal Salute a rare luxurious blend of fifty year old whiskies. There were only two hundred and fifty bottles of the blend in existence and at $10,000 a bottle he was delighted that he'd already bought ten. For him the smooth taste was elixir from the gods. And it was one idiosyncrasy he could well afford. Certainly it might help ease his frustration. As he savored it, he considered the change in plans. He could ensure continued medical attention for the professor at Paimpont and while there deal finally with the troublesome Tonnerre. He calmed down. It might cost a day, but it would rid him of the Breton. The more he thought, the more he considered it well worth the delay.

Chapter Ten

Buckingham Palace Mews, London

From his office window Sir Giles could just see the walls surrounding Buckingham Palace, known to most of them simply as Buck House or The House. Things were happening. There was a sense of crisis permeating the halls of power in London, Washington and Paris. In the past six months there had been the French president's assassination plus seemingly random murderous attacks on a number of churches in England, the United States, and Canada, not to mention several unsolved murders of prominent businessmen, journalists and politicians in all three countries.

All of the attacks used the same modus operandi—one or two shooters armed with automatic weapons opening fire. Leaving dead and wounded behind, the assailant escaped untouched, except in Tennessee. A lucky shot by an alert security guard killed one attacker although there was no ID yet. Investigations were continuing and security was tightened at many churches in anticipation of next Sunday's services. But how could you be secure against random assaults?

Heavy autumn rains raked against the windows. The door opened softly and Freddy Garret strode in, handing the director a file. "Thought you might want to see this latest intelligence Sir Giles"

He flipped through the papers quickly but thoroughly as was his wont. "Maddox saw? Professor loaded onto the aircraft? Wyndham as well?" One eyebrow was raised quizzically, giving Sir Giles what Freddy considered a "spockian" look after his favorite Star Trek character the unemotional but intelligent Mr. Spock.

"Plane going where?"

"A flight plan was filed for a small airport near Carmarthen. It's the old RAF base, Tregifor. Wyndham bought it some years ago during the military step down."

"Wonder he didn't buy a bloody aircraft carrier at the same time" Sir Giles sniffed. "Government hamstrung us. Sold essential bases and equipment cheap as chips." He huffed his way around the desk and plopped into his seat.

"Things are getting dicey. Heating up too fast. Men on the ground at that airbase immediately. See if we can intercept Wyndham and the professor. Must be some damn charges we can lay. Circumspect though," he warned, "No heavy stuff." He read further into the file. "Wallace? Connection to Griffiths and the Druids?'

The spockian eyebrow rose again. Freddy pointed silently further down the page.

"Ah. Get a copy of that Taranis article. See what else we can get on Wallace and Griffiths. He waved dismissal and then as Freddy turned away, he shook his head wonderingly. "Doesn't hold water. Him as suspect" he muttered.

As Freddy left, the guvnor leaned back in his comfortable oversized leather chair. There were all sorts of loose threads flying around; assassinations, political resignations, bombings, kidnappings, random mass murder. Until he sorted them and tied them together in some comprehensive order, he could do nothing. Only then would he require action from his specialized and special teams. He never placed them in jeopardy unknowingly and prided himself on keeping them as safe as possible in their underground world. Except, he thought, for poor Harry Lange. Bungled operation. Bungled investigation. He shook his head in disgust.

He picked up the red 'eyes only' file folder again. From it he extracted reports from his North American operatives including Lange, Broderick and Maddox. Despite Sir Giles's grudging nods to modern technology, he much preferred tried and true paperwork. Hard copy which could be read and re-read was the bedrock of his thinking process. He literally absorbed any information on paper, convinced there was something tangible in his ability to handle, touch, and feel the information rather than staring at it on a screen. Paper reports were a staple in his office and woe betide any staffer who relied solely on digital input.

He reviewed the Murphy report again, looking for more threads. He tut-tutted to himself, intrigued that Murphy entered the country under an alias only to disappear into the Welsh countryside. His agents could only surmise he was meeting Rhiannon. The reports also suggested as yet unproven connections between Murphy and Sir Damien Wyndham which, if true, would explain Murphy's bottomless funding.

He felt the hairs on the back of his head begin to tingle. Whenever he sensed them vibrate, he knew he was on the trail. Sir Giles thought for a moment, doodling idly with his pencil then, sitting back with a pleased look, he punched a button on his phone.

"Freddy. Activate Charlie immediately. I want on-ground information."

Security Intelligence Directorate; Chantilly, Virginia

Chad shifted in his uncomfortable straight back chair. Across the desk he waited patiently for response from Calvin Tyler, SID's Director and Chad's covert operations boss.

"Good job hustling Wallace and the girl out of town. There are senior people at Homeland Security determined to put Wallace away."

"Yes sir, but how long can we keep them out of sight? The Bureau is involved and the DC, Virginia and Maryland police are all looking for the two of them. It's a put up job yes, but who?"

"Yes indeed, who?" Tyler scratched his chin.

"Ever run across a man by the name of Harry Lange? British fellow."

"No sir." The abrupt change of topic was typical of any session with Tyler. Chad knew the circle would close eventually.

"Murdered in the District a couple of months ago. He was working for my British counterpart Sir Giles Broadbent. We had a scoop arranged to pick up a particular individual but the CIA totally scaled back the operation without telling me or the Brits. I can't find out who made that decision. In fact I've been told officially to drop the subject". Swearing, he angrily jabbed a finger at Chad. "A complete 'cock up' as the Brits would say. Lange stabbed to death just across the street from the Agency's team and yet no witnesses. It stinks to high heaven…and nobody tells Calvin Tyler to lay off a security issue like that."

He picked up a pen and began tapping it on his desk.

"The thing is. Lange was working on American connections with the Celtic groups; highly placed connections too. Now we've got the attempt on Professor Griffiths' life and the sudden intervention—or should we call it kidnapping—by Sir Damien Wyndham." The pen stopped. "Something's coming down. I can feel it. I can smell it."

Chad shifted again, hoping Stone would understand and forgive his breach of confidentiality. "I might have some information there," he said quietly. As briefly as he could, he brought his chief up to date on the Arthurian connection and the monk's document,

Tyler stood and wandered around the desk, leaning on it in front of his seated associate. "And you say the professor was all hung up about King Arthur's sword, a medieval monk and a Druid's grab for European and maybe world power?"

Chad smiled slightly. Sound bizarre, I know. But I've read some of the monk's letter and if it's authentic…well, there may be more to this than fairy stories."

Tyler was quiet for a moment. He twirled in his office chair.

"Chad, you are now officially sick! Stress and a flu bug or whatever you want. I'll have a doctor call your precinct captain right away. He'll backdate your medical visit to yesterday morning, so there won't be a link between you and Wallace's disappearance." He leaned forward. "Wallace is the key. We've got to keep him under the radar and out of jail. If he's picked up it effectively puts him on ice. So your job is simple. Keep him close and keep him safe. Right now he's the only lead we've got."

His face creased into a small grin. "One good thing. At this point they're only looking for Stone Wallace. Nobody, other than you, and possibly that half-baked doctor at GW hospital, seems to be aware that Griffiths' daughter is in this country. Keep it that way."

Atlantic Ocean 35,000 feet

After confirming a new flight plan, the pilot turned control over to his first officer and disappeared into the back. He knelt beside a dozing Wyndham and nudged him awake.

"Sir. Our new flight plan will not allow us to get into Rennes. If the gale strength increases as expected we will have to land somewhere in Scandinavia for refueling. My recommendation is Helsinki. We can get there easily by taking the northern track and we'll be far enough away that the storm won't hit us badly. At best they're calling for wind gusts and rain. We can make a decision then on whether or not to head directly for Carmarthen."

His eyes still closed, Wyndham acknowledged the pilot's information with a nod, then added. "Rennes. We still head for Rennes. We will go to Carmarthen after."

The pilot stood and headed towards the cockpit, pausing when he heard Wyndham call out

"Heatley?"

"Yes, sir?" He turned to face the business mogul.

"Don't ever touch me again."

Near Winchester, Virginia

Given the stressful days and sleepless night, Stone expected a quiet drive once they picked up the car. In fact it was the opposite. Mandy was determined to mine him for all he could remember about Huw's visit. Together they swept unseeing through the green Virginia countryside, Mandy probing each comment Stone could remember from his conversations with her father and adding her own remembered information as well. She was still fuming, still questioning why Stone was involved.

"And you're sure he said he only gave Evans a copy of a piece of the parchment, that he'd hidden the real thing somewhere?"

"Mm. He said the original was in safekeeping somewhere. He didn't say where. He had photocopies made. One he destroyed at George Mason University after he scanned it into my disk. He sent part of another to Father Joe in Rome."

Mandy glanced across. "There's probably another in the parcel he sent to me; the one I wasn't to open unless something happened to him". She gave a quick laugh devoid of any humor as the irony hit her. "Now that something has happened to him, I am thousands of bloody miles away from it." She sat huddled in the passenger seat, arms folded tightly around her.

"None of this makes sense Stone. None of it."

They both stared silently at the highway ahead before Stone spoke again.

"Huw's find is really a record of the monk's activities before, during and after he began copying the Excalibur parchment, the one written by St. Byron. Now, Huw said he only found Thomas's journal and not the copy of the original parchment. Which means the parchment or its copy is either lost or it's in Rome." He thought for a moment. "My guess is Rome, unless Father Joe already has it."

"Why?"

"The good Father was shifted away from Rome suddenly. He must have found something or touched a nerve. Don't forget, we're actually hunting two, maybe three documents."

Mandy thought for a moment. "Yes, you're right. The monk's copy was verified by a second document from the Abbot and sent to Rome. That would mean the Excalibur parchment and the Abbot's verification letter. Two documents sent to the Vatican and there's also Thomas's journal which Da found a portion of."

Stone nodded, his mind muddled and his self-confidence and pride gone. He was no longer sure what to believe or which way to turn. Mentally he wrestled with a multitude of options from being a throw-caution-to-the-wind superman who'd chase the bad guys, to doing the smart thing and letting the authorities handle it.

Unbidden, Huw flashed into his mind. Stone remembered a brief conversation in Philadelphia. God does care about you Bradstone, Huw had said. All you have to do is talk to him about your problems, your issues. We call it prayer. Stone scoffed at the idea of 'talking' to a silent, unseen non-entity. It would be easier to talk to Peter Pan or some other fictional being he'd chided Huw. You'll never know till you try it, Huw countered.

As they drove deeper into Virginia, Stone muttered under his breath, Huw, I hope you're praying right now because we both need help. He half-listened to Mandy as she detailed her own explorations of the Druids.

"…they're as much matriarchal as anything. Women were considered just as strong and wise leaders as men. That's why Rhiannon was able to obtain power and keep it. Make no mistake. She's the one in charge. All the others report to her."

Stone looked at his watch. It was almost time to check in with Chad who in the past few hours had become an enigma. Until today Chad had been a reliable, if sometimes overbearing, friend. But now there was this new, different Chad Lawson with an identity and role well hidden even from his buddy. The question is, Stone asked himself, is can I still trust Chad? A few miles further on they pulled into a rest area and waited. Almost on the dot of the promised two hours, the phone buzzed sharply.

"You're on somebody's hit list!" Chad ignored the niceties.

"They've got an intercept and hold order on you. Every police department and FBI office in the region now has your photo and ID. If they don't pick you up soon, the rest of the country will have it. The good news is they think you're still in the District. A cop recognized you at the Metro station and they think you've gone to ground somewhere in DC. The other good news is that right now, nobody other than you and me and my boss knows that Mandy is with you, let alone that she's in the country."

As Stone listened, Chad outlined his plan to protect Stone and Mandy. Stone made no comment during the brief conversation, thanked him and hung up.

"Well?"

"He wants us to head to a safe house in the Shenandoah Valley. Says we will be protected 24/7 until they can get to the bottom of this whole mess."

"So how do we get there?"

Stone didn't answer immediately, staring out the windshield lost in thought. Sensing the battle inside him, Mandy kept quiet as well. After a minute his temper and frustration poured out. He pounded the steering wheel, swore and twisted in his seat to look at her intently.

"I'm sick and tired of being a pawn in this whole damn mess. Everyone has information or knowledge that's either been withheld or dribbled to me in tiny bits and pieces," he glared at her.

"Sure, you're right. I'm just a reporter not a historian. Show me a computer or a camera and I'm comfortable. And yes, this is beyond my comfort zone. Way beyond." The intensity and vehemence of his words silenced any response from Mandy.

"Well this simple reporter is tired of playing everyone else's games, including your father's and Chad's. I'm putting a stop to this stupidity. I'm calling my own shots from here on in, and no one, not even you, will stop me. Stone Wallace is not a poker chip in a cosmic game of chance. It may cost me everything, but I'm damned if I'm going let them push me around anymore."

Mandy sighed and looked down for a moment before looking Stone in the eyes. Softly, her lilting voice broke through his self-absorbed diatribe.

"Answer me one thing Stone. Do you believe Da? Do you believe there's some kind of Druid conspiracy under way? Or is he barmy and you're only trying to humor him out of friendship."

Stone eased his vice-like grip on the steering wheel. She'd voiced the question that had plagued him the past two days. "Up to a few hours ago, I confess I wavered on that one. Huw's story is so surreal, that any ordinary person would dismiss it out of hand. But there are so many coincidences and events over the past few days." His voice trailed off and he was quiet for a moment. "Paraphrasing Sherlock Holmes, he once said that if you eliminate all the obvious answers, then even the most fantastic one must be the truth. So, I guess my answer is yes, I do believe him."

He handed Chad's cell phone to her as he pulled out onto the interstate.

"I'm not going to any safe house. I'll drop you off in Winchester. Call Chad and have him pick you up there. Me? I'm going hunting in Venice and Wales for some answers."

Mandy struggled with her thoughts. Should she take the safe route and put herself in the hands of this American policeman or sally off into the unknown with Stone? Either way, she considered, her quiet studious life was going to be turned upside down. As they neared Winchester she suddenly rolled down the car window and tossed the cell phone out.

"I'm going with you. I still dislike your involvement but I know you a bit more than that policeman. You're stuck with me. But you've forgotten something very important. You are a wanted man. How are you going to get out of this country? Have you even thought about that? We can't return to Dulles and catch a plane. Nor any other airports. And what about tickets? Did you think of that Mr. Smart Reporter? Great idea, but we're blocked before we get started!"

Her deflated voice mirrored her gloominess. "Maybe we should go to that safe house after all."

For the first time it seemed in days, he grinned. "Ah. Leave that to me. This Mr. Smart Reporter might know of more than one way to leave the country."

Chapter Eleven

Wales, 1301 • Bryn Penbarryn

My memories of that cold harsh climb up Bryn Penbarryn are thankfully fading. After telling Owain my story, I watched him carefully out of the side of my eyes as we trudged painfully and slowly up the mountain.

"And this sword you carry is Arthur's?"

"I believe it so."

"And the parchment you copied is one written by the blessed St. Byron?"

"I believe it so."

Owain stopped and took a deep breath. "Then it is good. St. Byron himself protected the sword in the past. He will protect and guide us now."

Without further word, he began climbing again, the gorse tearing once more at my unfamiliar leggings as I staggered after him. I had long ago acknowledged his leadership in our new relationship.

After yet another hour I remember begging Owain to have charity on us both and allow us rest. He grunted acknowledgement and led us to a small depression in the mountain side. We dropped to the ground exhausted. I remember the silence. Apart from a slight rustling made by the wind, I can recall no other sound than that of our heavy breathing and my own belly rumbling with hunger. No animal noises. No night birds on the hunt. A silence as deep as my own thoughts. As we lay flat on the grassy slope my embarrassment I felt at my weakness dissolved when I heard Owain's own belly rumble sufficiently loud to startle sheep had they been present.

"Ah Thomas, what I would give for a trencher and ale right now. A good slab of beef or mayhap some elegantly cooked trout from that stream far below."

"Best not to think of these things. Consider that we are on a fast and must needs ignore our cravings to satisfy our fleshly bodies."

"Perhaps so, but we are most definitely not on a fast. We sit not at prayers, our bodies at rest while we refrain from food. No, we have run miles through deep woods and are now climbing, or should I say stumbling, up a goodly size mountain, and it draws all our reserves from us," he said glumly, He turned to look at me. "We need food and drink. And we need it soon."

I could not in truth see his face, but his soft voice probed me. "Would you like me to relieve your burden and carry the sword for a spell?"

The words were said quietly and with compassion. But the task was mine and mine alone. Though I had failed in many ways so far, this is one that I would not. I and I alone would carry Excalibur. I refused his kindly offer gently but firmly. In the darkness I saw him nod silently as if he had expected no other answer but offered himself only as a way of expressing support.

I pulled the oilskin parchment bag from my beneath tunic. "I would be grateful, however, if you would carry this." I offered it to him. He grinned and took it reverently with a shy smile on his face.

We rested some more, then with a heavy sigh, forced ourselves up and began climbing again. Not an hour later we crested the mountain and I saw the banwen—the bleak high upland moors spread before us. Behind us somewhere in the gloom of night was Cwmllyn, my home for many years, the center of my life and now the source of my nightmarish days. Ahead lay the unknown. I feared whether we would indeed find safety in Owain's village. I feared for Alys and her family. But most of all I feared Gethin.

Avoiding the banwen, we headed down to the next valley below. The journey down was even more difficult and wearying than the climb up. My legs ached from the jarring they took heading down, almost wanting to flee headlong by themselves without restraint, while my tired body stiffened to fight against that desire. We slipped and fell numerous times, catching each other from time to time but mostly trying simply to hold ourselves upright.

Dawn found us safe within the depths of yet another narrow wooded valley and we fell in an exhausted heap.

"We have not eaten since we broke our fast yesterday." Owain's statement of the facts was less for my benefit, I believe, than it was his own wishful thinking.

"Aye. And I cannot think to find sustenance since I don't even know where we are."

"Thomas, Thomas," he chided as if to a child. "Have you never spent time in the woods?"

I shook my head. In truth my early life was on a small farm holding and then the monastery. I knew naught of the woods and its creatures. God knows, as a child I had feared the dark forests around my home and yesterday's terrifying race through the woods did nothing to enhance my desire to know more!

"There is food all around us, look you."

To show me the truth of his statement he poked around in the brush under a tree for a moment or two and then triumphantly produced a single wild mushroom. He brushed the dirt off, broke it into two pieces and handed one to me. The other he quickly popped into his mouth. "See? You can always find something to eat in the woods."

I gobbled the mushroom piece quickly, grateful for it but at the same time yearning desperately for more. I looked up as Owain bade me stay where I was and disappeared silently into the forest. As he went I lay on the bracken and closed my eyes. Blackness descended over me again. Not clouds that blocked out the sun but a blackness of the soul, not of sight. Ever since we fled the abbey I had been aware of it. In the cave it crept upon me. Now it descended like a hammer on my heart. I had broken my solemn vow to Abbot Godfrey within days of its making, and now was suffering physical, mental and spiritual anguish. Surely it was a foretaste of my eternal damnation.

I rolled over onto my belly, plunged my face into my arms and sobbed my heartfelt confession before God. "O mighty God, giver of life and all that we are and have, I plead my soul before you. I have failed Father Abbot, I have failed in my task and above all I have failed you."

The resonant chanting prayers of our Offices eluded me. In truth they did not seem even appropriate. None of our chanted prayers could even begin to fathom the deep dark pit in which I found myself. Truly I bared my soul before God, but I had to do it in my own words. I did find comfort and words for my prayers in the remembered psalms of King David. He alone, it seemed, understood the depths of my despair.

I prayed for what seemed an eternity, broken and sputtering rather than eloquent. At times I panted with remorse; at others I was silent, not able to put words to my thoughts and fears. I pleaded for salvation from Gethin's revenge but I also yielded my life, recognizing it was forfeit because I had broken my vow.

"Sweet Jesu, in your goodness and compassion save me. Lift this darkness from my soul and guide me in my task so it may be to my eternal benefit and balance my mortal sin." I paused. "And, Holy God, mayhap a sign of your forgiveness and your favor upon this lowly sinful follower." My penitent request was whispered with slight expectation that it would be fulfilled.

I lay prone with my head buried in my arms. Was it an hour or merely minutes? I know not. I heard a sound, the flittering of leaves and branches. Owain was returned. I struggled to sit up and looked around for him. I heard the noise behind me and twisted to look. There, not an arm's length thither, was a pure white dove. It cocked its head, and stared at me, eyes unblinking, while it cooed.

I stared at the bird, tears flowing freely down my face. I had asked God for a sign. He favored me with the gift of this dove. Was the dove not a sign for the blessed Noah? Was a dove not sent by God at Jesus' baptism? I rejoiced. He was not finished with me. He was not angry with me. He would guide me.

The sound of branches breaking startled the bird and it flew off. I cared not for its job was done and I had my answer. Owain burst through the bushes, his jerkin held up like a sack. He spilled the contents before me. "Food, Thomas! Nuts and berries and mushrooms. Sweets and savories for our repast and there is a stream not far so we can drink as well."

He dropped beside me and began eating. I joined him joyfully, the weight gone from my soul. We rested for some time then struggled up. I girded Excalibur about my body. Somehow this morning it seemed lighter. We moved forward, following the little stream, seeing only a few wary foxes and scurrying hares. Hearing the chirping, singing birds.

Behind us was Bryn Penbarryn. Ahead lay Tir Iarll, 'the Earl's land', and this I worried about, for it was open country, part of the holdings of Sir Payne de Tuberville, Lord of Glamorgan, The uplands were cleared, largely to prevent Welsh raiders and armies from attacking de Tuberville lands. Anger and conflict still raged sporadically through much of Wales as it had in the more than two hundred years since the Conqueror. From the time of the first Lord of Glamorgan, Earl William Fitz Robert, the memories of bitter fights lingered heavily for all.

Though we in Cwmllyn Abbey disdained earthly things like politics, we were none the less aware of the situations that surrounded us. The English hold on our land was still tenuous. Just recently we heard that Edward I, King of England—Edward Longshanks was one of the nicer things we Welsh called him—having crushed much of our land had the effrontery to declare his own English infant son as Prince of Wales. The sheer audacity of the man!

The bleakness of Tir Iarll allowed de Tuberville a clear view of whoever travelled across his lands. It bought him early warning of armed men moving into the rich, fertile vale of Glamorgan. From his fortresses at Coity, Ogmore and across to Kenfig, de Tuberville stretched a barrier of castles across his lands to protect and secure his holdings in an iron grip.

I feared Tir Iarll because of its openness. Two figures, small though we might be, would be seen for many leagues. Gethin's followers would see us easily and De Tuberville's men patrolled the area as well. If they to come across two wanderers, landless peasants (for such we would seem) with no proper explanations…well the thought of our fate in their hands gave me no comfort either! Especially if they had word of the murder of our Abbot.

At the edge of the woods, we stopped and looked at each other. We said not a word. In the distance, we could see an armed party of men, some on foot and some on horseback, cresting a smaller hill away from us. I counted fifteen in all as they disappeared from view. From the shadow of the woods we could not see if they belonged to Lord de Tuberville or Gethin. It mattered not. We must not be seen.

We hastily covered ourselves with bracken and brush, lying against the warming ground, and waited, anxious that a second band of men might follow the same pathway. After a goodly time, we crept out of the woods and slowly made our way across the open lands and up a small hillock. There, scrunched low so we could not be seen, we peeked over the hill.

In the distance we could see the soldiers (for such I thought them) disappearing down the valley. Some paused at the top of a small hillock. We waited momentarily then as the last seemed to vanish from sight, we looked at each other and in unison broke ground and quickly ran down the hill, across the open meadow land, plunging into the safety of the next copse of trees.

Our needs were many; more food and drink of course as well as shelter and rest. I asked Owain in jest if he knew of any other hidden huts or caves. He shook his head, smiling somewhat guiltily. I prayed as we walked. This new commune with God was strange. Far from the ordered daily regime of prayer, work, food and sleep, my past two days had been filled with sharply discordant blows of terror, hunger, penetrating cold, physical, mental and spiritual exhaustion. Yet as of this morning I had also experienced a new freedom of speaking my thoughts directly to God, and he answering me. I felt a lightness in my soul that I had not had since the day Abbot Godfrey first sought me out. No. I tell an untruth. It was a lightness of soul such as I had never experienced in my whole life!

It was close to mid morn when we stopped. We agreed to travel in the early morn and at night when other men were not as likely to be abroad. So we spent the next hours in rest, one watching while the other slept. At times Owain foraged for more berries and nuts. Through my watch times I was less ambitious, but I warrant my contribution was just as valuable. I prayed.

In the evening, we moved on. The sun was going down and we were loping along aiming at some large dark trees part way up the hill. The storms that held off all day were gathering once again. Dark clouds covered the moon and occasional splatters of rain dropped down on us.

Other than the soldiers of early morn, we'd seen no other people. But as we wandered across the open ground I heard a sound that turned my belly to water and my legs to quivering sticks. Hounds. I heard the baying of hounds.

"Quick. We must crest the hill."

Owain began running at his best speed. I trailed, Excalibur banging painfully against my back with each stride. At the top of the hill we searched the horizon. Not that far off, we could see the light of blazing torches. They spread across the valley between us and Mynydd Margam.

Owain turned around and we ran back into the woods. Still the hounds bayed closer. I know not whether they really were closer or if the winds merely carried their sound. I cared not either way. We stumbled into the river and Owain stopped immediately.

He pointed to his left. "Stay in the stream. It will destroy our scent. We must slip past that line of men."

We slowed our pace for we did not want the sound of our splashing and stumbling in the dark to give us away. The river widened after a while and we found ourselves at times chest deep. "I know this river now," Thomas whispered.

Still the hounds came closer.

More frequently I could see glimpses of the torches through the trees. They were coming closer and closer down the bank towards us. I heard hounds howl as if they were at our feet. We turned a bend and saw a mud cliff under the bank. Storms had obviously washed away some of the cliff, for a tree perched perilously on top of the bank, its roots holding grimly onto the soil but with a small hollow beneath. I grabbed Owain by the arm and pulled him over to it.

We huddled in silence, sheltered by the tree roots. Owain reached down and spattered mud on his face and hands to take away the whiteness. I did the same.

As we clung to each other willing our bodies into the muddy sides of our shelter we heard, then felt, the thudding of feet along the side of the river.

"They are in these woods. I know it. I feel it."

A guttural voice panted as he stopped not yards from us. "Here from the top of this bank we might see. Bring me a light."

The voice clambered up, a light held over his head he searched, twisting his body to see behind him and around him. At one point he stepped onto a root of the tree to peer across the river to the far bank. Had he looked down he would have seen our muddied faces fearfully peering up at him.

Chapter Twelve

Northern New York State

All morning and afternoon Stone and Mandy drove north from Winchester on Interstate 81. They talked and then all was silent as she cat-napped, only to begin talking again once she woke. They stopped for quick rest stops at gas stations where Mandy jumped out to get food and drink while Stone pumped. As long as she remained unidentified, she could interact with the public. Stone kept his face down and away from curious eyes as much as possible. At their first stop, she'd bought him a ball cap he could wear to tone down the TV image. He grudgingly agreed to wear it at stops but absolutely refused to wear it in the car

"Where are we going? I'm completely lost, look you." Mandy pushed some loose hair out of her face. "If we are going to work together, we must work *together!*"

"I know. I have something in mind. It may not work out—depends on the guy we're going to see—and it will be completely illegal. But it may be our only chance to get away. It's a long shot for sure and I don't want to say anything until I know for sure." He looked across. "Trust me just a bit longer?"

Driving through the heart of downtown Syracuse in heavy traffic increased Stone's fear they might be spotted. Already, breathless radio newscasts reported that INN reporter Stone Wallace was wanted for questioning in an attempted murder. North of Watertown, he left the interstate, followed signs toward Millar Bay then turned on a side road. They drove along a scenic road that flirted with a river. "The St. Lawrence River and the Thousand Islands," he quietly explained. Five miles later Stone suddenly turned down a gravel driveway toward a white blue-trimmed two-storey wood frame house. Beyond the house she saw a dock sticking into the river with three boats of varying sizes tied up.

"Wait here." Stone got out, jammed the ball cap low on his head and walked up to the house. Mandy watched him step onto the porch and knock. The screen door opened. Within seconds he was inside and she was alone.

Chantilly, Virginia

Chad thought his report was received surprisingly calmly. Tyler wasn't overly upset that Wallace spurned the safe house offer and disappeared. His only response was a muttered grunt.

"We put a name to the heavy who attacked Griffiths." Tyler shuffled a paper on his desk. "French embassy security guy named Louis Carveau."

"Figures. I took all kinds of crap because some French embassy guys were hanging around Stone's block the night before the bombing."

Another grunt. "Can't do much about Wallace right now. He's charting his own course."

Tyler tossed a package across to Dom. "Passport, ticket, credit cards, Euros, everything else you need. You're heading to France tonight. I want you to scout around Tonnerre's set up and see what you can find."

Quickly, Tyler briefed Chad. He'd be working with the British Crown Security Bureau who had already exchanged information and concerns with Tyler about the growing Druid movement in both Wales and France. Plus they'd made a crucial connection between the Druids and American leaders, including the Presidential candidate Senator Murphy. "I want you to look around the Taranis setup and see what you can get on their leader Andre Tonnerre. I've given you everything we have on Tonnerre. Sir Giles is concentrating on the Welsh end. See what you can dig up that will connect this whole mob together."

Chad rifled through the package. "My cover?"

"A tourist exploring Normandy and Brittany, showing interest in the history of France, particularly connections between them and the British; the hundred years war and that sort of stuff." He looked up seriously. "Be careful Chad. We know this outfit is sophisticated. They have money and excellent communications. Our guys have broken some of their satellite uplinks and say it's as good as anything we have. The Brits have men in the area so if you need help there's contact information in the briefing notes. Memorize and destroy.

Helsinki-Vantaa Airport, Finland

The jet landed in early morning and taxied to a remote stand far from the main passenger terminals. It sat there waiting for refueling.

Wyndham was perturbed. The stop was an unwelcome delay. Nevertheless, he'd consulted the doctor and agreed that it was better safe than sorry. For the professor's sake a bumpy ride through turbulent weather was not on. Griffiths was too valuable. Even so, he vehemently rejected the suggestion that they move Griffiths to a hospital until the storm subsided. As it was, heavy winds and rains rocked the craft as it sat on the tarmac.

"You can take care of him just as easily here," he'd barked. "We brought everything we could think of with us. Anything else you need, my crew will arrange to get. But you and the professor stay on board." He softened the harshness. "We need to be ready to move as soon as the gale blows over." Abruptly, he walked out of the rear cabin

In the cockpit, the two pilots argued with airport officials over the radio. No, they needed no servicing other than fuel. No, they didn't need customs and immigration since nobody was deplaning. Yes, as soon as possible they would depart for Rennes. No, they were not offloading cargo. Yes, the gale now lashing the UK and France was responsible for the wide diversion over Scandinavia and into Finnish air space. Yes they knew the A319 aircraft could handle the heaviest turbulence, they just had a very fussy owner who was terrified of turbulence and ordered them to wait out the storm on the ground.

Finally, after repeating the arguments and with solemn promises to keep the aircraft doors closed, permission was granted to remain in solitary splendor on the isolated stand. Even so, the co-pilot gestured outside the cockpit window. As rain pelted down in the grey early morning light they saw a police car discretely position itself to keep the aircraft in full view at all times as the fueling began.

With nothing more to do, the cockpit crew called for a breakfast from the flight attendant. In the rear cabin, the doctor and nurse fussed over their patient and made him as comfortable as possible.

In the main cabin, Wyndham nursed a second glass of whiskey ignoring the food laid before him, waiting impatiently for a break in the weather.

Thousand Islands Region, New York State

His voice startled her. She'd dozed off momentarily, hunched over in the front passenger seat. "Mandy, come on inside."

She scrambled up as Stone gestured toward the house. As the bright blue wooden door closed behind her, Stone introduced Greg Michaels, a barrel-chested non-nonsense man with a two day whisker coating on his face. Stone pointed at Michaels and outlined his plan to her. "He's going to help us leave the USA by taking us quietly across the river to Canada."

Michaels smiled at her. "I don't believe all this stuff about Stone murdering someone. Stone did a report on our Thousand Island cruises three years ago. Our business was almost belly up, but his story meant the difference. We're grateful sure, but since then we've become friends. I have his word he's innocent and that's good enough for me. So if he asks me to take him across the river, then across the river we go. Even if it is illegal"

Mandy looked at Stone. He explained that boating guidelines on the Great Lakes meant anyone from the US or Canada landing in the other's country needed to telephone the appropriate customs and immigration authorities and report immediately they arrived.

"It's a good system, well-handled on both sides of the border and even in this post 9/11 era it works well. Boaters generally are a lawful bunch. In this case, however, we're going to take advantage of that fact and enter Canada illegally."

He beckoned Mandy over as he hunched over a map. "We'll cross over tomorrow morning and do a touch-and-go. Greg will just pull alongside the dock in Gananoque. We hop off and head into Kingston." He pointed at the city. "We can get a train to Toronto and from there we'll grab a flight to Italy tomorrow evening, then Venice the next day. We'll be in Canada unlawfully for less than a day."

He pulled out some credit cards with different names. "I use them when I don't want hotels, airlines or restaurants to recognize 'Stone Wallace the travel reporter'. It helps me travel anonymously. This way, we purchase tickets without leaving a trail. The FBI is no doubt already checking my credit and debit cards. The longer it takes to track these fake cards and follow us to Italy, the better. By then we'll have met with Father Joe, obtained whatever information he has and be in the UK rescuing Huw, find Excalibur and put the whole mess to bed. Easy!"

Easy. But so complicated. And so fraught with danger and potential complications, she thought. He must be crazy to have even thought of this plan. "What about the Canadian police. Suppose they're looking for us?"

"Why would they? I doubt the FBI or police will think of us heading to Canada. They're probably still convinced I'm hiding out around DC. Even if they do think of Canada, everyone on both sides will be watching the main border crossing points, not this.

Anyway," he shrugged lamely, "it's the best I can do. Unless you can think of something better."

Throughout the conversation Greg was silent. He pushed himself away from the table. "Seems to me you two need food and a place to sleep right now. We need to get going about seven in the morning." Without waiting for a response he headed into the kitchen.

Mandy sighed and pulled out one of her ever present books.

Stone wished he'd remembered his iPod so he could hear the calming, soothing strains of Bach or Handel.

Buckingham Palace Mews, London

The rain beat even heavier and he cursed himself for leaving his umbrella at home that morning. Sir Giles eschewed the trappings of Westminster power, never using the car and chauffeur allotted to him despite the bleating of his own security people. Hopefully the rain would end before he plodded his way along Buckingham Palace Road to Victoria Station and his train home. Otherwise there was going to be one very wet and very grumpy Sir Giles rampaging around his house that evening.

The irrepressible Freddy, never daunted by weather or the guvnor's moods bounced into the room. "Something interesting from our Welsh contact, sir." The red file folder was placed on the desk. "Seems Professor Griffiths has a daughter and she did a bunk. Twice!"

"Explain."

"She left Caernarfon University about three months ago without explanation. Just resigned and left her flat as well. We finally tracked her to St. David's in South Wales but before we could connect with her, she'd gone again."

"Bloody hell."

"Ah, but there's more." Freddy smiled, not at all intimidated by his boss, "Our man spoke with a neighbor who told him she'd had a call from a friend in America. Her father was in an accident and she left immediately for Washington."

"Must be with Wallace. Tyler know that?"

"Probably, but our man's also checked phone and email records for the good professor. Seems that along with all his research into Druids and the like, he's been in contact a couple of times with a Father Joseph Panterra, an early Medievalist working at the Vatican. Or at least he was until ten days ago."

Sir Giles cocked an eyebrow. "Go on."

"Father Panterra was apparently searching Vatican archives looking into documents and correspondence for Pope Boniface VIII. He let slip to one of the archivists that he was looking for some kind of documents sent to Boniface from Wales." Freddy paused. "The documents apparently concern King Arthur."

The normally unperturbed Sir Giles whistled. "And our boy Huw Griffiths put him up to it? Interesting!"

"What's even more interesting is that within days Father Panterra was summoned to an internal Vatican meeting. Less than a day later he was packed off to a cloistered monastery on the island of San Bernardo in Venice. Officially he's there to research Venetian medieval documents but our Rome contact says he's likely there to keep him quiet or to keep him out of sight. Either way, he'll be difficult to get to."

"Need more information. Run Panterra through the computer. Double check the Griffiths connection." He thought some more. "And more on this San Bernardo place."

As Freddy made quick notes, Sir Giles stood and looked out the window. The rain hammered harder. From the window he could just make out the red double deck buses, multi-colored taxis, cars, lorries and vans jamming the streets, slowed by the incessant downpour. So much for the congestion charges cutting traffic in central London, he thought idly.

He looked at Freddy again. "Something else. Tyler's sending one of his men to Brittany. Checking out Tonnerre. He's got our contact numbers. Treat him as one of our own. Name's Lawson. Whatever help he wants, he gets.

"Oh, and Freddy. Maddox and Broderick. I want them in Venice. Brief them."

St. Brigitte's, Paimpoint, France

"He is here." Jean-Marc stepped aside and Belenos walked hesitantly forward stopping short of Tonnerre's desk. Noiselessly the door closed behind him. They were alone.

The silence increased the tension. Belenos stood still, trembling slightly, aware of both Tonnerre's infamous temper and his well-known penchant for revenge—slow, painful revenge. He dared not speak as Tonnerre stared at him, no words of anger or scathing denunciations yet falling from his lips.

Glancing beyond Belenos, Tonnerre's eyes focused on the effigy of Taranis. Seconds that seemed like hours passed. Finally, without shifting his gaze, he spoke.

"You disappointed me, Belenos." His voice was quiet and his demeanor peaceful, totally unlike the raging demagogue Belenos had seen many times. "I trusted you with a major job but to do it discreetly and successfully." Tonnerre played with a pen on his desk. "The mission was simple. Silence the writer and bring the professor to me. Instead of that, you shattered the professor and the writer escaped unharmed." He looked directly at the bull of a man standing in front of him. "You were honored with the name Belenos, the sun god. It is now taken from you."

He raised his hand, palm out, as Belenos began to open his mouth. Not a sound emanated and he closed it again. "Louis Carveau you came to us, Louis Carveau you will leave," Tonnerre intoned. "We will not speak again." At those words the door opened and Jean-Marc stepped in, summoned by a silent signal. He led the terrified Carveau out.

When the door closed, the cool, icy calm left. Tonnerre shook with both anger and apprehension. An hour ago he'd found out that Griffiths survived the blast. Worse, that Wyndham scooped the professor right out of an American hospital and was returning him to Wales. He balled his fist in frustration. If Wyndham had Griffiths, who knew what might happen? Depending on his injuries, the professor might die and that, for sure, would be laid at Tonnerre's feet. But if he lived and provided information—voluntarily or not—then Wyndham got the credit and a huge advantage. Both scenarios were unacceptable. How, he wondered, could he turn things to his benefit?

He pressed the signal button again. Jean-Marc returned.

"We will hold Belenos' trial tonight. Ensure no one speaks to him or acknowledges his presence if they see him. The torment of utter silence will begin to build in him. Stoke it. Make sure his food is tainted so he suffers. But give him nothing to ease his misery. Let him feel the pressure mount. Leave his light on constantly. He will know no more darkness until the end."

He waved dismissal and stared out the window at the other buildings in his fiefdom. Rain deluged down, whipping with such ferocity and strength the buildings disappeared from sight at times. Beyond, he could see the gale force winds raking the trees of the Broceliande. The winds were strong, stronger than he'd seen for many years. He wondered briefly if the old oaks in the sacred grove would be damaged. Tonnerre turned away and sat at his massive desk. Now for the difficult part of this day. He lifted the receiver. A few words and he was connected.

"Rhiannon." He tried to force a smile into his voice. "I understand you will soon have Huw Griffiths safe at Llanmerddyn." He spun his limited knowledge to try and seize momentary advantage but was cut short. He listened as she poured out her bile then jerked upright as she continued. "When?" he blurted as she delivered the bombshell news that Wyndham was on his way to St Brigitte's with Griffiths safe in hand. He listened carefully. As she explained Wyndham's situation he switched gears and his now honeyed voice soothed her anger.

"*Mais oui*, of course we will look after them both. It is our desire to serve you Dragon Master and ensure that the good professor is well cared for. We can have a doctor out here from Paimpont *immediatement!*"

Smoothly he assured her that his rogue follower Belenos was already dealt with. His profuse apologies for Belenos' overzealous stupidity were accepted. In minutes the conversation was over. Rhiannon was mollified. Ogmios, the god of eloquence, had led him yet again.

Bien! Wyndham and Griffiths would arrive at St. Brigitte's as soon as this cursed storm eased up. He snorted and stared out of the window again, rubbing his hands gleefully. He couldn't wait to come face to face with the famous and elusive Professor Huw Griffiths.

Outside Paimpont, France

The road sign indicated only five more kilometers to Paimpont which was just fine with Chad. The overnight flight to Paris and hasty train connection at Gare Montparnasse had left him little time to reflect. Thankfully, Tyler arranged a car between the airport and train station. On the TGV to Rennes he'd reviewed the briefing notes yet again and, on arrival at Rennes station, he'd stopped in the men's room and slowly and methodically ripped his notes into tiny pieces then flushed them into the French sewers.

The more he read about the Druids, the less he liked them. Tonnerre and his gang oozed zealotry and violence. Interestingly, one of the softest reports he read was Stone's. He'd absorbed the information as best he could but he much preferred to rely on his own instincts and findings rather than bureaucratic documents. Rely on your own senses and intelligence was a mantra built into him by his father, a military intelligence officer in Korea and CIA agent during the cold war. Other sources and their perceptions were only supplements. On the ground intelligence—his—was the most trustworthy.

He concentrated on the road ahead. The gale, which made the flight from Dulles to Paris extremely bumpy and nerve-wracking, had barely eased through the day. His car's wipers fought to keep up with the torrents of rain. Using the rental agency's map he followed the N2024, and then wound through Pielan-le-Grand, negotiating the narrow streets carefully to avoid scurrying pedestrians trying to get out of the storm as well as the numerous awkwardly parked cars and vans. Slowly he threaded his way north east. He was proud of himself for finding his way and only doubling back once before he found the D38. He turned onto it and sped up the more open highway towards Paimpont. Ahead through the low clouds he could see a large dark forest of trees on all sides of the hedgerows

"No! I don't believe it!" he blurted. Chad suddenly jammed his brakes, grateful there was no one behind him. He quickly reversed to the driveway he'd just passed. Outside, a small sign advertised vacancies at the *Auberge du Roi Arthur*—King Arthur's Inn.

Quickly he jumped out, and ran into the cozy little lobby shaking water off as he entered. In the background a clock ticked quietly. A large black cat snoozed, sprawled over the reception counter top. He coughed but there was no response—not from the cat and not from the back rooms of the Auberge.

"*Bonjour?* Hello?" Chad called out.

"*Oui. Allo? Un moment, sil vous plait,*" a silvery voice called out from a side room. Seconds later a cheery looking, red-cheeked woman bustled out. Her black dress covered her like a tent—a sizeable tent. Obviously the food at this inn was a feature if her girth were any indication.

"Pardon, Madame. *Parlez vous Anglais?*" Chad looked at her hopefully, his total French knowledge virtually exhausted.

"*Oui, M'sieur. Un peu.* I 'ave a little English." She smiled at him and bustled around the counter, dislodging the black ball of fur.

In a few moments of fractured English and French Chad had rented a room. It was further from Paimpont and Tonnerre's compound than he'd planned, but in retrospect removed him from immediate observation by the Druid's followers. She led him upstairs to a small room dominated by a four-poster bed. A small armchair covered in nondescript brown material faced an equally undersized three drawer cupboard. Sitting on top was a small TV. To the left a large window facing the D38 and to the right a small sink and washstand completed the room. He pulled open a door and looked into a closet.

"The toilette, she is down the 'all M'sieur," The woman pointed. Chad nodded his thanks and took the key she offered. "Madame. One question. Why is this inn named after a British king?"

She spat in disgust. "British? Pah! *Tout la monde*, all the world, knows *Le Roi Arthur et ses chevaliers* were from Brittany, especially Paimpont!" She swung her arms around, gesturing out the window at the nearby trees. "Is this not the Broceliande Forest? The 'iding place of the Holy Grail and burial place of Merlin? *Ici.*"

She led him downstairs into the reception area, rummaged behind the desk and emerged with a crumpled English pamphlet. She thrust it into his hands.

"Read, M'sieur. Read about Lancelot du Lac and the Merlin" With that she bustled off into a back room.

In his room, Chad sat in the chair to read. As the old lady had suggested, the region around the Broceliande Forest was a hive of Arthurian legend. No wonder Tonnerre had built his compound here. Merlin was the center piece. It was here, the brochure proclaimed with gusto and authority, that he was born. And here he was bewitched by the enchantress Viviane, and later buried. A small map highlighted the area's key Arthurian sites including Merlin's tomb. West of Paimpont was the village of Trehorenteuc where there was a Church of the Holy Grail. Chad whistled to himself. "Man, Arthur gets around. And so does Merlin or Merddyn or whatever they call him."

He mentally compared the pamphlet's map with the map in Tyler's briefing notes and realized that the St. Brigitte de Bretagne compound was almost exactly half way between Paimpont and Trehorenteuc, buried deep in the Broceliande. St, Brigitte itself was approachable only through Paimpont and then down a gravel private road. The forest abounded with walking trails for those who sought the legend but Tyler's briefing also noted that the Druids' aggressive closure of many trails infuriated countless Paimpont's locals.

Chad considered his situation. Following his gut instinct he decided to tweak his cover from that of a somewhat naïve American tourist, to a dedicated Arthurian pilgrim following the trail of the great king. He wished he'd paid closer attention to Stone's recap of the professor's research.

Jet lag crept up on him. He tried to fight it, but gave in and swung onto the bed. It was mid-afternoon. A short nap, he thought, and then he'd drive to Paimpont and look around.

Chapter Thirteen

Wales, 1301 • The Banwen

We held our breath. The voices were harsh and angry above us.

"Gethin will have your guts for garters if this is a wild goose chase. The hounds have found a trail going back toward Bryn Penbarryn. That is where we should look."

"I tell you I saw them come this way. I stood on that hill this morning and looked back. I saw two men run across the meadow towards these woods."

"You hung back on that hill because you're a laggard. You saw nothing you fool. Look around you. There's no living person in this part of the woods other than us and our men. Thomas and Owain are hiding near Bryn Penbarryn. The hounds have their scent. Come on, before the rain wipes out even that."

He must have grabbed the first speaker and tussled briefly with him, for someone slipped. Dirt and stones fell on our heads and a foot dangled just inches from my head. One look down and we were finished.

"Bastard!" The foot was pulled free and we heard them crash off through the woods.

A second time we were within feet of discovery by Gethin's forces. A second time we were protected. Owain nudged me. "This sword must indeed have magical powers, but they are from God not the evil one."

Yet again we waited then crept out into the river, this time keeping close to the banks. Silence descended on the woods and river once again. Where the river flowed into open areas, we half crawled, half floated, flat as we could make ourselves, pulling ourselves along by hand. It was a slow, laborious journey and more and more we were leaving the safety of the woods for the open spaces of Tir Iarll.

As morning broke—the third since our flight from Cwmllyn—we could see signs of human habitation. Fields of hay appeared on both sides of the river. A cloying white mist covered the mountains. We pulled ourselves slowly out of the water, peering through the hay. Beyond we could see some wattle and daub houses and barns. Already the villeins were stirring for the day's work for I saw smoke rise out of some of the huts.

"Maesgwynfi. My village," Owain smiled, relieved. "We can hide near here. Come."

Without looking to see if I followed, Owain crawled through the fields aiming, I could see now, for a small dwelling on the edge of the village. We slipped inside a dark animal byre. spackled by the early morning sun filtering through the straw thatch roof and flimsy door.

In the semi-darkness I could see Owain's warm grin. Without a word he burrowed down into the straw pile beside the sole occupant, a portly black and white sow who stared disdainfully at us and went back to the important job of gobbling her swill.

I could not help myself for my hunger was still not appeased. I reached forward quickly and grabbed a withered apple from beneath the pig's back hoof. She would not miss it. I crunched happily as I too burrowed into the straw, careful to place Excalibur beside me. We lay still a while, the strong smell of pig making me gag at times. Suddenly we heard a sound. Owain peeked out from his straw pile, finger to mouth warning me to silence, as if I needed it.

Cursing the cold morning a roughly dressed, solidly built older man limped in, switch in hand, ready to roust the pig into the morning mists.

"Alun!" A woman's shrill voice screeched from outside. "When you've got that pig out, see to the geese."

Grumbling he limped closer. The pig lurched and squealed as the switch hit her backside. Rumbling, she headed towards the ramshackle door and then outside. The woman's voice cackled again urging him to more work before they could break their fast.

Before he could move, Owain hissed at him and stood up. He clamped his hand over Alun's mouth lest a shout or shriek escape. "Peace, my friend. It is I, Owain." He dropped his hand and Alun stared at him. His dirty bearded face suddenly crinkled into a broad smile.

At the woman's next impatient shriek Alun shouted back gruffly. "Patience woman. I will see to the geese in a moment. Get you inside and finish your baking."

He waved Owain to stay as he backed slowly towards the byre's rough entrance and glanced out. The woman stepped into the living quarters. Alun straightened his back, smiled again and muttered amazed.

"Owain. What are you doing here? Know you not that men seek you all over the valley?"

"Aye. And my friend Thomas too." He signaled to me and I stood before Alun, brushing myself off ineffectually.

"Alun, we need help. Food, fresh clothing if you can spare it, shelter for the rest of this day. And we need a place to hide for a while."

Alun, it became obvious, was a man of few words. He stared at us both, taking in our scruffy sad state. He nodded silently, pointed to the straw and told us to wait before he limped stiffly out.

Owain turned to me. "He's a good man married to a shrew. Alun was wounded in one of the wars with England many years ago. His leg muscle was severed. For all the misery she brings him now, his wife saved his leg and his life back then. She holds it over him like a hammer and never lets him forget it."

Owain sat back on the straw as did I. We spoke in hushed tones, careful lest Alun's wife hear us and investigate. As Owain related tales of his youthful adventures with Alun, it was clear he had great affection for the old soldier. Remarkably, news of Alys and Owain's relationship had reached Owain's village. Alun's approval was important to Owain I could see.

As we spoke, the object of the stories returned laden with a leather pail filled with bread and cold roast chicken. Buried in the bucket was a clay jar filled with honey sweet mead, enough to slake any man's thirst.

"A foul black-visaged man named Gethin seeks you. He and his men were here yester noon. He has a deep hatred in him, that man, but said naught of why he seeks you." He paused a moment. "And de Tuberbille's sheriff was here not two hours later.

He pointed at me, "You, Lord Payne wants for murdering the good Abbot Godfrey of Cwmllyn Abbey." He looked at Owain. "And you for helping him escape the law."

He rubbed his grizzled greying beard thoughtfully. "As for this Gethin, well, he simply wants you." He was silent a moment. "From the look of him, I think I would prefer my chances with Lord de Tuberville. All he wants to do is hang you both! Gethin, I think would prefer a much slower, painful end."

He sighed deeply and looked at Owain with pain in his eyes. "Sad it is, my boy, but I must tell you that Alys' village was destroyed by fire two nights past." He struggled with his words and tears crept out of his eyes. "They found her body yesterday."

The news shocked me as much for its brutality as for the speed with which it had travelled. Owain and I had struggled across wild and open banwen, deep valleys and climbed barren mountains with villages and settlements far apart. Yet it was apparent that the people were somehow closely connected, in the Welsh way. They all knew what was happening in every village though many miles separated them physically.

A stunned silence gripped us. Owain turned white and tears coursed down his face, streaking his muddied features. His grief was palpable. Yet not a sound emerged. He buried his face in his hands and dropped to his knees, his body wracked with silent, heart-wrenching sobs. Ah God, it would have been better to hear him shriek with his pain and anger than to see him thus.

I knelt beside my sorrowing, wounded friend. I held him in my arms, silently sharing his grief. My mind sought to commune with God and at the same time I accused myself as the genesis of this grief. Had it not been for me, Alys would still be alive. Owain would have left the abbey and married the love of his life. Had it not been for me!

God kept us safe, but deserted Alys. Why? Did He keep us alive so we could experience the pain and suffering of her death and know that the excruciating pain of her death was at my feet? We, God saved. But she, he discarded. It was not fair. It was not right. I argued with God and my sweet communion was gone. I was angry with him.

Blackness descended on my soul again. I hated Abbot Godfrey for giving me this burden. I hated the malevolent piece of steel I carried. Perhaps my life would return to normal if I merely sought out Gethin and gave him the sword! All these thoughts and more crashed into my mind, battling with the part of me that still loved God and believed in his goodness. Yet here two good people—Alys and Abbot Godfrey—were cold and silent, killed for no good reason other than hatred and revenge. I could not comprehend it.

Owain's exhaustion and grief could not sustain him any longer. I held him tight against me. Alun, tears streaming down his face as well, merely stood above us. Strangely, I did not weep. No tears streamed down my face for grief and my pain was buried too deep inside. We held each other tight, saying nothing. After many minutes of horrible silent grieving, Owain pried himself from my arms and stood silently, brushing himself off. The pain and anger in his face was torture to me.

"Has God forsaken me?" he whispered. "Just because I wanted to leave the abbey, to leave my vocation." He sobbed again.

I had no wisdom to offer, no words of comfort. It seemed he was right. God had forsaken us.

Embarrassed and equally grief-stricken, Alun spoke. "You need a place to hide while this hunt goes on. Do you remember the old caves in the hill up the banwen? The one near Nantycoed stream?"

"Aye." Owain nodded. "But it lies right close to de Tuberville's ruined castle. He still keeps some of his men on watch up there does he not, even though it was destroyed in the uprising?"

"Exactly! What better place to hide from Gethin and his mercenaries than under the very nose of our overlord?"

Owain stared out beyond Alun, eyes fixed upon something seen only to himself. "Alun, Thomas is innocent of the charge of murder. He did not kill the abbot. I however am guilty because I willingly, then and now, helped him escape the evil of Brother Gethin."

Briefly, he filled Alun in on our experience at the Abbey, thankfully not mentioning the sword and parchments and charitably giving me far more credit than I deserved for the rigors of the flight across the mountains and into Tir Iarll.

Alun grunted. "I felt evil sweep over this place when Gethin appeared here yesterday. Whatever help you want from me, you will get." He pointed to the pail. "Finish while I find clothes. But take care. Some in this village would gladly turn you in to either Gethin or Lord Payne's men. The reward is great from both and there are many whose greed outweighs their humanity." Alun limped out into the afternoon sun, carefully closing the wicker gate behind him.

Owain spoke with a harder voice than I had ever heard. "Alys died for helping us. I grieve deeply and yearn to join her even now for I chose this path that caused her death." He looked at me. "I know things would be different had Abbot Godfrey not called you that day. We would be living in comfort in the abbey. But he would still be dead and Excalibur in Gethin's hands giving power to the enemies of Christ. No matter how deep the pain, that will not change." He paused momentarily, searching for his words. "We cannot change the path Christ has led us on."

He sat down to eat and drink, as did I. The afternoon passed in sleep. Then, as dark fell, Alun was back with two pails; one filled with good warm wool clothing, plain but welcome and the other with more food. We slept again, confident that Alun watched out for us. When I woke, I peered at Owain in the flickering dawn light. As I stirred, he turned his head to look at me. I had slept most of the previous day and through the night.

"You slept well?" he whispered. When I nodded, he stood and gestured towards the door. "We must leave soon, even though it is getting daylight. I have been much in prayer. I do not understand why Alys had to die; it is beyond my comprehension. I feel the pain deeply in my heart but yet find it hard to grieve. My tears are gone and I have no more. My love is no more and yet…" his voice trailed off into silence. Then he looked up at me, grey bags around his red-rimmed eyes. "…yet even in my sorrow I still feel God's strong presence. I accepted the task he gave me of helping you. I did not realize what it would cost."

Silence reigned for several minutes. Then with a great sigh, he heaved himself up. I was humbled by his words. He did not blame me. He who would have left holy orders was far holier than I; far closer to Christ in spirit and deed than I.

We stood and stretched. I felt refreshed not just from the sleep but also the food and clothing Alun provided. The plain garments felt warm and fresh against my skin, a welcome change from the clammy, sodden things I'd worn since fleeing Cwmllyn. The dawn skies were brightening into a sun-filled morning. We stepped back into shadows as we heard shuffling steps approach.

"Owain. Thomas." Alun whispered and limped slowly into the byre carrying a pail filled, this time with cheeses, meat and fresh baked loaves. He placed it before us and sat on a shaky three legged stool.

"It would be well if you left the village now." He gestured outside. "Most are out in the fields or tending the animals. Take as much food as you can and make your way into the woods beyond the meadow. If you keep to the woods you should make it to the bottom of the hill unseen. Stay hidden there. You should see the castle and any guards. When the way is clear, make your way to the cave. Its entrance is covered now with bracken and a large gorse bush, but you should be able to get in with little trouble."

Chapter Fourteen

Venice, Italy

This was his seventh visit but every time, the view from the steps of the Santa Lucia railway station at Ferrovia never ceased to electrify Stone.

The bustling Grand Canal, with its water taxis, vaporetti water buses, work boats, and barges and flitting back and forth like the world's busiest water spiders, was a sight that always uplifted him and put new life into his steps. Everywhere too were the black bobbing gondolas, their costumed gondoliers stroking fascinated passengers from canal to canal. Time and time again he'd arrived here as he did today, tired and disheveled, yet always this first glimpse of La Serenissima moved him. It was as if he stepped out of his theatre seat and up onto the stage that was Venice. Such was its repeated impact upon him.

Stone and Mandy stood quietly on the steps taking in the sight before walking down to the canal side ticket office and purchasing vaporetto tickets. They were quiet—he strategizing their next move, she taking in her first ever experience of Venice.

The journey from New York State to Venice was, thankfully, uneventful. The river crossing went without a hitch. With no prying eyes in sight they'd landed and walked quickly up the road to a gas station and used a pay phone to call a cab. Half an hour later they were at the Kingston station waiting for a train to Toronto. Less than six hours later they were at Pearson airport in Toronto, Air Canada tickets to Milan in hand. The rest of the afternoon was spent trying to relax in a quiet corner of an airside lounge waiting for the early evening flight.

There were a few uneasy moments as one security officer eyed them and approached. The tension dispelled when the officer smiled as he passed, waving at someone beyond. Stone was relieved. Their illegal entry into Canada meant the only time they'd had to show passports was to a bored gate agent checking ID's of each boarding passenger. They just might make it. He thought the whole illegal thing was a lark; law-abiding Mandy, normally upset at even receiving a parking ticket, was horrified.

The flight itself was uneventful. Each dozed and ate the plastic airline food. By the time they reached Italy, a truce had been declared. Their mutual determination to find Huw and Excalibur overtook Mandy's initial resentment and anger. They quickly cleared Milan passport control and within the hour were on the intercity express train to Venice. Stone had phoned ahead from Milan, booking two single rooms at a small family run hotel only a short walk from Ferrovia off the Campo San Geremia, so they headed there first.

The Montifrisi family was delighted to see Stone again; the bellman was secretly pleased that Stone remembered him and the maid couldn't believe he remembered she'd had a different hair style the last time he visited. Thirty minutes later, armed with a guidebook and map purchased at Toronto's airport, they headed out.

They stopped at the tourism office, a church and a couple of shops. A cold silence met their inquiries and none yielded information about San Bernardo the island or its buildings. Two less than helpful policeman merely looked at them, gesticulated briefly then suggested they ask the tourist office. They were stymied. Tired and discouraged Stone and Mandy pushed through clusters of tourists, each marked at its head by loquacious, conspicuous guides bobbing colored umbrellas up and down as they went.

"Let's get oriented," Mandy suggested, her logical professorial mind kicking into gear as they pushed through the crowds. "Maybe we can even find this blasted island in the lagoon on our own."

They opted for a crowded Number One vaporetto that puttered down the Grand Canal and across the lagoon to the long thin finger of sand, fancy hotels and expensive shops called the Lido. From there they planned either a walk or taxi south from the vaporetto stop hoping they might somehow see the island. Failing that, Stone said, they'd hire a water taxi for a lagoon tour.

Although their minds were jumbled with concern and fear mixed with hope, neither could escape the gentle enthralling pull of the magical city. The afternoon sunlight lent a placid warming color to the multi-hued grand homes or Ca's that lined the Grand Canal. Sweeping around the curve Mandy couldn't stifle an awed "oh" as they and the other vessels and gondolas skittered under the Rialto Bridge and lazily snaked down the Canal, criss-crossing to disgorge and collect passengers.

By the time they reached Arsenale most of the other passengers had gone. Stone and Mandy moved forward into the small seats near the bow as finally they headed out across the Lagoon. A cool breeze and light chop hit them as they moved into open waters.

Hunched over the map, Stone kept his finger on some unnamed dots south of San Giorgio Maggiore. His eyes kept darting up from the map to check locations. The boat easily wove its way amongst the hundreds of tall log pilings demarking shallow waters and dredged channels.

Just as the vaporetto made its final turn towards the dock at the Lido, he stared suddenly out into the lagoon. Just peaking between the islands of San Clemente and Sacca Sessolla was a tiny green patch marked by a fortress-like two story building, its red tiles offsetting creamy yellow walls. Stone craned his neck and noted a bell tower in one corner of the complex. He nudged Mandy and gestured unobtrusively. "San Bernardo, probably."

By agreement from the time they'd crossed into Canada, they kept their voices down and gestures muted in case they were somehow followed. In minutes the vaporetto lurched into the landing stage, a floating dock that marked the Lido "bus stop" at Piazzale Maria Elisabetta. They left the bobbing and swaying landing stage and quickly strode up the metal gangway to solid ground.

The difference between "true" Venice and the Lido was marked. Regular buses and taxis lined up waiting for or dropping off passengers. Crowds streamed around the docks and into the busy shopping area that led away across the width of the Lido to the Adriatic Sea. Together Stone and Mandy walked south along the path that lined the lagoon, past docks for various vaporetto lines. They stopped occasionally to admire the scenery and look back over towards Venice but their landside surveillance yielded little information about San Bernardo.

Looking around, Stone spotted a bookstall just past the main bus stop. He strode over and asked for a detailed map guide to the Lagoon. The bookseller shook his head. No, he had nothing other than the Venice guidebooks on display; nothing about the Lagoon itself. For that, he said, a bookshop like the university's bookstore Ca' Foscarini in Dorsoduro or perhaps the Libreria Sansovino in San Marco might be able to help.

"I'm interested in the islands in the lagoon," Stone extemporized. People keep saying Venice is sinking and I was wondering about the many islands in the lagoon." He pulled out his own map, "For example, I notice some islands here, San Clemente and Sacca Sessolla and I wonder if they too are sinking." Again the bookseller shrugged. "I also heard about a monastery on an island—San Bernardo—I think, and I wondered how the church was protecting it".

The bookseller jerked his head up suspiciously. He took a crumpled dirty handkerchief out and wiped his ruddy pockmarked nose anxiously. "What do you know of this place, Signore? It is not marked on maps. How did you know its name?"

Stone scrambled. "Uh, a friend of mine is a priest in Chicago. He was telling me about it some months ago when I said I was coming to Venice."

The bookseller's eyes narrowed. "Did he also tell you no one talks about this place Signore? That this island is a non-place?" He pulled his full stocky five foot six frame close to Stone. "Pah. You have no priest friend. I say no more to you."

With that he turned his back to serve another customer. Defeated, Stone retired. When he reached Mandy he took her by the arm, walking her diagonally away from the bookstall. From the corner of his eyes he saw the bookseller staring after them. They crossed to the Lido's main street, Gran Viale, and spied a shaded street café. Stone seated them so that he could face the street and ordered two lattes, remaining silent until the waiter walked away. Briefly he filled Mandy in on his conversation.

"So it's an island that nobody wants to talk about." Mandy said. "I knew it was a retreat centre, but my Vatican friend must have been only half-kidding when he said it was for troublesome priests. Obviously the church isolates them in a place nobody talks about and therefore cares about."

She slumped in her seat. "We're scuppered aren't we Stone? I mean how can we get out there? And, even if we could, how could we contact, let alone speak to, Father Joe." Her voice dropped in defeat. "If he's still there."

Stone stared across at the bookstall, studying the bookseller intently. "This undercover cloak and dagger nonsense is beyond me. But I'm a good journalist; a damned good one. That bookseller knows something. I just have to figure out how to speak to him privately and get it out of him."

They sat and sipped their lattes and Mandy tried to read. She surreptitiously studied Stone, conceding he'd shown ingenuity and easy confidence as he slipped them out of America. He was also a good companion, talking easily and knowledgeably about all kinds of subjects including those she considered her professional domain. Not only that, she glanced slyly at him, he was indeed good looking. Instead of her preconceived image of a shallow, plastic man, Stone Wallace was in fact an intriguing, sociable and stimulating one.

Stone, lost in thought about the bookseller, was oblivious to her scrutiny.

Less than thirty minutes later Stone noticed many of the fashionable shops were closing. It reminded him of two things: first it was late afternoon; second, they'd had an eventful two days. Jet lag was hitting him hard and probably hitting Mandy even harder since she'd done the transatlantic hop twice in just a few days with emotional shocks abounding all the while. He was about to suggest a return to the hotel when he suddenly noticed the bookseller quickly closing his staff and walking towards the vaporetto landing stage. He made an impulsive decision.

Throwing down some Euros, he grabbed Mandy by the arm and rushed her towards the Piazzale. Remaining behind the bookseller they hustled down the landing stage and squeezed onto the vaporetto jostling with workers and visitors returning to the city. They kept the bookseller in sight as he struggled to the opposite side and found a single seat beside the cockpit.

Stone leaned down and whispered to Mandy. "We'll follow him and see if we can speak to him alone."

Even before vaporetto made its turn to the stage at Ca'Rezzonico, the bookseller stood and headed to the exit. Stone diverted his eyes, but the man noticed nothing as he joined the crowd streaming off. Stone and Mandy followed. This was an unfamiliar part of Dorsoduro for Stone. They followed him up a narrow street, past non-descript doors and a tiny uninspired church. Down side lanes edging other canals were strings of multi-colored laundry strung across various balconies. They waited at the edge of a small campo until he'd cleared the open area before they too crossed. The crowds were thinning now. Stone hurried to close the gap.

"*Signore. S'cuse.*" The man turned, a puzzled look on his face.

"*Si?*"

"*Signore*, you seemed upset when I mentioned San Bernardo?"

A sudden flash of recognition crossed the bookseller's face. He crossed himself automatically.

Stone turned on his megawatt TV smile. "Signore, we mean no harm. We are merely people in need, looking for a priest friend. We believe he is on the island and we need to talk to him."

Mandy stepped up. "Signore, Father Joseph…Giuseppe?…Panterra was a close friend of my father's. We wanted to speak to him about my father but he's been sent to this monastery. Can you help us please? She looked pleadingly at him.

The bookseller shrugged and beckoned. "Come. We talk *privato*, No 'ere." Without another word he set off down a side alley. Stone and Mandy followed. On one side the canal's waters lapped against the stone. On the other, multi-colored doors led to hidden apartments and anonymous residents. He stopped at one, opened it and without looking back began climbing a worn staircase.

They followed.

St. Brigitte's, Paimpoint, France

"He what?! He's gone where?

Wyndham slammed down the phone beside his chair. He was sitting in Tonnerre's office. Tonnerre pensively watched him across the desk, eyes sporadically flicking upwards towards the statue of Taranis. Thirty minutes earlier, Wyndham had swept in and virtually taken over. Huw was placed in a private room. Dr. Horvath and the nurse, worried and confused by the strange people and place, were paid off with a handsome bonus and sent back to a four star hotel in Rennes where they could, at their convenience, make their fully paid way back to the US. Tonnerre's own doctor in turn took over the professor's care. He was stable, the doctor assured them. They could speak to him soon.

Both Wyndham and Tonnerre made polite conversation until they were completely alone. Each plotted his approach to the other, looking for an angle to put the other at a disadvantage and thereby confirm his own superiority. The phone call had interrupted the silent scheming.

Ignoring Tonnerre, Wyndham picked up the phone again and connected with his London office.

"Barker? Who do we have in or near Venice, Italy?" Wyndham's frustration and anger oozed over the line. "Wallace is in Italy. That's right, Italy.

And, I suspect, with Griffiths' daughter. Yes, the one you can't find despite all the cash I'm throwing at you!"

Wyndham barely took a breath. "They flew to Milan last night. That means they know Panterra was moved there from the Vatican. They're going to Venice. I feel it." He listened briefly, barked some more orders and hung up.

Tonnerre's eyes opened wide at the news then narrowed into glinty slits.

"One of my men in security at Toronto airport saw them boarding a flight to Milan," Wyndham said casually, freshly aware that sometimes good investigating can be trumped easily by blind luck. "He recognized Wallace from our alert. There was a young woman with him."

Wyndham rubbed his eyebrows again, as he thought. How had Wallace slipped through the security blanket thrown over Washington? And how in the world had he suddenly appeared in Toronto with the girl? Wallace might be smarter than he'd given him credit for, he grudgingly admitted. Nevertheless, it was time to be done with him. He had to be removed.

"I have a man at San Bernardo." Tonnerre's voice broke the silence. "He does laundry for the priests, but he's also a source of information at times." He paused. "It is San Bernardo they're heading for isn't it?" Tonnerre smiled smugly.

"What information needs could you possibly have from a Catholic monastery, Andre?" Wyndham scoffed. "They are the enemy, right?"

"*Cher Damien*, San Bernardo is where the church sends its problems. Where there is disagreement, disaffection or conflict, there is information. Information I can use." He gestured to the electronic map displayed on the plasma screen hanging from the ceiling. A quick word and multicolored lights flashed across Europe. He looked over at Wyndham and waved his hand in the air. "My informants. Everywhere."

"Impressive Andre. And yes, San Bernardo is their destination, I'm sure."

Despite his calm response, Wyndham seethed internally. In situations like this, he reminded himself, attack is better than defence. "None of this would be necessary, of course, if your inept followers had not screwed up." He glared at Tonnerre and began pacing the room. "Huw Griffiths is not twenty yards from here in serious condition because of your stupidity. He is the key! We can't find Excalibur without him and your men almost killed him." He roared at Tonnerre. "Samhein is less than a week away. All our plans revolve around London that day."

Tonnerre boiled inside but kept his voice calm "We can proceed without the sacred sword. We do not need it."

"Fool." Wyndham pounded the desk. "Excalibur is more than a symbol. Rhiannon believes it has power beyond this world. Whether you believe doesn't matter. She does! And with that belief comes our early legitimacy in power." He turned away, pacing once more, then spun and jabbed a finger at the electronic map.

"Give me the name of your man in Venice. I will have my men contact him."

Broceliande Forest, France

Chad's nap was an exhausted fourteen hour sleep. A cock crowing in the inn's back yard woke him just as light was peeking through the half drawn curtains. He struggled up, barely aware of the disheveled and crumpled clothes he'd slept in and splashed water from the tiny sink into his face.

An hour later, greatly refreshed, he drove into Paimpont. The dark clouds and raging rains had gone, though strong winds still howled. A washed-out sun peered weakly through the thinning clouds. As he approached the center of the village, Arthurian connections amplified a hundred times. The D38 became *Rue du Roi Arthur* as he entered town. It connected at the end, close by a small lake, with *Rue Chevalier Lancelot du Lac* and just around the corner was *Rue de L'enchanteur Merlin*.

A few shops dotted the streets flogging trinkets and souvenirs from books about the legends to mystical crystals and symbols—all attesting to the 'power' endowed by the mere presence of Merlin. He remembered Stone's complaint about tourist traps in Britain claiming Arthur and selling junky mementos; same apparently in Paimpont.

He parked and wandered down to the lake side to get his bearings. His innkeeper, Madame Lecavalier, recommended he start his tour of the "route d'Arthur" at a small bookshop close to the Abbey. "*Mais certainment zey 'ave books en Anglais*" she'd smiled at him, mixing her languages but getting her point across.

He poked about the bookshop admiring some prints and books depicting the Breton versions of the Arthurian legend then opened up an ongoing discussion with the sprightly old shop owner. Fortunately the man spoke intelligible English. "A result of the war, m'sieur."

In between other customers Dom got a skeptical but humorous Cliff's notes version of the legend. "Of course it is all nonsense *M'sieur*" the old man twinkled, "but it keeps the tourists coming and pays for my three wives, *n'est pas?*"

Chad paid for a couple of books and wandered down to the lake once again. He sat on a bench angled in such a way that it offered views of both the lake and the church. Quickly he perused the two slim volumes he'd bought. They filled in some holes in the legend pertaining to Brittany. It was obvious Arthur was as much a 'hero king' around here as he was in Britain.

The warming sun was tempting but he had to find a way into Tonnerre's compound. He walked back to the car and dropped the books onto the passenger seat. Just as he turned the engine on he noticed two swarthy men wearing white robes with a stitched black dragon on the front, emerge around a corner and enter the bookstore. Tonnerre's followers, he thought. He waited until they left then strolled over casually and, turned into the shop once again.

The old bookseller looked up, startled to see Chad once again. "*M'sieur?*" His eyebrows rose quizzically.

"Ah," Chad hesitated. "I wondered if you had a more detailed map of the forest region. One that shows where the various Arthur and Merlin sites are located." He smiled innocently at the bookseller who nodded and turned to a set of drawers behind the counter.

"By the way," Chad continued. "I just happened to notice two men in robes. Are they involved in some kind of play or pageant? Can I buy tickets?"

The old man turned, and looked quizzically at Chad. He put the a folded map on the counter and spat forcefully on the floor. "Those? *Merde! Excrement m'sieur*. Nothing but vermin."

The ferocity of his response startled Chad. I'm not sure I understand."

"They are frauds and liars, m'sieur, not actors." He shot a glance at the shop door and windows. "They are *voleurs*, thieves, who are destroying this village with their greed."

Surprised by his own vehemence, he looked keenly at Chad. "*Pardonez, m'sieur*, but neither do I believe you are what you seem." He pushed the map across the counter, his squinting blue eyes staring at Chad the entire time.

Chad shrugged. "I don't know what you mean."

"Do not take me for a fool, *m'sieur*. There are very few tourists, especially Americans, at this time of year so deeply interested in Arthur. Nor does one who is following King Arthur ask simple questions a true specialist would know the answers to." His hand still on the map, he waited. "I ask again. Who are you and what do you want in Paimpont?"

Chad cursed himself for not being more circumspect in his questions, but steadily returned the old man's stare. "One who is interested in Arthur and his impact upon this region."

"As I said, *m'sieur*, do not take me for a fool." He looked up as two men entered the shop.

Chad turned and saw a hefty man in a grey winter jacket, close the door firmly and flip the sign to '*Ferme*'. The second, a fair haired man in a jacket, sweater and jeans, approached Chad and the shopkeeper.

"Remy," he nodded to the old man and then turned and faced Chad squarely. His casual black jacket flopped open, deliberately Chad thought, as he spotted an underarm holster.

"And now *m'sieur*, what is your name and why are you in Paimpont," the fair haired man asked belligerently?

Offence being the best defense, Chad turned angrily on shop owner. "What is this?" he shouted. "I ask some simple questions and your two thugs come blustering in like Hollywood heavies. What's going on here?"

The old man ignored him and spoke directly to the lean fair haired man behind Chad. "He is not with Tonnerre, but he asks too many questions." He watched Chad carefully, "too many naïve questions."

Chad turned to the fair haired man who he'd already pegged as the leader when suddenly everything went black and he crumpled to the floor. Remy caught his body as he fell.

"You didn't need to hit him that hard, Remy." He threw his jacket off and signaled his companion at the door. "Close up while we take him in the back." He lifted Chad's feet while Remy grabbed Chad under the shoulders. Together they staggered behind the curtain into a chaotic book-filled room behind the shop. The man at the door moved quickly, turning off the lights and pulling down blinds to reinforce the closed look.

Chapter Fifteen

Wales, 1301 • Maesgwinfi

Owain led the way, weaving through the woods following a trail only he could see. Then he held up his hand and crept forward. He signaled me beside him and whispered that we'd reached, Nantycoed. Carefully we looked around before we splashed across and melted into the trees again. Our unseen path now moved upwards. We kept climbing, then a quick turn then Owain stopped and pointed. I stared but saw only large clumps of gorse and heather with some small trees scattered around a rock fall. "Our new home," he whispered.

A cold cloying mist descended the hill. Already, the castle ruins were barely visible. Wrapping our new cloaks around us we scampered up and Owain quickly moved some of the gorse aside before slipping out of sight. I crawled in after him. In the gloom my eyes slowly adjusted and I found myself in a cave, partly natural but further in, largely man-hewn.

"This has long always been held secret by our people. It was a refuge during the risings against our English overlords. Our stories say that one time, many years before the first Earl built the castle, our entire village—men, women and children—were protected from an army for days."

By Jesu, I could believe it. The cave stretched back well into the hillside. As I explored more in the following days, I found smaller side caves and tunnels extending all directions from the main cavern.

"Ah, thank the Lord, Alun has been here before us." Owain pointed. There, leaning against the wall were more clothes, woolen blankets, some wood and food. Quickly we gathered the supplies and carried them into the bowels of the cave. At one point, part of it curved away from the entrance. We followed until we came to a smaller cave obviously deep under the hillside. There we dropped everything. Owain reached into his jerkin and pulled out a flint. He struck it against the stone walls and lit a reed torch that had obviously been used in the past. In the flickering light I examined our new abode.

Against the far wall was a shallow pit where I could see the blackened cold remains of earlier fires. Against another wall there were ledges hewn out of the rock sufficient to make sleeping platforms up from the cold earth and close to the warming fires.

I looked carefully at my companion. A cool calmness had surrounded him since Alun had told us about Alys. But calm as he was on the outside even in those flickering flames I sensed the deep sorrow. I reached out to him and he collapsed in my arms, heaving huge sobs of pain. It was as if the relief of reaching the safety of the cave allowed him to release his enormous hurt.

Again, the Offices would not meet our needs that day. But I prayed. Lord Jesus how I prayed!

As I comforted him I felt the calmness of God infuse my being. The psalms of David now became real, where before they had been half-listened-to chants. A week ago I would have repeated them by rote. But now they came out of my own soul as I sought to comfort him.

I repeated the psalmist's words. "How long, O Lord, will you forget me? Forever? How long will you hide your face from me? How long must I wrestle with my thoughts and every day have sorrow in my heart? How long will my enemy triumph over me?"

Owain lifted his head and said softly, brokenly. "Aye, Thomas that is my cry; that is my heart."

"Then listen carefully and remember this, Owain. Does not King David also say God is a refuge for the oppressed, a stronghold in times of trouble. Those who know his name will trust him for he has never forsaken those who seek him. That includes you and me Owain.

"No matter how difficult or painful our days, he loves us and guides us. He has given us a great challenge—to protect the church and to destroy those who seek to destroy her. I know not how or when this will end. But this I do know. He has led us and preserved us thus far. And he will not forsake us now."

Owain nodded grudgingly. I was amazed myself that I had remembered those comforting words. They had come easily and flowed out of my very being. I remembered them for Owain. Why did I not always remember for myself?

He pulled away and wiped a rough sleeve against his tear stained face. His ragged, uncut and untonsured fair hair hung down.

"Fine words Thomas. Have you ever considered becoming a monk?" He smiled weakly at me, but I knew that his old sense of humor was battering its way through his grief.

He picked up the wood and began stacking it in the cold fire pit. Quickly he lit the fire with the reed torch and soon the fire's warmth began to reach into us. As we sat and talked Owain told me that the honeycomb of tunnels and smaller caves was actually well planned and carved out by those who'd inhabited the area many hundreds of years ago. Indeed, one long cave system even extended through Mynydd Margam and ended close to Margam Abbey.

It was good to know this. Should Lord De Tuberville or, worse, Gethin discover our hiding place, we needed an escape route. To be trapped like a badger was now my greatest fear. It was comforting to know there were ways out so I spent many hours the next few days exploring and memorizing various paths and tunnels, seeing where they would lead.

One time Owain and I followed a very dark tunnel that felt like an unending tomb seemingly climbing ever upward. We saw a shaft of light at the end and soon found ourselves crawling on our bellies to a point where we could peer out through some bushes looking down on what seemed like an open meadow. At the far end of the meadow there were oak, hawthorn and ash trees but the meadow itself seemed undulating. There were circular looking mounds that created what I can only describe as an amphitheatre. The place was silent and deserted. I could not even hear the birds. Beside me, Owain shuddered.

"This is an evil place. People in the villages around believe it is haunted by ghosts. My father claimed he heard them moaning one night when he was out hunting. It is called Maes Haberth, the field of sacrifice." I sensed his discomfort as we edged our way backwards and turn back toward the main cave.

Yet another time, while Owain rested, I explored the tunnels alone. I came to a crack in the rock face. As I studied it further, I saw that many smaller rocks were stacked one upon the other to block yet another entrance. I moved some of the stones, just enough that I could clamber on top and look out from the hidden entrance. In the distance I could see yet another forest and, sparkling through the trees, the river. I had a fine view of Tir Iarll's upper reaches.

For five days we hid. Alun was faithful. Over the days we found fresh baked breads, newly caught trout, haunches of venison, beans and one time even a fresh butchered mutton. We never saw Alun. The supplies just appeared most mornings at the cave entrance. We gathered our bounty to our living area where we partook of the blessings God provided through Alun.

Those days took a toll on both of us, Owain in particular. We knew not what was going on in the world outside our underground home. I began to feel like a penned up rabbit, despite the steady supply of food and sustenance. Owain felt it more than I. The village was his home, yet he was cut off. The agony of Alys' loss was obvious. Several nights into our confinement I woke to his thrashing and moaning. I jumped up and went to him, but he was asleep, suffering over and over in his dreams.

Even in our exile, I tried to maintain the discipline of the abbey. Although I had no copies of the scriptures, I remembered enough to speak them aloud for my own encouragement and Owain's. I prayed aloud. Even Owain remarked on the change in my prayers from memorized words to heartfelt cries. He said my tonsure might be disappearing, but the power of the abbey and God himself, was very much alive in me. I doubted that, but I was touched.

On the seventh morn we were breaking our fast. Owain idly played with a stick then suddenly flung it against the cave wall. "I shall go mad, Thomas, if I don't find out what is happening." He jumped to his feet. "Alun, bless his heart, provides, but he cannot read or write. He leaves us no information." He paced rapidly up and down in front of the fire. "I must go into the village and find out if we are free yet to leave this place."

I argued that seven days was not enough time for us to be forgotten. Why, I said, Abbot Godfrey was still only fresh in his grave. The hue and cry for his killer would not be dropped this suddenly. Alun would tell us when it was safe. And there was still Gethin. His hatred for us and the church was exceeded only by his desire to get his hands on Excalibur!

Excalibur. It lay with the parchment sack, covered by a woolen blanket on one of the rock ledges. We had not mentioned the sword or our burden for days but it was never far from my thoughts. Jesu, I quailed at the task yet before me. What was I to do with this great sword even if I should escape Gethin's clutches and the accusation of murder?

Owain and I argued all morning but my words fell on deaf ears. Owain would not be persuaded. Nothing would do but he had to find out where Gethin was and what Lord de Tuberville was doing. Was our overlord still hunting Godfrey's killer or had he withdrawn to his mighty castle at Coity? Finally, he agreed that it would be folly to leave the cave in daylight. If leave he must, t'would be at night.

We argued again when I said I would join him. His insistence upon my staying was bolstered by the fact that I did not know the area or the village. Further, moving around woods at night was not a talent of mine. I could not disagree, so we came to the same mind. I would pray him safely through his visit to the village.

Somewhat mollified, he moved close to the cave entrance, the more to look out over the village. The afternoon passed slowly. I spent it close to my friend but in silent prayer. His restless spirit would not welcome words from me now. He watched, jumped up, paced and just as quickly lay down to peer out once again. Thus was our pattern until dark began to creep in.

When night was fully upon us, he could wait no longer. Quietly and carefully he slipped out of the cave. In fear and trepidation I settled myself down to wait at the opening, staring into the gloom, and picking mindlessly at the small loaf I laid in my lap.

I sat there all night. Only the occasional owl hooted. Once I heard rustling in the long grasses on the hillside but it was only a small animal, a fox mayhap. Truly, the hours of looking awake while catching cat naps during our vigils at the abbey served me well this night. In my semi-sleep I was able to both pray and keep watch.

Dawn broke. I stirred, stood and stretched. I peered out as far as I could without exposing myself. I saw nothing except the trees and, beyond, the river. Not a soul moved. My concern for Owain grew. Hours passed. During my vigil at the cave entrance I hoped also to see Alun as he arrived with food for he would surely have news. But he did not appear either. My worry increased and so did the fervency of my prayers.

The sun was high in the sky. As I stood and stretched, I noticed a slight movement in the woods below me. I peered closer, again trying to get as far out of the cave entrance as I could without showing myself. I saw the movement again. Suddenly, a figure burst forth quietly but quickly, pounding up the hill towards me. Praise God, I thought, it is Owain. Within moments he'd reached our lair and slipped inside.

"Thank God, Owain. I was terrified you'd been caught."

"I nearly was. Gethin and his men are still scouring the area for us. They slip into the village quietly and wander about asking questions. The villagers are terrified." He was still gasping for breath after his run uphill. "Alun had to hide me in his byre." He sniffed his sodden muddy clothes and made a face. "I wallowed in pig muck for much of the morning, and only now was able to take some time to try and wash myself quickly in the river before coming back." He slipped a sack off his back. "Our food."

As we ate he told me his news. It was not good listening. Gethin knew this was Owain's home village and was willing to wait patiently, convinced that sooner or later we would show up. Gethin had warned the villagers that the gods would not look kindly on those who protect the Christ followers, invoking fears of the underworld that lay buried just below the surface of their minds.

As we talked he told me that Alys was killed by Gethin himself. Owain's anger and pain built as he recounted the story. One of her own villagers told

Gethin that she knew Owain. His men pulled her out of the hut and into the mud. Gethin demanded she tell him where we were. He paused, tears filling his eyes. "She began to pray—for you, for me, even for Gethin. In his rage he slew her." He stopped and took a deep breath. "I will see Gethin damned and dancing in hell if it is the last thing I do."

I held his shoulder silently. There was nothing else I could do or say.

Chapter Sixteen

Venice, Italy

Stone and Mandy left the bookseller's apartment elated by his reluctant agreement to help them. Once in the confines of his flat, the bookman, in halting English, confided that the monastery at San Bernardo was so cloistered few in Venice really knew of or spoke about it. It was as if the island monastery did not exist. "My own priest… not talk of dis place."

"How do you know about it then?" Stone stood up from the battered armchair.

"*Mi cugino*, my cousin is the head gardener there." The bookseller shrugged. "'E tells me things."

Excitedly, Mandy leaned forward. "Could he help us get in and talk to Father Giuseppe?"

"*Signorina*, no. San Bernardo 'e ave no *visitatori*. Please, no more talk of dis place." His hand swept across his forehead as if erasing something from the mind then throwing it away.

"Signore please. We need to talk to my father's friend…"

"If we don't speak to Father Joe," Stone interrupted, "it will mean disaster not only for the Church but perhaps Europe itself."

For more than an hour they argued and pleaded with the bookseller. Without divulging the full depth of their knowledge and fears, they slowly convinced him that Father Joe was the key to stopping an evil force. Warily he finally agreed and slipped into a smaller room taking his cell phone with him.

They waited. Minutes passed. Finally, he emerged shaking his head. "He will help you Mario, 'e thinks you are instabile; malato di mente," circling his finger around his head in the universal sign for "crazy".

His cousin would speak to Father Joe if possible the next morning. They were to meet that afternoon at the bookstall to find out if and how they could meet with Father Joe. With that they had to be content.

They left and found their way to the Grand Canal. One good thing about Venice was that it is an island where nobody ever really gets lost. No matter which direction you went, Stone knew they would wind up somewhere by a canal. Then it was simply a matter of finding a landing stage and hopping on the water bus. Soon they were motoring across to San Marco. As they chugged down the Grand Canal, Mandy impulsively reached over, "You know Stone, we actually make a pretty good team. Better than I thought we would." She gave him a quick peck on the cheek. "Sorry I was such a crabby cow about everything. Including you."

Stone smiled back at her. "Yeah, well I wasn't too happy you came along myself. Always worked alone. Never needed anyone's help. Huw was the first one I could trust and open up to. That's why I had to help him."

The vaporetto lurched as it hit the landing stage. They disembarked and walked into the Piazza San Marco, passing the Doge's Palace and the Campanile and pushing through the tourist throngs leaving the Basilica. They crossed the piazza slowly, the masses of pigeons in front of them exploded in flapping wings and noise, settling just as quickly behind then. Stone explained his unique relationship with Huw as a surrogate parent. "I'm not sure how much he told you or even if he understood exactly how much he meant…means…to me."

Mandy nodded. "He has that way with him of making you feel that you are the only person in the world who matters." They walked along silently for a few minutes and she shrugged and heaved a sigh. "I think that's part of why I resented your involvement in his research."

Stone grunted acknowledgement and touched her shoulder. "Let's start again. Friends?" Mandy grinned and linker her arm in his. "Friends!"

There was nothing more they could do and a heavy tiredness was setting in so they agreed on a quick meal then back to the hotel. They hurried across the rest of the piazza then headed up the Mercerie, Venice's main shopping and restaurant district.

As they walked along a green jacketed tourist leaning casually against a wall glanced over at them. Quickly he pulled out a smartphone and checked. The picture on the screen matched the face he'd just seen. He signaled to another man across the square and hurried over, keeping his eyes on Stone and following him discreetly.

"That's him. And it must be Griffiths' daughter with him."

The taller of the two swiftly tapped the other on the shoulder as their targets suddenly entered a small restaurant. They passed by without looking in and then stopped a few yards up the Mercerie ostensibly to admire a shop window full of Venetian masks.

The loftier one then reversed course, walked past the restaurant, stopping to look at the menu posted outside. Through the window he noted the pair seated and talking with a waiter. Moving slowly on, he stopped three doors down took out his own cell phone, leaned against the wall and made two hurried calls, one local, one to London.

Shortly, three casually dressed men strolled nonchalantly down the street, stopped to admire the mask window and then ambled a bit further. A few whispered words and the trio split up, one staying still, one continuing down the Mercerie before turning left into a side street, while the third walked slowly back to the restaurant entered and took a small corner table away from Stone and Mandy. The coverage was in place.

"I don't see that we have any choice," Stone said quietly. "Who knows if this Mario can be trusted but I don't see any other avenues open to us."

"If we do get on the island to talk to Father Joe, let me do the talking." Mandy tapped a napkin against her mouth. He knows me and he trusts Da." She leaned back against the chair and laid down her knife and fork. "I just wish there was someone we could turn to, someone who could help. What about Chad and his agency?"

Stone shook his head vigorously. "I burned that bridge when we didn't go to the safe house. "Nope. We're I'm afraid we're on our own."

"And if we get to Father Joe and get the information?"

"Then I guess we play that by ear. Maybe we trade it for your father's safety."

"Never. Da would not want that. Ever. Even at the cost of his life. No. We use the information to destroy that Druid movement once and for all." Her voice rose slightly in indignation and Stone hurriedly waved her silent.

They finished the meal quickly, paid the bill and left, pushing through the crowded lane toward San Marco. They didn't notice their shadows gradually head in the same direction, one ambling several yards in front, the other two casually leapfrogging each other. Inside the restaurant, the other man paid for his meal and sauntered out into the street, ear glued to his phone speaking rapidly but quietly despite the noisy late evening crowds in the street. He nodded silently at his instructions; follow, do not intercept. Wait.

St. Brigitte's, Paimpont, France

Carveau cringed in his chair before the silent Druid priests arrayed in a circle around him. Black circles under his sunken eyes and unshaven whiskers gave him a cadaver-like look. He was disoriented, his sense of time washed away by the constantly shining cell lights. His body wracked with pain once again. A groan escaped his lips. He knew he'd been poisoned in some way—not enough to cause the blessed relief of death, but enough to create excruciating pain to wash over him in wave after wave.

The poison also impacted his mind and ability to speak coherently, to tell them that everything he'd done was for the good of the community and on instructions from Tonnerre himself. None of his sentences made sense. The stammered explanations of his decisions and actions in Washington jerked off his tongue phrase by phrase but in jumbled mixtures of Breton, French, and even some English. He struggled to control his mind and make his tongue obey. Tears flowed down his dirt and drool encrusted face.

Tonnerre dominated the room in his pristine white robe and golden-garlanded head. The massive staff, held in both hands was topped by a sculpture of the wizened god Taranis. In ringing tones his deep voice consumed the room.

"The council is agreed. There can be only one response to your crimes. One punishment." As he spoke, two hooded figures slipped into the room and quickly whisked a cover over Carveau's head and one held a hand over his mouth to stifle the screams. The second quickly jabbed a syringe into his arm. In seconds the struggling ceased. Carveau was removed from the room. Tonnerre remained standing. His voice lost its ringing tones but kept the steely determination. His eyes swept the room again.

"We meet at the grove in two hours. Ensure that all are present. Everyone must witness what happens to one who disobeys and fails me."

He stalked out of the room. Wordlessly the others waited a few moments and followed.

Buckingham Palace Mews, London

Freddy entered armed with the latest field reports.

"Summarize."

"Wyndham landed in Helsinki and waited in solitary splendor for almost three hours before taking off again. Other than a visit from the fuel tanker, nobody approached the aircraft. It landed in Rennes just over two hours later. Passengers, including we presume, Sir Damien, disembarked. A stretcher passenger was loaded into a waiting ambulance. The entire party then left the airport." He looked up at Sir Giles.

"Our people in Paimpont later reported an entourage of three cars and an ambulance racing through the village and up towards Tonnerre's compound."

Sir Giles harrumphed. He flicked the pages. "Have to move quickly in Paimpont. Get Griffiths out." He paused, his brow and bushy eyebrows furrowed in thought. "Mustn't get the French involved though. Too much of a sticky wicket. Use our own people on the ground there." He dismissed Freddy then shouted as he disappeared through the door. "Let me know when we get word from France or Venice. "And set up a cot in the bloody boardroom. Be spending the night here, I'll warrant!"

Paimpont, France

Flickers of light and awareness flared through his mind. Slowly, he became aware of his surroundings.

"Ah, M'sieur, you are back with us."

Chad struggled to sit up, holding his aching head. He opened his eyes, recognized the French bookseller close to his face staring at him intently. Behind him, the fair haired man also looked anxiously at Chad.

"You'll have to forgive my overzealousness to protect this place," Remy blurted. "I merely wished to know who you were and why you were so curious. We worry that Tonnerre's creatures will wipe out our mission. Your name, it is known to us Agent Lawson." Remy helped Chad stand, handing him his wallet. An incredulous look crossed Chad's face as he tucked it in his pocket.

"You have the advantage of me then. Who are you and why the crude tactics?"

Remy nodded. "Remy Gaspard, *a votre service.*" He looked quickly at the fair haired man.

"As Remy said, Mr. Lawson, we are deeply sorry for the way you were treated. My fault, I'm afraid." He stuck his hand out. "Fowler, John Fowler. I'm with the Crown Security Branch, Sir Giles Broadbent's crowd. Only just found out you were going to be in the area, I'm afraid. We thought you were one of Tonnerre's stooges looking to eliminate Remy and his operation. They can't stand him because he mocks them, but we're sure they suspect he's a pipeline of information to the authorities."

Ruefully, Chad shook the proffered hand. "My fault too. I tried to wing it with the 'Arthurian-nut' cover but not enough background to fool a schoolgirl. Rule number one; know your background cover intimately. Trouble is, until the day before I didn't even know I'd be in France, let alone the heart of King Arthur country."

"Yes, well, mistakes were made on both sides but no real damage done thankfully." Fowler pulled a chair closer and beckoned Chad to sit. "We've got a real problem now, though. Happened just after we slugged you." Quickly he reported several cars and an ambulance had raced through Paimpont headed toward the Taranis compound.

"London's fairly certain it was Wyndham and the ambulance had Professor Griffiths in it. Sir Giles wants us to mount a quick rescue operation. Determine if the Professor is there and then get him out."

"What if he's not capable of being moved? What if anything like that kills him?"

"No choice. We have to get him out. Those are our orders."

Fowler glanced up as a third man walked into the tiny back room. "London's arranged a medevac helicopter. It will arrive at Beauvais this evening."

Fowler turned to Chad. "We've been watching St. Brigitte's for months from a small, isolated farm at Beauvais, about fifteen kilometers west of here. That's our HQ. So, we've got to come up with a plan, nip in, find the professor, close down Tonnerre's operation if we can, whistle up the helicopter then nip out again with professor neatly in hand. Simple, really!"

"Yeah, simple!" Chad's headache returned with a stabbing vengeance. Only this time he doubted the head shot was the cause.

"Come on, old man," said Fowler. "Let's get over to Beauvais and get you geared up."

Venice, Italy

After an anxious morning of desultory sightseeing, Stone and Mandy stepped off the vaporetto and walked slowly over to Giovanni's kiosk. Stone picked up the day-old copy of *USA Today* startled to find his own picture staring at him with blaring headlines calling him a fugitive. Not that it would make much difference but he scooped all the available copies and quickly scanned the *International Herald Tribune* relieved to find it had not yet picked up the story. Wordlessly, he handed the pack of papers to Mandy and several ten Euro notes to Giovanni.

The bookseller accepted the notes and offered no change. Instead he spoke directly to Mandy.

"Mario 'as spoken with your priest friend. He asks proof you are right person. Father Giuseppe wants to know name of favorite book your father read to you when you little girl."

Smiling, Mandy answered immediately. "Tell him it was *The Lion, the witch and the wardrobe* by C.S. Lewis."

Giovanni nodded, served a customer then took out his cell phone. He spoke rapidly in the Venetian dialect, adding "si" every couple of breaths. His black eyebrows jumped up and down expressively and his arms waved as he talked. Within moments he was finished.

"He will speak to the priest. Come back, one hour." He turned to a green jacketed tourist.

Stone and Mandy walked away, stopping only to discard the papers in one of the infrequent trash bins. They strolled to a café, sat down and ordered, oblivious to three men in a café across the street. They said little, anxiously waiting for the hour to pass. Precisely on time, they walked over to the kiosk.

"Mario will meet you here in two more hours. He will then take you across la Laguna to meet your priest."

Finally, the time was up. Across the Lagoon the sun was setting behind the clouds. By the time they got out onto San Bernardo it would be dark. They lingered briefly by the shop watching the news vendor carefully until another man joined him. They walked over. Mario looked them over briefly acknowledging their presence with a nod, and beckoned them to follow. He shook his head disbelievingly that they still wanted to cross to the island. He led them to a small moored motor boat. Mario waved them to sit, untied and headed slowly off into the lagoon. Stone pulled his light zip-up jacket tighter, grateful he'd remembered how cool evenings could be in the lagoon.

Behind them, the fair haired man and his companion quickly waved up their own boat and jumped in, joining two others.

They lagged behind Mario's boat watching carefully as they headed across the lagoon towards San Bernardo. Once sure of Mario's destination, their own boat set off at speed across the lagoon, crossing behind the island. In the dark of the eastern side of the island, they dropped speed and approached stealthily, winding carefully over the shallows, closing on a stone embankment. As they closed the gap, two jumped out and disappeared against the shadowy walls of the monastery. The boat slipped silently away, out of sight yet within easy call.

Quietly the men edged their way around the wall.

St. Brigitte's, Paimpont, France

Wyndham eased himself into a chair beside the patient. He rubbed his eyebrow compulsively as his hawk-like eyes watched the French doctor remove Griffiths' oxygen mask. Tonnerre entered the room, cast a cursory glance at the professor and turned to Wyndham. He brusquely waved the doctor out

"This is going to delay Crowning Glory." It was a statement rather than question.

Wyndham glared. "Shut up you fool. Nothing will delay it. Do not speak of it unless we are totally alone."

Tonnerre nodded his head at the hospital bed. "He's sedated. He doesn't know what we're talking about."

"Nevertheless, keep your mouth shut!" Wyndham turned and leaned closer to the patient. "Professor Griffiths?" He waited and watched as the professor laboriously turned his head and focused his eyes on the voice. His head was swathed with bandages as were the arms that poked out beneath the sheets. There was no response. A myriad of tubes ran from his body to various machines and IV bags.

"Professor. My name is Damien Wyndham. I know you can hear me. I have read the doctor's reports. You are out of danger now and I am pleased that we have been able to help you." The patient stirred. "I want to get you home to Wales as quickly as possible, but we had to make a necessary stop in France. You will be well taken care of here and we will get you home hopefully as early as tomorrow." Wyndham paused. Patience and sympathy were not his norm. It was too frustrating. He wanted answers and he wanted them now. But he also needed Griffiths' trust and cooperation.

"Professor, I want to help you, but you can help me as well. I know that you are working on a historical discovery that will set your name down in the pantheon of British historians. I need you to answer some questions for me." Griffiths' eyes fluttered briefly. Perhaps he was getting through to him.

"Before your accident you were doing research into King Arthur?" Again he paused, waiting for a response. "Dr. Griffiths, your country is depending upon you. You have the key to great things for the Welsh people, indeed for all Celtic peoples around the world. You have information that could help your people. Can you tell me what was in the parchment you found? Tell me what became of King Arthur and Excalibur?"

The bandaged head stirred slightly. A quiet whisper escaped his lips and the right hand seemed to painfully beckon Wyndham forward. He exchanged eager glances with Tonnerre and leaned in, putting his head close to the professor's lips.

Huw's head turned slowly, painfully until he faced Wyndham. His eyes gripped Wyndham.

"Yes, professor? What is it you want to say?"

"Get....stuffed!"

Chapter Seventeen

Broceliande Forest, France

It had taken nearly two hours of arguing, agreeing, critiquing, constructing, deconstructing and reconstructing but they finally, reluctantly, agreed on a plan. It was not a great plan, not even a good plan, but it was the best they could do under the circumstances.

Chad, Fowler, his brawny colleague Will Hamilton and the third agent Keith Rumsford collectively agreed they would enter St. Brigitte's through what they perceived as the weakest link in a formidable security system. They'd huddled around a map of the forest and satellite images of St. Brigitte's spread out on the farmhouse's massive wood kitchen table. Tonnerre's compound was outlined with red marker, solid in places, dotted in others. A blue X identified the farm at Beauvais and blue lines marked potential routes from the farm to the compound. A black circle surrounded the main building where they believed the professor was held. A large grass lawn area in front of Tonnerre's personal quarters was marked as the potential landing site for the chopper.

"Their security seems first rate. We know that their electronic surveillance is tops. They have high tech communications facilities that keep them in contact literally around the world. The perimeter is entirely surrounded by wire or, in places, electronic security fencing. Plus there are personnel patrols along the boundaries every half hour. The roads, in particular, are monitored by camera and movement sensing devices.

"But we've noticed at times that small animals—deer, foxes and the like—have sometimes caused the electronic fences to send out breach signals. It happens so frequently that the guards have become a bit lapse in responding quickly and efficiently."

Fowler looked up at the group. "That may be our only opportunity. If we can get through the electronic fence and clear the area quickly, we just might have a chance."

Will Hamilton leaned forward and stared intently at the map then turned his attention to the satellite photos once again. He jabbed at the photos. "I think we can up our chances slightly."

He took a black marker and carefully outlined a small section to the north and west of the compound's buildings and approximately two kilometers from the western boundaries.

"It means taking a roundabout route, but if we breached the compound here," he designated a dotted line some four kilometers north of their planned entry point, "and moved quickly down here, there's less chance of being spotted."

He drew a small circle and planted his finger in the center.

"That's their sacred grove. Tonnerre's people think it's a mystical place to be feared. They try to stay away if at all possible." He stood and stretched.

"If we move quickly and quietly through the fencing and get down into the grove, I don't think we'll be bothered. The bonus is it's only half a kilometer to where we think the professor is. We should be able to cover that quickly in the dark. They won't be expecting anyone coming from that direction."

Fowler brought him back to earth. "What about sensors or video triggered by movement?"

Hamilton's smile disappeared rapidly. He shrugged. "Didn't say it was perfect; just said it might improve our chances."

For several minutes the mental head scratching continued as they stared at the map and photos, searching for flaws or, better yet hoping a superior plan would drop on them out of the blue. Finally, Fowler stood up.

"Don't see that we have much choice, do you?" He turned to Chad. "We have night vision equipment for ourselves, but none for you unfortunately, so you'll have to stay close to me. "Anyway extra gear around might make it tougher for you to enter and search for Griffiths. We'll go in with you, but you're the only one who can actually identify the professor.

"The thing is," he mused, "they might bandage a decoy and slip him into a bed. We won't have time to ask for ID and the professor may be out of it. We need you to verify it's him. Then you can evacuate with him in the chopper. We'll cover you."

"What about you and your men?"

"I'll arrange with Remy to have a vehicle hidden near their main entrance road. We have to trust that Tonnerre's security plan is aimed at preventing a break in. Let's hope he hasn't thought of anyone trying to break out! If we can take out the security guys at the gatehouse, make it down to the main road and get to Remy's vehicle, we should be OK."

Fowler stepped away from the kitchen to make a quick phone call to London. He returned and swept his hand towards the map. "Sir Giles has given us the go-ahead. The Guvnor also says we're to apprehend both Wyndham and Tonnerre and shut down the operation. He's standing by to alert the French authorities. They suspect Tonnerre had a hand in the president's assassination. As soon as we let him know we've got the pair of them and the professor's safe, the French will move in.

"Chad, he's spoken with your chief. Technically you are now seconded to Crown Security and will work closely with us. By the way, he also said to tell you that your friend Stone Wallace is apparently in Venice hunting down a priest who might have some information regarding an old document."

Relief and confusion flooded Chad's face. He knew Stone was resourceful, but how the devil had he made it there? Knowing Stone, he figured the story of "how and why Venice" would be both simple and complicated. He couldn't wait.

Fowler distributed the kit they'd need including Viper night goggles complete with head gear. Fowler himself kept the thermal imaging gear. He handed out Heckler & Koch MP7 submachine guns and silencers reminding them the guns were just to be used as a last resort. "Stealth. That's our main weapon."

Only when they heard the approaching helicopter did they push themselves away from the table.

St. Brigitte's, Paimpont, France

Wyndham fumed. Tonnerre smiled to himself as Wyndham stalked out of the professor's room and back to Tonnerre's office. "The bloody fool! I could have strangled him there and then. Insufferable, pompous ass!"

The tirade of cursing continued all down the hall and up the stairs. The door to Tonnerre's private sanctuary slammed hard behind Wyndham as he followed the Breton into the room. Before either could say anything, the phone rang. Unthinkingly, Wyndham pushed past his partner and immediately grabbed it, ignoring Tonnerre's angry look.

"Speak English, dammit! This is Damien Wyndham," he told the surprised caller. He listened intently, his palm face up towards the Breton's face, holding off his recrimination.

"Very good. Tell my men to take the girl and let me know the minute you have her. Eliminate the others. Permanently."

"That was your laundry man. The priest is meeting with Wallace and the girl tonight during the hour the monks are allowed to wander the island unaccompanied. The abbot there apparently thinks it is good for them to have moments of personal freedom. That will make it easier for my men."

He paused and looked up. "Oh yes, as soon as I knew they were in Venice I sent my own team in. They're going to grab the girl and get out. I have planes standing by for just such a purpose." His face turned blacker with anger. "As for the worthless priest and reporter, their time for reflection will be eternal." The malice and anger in his voice was palpable. He slammed his body down into a chair and looked up at Tonnerre.

"Make no mistake Andre, this entire screwed up mess is your fault! My whole plan has been jeopardized by your idiocy. You are bloody useless and your followers are even stupider than you are! One foul up after another. One stupidity after another." He jumped up, his lips curled into a sarcastic sneer

'By the gods. Your whole operation is a foul stench that must be eradicated. You should be joining this Belenos in punishment tonight!"

Ashen with anger and shock, Tonnerre thrust his taller frame into Wyndham's personal space. The two lashed thunderous invective at each other in voices that even Jean-Marc heard through the solid oak doors across the hall.

It was not going to be a good night.

San Bernardo Monastery, Venice

Mario's boat motor cut out and they drifted slowly in the dark towards the monastery's wooden dock. The moon had long since disappeared behind clouds. In broken English, he urged them to lie down and tossed a putrid canvas tarp over them.

"Stay 'ere. No speak! I land, take away monk. You watch, then come 'ide by bushes near wall. Father meet you by bench." He gestured weakly to the left, picked up a bottle and dropped a fish stinking canvas on top of them.

Clumped tightly together, Stone and Mandy felt the boat nudge gently against the wooden pilings then tip precariously as Mario stepped onto the dock. They held their breath. In the quietness of the night, they heard soft but cheerful voices as Mario engaged a man in familiar conversation.

Peeking out from the tarpaulin, Stone waited until his eyes accustomed to the inky darkness. Mario, arm around the shoulder of the monk was calmly guiding him away from the dock and along the shore to the right. He offered a bottle and the monk tilted it back, letting the finest Veneto red wine trickle down his throat. Mario slapped him heartily on the back as they disappeared into the night.

Stone and Mandy slid out of the boat and gingerly walked across the dock. Unseen, they pushed into the bushes against the wall. They could barely see the bench in the darkness even though it was only a hundred yards away. As carefully and quietly as they could they edged their way along the wall, checking constantly for anything suspicious. A steady wind rustled the leaves and water slapped noisily against the shore. Stone was grateful the noises masked their own stumbling steps.

Finally they were in the clumped and dark bushes directly behind the bench that rested just off a narrow stony path no more than two persons wide at its widest. Stone figured more than ten minutes had passed. He worried that Mario would return and want to leave before Father Joe appeared. Then Mandy gripped his arm. A shadow appeared, walking slowly along the path, speaking gently, hands clasped in front. The figure's feet crunched the stones as he approached. She squeezed his arm tighter as the shadow sat down.

"Father God," the deep resonant voice said in English, "I thank you for the lion that reminds us of your strength. I ask that you command all strong people to stay still and speak quietly if they are indeed to serve you."

Mandy lurched forward but Stone gripped her tight. "No witches now in Narnia Father Joe," she murmured.

The priest studied the gloomy darkness. "Ah, Mandy it is indeed you. Shush, don't move. I still fear we may be watched. Who is with you? It's not Huw is it?"

Mandy whispered "no, it's a friend". Before she could continue, Father Joe interrupted. "Listen carefully. I have the document your father wants."

He sat down and a package plopped out of his voluminous robes. He carefully kicked it underneath the bench. He sat sideways speaking but not looking at them. "Huw opened a can of worms with this request. I found what he wanted and was able to smuggle them with me when they sent me here. I did a quick rough translation like he asked me to. An incredible story if it's true! I'm surprised he sent you though. Where is he?"

Emotions suddenly poured over her. Worry, jetlag, gratitude and relief all washed away restraint. She lurched forward, freeing herself from Stone's grip and running out to Father Joe. As she appeared out of the shadows, voices shouted as they ran toward her. Father Joe rose and faced the men running towards them.

"There she is. It's her! Him too!" In the confusion and shouting Stone heard a shouted "damn" from further away.

The closest thug grabbed Mandy by the arm and pulled her away from Father Joe's grip and began to back away half holding, half picking her up. The second calmly stood and raised his arm. Stone heard soft plops and watched Father Joe crumple to the ground a millisecond before searing pain also hit him.

The two men threw Mandy into a boat that had drifted quietly in next to Mario's. It fired up and disappeared in the dark lagoon night.

Stone half-crawled to Father Joe, clutching his bleeding side. The priest lay on his back, mouth open in surprise, eyes staring in sightless death. A growing pool of dark oozed out from under his body. Stone was beginning to lose consciousness. He mustn't. He had to get to Mandy. He reached under the bench, pulled the package to him and painfully stuffed it inside his jacket. He tried to struggle to his feet but fell backwards. Before he could hit the ground, firm hands gripped his shoulder. More arms grabbed him around his waist.

"We've got you!"

He went blank.

Chapter Eighteen

Wales, 1301 • Maesgwinfi

I stared out the cave entrance unseeing.

A watery milk-like sun drizzled its warmth through rapidly disappearing mists that swirled impatiently. Above I could hear birds chirp awake. Owain slept fitfully while I had sat there and prayed. My eyes were open but my mind was not connected to them. An entire army of Roman legionaries or King Arthur himself could have tramped past and I would not have noticed. My mind was in another place entire; a place so black and dark I never want to go there again.

I stirred at noises in the darkness of the trees and bushes in the forest below. I saw a man pushing his way through, glancing fitfully behind him and upwards towards the castle ruins as well. I looked closer. The man dragged a foot behind him. Alun!

"Quick," he whispered, pushing his way past me. "Cover the entrance well."

I hustled around pulling more branches and bushes into place, blocking out the light and covering our secret opening as best I could. Alun lurched deeper into the cave looking for Owain. Awakened by the noise, Owain was up and grasping a short dagger as we plunged into our living area.

"You must leave now. Go over the mountain to the coast. By all that is holy, find a vessel that will take you from these cursed shores." Agitated, he ran a rough hand over his bald head. He ignored me totally, addressing Owain alone. "Boy you must get away. They are coming for you! They know you are here!"

He turned to face me and snarled. "God curse the day you met our Owain and ensnared him in your unholy deeds."

He would have gone on but Owain stepped between us and rebuked him, reminding him of our story poured out the day we met. Alun was not easily placated. He spat in the dirt at my feet. The anger dissipated somewhat, but his distrust of me was immense. He turned again to Owain.

"You were seen in the village yester noon. Idris the swine herd saw you leave my pig barn. You disturbed the geese when you crossed onto the common land and he remembered you." Idris immediately sent his half-witted daughter Enith to find Gethin's men and collect the promised reward.

"They arrived this morning. Came right towards my hut led by that slovenly Enith. Lucky it was that I saw them early enough and slipped out before they got there." He shuddered at his narrow escape. "Angry faces they had, boy. Angry faces." His grim look took us both in.

"My wife will not be able to tell them much, but I doubt that will stop them. I left her a death warrant!" He shoved Owain. "Come boy, get what you need and get you gone!"

Startled into action, Owain began gathering our few meager belongings. I did the same, securing Excalibur to my back and pushing the oilskin package into my jerkin. Even in the flame-licked darkness of the cave I saw Alun's eyes narrow as he watched me.

"What needs a monk with a sword, boy?" he sneered, seizing my arm to spin me around.

"Alun. Leave him be!" Owain's voice crackled with authority.

"He has a right to that sword. He is my leader in this undertaking. The sword is his and I will guard him and it with my life. If you value our friendship, value him!"

Slightly mollified, Alun dropped my arm and began helping us stamp out the fire. He glanced over at me with new respect. I noticed he carried two swords. One he kept. The other he threw to Owain.

"Few there are in the village who truly know about this cave and its location. We have not needed this old refuge under the lordship of De Tuberville."

Comforted somewhat by that news, we finished gathering our things and hurried to our entrance. Silently, Alun parted the bush leaves.

We were horrified by the sight before us. Smoke and flames raced through the village below us, glowing and rising above the tree line. We could hear the crackle of fire and the screams of the villagers. Gethin's revenge was swift and sure.

As we looked down we saw armed men working their way up the hill, thrusting swords and spears at each bush and clump. "We cannot leave this way."

We returned to the living quarters and sought our way out through the side tunnels. As we stumbled along, Alun mused on Gethin's swift attack on the village.

"Clearly he believes he can either capture or kill you both, before De Tuberville can send his men up from Coity Castle. I wouldn't doubt they've killed the soldiers manning the castle above us."

"He will leave no witnesses alive," Owain agreed.

In the dark, we stumbled along. I banged my head painfully against an outcrop of rock, but could not stop to soothe my hurting, bloody skull. There was no use heading for any of the smaller cave openings that overlooked the village. We had no choice. We began to squeeze our way through the smaller tunnels towards Margam. I do not recall how long it took us. My mind was racing. Fear was interspersed with prayer and trying to remember the tunnel paths I had explored in the days before.

We must have taken a wrong tunnel path at some point. We were forced to bend and hunch over as we finally saw some light ahead. We paused to regain our breath. Owain pressed up beside me then pushed ahead to see where the tunnel would bring us out. Carefully he pulled some branches back and peered out. He hissed to himself then turned to us grimly.

"Maes Haberth."

Alun did not like me; he'd made that clear. Yet I confess my admiration for him at this time. He was deathly afraid—afraid of Gethin and what he brought to the village and afraid of the terrors real or imagined of Maes

Haberth. But the old soldier in him surged forward. Silently he pushed past me and pulled Owain back from the opening.

"Let me, boy!"

With that he carefully peeled back the bushes covering the opening. As silently as he could, he squeezed through. Up here, higher than our main cave entrance, the mists were still grey and clinging. Like a snake, Alun slithered along until he was fully out. He stayed still, his head twisted to the side, straining to hear the slightest noise that would betray our enemies. All seemed quiet. Resting heavily on his good leg he slowly stood glaring around at the mist. There was nothing.

He beckoned to us and we followed him out. He sniffed the air and pointed off to his left.

"Mynydd Margam. We must get over it and to the shore. Mayhap we can find a boat there to take us away from this cursed country."

We tried to move silently in Alun's path, following him down the slight hill. As I got closer I could see the large bank ahead of us. As we scrambled up the well-formed mound I realized that this was no natural creation of God's hand. No, it was man-made; an earthen wall enclosing an area at least a hundred rods across. It encircled a grassy area dampened by the morning dews and mists. The grass covered walls were six or seven feet high, sloping up then down into the enclosure.

I shivered, not because of the cold, but the sight inside Maes Haberth. Bones littered the ground everywhere. We slipped down the inside of the walls. Alun limped steadily forward across the ground, eyes staring fixedly ahead. He neither looked to the left or right nor down. I could not help myself. I stooped down and stopped.

These bones were not animal bones. They were human. We crossed the encircled death ground as quickly as we could. As we approached the center I saw the remains of a fire pit. Blackened wood and grey-white ashes mixed with the shards and stumps of what I could only imagine were arm or leg bones. Although the mist was lifting rapidly, a heavy darkness swept down over me. We approached the far end of the circled enclosure. Beyond were some oak trees.

"Jesu!"

"Sweet Jesus"

The oaths escaped involuntarily from both our mouths at the same time. Alun glared silently back at us then saw where we were looking.

At the foot of the enfolding mound ahead of us were four human skulls, laid out ritually around sprigs of holly and oak leaves. Their black open sockets stared up at us, jaw bones attached still and propped open by small sticks as if they were still crying out their death agonies.

Waves of sickness swept over me. This was a place of evil; of human sacrifice. I had read and heard about such things happening in ancient times while at the Abbey, but never had I thought to see such a place with my own eyes. My mind rebelled against the truth my eyes saw. Such things were not done in this day!

I was pulled back to the present with a rough hand on my shoulder. Alun had me in a tight grip and began dragging me forward. I could not release my eyes from the skulls. They seemed to follow me, crying out to me, as I stumbled along. He thrust me against what I knew now to be a wall for this enclosure. Only then did I realize that he had dragged Owain in the same way for his eyes too were in the clutch of those skulls.

In spite of the brisk clammy mist, I was now sweating. We had to get out of here. Involuntarily my hand grasped Excalibur's hilt. I wanted to take the sword and sweep those skulls away, destroy Maes Haberth if I could. Horror and anguish swept over me. I lay my head back against the earthen walls gulping air down my throat. I closed my eyes but could not wipe out the vision of those open-mouthed skulls staring at me.

Alun suddenly clasped his hands over both our mouths.

"Shush. I hear something."

We all stood straining to hear. In the distance we could hear a horn blowing, hounds baying and men shouting. Alun whirled and pushed us both, straining to force us over the wall.

"Move your arses. They come!"

We clambered over and ran. As we did I glanced back. At the top of the hill overlooking our secret cave we could see armed men rushing up and over. One suddenly saw us and shouted, pointing. The horns blared and the men raced towards us. We ran. Alun's limp meant he began falling back as we ran across the meadow to the safety of the forest.

Suddenly Owain stopped. Alun had already turned to face the half-dozen men who raced down the hill pell-mell. He spat in the ground, planted his feet and drew his sword. Owain turned to face me once again.

"Run. Save the sword! We will hold them while you escape."

I stumbled on almost backwards. I could not leave them. Urgently Owain waved me onwards. I saw a look of calmness sweep over him. "My task is done, Thomas. Let me do this one more thing for you."

He ran up to Alun, his borrowed sword drawn.

Quickly I glanced towards Maes Haberth. The armed men had mounted the wall, jumped into the enclosure. For a brief moment we were out of their sight lines.

"Go," he urged.

My heart and mind will ever remember that time. I still feel guilt that I ran like a coward into the safety of the trees, stumbling and crashing through the gorse and heather till I was hidden by the greenness, leaving Owain and Alun to fight. There was no river or rain to protect me now. As I ran I searched wildly for some hiding place. A thought came to me. From God? Mayhap. It was almost like a voice speaking loudly but calmly to me. "Up," it said. "Go up."

I lifted my eyes. A large yew tree beckoned. Hoisting Excalibur in its makeshift scabbard on my back, I began to climb. Up I went. I was breathing so rapidly and loudly I was sure Gethin's men would hear me. I climbed to a particularly sturdy looking, leafy branch and crawled along, spreading myself as flat as I could. I was grateful that the crude brown woolen clothes Alun provided, now might protect me from prying eyes.

"Sweet Lord," I prayed. "Keep their eyes on the ground. Let them not look up."

In the distance I heard the clash and clang of sword on sword and the cries of anger and of extreme effort. Then I heard cries of pain. In a short time there was silence. A short time later I heard crashing as men pushed into the woods.

"I swear I saw three." I heard the harsh voice nearby.

"We were told there were but two"

"Aye, but there were three running. One has escaped. I am sure of it."

I peeked out, straining to see without giving myself away calming my breathing forcibly, not wanting to give myself away. In the near distance two men stood panting. The taller one bent double, recovering from the exertion. He straightened and rubbed his grizzled, bearded face. Blood stained the open sword he held in his hands. His shorter companion wiped a dagger on a filthy leather jerkin. With a gesture from the bearded one, they began to half-heartedly poke about at the bushes, stopping on occasion to listen. They moved out of sight slowly, poking and thrusting as they went.

I dared not move. The mist had truly lifted and the sun broke through, its warming rays landing squarely on my back and legs it seemed. But I had no thought for its warmth. My soul was cold with fear for Owain and Alun.

I heard more noises and saw movement below me. They were returning up the hill and passed not more than two rods to the left of my yew. At no time did they look up, thank God.

I noticed that the bearded one held his arm clasped tightly to his side obviously in pain. Perhaps, my heart soared, the blood on the sword was the man's own! But even as I thought it I dismissed it. They would not have run after me had Alun and Owain still fought. I commended both of them to God's mercy, closed my eyes and prayed for my companions.

The pair retreated back to Maes Haberth. I still did not move. Doubt crept in. Perhaps it was a trap? Were they seeming to give up, hoping I would show myself? I waited. In agony I waited. The bag with its quills crushed against my breast; Excalibur weighted my back. I could not help it. I shifted slightly to relieve the pressure of the tree limb pressing the bag into me. My feet were propped against another branch and so I was able to push against it carefully, using the pressure to lift my body slightly. With a free hand I adjusted the bag.

Silence pervaded my wooden lair. If there were eyes watching or ears listening for my presence, they were well hidden. I must have stayed in the tree more than an hour, shifting carefully and quietly every so often to relieve the pain. I lost feeling in my one leg. My arms ached from grasping the limb. I had to get down before I fell. Besides, I suddenly and ruefully realized I had a sudden urge to relieve myself.

Gently and quietly as I could, I levered myself down. At the base I crouched ready to flee at the slightest sound. Nothing. I paused and took my relief.

Some might say I should have made my way over Mynydd Margam as Alun urged. But I could not. My friend and faithful companion Owain had protected me, aided me and guided me. It cost him everything; the Abbey, Alys, his home and possibly his life. I could not walk away unknowing, though I know it was what Owain would have counseled.

It was now near mid-day. I crawled quietly and ever so gradually back towards Maes Haberth. I did not want to betray my position. My burdens demanded that I move slowly. The king's sword thumped against my back and at times got caught in gorse branches as I half-crawled, half-crouched my way back to that wicked place.

Such was the evil nature of Maes Haberth I swear I heard no living things in the woods that day. No birds chirped or sang. No rabbits, foxes or other creatures scurried through the grass. It was as if life itself was sucked out of the area.

I lay watching carefully. The whole of the deathly mound was open to my eyes save for the walled mass nearest me. If any hid, it must be behind that wall. I crouched behind a bush, again ready to flee. Nothing broke the silence. I stood carefully and quietly, and then moved slowly forward. I half crawled up the lip of the mound and peered into Maes Haberth.

There were four bodies scattered at the center. A fifth was flung against the grassy wall. I ran over to the fifth, for I had recognized it immediately. Alun!

I pulled his limp body into my arms. Dried blood stained his jerkin; a gaping wound in his side. As I cradled him, a sound escaped and his eye fluttered.

"You," he croaked. "You should not be here. Flee." His arm flopped vainly trying to point me away. "Owain, taken," he rasped.

The effort to speak drove the last spark of life from him. I embraced him and wept, holding his body close to me. Moments passed before I laid Alun gently and reverently down. He had not trusted me for his loyalty was to Owain. But he had died protecting me. I asked God to keep him in his care. I could not flee. I had to find Owain.

Tears coursed down my face. I shifted the weight of Excalibur on my back and adjusted the package on my breast, climbed back over the wall mound and headed back to the safety of the woods. "What now Lord? Where do I go now? Owain was my guide."

I had just clambered over the smaller wall at the south end when I heard shouting. Above Maes Haberth more men came. Some small bushes clung to the brow of the wall. I crouched behind them relieved they had not yet seen me. They climbed the north wall and moved into the centre of the compound carrying wood and piled it in the centre.

I flattened myself as best I could, but they were disinterested in looking around them. They ignored Alun's body as they ignored their own dead. Their work done, the men fixed their eyes upon the brow of the hill. Topping the hill were the other two men, this time carrying a form covered in a blanket of some kind. I gasped silently. Behind them, an unmistakable figure draped in a white cowled robe stalked in their footsteps. God curse him, it was Gethin!

I was frozen in place. Fear erupted throughout my body. Even beneath the cowl I could see his cold eyes and black bearded face. Silently the procession entered the mounded ring.

They placed the body on the wood. I noticed that even though the form was covered, his arms and legs were bound to a trunk of wood that the men now placed upright. Gethin banged his gold covered staff on the ground. As he did, one man took a flaming torch and lit the wood. Flames jumped immediately and the form twitched under the blanket.

Hoof and horn, hoof and horn
All that dies will be re-formed
The mother goddess for enemies waits
Let all men know, this shall be their fate.

At another silent signal from Gethin, the covering was snatched from the wretch on the fire.

"NOOOOOO!"

My cry was involuntary as I stood and ran towards the horrific scene, for Owain's broken and bloody body hung bound on the log as flames crackled at his feet.

Gethin spun at my cry, a snarl curled on his face. I saw lips move but did not hear him scream at me. Nor did I hear the men start shouting. My eyes were fixed only on Owain as the smoke and flames from the dried wood began to devour him.

Unconsciously, I freed Excalibur and swung it carelessly about my head as I charged towards Gethin. My eyes blurred with tears. Gethin stood unmoving as two of the men ran towards me. I am no trained swordsman, though I had hefted rudimentary arms when a farm lad. Yet I believe God was truly with me that day as I smote first one then the other. My eyes were fixed on Gethin and Owain. Jesu help me kill my enemy and save my friend, I cried silently.

More shouts penetrated my mind. I heard horses' hooves pounding and out of the corner of my eye saw a mounted soldier of some kind leap over the mound and into the centre, chasing two more of Gethin's men.

I ran towards Gethin, anger and hatred flooding me. He placed himself between Owain and me turning his staff into a protective weapon, so confident was he in my lack of swordsmanship. But as I raised the sword it glinted in the warming sun, its jeweled hilt sparkling and blazing. I felt a warmth flow from the sword into my hands and a new strength surged into me. Gethin suddenly stepped back.

"Excalibur," he hissed. "You had it all along!" He dropped his staff and struggled to pull a short sword from beneath his robe.

Before he could speak again I slashed at him and he stumbled backwards against the fire. In my rage I swung Excalibur like a madman, pushing Gethin back against the flames until suddenly he lurched and thrust his hand out to save himself from falling against the fire. He mistakenly pushed against the log holding Owain's body, tipping it over and out of the blazing, smoking inferno.

Gethin screamed in agony as flames seared his hand. I yielded not a moment of time to him. I swung the sword again. Vainly he tried to ward me off. I felt the sword slice into his arm and his burnt hand suddenly hung by bloody tendons. Fear ripped through his face and he dropped his sword into the fire.

"God curse you and all your demon kind" I screeched at him.

He backed away, holding the stump of his hand.

"God curse you and your Druids." I swore at him. "God curse you for your killings and your evil." I kept swinging Excalibur, slashing at his body again and again. The white woolen robe quickly stained with blood. He dropped to his knees, face bloodied and filled with hate.

I stopped momentarily, panting with exhaustion, frustration and fear. I raised the sword again.

"This for Abbot Godfrey, for Alys, for Alun and especially for Owain."

I stepped back and with one almighty thrust, I plunged Excalibur into his cold black heart. I pulled the sword out and watched his lifeless body drop. Quickly I ran over to Owain. Only then did I notice that liveried soldiers, some mounted, were inside the circle. As I dropped at Owain's side they came near but did not touch me.

O cruel God, I screamed inside. Must everyone die to save this cursed sword? I wrestled with my grief and yes, anger with God as I knelt beside Owain's still tortured form. His eyes opened and recognized me.

"It is safe?" His broken voice was barely a whisper. I nodded, knowing what he meant.

"Gethin is dead. We need fear him no longer."

Owain closed his eyes and I swear a smile cracked across his burnt face. He opened them again. "It is good, Thomas. I go to Alys." He closed his eyes again, this time forever. My heart was broken, my body wracked with sobbing.

A hand grasped my shoulder and pulled me up roughly. The armed man held me tight. He looked away at another, this one mounted and wearing a surcoat with a coat of arms over his chainmail. I looked frantically around. All of Gethin's men lay dead on the ground. A dozen helmeted and liveried soldiers stood firm with bloodied swords and pikes watching me. They had seen the final moments of my fight with Gethin and my grief at Owain's death. The mounted man turned his horse and trotted towards the opening. He turned back and pointed.

"Bring him. Bring his sword too."

My arms were tightly bound behind me and, by a rope, lashed to a horse's saddle. The man who tied me leaped onto the animal and began riding after his leader.

I stumbled sobbing and praying behind him as his mount jerked me my Lord only knew where.

Chapter Nineteen

Broceliande Forest

As they crept along, Chad suddenly saw lights and heard a strange moaning chant in the distance. A frantic whispered command and hand gestures dropped all of them to the ground. Fowler used his night goggles to peer through the brush. Flickering lights danced against towering black trees while the mournful chanting grew even more frenetic. Fowler whispered to remain motionless until they knew the source and reason for the lights and noise.

Until then their penetration of the compound had gone according to plan. It was surprisingly easy to identify the electronic fence points then cross over before swiftly moving into the denser portion of the woods. As planned, they waited to see if anyone came to investigate the breach. No one did. Moving rapidly but silently, avoiding wayward twigs or leaves that would betray them, they moved forward. Then the lights.

Fowler waved the others cautiously to him, gesturing ahead to the shadows moving and swaying. "Some sort of party or ritual."

"Can we go around?

"No. We need to get into the buildings quickly." Fowler thought for a moment. "This might work to our advantage. They're so involved in whatever they're doing they won't be as vigilant for intruders."

He glanced through the night vision goggles again then signaled the group towards a black mass of trees south of the grove. Cautiously they began moving again. As they got closer the chanting increased in volume. Mournful wailing pitched higher and faster. Flames and shadows flickered and danced higher and brighter across the darkened tree trunks. It was an unnatural spectacle of other-worldly sights and sounds made more intense by a moonless, starless night.

Suddenly, as screams penetrated the night, an expletive exploded from Fowler's mouth. The party dropped as one, each frantically looking around for the cause of Fowler's oath and, crucially, any consequences. Apart from increasing screams and the strange wailing from those in the grove, there was nothing. Fowler gestured urgently, drawing them to him. He tore off his goggles and flopped onto his back reaching for his weapon. Pointing at the grove, he thrust the night equipment to Hamilton.

"My God," was all Hamilton said, handing them to Chad. The ghostly green images in the eyepieces popped into focus.

The Sacred Grove

Silent black-robed figures, faces hidden by dark oversized cowls, glided slowly down the gravel path holding massive flaming torches and moving towards the center of the grove. Behind them Tonnerre swung his long bronze staff of office in front of him with each step while still more robed figures paraded behind. Trailing them all was Wyndham jarringly out of costume in his Armani suit, a distasteful sneer gripping his mouth.

As they approached, the devotees chanted a bizarre tuneless dirge that sounded more like a rolling moan pierced with high-pitched shrieks. In the middle of the grove a huge mound of wood was topped by a peculiar shaped steel cage, its gate hanging open. From the cage's small square base, steel frames stretched upward then buckled in, waist-like only to expand up and out again in a travesty of a woman's body. Below it were piles of wood.

As Tonnerre arrived, the wailing and chanting increased in volume. Shadows and torch flames danced over his face, but no expression showed. Only the ice cold grey eyes, hidden under his cowl flickered with emotion. Now Wyndham would see power, he thought. Now the pompous fool would acknowledge Tonnerre's overwhelming supremacy.

He raised his staff slowly until it stretched high above his head. As it rose, the chanting lowered in volume until silence ruled as the staff hit its zenith. The only noise was the crackle of flames. Behind him, Wyndham sneered inwardly at what he considered inane showmanship.

Tonnerre suddenly and wordlessly waved the staff in a circle then pointed down.

As it dropped, Wyndham was startled by an unexpected painful moaning behind him. He stepped aside as two heavily built guards thrust a staggering, drugged figure before them and thrust it at Tonnerre's feet.

As he glared at the wretch before him, Tonnerre's voice took on a hypnotic, sonorous tone. In the quietness of the forest, it boomed. Using the Breton tongue he detailed the faults and sins of the broken man before him then smoothly, for Wyndham's benefit, he switched to English.

"This creature disobeyed me and through that insubordination jeopardized our security and our mission. Failure will not be tolerated. The gods demand total obedience. There are no exceptions." He turned slightly to make sure he had eye contact with Wyndham. A deeper level of hardness entered his voice. In Breton and in English he shouted again.

"Taranis, the god of thunder, demands sacrifice. Let all see the punishment of those who cannot or will not obey." His staff moved and pointed to the figure before him. "Behold the fate of one who fails us. We return him to the gods."

Tonnerre's gaze locked on Wyndham's stony features, engaging in a brief battle of the eyes though nothing flickered across either face. Finally, he turned away.

The guards pulled the nearly comatose Belenos to his feet, dragging him towards the metal cage. Realizing what they intended he struggled and twisted to get away, but his drugged body betrayed him. He screamed and wept, powerless as they pushed him into the cage and locked it.

All eyes were now on Tonnerre. As he raised the staff, each disciple touched his fiery torch to the gasoline soaked wood. The chanting began again, increasing in pitch and volume. Belenos screeched and grabbed the frame shaking it to somehow free himself. Smoke and flames licked at its base and Belenos' screams reached a fever pitch. The chanting became frenzied.

Broceliande Forest

Hamilton stared into the night. "They're going to burn the poor devil to death" he blurted out to no one in particular. More screams wrenched their eyes to the grove.

"Call in the chopper and the French. We can't let anyone die like that," Fowler raised his machine pistol and began to unscrew the silencer. "Chad, you and Will head for the compound immediately, find the professor." He waved Rumsford forward. "Keith and I will distract them."

In an instant, Fowler and Rumsford were up running towards the grove unconcerned with being seen or heard by eyes already mesmerized by the horrific scene before them. Chad grabbed the night gear and joined Hamilton, racing towards the compound the map said should be just over the slight hill.

The Lagoon, Venice

It was a dream. A bad dream.

Sharp piercing pain shot through him; a hazy dark mist drugged his mind. Sleep. He just wanted to sleep. He jerked suddenly as another dart of pain struck.

"Come on Mr. Wallace. Stay with us."

His fogged mind grappled with the unknown voice, aware that someone was holding him under his arms and other hands were wrapping something around his side. The fog began to dissipate. Mandy. My God, Mandy. In a stupor he wrestled with the arms, trying to stand.

"Whoa, Mr. Wallace. Steady on." Firm hands held him down. He blinked, trying to focus on the darkened hazy face peering close in at him. "Ah. You are still with us. John, hold him still while I finish with this bandage."

Stone closed his eyes again, and then blinked them open as the hands finished their work. He sensed rather than saw movement, bouncing movement, which intensified the pain at each bump. Boat. He was in a boat. The island. Mandy. Father Joe. In the murkiness of his mind, it started to come together. He tried to sit up but again, firm arms held him down.

"I must get up….find Mandy…help her…help him". His mind struggled to come to grips with what had happened.

"Easy. You're safe with us."

Stone's mind raced, his hand automatically going to the pain on his right side. "Who are you?" He struggled again. "Got to get help, quick."

"Mr. Wallace. We know who you are and what happened. You've been shot. It's just a flesh wound, but you've lost blood. Miss Griffiths we think has been kidnapped." He paused. "The priest you were talking to is…dead."

Stone tried to take it in. "Who are you?" he asked again, twisting to see the man's face in the dark. Dimly he was aware of another holding him and yet another in the cockpit eyes focused ahead driving them on.

"Colin Maddox, Mr. Wallace. John Broderick is holding you up. We are with a special branch, of British intelligence." Briefly he explained their mission dealing with the Druids and how they knew about both Stone and Mandy.

"My men have been following you and Miss Griffiths. John and I arrived two hours ago, just in time to catch up with you as you got on the Italian's boat. Unfortunately, we still botched the job."

As he spoke Stone began fumbling for the package in his jacket. It was gone. Maddox noted the movement. He reached behind him, picked up the package and handed it to Stone. "This what you're looking for, Mr. Wallace? It's safe. Unopened."

Stone reached out and accepted the package. He nodded but said nothing. "Where are we? What's happening?"

Maddox turned to the man piloting the boat. A brief conversation in Italian followed.

"We're following the men who grabbed Miss Griffiths. We saw them head north across the Lagoon, probably heading up past Punta Sabbioni, maybe up to Lio Picollo. We're closing on the northern tip of the Lido. Fortunately there aren't many boats out this time of night moving fast enough to leave a bow wave every so often."

As Stone drifted in and out of consciousness each thump of the bow caused a bolt of pain. As they sped across the lagoon, the roar of the engine and the hiss of water were the only noises Stone could hear. Water splashed in on him every fourth or fifth wave bounce, but he paid little attention.

"Damn. He's lost them". As Maddox spoke the boat slowed and bounced gently in its own wake. He and Broderick held a hurried conversation with the man at the helm. With a shrug, the helmsman spun a tight turn taking them back over their wake.

Stone struggled to sit up. Slower now, they retraced their route looking sharply along both sides of the vessel. Maddox leaned out, forcing his body forward as if that would help him see better. As they bounced across longer portions of surf he told Stone they were crossing one of the entrances to the lagoon. "That's the Adriatic forcing its way in. If he went out there we'll never get him."

While he scanned left, Broderick tried to make out the murky depths of the islands inside the lagoon. All eyes and ears were focused, hoping for a glimpse of wake or the sound of a boat. Maddox abruptly stiffened, ears alerted to a noise, and ordered the boat's engine cut. The sound slowly gained intensity. Instantly they realized that it was a small aircraft rather than a boat.

"San Nicolo airfield" the Venetian pilot pointed as the aircraft gained height and flashed northwards across the Lagoon.

Maddox reached over and spun the wheel, forcing them towards shore. The pilot took control again, threading through the deep water channel pylons. Shortly they saw a darkened boat bobbing up and down tied to a small dock. As they drifted up the pilot reached over, felt the outboard motors, grunted and spoke to Maddox.

"The engine is still hot. This is their boat. Damnation!" He turned and stared upward as if willing the plane to circle and come back. "I didn't count on this. Bloody hell! What a hash a job start to finish." He slammed his fist on the cockpit roof. "Best call the guvnor and get it over with."

Broderick grasped his cell, punched one button and was soon speaking softly. A few moments later he ordered the pilot to head to the city. As they crossed the lagoon he leaned down and spoke to Stone, reassuring him.

"We have a doctor who does discreet work for the service. We'll get you patched up in no time. Plus our guvnor is already onto the Italian authorities to see if we can track that plane. Don't worry, mate. They obviously want her alive. We'll find her."

Venice's lights, bobbing in the dark, drew even closer. They avoided the Grand Canal, steering across its entrance, around the island of San Giorgio and slipping south of the floodlit Salute church into the Giudecca canal. They continued down the wide channel, slowed and turned into one of the smaller canals in the underbelly of the Dorsoduro. After a few more baffling turns into other canals, they drifted silently up to some steps.

Maddox and Broderick spoke briefly, dismissed the pilot and took hold of Stone, hustling him off the boat and walked him quickly through a silently opened door. A strapping figure slid past them, took up station outside and quietly closed the door behind them. As it closed a light suddenly flicked on and they eased him into a hard chair where the doctor waited.

Stone felt broken with profound loss and failure. He'd failed Huw, dragged Mandy half way around the world only to get her kidnapped and to top it, he'd got a priest killed. He pounded himself mentally for constantly trying to do things himself and not trusting others. His once palpable confidence was shattered. He'd had no business getting involved because he had neither the expertise nor the experience. Mandy had finally trusted him as

Huw had and now both were in the hands of the Druids. God what a mess! And here he was, helpless and hopeless with nowhere to turn.

In desperation he remembered Huw's talks about prayer and his confidence that God cared. Stone turned his mind to that half-remembered God, his mind fumbling for words. How do you address a God you've ignored for so long? Would he even listen? As he wrestled with his feelings the doctor ministered to him quickly and with minimal pain.

A cell phone ring broke the silence. Maddox took the call, listening mostly but speaking softly several times. The plane had filed a flight plan for Trieste he reported. Maddox sat down and faced Stone as the doctor finished bandaging him.

"Interestingly, there was an Air Celtica jet in Trieste. Unless I miss my guess they've transferred her."

"Can we stop them and get her off?"

Broderick voiced Stone's own buoyant thought but Maddox shook his head.

"The Italians can't—won't—move without cause or proof. We've no evidence she was even on that plane let alone now on the jet. And even if we did they will have left before the police could do anything."

"Has the jet filed a plan? Could we find out where it's going?"

Maddox and Broderick smiled. Stone's lucid questions showed he was back in the land of the living. He was already buttoning his shirt as the doctor slipped out of the room.

"Already got it. They left for London Gatwick airport ten minutes ago. They're taking her home. He smiled down as Stone finished pulling his jacket back on. "So we're going to join them as well. The guvnor wants us back in Britain. You too."

St. Brigitte de Bretagne, Paimpont

More than anything, Chad remembered the screams.

First there were the unearthly screams of the doomed Belenos. Suddenly there were other screams and shouting accompanied by thrashing about in the forest as the British agents showed themselves and began shooting, first in bursts above the devotees heads, then into the crowd when a few tried to continue the sacrificial immolation.

As they exploded out of the trees, Fowler and Rumsford yelled and shouted at unseen allies. Panic set in. Tonnerre's followers later swore they saw many dark shapes--at least fifty some claimed afterward--hurtling at them firing all manner of weapons. Screaming and trampling over each other, they tried to flee into the forest. The shrieks of the wounded added to the nightmarish scene. Above all the confused noises were the chilling, unholy squeals and cries of their sacrifice. The few who tried to remain calm and in control looked frantically around for their leader only to find him gone.

At the first explosion of noise and firing, Tonnerre swore, dropped his staff, picked up the hem of his robe, turned and began running down the path, back to safety. Wyndham didn't hesitate. Flushed with fury, he spun and ran after Tonnerre, pulling a concealed gun and pausing to aim shots at his erstwhile partner.

"Cowardly damn traitor. Go to Arawen you gods-forsaken slime."

The Breton did not stop, only hitching his robe a little higher to lengthen his stride. Wyndham fired again at the fleeing Druid. Suddenly Tonnerre stumbled and sank to his knees, one arm propping him up. Wyndham skidded to a stop and snarled at the cowering figure before him.

"You never could do anything right Andre. Thank the gods I was never depending on you for the future. Crowning Glory would never have succeeded with you around."

Tonnerre's bloodied right hand clutched his chest trying to stem the blood spurting from the massive exit wound and staining his priestly robe. He glared hatred at Wyndham but said nothing. Wyndham squatted beside him and heard Tonnerre's gurgling gasps for air.

"Best make sure." He coolly fired one more bullet into the Breton's body and one to the head. "Ta muid amse. The Master has spoken."

Without looking back Wyndham ran towards the compound's buildings. He stopped just short of the forest edge, startled by the unmistakable rhythmic thumps of a helicopter as it descended. Seeing two men run towards him out of the corner of his eye, he raised his gun again.

Chad and Hamilton raced towards the compound. The building's positions were fixed in Chad's mind as he ran. He tried to blot out the screams and other noises. Dimly he was aware of the helicopter approaching in the dark. He ran even harder.

Together they burst out of the trees and raced across the compound. Already the helicopter was dropping onto the grassed space in front of the main building. Unseen, Wyndham raised his gun and fired to stop them. Chad felt rather than heard a shot flit by his head. Automatically he turned in the direction of the shot.

"Over there, he's shooting from over there" Chad pointed and kept running while Hamilton returned fire.

Wyndham flung himself down as bullets hit the trees beside him and splinters of wood sprayed his body. He rolled into the bushes and raised his gun again only to suddenly realize he was out of ammunition. He flung the weapon to the side, rolling deeper into the darkness of the wood and watched helplessly as his targets kept running toward the building.

"Must have hit him. Get the professor." Chad and Hamilton dashed across the path, racing up a set of steps and into the main entrance.

Desperately, Wyndham stood and flung his head back and forth looking for escape. In seconds he raced around the edge of the trees towards his parked car, flinging the door open. At his standing orders, a driver was always with the vehicle. This one stood with eyes wide with fear and puzzlement at the flash and fury in the woods and sudden appearance of a helicopter. Wyndham flung the passenger door open. "Drive! Get me away from here! Take back roads to Rennes airport."

In the distance he could hear the 'mee-maw' wailing of police sirens. At the compound exit he urged the driver west, away from Paimpont. He wanted no run-ins with French police. Not now. They roared onto the D40 and disappeared down the tree fringed road, rounding a corner just as the first police vehicles appeared.

Inside, Chad and Hamilton raced quickly but efficiently through the empty building realizing that the occupants were likely in the mob at the grove. Suddenly they burst through a door and saw Jean-Marc kneeling on the floor about to start smashing computers with a heavy ax. Without hesitating, Hamilton ran over and clubbed him.

"Find the professor. Quick. I'll grab things here in case there's anything we can use."

Hamilton began throwing papers, files and laptops into empty boxes as Chad raced down the hall, flinging open the last door to find a figure wrapped in sheets and bandages, pulling IV needles and tubing out of his body.

"Thank God. The US cavalry! Thought you'd never get here." Huw winced as he pulled the last tube free.

"Nice to see you too, professor," Chad smiled as he shouted to Hamilton for help. He stepped forward quickly enough to catch Huw as he fell.

Chapter Twenty

Buckingham Palace Mews, London

"Blast it!" Sir Giles hammered the phone down on its cradle, frustrated by the oh-so pleasant yet oh-so unhelpful bureaucratic mindset that stymied his attempt to ground the Air Celtica flight and search the aircraft. "I'm the bloody director of bloody Crown Security but I can't blast those stodgy minds into action!" he roared to his empty office.

He shook his head in disgust, mimicking his pointless discussions: 'no Sir Giles, I'm sorry but we cannot divert that aircraft just on suspicion…'; and 'yes Sir Giles, I'm well aware that it is of the highest national urgency, but without legal justification…"

"Blast it. Freddy! Update now." He shouted, drawing his assistant into the office.

"Bloody minded clerks. That's all they are Freddy, bloody minded clerks not able to think for themselves," pounding his desk in frustration.

Calmly Freddy responded. "Well, Sir Giles, it is the middle of the night. Very little they can do at this hour."

"Bollocks!" The security chief thundered around the corner of his desk, finger jabbing at Freddy. "If Churchill had had fools like that running the show we never would have won the war. Same for Maggie Thatcher and the Falklands!"

Used to the furious but short-lived rages, Freddy waited until Sir Giles lowered himself into one of the office's perks, a comfortable if somewhat worn black leather couch.

"More problems sir. We've lost track of the Air Celtica flight."

As his guvnor's face flushed with anger, Freddy hurried on.

"They filed a flight plan for London from Trieste. They were closing on Strasbourg and requested diversion for mechanical problems."

"And the other aircraft? Wyndham's private jet?"

Freddy shuffled the papers in his hands.

"Left Rennes within a half hour of the raid on Tonnerre's compound and landed at Southampton airport twenty minutes ago, though how he got permission to land in the middle of the night is still a mystery. Sir Richard was picked up immediately by his chauffeur and disappeared."

"Don't care what you have to do, whose nose you put out of joint, but get on board that plane. Search it. Warrant or no warrant. While you're at it, get someone over to Wyndham's flat in Mayfair. Break in if you have to. Whatever it takes. Same for the other aircraft. If it lands, get it boarded. Let me know the second you have any information"

He stood up. "No mistakes Freddy. I want Wyndham's head on a platter!'

Freddy was silent for a moment. "Maddox and Broderick should be landing at RAF Northolt…" he glanced at his watch, "…within the next five minutes or so. I've ordered them to report here immediately. Wallace was wounded. Maddox says he's been triaged but refuses to go to hospital. He's coming with them."

Aboard Air Celtica

The virtually empty aircraft settled into its new flight level. In the cockpit, the pilots quietly but efficiently entered a new course and identity into the autopilot. Under a new guise the plane banked gently to port, headed for a new destination in Wales.

Below them, in Strasbourg air traffic control, one of Tonnerre's followers, an ATC controller, carefully but quickly covered up the flight plan change, before passing off to the next controller. To all intents and purposes the Air Celtica flight had disappeared. His fellow controller had the "new" aircraft while he finished covering the tracks of the old. He waited a few more minutes, then reported that Air Celtica was diverting to Metz to check their instrumentation. That would forestall any search and rescue. By the time Metz reported that no such aircraft landed he would have disappeared.

In the darkened aircraft interior, Mandy was in shock. She had not stirred from her seat from the moment her captors had bundled her on board and stuffed her into it. Across the aisle, a hefty mustached guard grimly watched but made no move towards her. He'd said not a word the entire time.

She had hazy memories of shouts and flashes of fire and remembered Father Joe dropping at her feet. Before she could react, she saw Stone fall as well and heard a voice say they'd got him. Oh God! Two men killed before her eyes. She forced herself to remain calm. She would not give them the pleasure of seeing her whimper like a frightened female, demanding to know who they were and why they had kidnapped her. She knew. Rhiannon and Wyndham had finally caught her. She knew it before she even saw the proud Air Celtica logos splayed all over the jet.

Think, she told herself. Nothing in her life or career had prepared her for this, but her precise logical mind kicked in. As she'd told Stone, Wyndham and the Druids needed her father alive for the information they believed he had. So it is logical that they want me alive for the same thing, she reasoned. Very well, she thought. I know nothing but I can certainly string a good line.

A sickening thought suddenly hit her. Father Joe kicked the package under the bench. Was it still there? Her kidnappers didn't seem to have it or they would have flaunted it. Would it be thrown away as trash or would the priests take it back inside the monastery and have it consigned to the Vatican depths again? A sigh of despair escaped. Her guard looked over and smiled maliciously.

She tried to pray. Her pleas mingled with guilt and doubts and a pack of 'if only's; if only they'd gone to the safe house in Virginia; if only they'd not tried to find and contact Father Joe. She stifled another sigh but Da was right. 'If onlys' were a fool's game that did not take into account what he called God's own perfect plans. Perhaps Stone and Father Joe were still alive. Please God let them be alive.

Think, think. They still didn't have Excalibur nor did they know how to get it. But then, neither did she, she thought glumly. Should she just give in and help them? No, they were ruthless enough to kill Da and herself once they got what they wanted. Her mind spun again.

Oh God! She turned her head to look out the window.

Dark, like her hopes.

Buckingham Palace Mews, London

The office was a busy place for the pre-dawn hours. In short order, Freddy burst in with news that the Air Celtica plane had diverted to Metz. A quick call to French security ensured that the plane would be boarded and searched and would not be allowed to leave "until the last bloody rivet was searched, and not even then" Sir Giles thundered at his French counterpart. Moments later an exhausted Broderick and Maddox entered, followed by Stone Wallace,

"Glad to see you, m'boy."

The old spymaster gripped his hand and shook it vigorously, causing Stone to wince in pain as his arm shook. Embarrassed, Sir Giles waved the reporter to his favorite couch and turned to his team.

Though he'd been briefed by Freddy, he still expected Maddox to walk him through the entire litany of events from the arrival in Venice until they returned. As they spoke, he nodded from time to time, mentally making notes but offering no recriminations or criticism. It was his matter-of-fact acceptance that his team did the best they could at all times, that endeared Sir Giles to them. It drove their intense loyalty. And made them feel worse than fools when they failed. They were part way through the briefing when Freddy poked his head in to say that no Air Celtica flight had landed at Metz in the past three hours.

"Damnation!" The oath uttered, Sir Giles signaled Maddox to continue. It was what he'd suspected. There had been no malfunction and the plane never headed to Metz.

Ten minutes later Maddox and Broderick concluded their report. Silence permeated the office. In the distance Big Ben tolled the quarter hour and muffled traffic noise seeped into their sanctum as the great city began to wake. Sir Giles unconsciously ran his hand through his snow white hair.

"Did well. Best that could be expected in the circumstances."

"Best that could be expected!?" Stone's roar startled them. His fear, frustration and exhaustion snapped him out of a painful stupor. He jumped up, stepped forward and shouted into Sir Giles' placid face.

"Best that could be expected? Mandy's been kidnapped, Father Joe is dead, Huw was almost killed, then kidnapped, I've been shot and I'm wanted back home for god knows what kinds of crimes, and all you can say is 'best that could be expected'?"

Stone's fist cracked down hard on the desk. His fury dissipated as pain shot through his body again. He sank down exhausted and discouraged into the couch, face cupped disconsolately in his hands.

"Yes, quite." Sir Giles apologetic huffing surprised his team. It was not often anyone, especially a stranger, took the wind out of the guvnor's sails. He signaled them to stay seated.

"Aware of the problems still remaining, dear boy. But there is good news."

He began to flick his fingers up as he counted; "First, Mandy is still alive. They obviously need her. As long as she is alive, we can find her. Second, the professor is alive and well. In tough shape, but we've got him safe."

Stone started and dropped his hands at the news. Broderick and Maddox jerked their heads up as well.

"Hmm. Yes. Wouldn't know of course. Raided St. Brigit's earlier tonight." Sir Giles looked straight at Stone. "Your friend Lawson helped get him out."

He held his hand up to forestall questions. "Just arrived here an hour ago. Have him in a safe private hospital. Getting the best of care. Third, Tonnerre is dead. Killed in the raid. French have shut down the compound. Finding all sorts of useful intelligence. Taken some of the steam out of the whole mob no doubt." He paused, wrinkling his forehead as he considered his net words. "Make no mistake, we still have problems. Lost track of Wyndham. He was in France, but eluded us. Back in this country somewhere."

He asked Freddy to bring them up to date. When the briefing finished, silence saturated the room again. Before anyone could speak, the sharp double ring of the phone broke the silence. Sir Giles picked it up, listened carefully, grunted a couple of times and hung up.

"Feel up to a short trip dear boy?" He directed the question to Stone. "Professor Griffiths is asking for you"

Stone's exhausted mind still reeled trying to absorb the information. Huw alive? How did Chad get here? As he twisted to face Broderick, he felt Father Joe's package still stuffed untouched in his jacket. He almost pulled it out but decided to leave it. That information cost Father Joe his life and was something Huw had set in motion. He would wait until he was alone with Huw.

Chantilly, Virginia

Calvin Tyler replaced the phone thoughtfully.

The call from his British counterpart clarified some things and confirmed others. Tyler was surprised that Wallace was in London after a trip to Venice. He couldn't wait to find out how he had eluded police, the FBI and

Homeland Security and made it all the way to Europe. Very resourceful, he mused; someone with potential.

Documents retrieved in the raid outlined a massive conspiracy to disrupt several European governments, aided and abetted by collaborators in the United States and Canada who supplied much of the Druid's financing. They also confirmed that Tonnerre had orchestrated the assassination of the French President. That alone would mollify French sensitivities over the raid by British and American agents on their sovereign territory.

Things were falling into place with the new intelligence adding details to Harry Lange's murder and the sudden reversal of plans for the pickup of Murphy's aide. Tyler was awed by the sheer audacity and scope of the plot. He reached forward again and picked up the grey phone sitting on his credenza, punched a button and waited.

"Mr. President? Sir, we need to talk."

Hampshire, England

Despite the cool autumn pre-dawn, Wyndham was sweating. He was safe for now. Thank the gods he'd bought this isolated country house in the New Forest some twenty years ago. It was ideal for his secret meetings with the movement's various leaders. Today it was a welcome refuge where he could go to ground.

What in the name of Lleu had happened he wondered? The shock of the unexpected and deadly attack on Paimpont was only now hitting him. His panicked escape was a blur. Tonnerre's security had obviously failed, as had his nerve and therefore his usefulness. Killing the Frenchman bothered Wyndham no more than swatting a fly. But how did they—whoever they were—know to attack that night?

He vaguely recalled one of the attackers calling out to get the professor. So they knew that Griffiths was at the compound. A leak somewhere? It stood to reason they knew Wyndham had been on site as well. Well, if they were still searching for him, they wouldn't look in the New Forest. Wyndham walked over to the bar in the darkened room and poured a drink. He would keep the lights off for now. He thought better in the dark.

British security. It must have been them. He remembered hearing their accents during the attack. Then he dimly recalled an American voice; not that Wallace either. So, the Americans were involved in some way too. He had to talk to Murphy. Wyndham swirled the drink in his glass without sipping. Grilling Murphy was the easier part of his task. He would call the Senator later in the morning.

The biggest challenge was informing Rhiannon about the night's debacle. At least there was some good news there. The girl was on her way to Llanmerddyn. Let Rhiannon deal with her. But there was Tonnerre's death—best not say anything about his role in that—and the raid on Paimpont, not to mention the fact that the professor had slipped from their grasp. Should I give her the good news first, or the bad? He grimaced at the fact that this 'powerful business baron' as *Time* had called him, was conflicted on how to break news to a woman. Lleu, what a mess!

Dawn was slowly breaking and though early morning light crept in, a cold sweat still trickled down his neck. He swirled his drink nervously again. For the first time in his career, indeed his life, he faced a situation where he was not in control. It was an uncomfortable feeling. He would not describe it as fear. Not Damien Wyndham. Still there was this niggling doubt that his well laid plan was unraveling on the fringe. He stood suddenly raising both arms spread high above his head.

"Great god Cerunnos, God of the underworld, take those who would thwart our plans and destroy them. Give me the power, O horned one. Hoof and horn, let them be torn; deliver them to me. Let them be mine!" His entreaty continued, hurling epithets against Wallace and Griffiths and calling down the wrath of the gods on their heads. He stood unspeaking, arms still upraised for several minutes.

Then, he slammed the glass onto the coffee table, his precious whiskey spilling unnoticed. Right, he said to himself, time for action. He walked over and picked up the secure phone on his desk. As always, he mentally ticked off his plan of action. Only when he had gathered all the information about the Paimpont debacle and had a preferred course of action would he call Rhiannon.

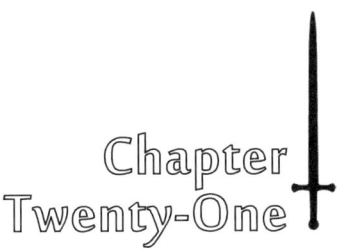

Chapter Twenty-One

Wales, 1301 • Coity Castle

For four days and nights I rotted in the dank, fetid dungeon of Coity Castle.

From the time of my capture to the time I was thrust into the cell, I was treated firmly but with silent wariness. I found out later that de Tuberville's Constable led the attack searching for those who'd slaughtered their own at the castle ruins. T'was naught but luck brought them to Maes Haberth that day.

The sight of a wild man, filthy matted hair, unkempt beard and ragged clothes slashing his way through the Druids awed them. That I wielded a great sword in the carnage of that godless place and killed Gethin—a man they'd been hunting—left them more than a little frightened of me. What manner of man was this who screeched and howled while swinging his sword crazily and killed uncaringly yet at the same time wept bitter tears beside one of the bodies?

There in the gore of that damnable place their superstitious minds made them wary.

For what they perceived as their own safety, they tied me to the horse and confiscated the sword. But they spoke not to me; not when we struggled our way down the hillside and across the river, nor through the meadows and woods and not as we passed the west gatehouse leading into the Outer Ward of Coity Castle.

Word preceded us, for while many crowded into the ward to watch, not a few crossed themselves and held up their hands and fingers in a cross sign to ward off evil. They formed a hushed and still mass, those men-at-arms, smiths, barefoot dirty-faced children, butchers in blood-stained aprons, scullions, and women both finely dressed and in ripped and ragged kirtles. Scavenging dogs and wandering chickens pushed through the crowds to snap and peck at our heels only to be kicked aside.

We passed through the middle gatehouse and I was immediately thrust through a doorway, down rough stone steps and into the dungeon. I collapsed in fear and fatigue in a small pile of dirty straw in the corner and thus passed my days in filth and degradation, unseen and unspoken to by any human.

My captors had not searched me. So I quickly removed the precious package from under my jerkin and shoved it beneath some of the straw, hastily arranging it so the pouch could not be seen. I did not know what else to do. I first knelt on the cold stone floor then lay prostrate on the icy cold stone, beseeching God. I had no doubts of my fate.

"I have failed my heavenly father," I wept. "Owain is dead, the sword taken and my quest in ruins. I now give myself up to the judgment of Lord de Tuberville and you, Sweet Jesu. I pray that you will greet me in paradise once I am executed."

I paused, fully expecting that some voice from heaven would respond. The stone walls rang with silence. I asked God that my death would be swift, not to spare me pain and suffering, but rather that this whole tragedy would just be done with. I then asked God to find another man—perhaps even in de Tuberville's retinue—to carry out the task that I had so foully ruined.

Although I heard no voice, I did sense a tremendous peace as I prayed. I had a deep assurance that, somehow, God's will would be done and the quest accomplished. With that I spent my remaining waking hours preparing for death, even welcoming it before I fell asleep.

Each evening, my food—if it could be called that—was slipped silently through the doorway on a wood platter.

I awoke the fifth morning to banging on the dungeon door. I knelt in prayer, my hands clasped around my knees, in the furthest corner.

Death awaited.

The door opened and a spear-carrying guard entered. Behind him was a man I later learned was de Tuberville's Chief Steward. He approached me carrying a small stool encumbered with cloth. Two others entered behind him.

"You are Thomas of Gwent, a monk of the abbey at Cwmllyn?" the Steward stated rather than asked, though not unkindly. I nodded. "Lord de Tuberville requires your presence in the Great Hall. Prepare yourself."

He put the stool down and picked up the cloth which I instantly identified as a Cistercian habit. He gestured at the stool and bade me sit while the third man, obviously the castle's barber, stepped behind me with a bucket of warm water and doused my head.

I jumped in shock, but he proceeded to vigorously massage my head with soap and, with familiar strokes, began to shave my tonsure and crop my unruly hair. At the same time, another stropped a razor and attacked the unkempt beard on my face. Those jobs done, I was asked to remove the mucky and soiled clothes that adorned my body. When I finished, buckets of tepid water were sloshed over me, and I was instructed to dress myself in the habit.

Ablutions done, the Steward asked me to follow. I did so with a new step. Whatever was now to befall me, I cared not. I looked once more like a monk! I would not fail in my duty again. I would die as a man of God, knowing I had done no one other than Gethin ill, no matter what others or evidence might say.

We proceeded sedately out of the Keep and across the Inner Ward to the Great Hall. The curious acted nonchalant, carrying out their respective duties while yet grabbing quick peaks. No doubt they wondered who the monk was—surely he had been hearing the confessions of that wild killer brought in four days before? I tried to smile bravely as we crossed the ward.

I stopped at the entrance of the Great Hall before being nudged forward by the Steward. Across the open space of the hall was a roaring fire. Before the fire stood Lord Payne de Tuberville himself.

I had seen him once before when he rode into the Abbey forecourt to visit Abbot Godfrey. Then his sturdy frame sat astride his destrier, head and neck covered in chainmail and his whole armored body covered by a white woven surcoat emblazoned with the de Tuberville coat of arms.

As I approached him this day, he wore a simple blue wool surcoat over white cotton shirt and black leggings, a fine leather belt outlining his ample but still discernable waist. His feet were clad in what looked like fine doeskin boots. I looked up and saw that his shock of black hair was laced with grey as was his short, finely coifed, beard. He turned at my entrance.

"Thomas of Gwent?"

I stepped forward and acknowledged him with a bow of my head, my hands clasped in the voluminous sleeves of my habit. He studied me fiercely, his eyes taking in every portion of my being from head to toe. He grunted, left the fire and sat in a fine carved wood chair. He pursed his lips and spoke in a firm ringing tone. His Welsh was impeccable, though I knew it was not his first Language.

"You are an intriguing man, Thomas of Gwent. You are a foresworn monk of the abbey at Cwmllyn yet you are accused of murdering your own Abbot Godfrey and proscribed therefore as an escaped felon. You eluded me for several weeks and are suspected in the deaths of my men at Castell y Coch. Yet you are found acting like a demon-possessed man, smiting four including one who was your abbey Sacrist. Lastly, you are found on your knees wailing at the bound and charred body of yet another monk from your abbey who like you disappeared the night of the murder."

He paused and stared at me, his fingers rubbing his chin thoughtfully, elbow resting on the chair's wide wooden arm. "Intriguing is not the word for you, Thomas," he suddenly barked.

"You were seen killing with this great sword!"

His arm swept across the room where, in the shadows was a side table I had not noticed. There lay Excalibur and the purple wrap.

"What say you? What of these charges and how came you by this wondrous weapon?"

I clenched my hands inside my sleeves. They were sweating, but I felt a calmness sweep over me. I could not tell him about the sword yet I had to speak truth.

"My Lord de Tuberville, my answers will be honest, but I fear that they will make little sense." Before he could respond I plunged on. "The sword is a possession of the Abbey in the sole protection of the Abbot. I was charged by Abbot Godfrey with keeping it safe and out of the hands of the enemies of the church. When my lord Abbot was murdered—I had no part in that—I fled the Abbey with the sword and with my brother monk Owain."

Before I could stop myself, the story of the murder, our flight and our knowledge of Gethin's sinister duplicity poured out. Gethin the Sacrist was none other than Gethin the evil-filled Druid, hater of the church and all within its holy care. I told him how Gethin had destroyed the village and its inhabitants and how in hideous wickedness, sacrificed Owain by torturing him and then burning him alive.

I looked up at de Tuberville and met him square in the eye.

"Aye, my Lord. It is true. I am guilty of slaying those Druid followers and Gethin, the arch Druid himself." I drew myself up tall, keeping my eyes glued to his. "I am proud that I was gifted with the strength and ability to rid this land of such a cursed man. Do with me what you will."

He looked at me thoughtfully, rubbing his chin, fingers combing his beard. More questions flowed about Gethin and the sword. I was as honest as I could be while still protecting the sword's identity. Finally, he stood and snapped his finger. The Steward left the room.

"I am not satisfied with all your answers, Thomas. I sense, nay I know, that you are telling some truth and yet holding more." Astonishingly he then smiled briefly at me. "Nevertheless, I am prone to accept your story." As he uttered those words I heard the door opened again and a familiar voice called out to me.

"Brother Thomas!"

I whirled unbelievingly and there stood Prior Edwin. Or rather the former Prior, for he now wore the robe and accoutrements of Abbot. He rushed forward and embraced me.

"Thank God you are safe." He smiled down at me and then pain coursed across his face. "We mourn the loss of our dear Brother Owain. May he rest in God's safe keeping." As Brother Giles embraced me, de Tuberville nodded smilingly.

"Prior Edwin was appointed Abbot of Cwmllyn one week ago He has vouched for you and Owain. He has also condemned Gethin as a killer and a Druid and, as he called him, 'a vicious wolf pillaging the sacred sheep fold.' Nevertheless, I remain intrigued by this great sword and why the Abbey should have such a weapon in its possession."

Prior Edwin (I still found it difficult to call him Abbot) smiled conspiratorially at me and told de Tuberville only that the sword was a relic left in the care of the Abbot of Cwmllyn. The killing began when Gethin desired the sword for himself to be symbol of his Druidic command, Edwin continued. I was in awe of his tale spinning. But how much did he know and how much was guesswork?

After a time, de Tuberville had food and drink brought in. We talked, or rather de Tuberville probed and questioned while I answered as I greedily grabbed at the bread and venison laid before me. I was famished and he acknowledged ruefully that the food in his dungeons left much to be desired. I merely smiled and drank his fine wine enjoying its sweetness as it warmed my body. De Tuberville's grizzled face caught my own. He scrutinized me steadily.

"My Constable still thinks you have much to answer for and that time in the dungeons would serve you richly. However, I myself am satisfied with your answers and the fact that Abbot Edwin vouchsafes you. You are free to go!"

I suddenly remembered the parchment. Sweet Jesu, it was still in the dungeons.

"My Lord de Tuberville," I almost shouted at him. "I thank you for your justice and your kindness. I promise to serve you well in the future. However, I have a boon."

"Ask."

"When I was in the dungeon I prayed to God that he would protect me and guide me. I spent hours prostrate on that floor. My Lord, I would ask permission to return to the dungeon and give thanks and praise to God there for my salvation." It was all I could think of, weak as it was. Breathlessly I waited for his response.

"Be it so."

He gestured to the Steward to take me back. Abbot Edwin went with me, but I asked him to remain outside while I prayed. I slipped inside and as the cell door closed behind me I dropped to my knees in gratitude. My prayers finished, I grabbed the pouch, hid it in my habit and left that awful place.

By now evening was drawing on. I was assigned a small pallet in a room in the keep. Abbot Edwin escorted me there and, once we were assured of privacy, told me that he'd read a letter passed down from abbot to abbot always kept safe for the next to read. I sat on the edge of the bed. "It is Excalibur is it not?" he asked quietly.

I agreed, knowing I could trust him and reasoning that as Abbot he was fully entitled to the knowledge Abbot Godfrey entrusted to me. I told my tale. When I finished he shook his head fiercely.

"For all that I loved Abbot Godfrey, I fear he was wrong to involve His Holiness. Excalibur is for Wales and a united kingdom here on this island, not for the Pope to hold."

I was startled at his vehemence. But his concerns mirrored my own. Abbot Edwin paced the tiny room incessantly, at times peering out the slit towards the coast and at others pausing by the door, listening intently to ensure we were not overheard. Throughout he verbalized his every thought and fear, running his hands up and down his sleeve in nervousness.

"If word should get out, it would cause a holy war within Wales and England. The King and barons are already on the verge of war. Edward bleeds the nation dry with demands for gold to pay for his unholy wars in Scotland while the barons refuse more men and money. I have no doubt Edward would seize the sword and use it against all our peoples."

He sat on the pallet beside me, wringing his hands. "Also, no matter how secure we thought it might be, if Excalibur were sent to Rome, others would find out about it. People would kill for it." He stood and paced again. "Excalibur belongs here!"

He faced me and told me that he although he trusted me he would not send either me or Excalibur to Rome. "You've shown yourself faithful, courageous and resourceful. But I cannot send you on such a quest. There are more Gethins out there, who want to overthrow the church and all we hold dear. They are prepared to kill and the threat will not disappear with Gethin's death. No my son, this will remain our secret and the burden of Excalibur must remain with the Abbey."

My heart sank. All the killings, all the deaths and for naught. I was pleased at the Abbot's praise, but could not help the resentment beating in my breast at the futility of it all. Suddenly, there in the stillness of that turret room I heard a small still voice inside me confirming his words; it is yours, my son. The burden is yours.

Edwin stopped pacing and perched on the pallet beside me.

"Did you know that Lord de Tuberville recommended I accept you as the new Prior at Cwmllyn while I wait confirmation of my own appointment?"

He smiled as a multitude of emotions spilled over my face. "I could not find a man better suited to that role than yourself, Brother Thomas, in spite of your youth. Indeed, I think you would do well as Prior and, mayhap in the fullness of time, as Abbot." He pressed his hand against my arm to quiet me as I began to sputter and protest at his kind words.

"But I have a bigger task for you, Thomas. It requires you to carry a heavy load and give up all your ambitions, hopes and dreams. I ask you to carry the burden of Excalibur and your knowledge of it for the rest of your time on this earth. We must hide the great sword, yet keep it close. I am asking you to bear the responsibility."

Since de Tuberville released me I had been praying silently, asking God to guide me. If I had learned anything through my doubts and fears on this journey it was that God loved me and had preserved my life while others fell—I choked back tears for Owain yet again—and that he had done so for a purpose. Who was I now to refuse that task? I knelt before him. He then stood and blessed me.

"Thank you, my son. You know that we have endowed and rebuilt St. Dyfrig's. I name you to be parish priest in that church and ask that you hold Excalibur and its secret safe within its confines."

I remembered when the small new sanctuary had been blessed and re-dedicated. It was dressed in warm whitewash and dominated by a beautiful stained glass window showing St. Dyfrig holding the Bible. Dyfrig was made Archbishop of Wales at the time of King Arthur so it seemed fitting that the church should now hold the sword as it had before the abbey was constructed.

My mind reeled. I had not expected this. I thought for several minutes, aware that he awaited my acceptance. Unexpectedly, a thought came to my mind. "My Lord Abbot, may I ask one favor?" When he said yes, half-formed thoughts began to take shape.

"Would you give me charge of two churches? St. Dyfrig's yes, that I will make my prime responsibility. But allow me also to build a new church near to where Owain was sacrificed. He died for me and for the Holy Church. I seek to honor him. I would place the church high on the ridge, close to his death place that we would cleanse with holy waters."

I stumbled enthusiastically on, tongue tripping over words as I laid out my vision. Reluctantly Edwin began to agree, concerned about the onerous duties it would place upon me but more, I warrant, the cost. I promised the cost would be minimal with much of the labor and materials coming from those remaining of Alun's villagers. I was sure we could get de Tuberville to agree to their helping and, I reasoned, since we had helped rid Tir Iarll of murderous Druids, he might even provide some coin.

"We cannot call the new church after Owain, of course, no matter that you personally see him as a saint." I smiled appreciatively, realizing that he had just agreed to my entreaty. "What do you propose we name your church?"

I doubt that any parish priest had ever before been given the privilege of naming his charge, but I was prepared for that too. My mind flooded with assurance. "Llanffyron, after St. Byron, the man who swore to protect Excalibur and turned to mother church and to protect his secret."

Abbot Edwin and I left it that night in God's hands.

In the morning I was again summoned to de Tuberville's presence. He and the Abbot waited, smiling, a good omen. De Tuberville told me the sword would remain in the protection of the Abbey and that I would not only be given St. Dyfrig's but also allowed to build Llanffyron.

"I will not rebuild the castle. It has no further strategic value. You may use the stones there to help you build." He handed me a small but heavy pouch that jingled with coins. "Let this too be a start."

He walked over to the side table where Excalibur still lay. He stroked the helm and pulled the blade out. I saw it had been cleaned of blood and grime, sparkling in the shafts of sunlight that poured through the Great Hall's window. Wistfully, he caressed it.

"I still have my doubts about letting the Abbey keep this wondrous sword, but I have given my bond before God and before this good Abbot. Be ye gone, brothers. My Steward will provide provisions and horses to return you to the abbey." With that we were dismissed.

Our journey back was quiet and uneventful. Abbot Edwin and I spoke little about the events of the past weeks. I prayed, a new joy lifting my heart, a new purpose in my soul. A monk I would always be, but not of the rote and methodical unthinking of many of my brothers. I was freed! I had a new relationship with God and he would see me through whatever trials and tribulations still awaited. The smile never left my face. My task was set. I would see it done in joy and thanksgiving

---

I am an old man now. I pen these words as commanded by God, to close the story of Excalibur and the Abbey at Cwmllyn. Our church, Llanffyron, was indeed built high on the hill overlooking Maesgwynfi. Soon after, I led a group of villagers and monks from Cwmllyn to the place where Owain died. There we held a solemn exorcism of that evil spot and dedicated it to God. To complete the act, the grove of oaks was completely cut down and the land surrounding Maes Haberth cleared and leveled. The wall mounds I left up as a memorial to Owain and a remembrance that wickedness and hatred of the church will always be present. They remind us that the church must always keep our own spiritual walls in good order.

In time a small village grew up around the church. It became a place of refuge and a stopping point for many pilgrims on their way to the great cathedral at St. David's.

I thought about Excalibur long and hard over the years. Abbot Edwin was dead, taken by the plague only a year after his installation. He had not passed along the secret. Fear and worry ate at his soul. One day he burned the letter each Abbot had passed along to the next. He was remorseful ever after, but the deed could not be undone. I struggled anew with the burden. Edwin was a good man, a kindly gentle man, but not a wise or discerning one.

Some years later I carefully took Excalibur out of its temporary hiding place at St. Dyfrig's and took it up to Llanffyron. A master cutler I brought in from England inscribed words upon the sword at my direction, 'Christus Supremus Omnis; Christ above all.' I was fortunate that the cutler, while skilled, was most uncurious about his task. The job done, he greedily grabbed his money, smiled and left happily for his next commission.

In my most careful hand on the finest parchment I wrote 'Ad Gloria Dei', to the glory of God, and carefully laced it with thongs so it was bound tight to the sword and king's robe. All of this I gently wrapped in the best and softest doe hide leather, greased it and wrapped all in a leather hide tarred with pitch until it was completely sealed for all time against destruction and decay. I placed the entire package into a long shallow iron clad chest I commissioned from a craftsman in Bristol.

In the dark of one night, I slipped out of St. Byron's church alone. Only the occasional glimpse of the full moon guided me that cloudy threatening night, but I stayed as close to shadow as possible lest someone who also strayed at night might see me. I stumbled slightly over loose branches and stones, struggling with the weight of the steel bound chest upon my back. I determinedly stayed on the path I had memorized every time I visited the church.

It led away from the church building towards the west. Once past the few wattle buildings at the extreme end of the village I hastened to our tithe barn. I turned to my right after one hundred paces, turned left and staggered down the slope of the hill. Halfway down I stopped and probed around the bushes with my wooden staff. I felt the bush give way and, on my knees, hastily parted the leaves.

It was the entrance to the caverns. I crept inside and then felt in my pouch for a flint and some tinder. I lit it and poked my way further in. I lifted the heavy box from my back where it was tied and gently placed it down, said a prayer, then backed out.

Once outside, I reached into my pouch and brought out a handful of hardy yew seed pods a woodsman had given me, along with a blunted knife. Swiftly I dug into the soil with my knife and buried the seeds. God willing, those seeds and their successors would grow tall and mighty, marking the place where Excalibur rests.

I brushed myself off and looked up again at the clouds. Yes the storm was rolling in. Good rains to water thirsty seeds. Rain forever has been a sign to me of God's favor and protection. I hastened back up the hill and into the church where I spent the remainder of the night in prayer.

That was near twenty years ago. I have seen the yews grow since, strong and unbuckled by the fierce winds and storms that so often rage in this area. I am convinced that God will protect that sacred spot.

Five other popes have ruled since Boniface. Our new pontiff, Clement VI, seems more interested in the politics of France than in matters of Britain, thank God. It matters not now. Should Papal emissaries come looking for Excalibur, they will not find it. Not at the Abbey, not at St. Dyfrig's nor at Llanffyron.

My eyes grow dim now. I find it hard to write, my hand not as sure as it once was.

Praise God. My journey is done, my task complete. I have kept the faith.

Chapter Twenty-Two

Budleigh Hampton, England

The light early morning traffic meant that within forty minutes Stone and his escorts were out of London and into the late autumn countryside. Unobtrusively their Jaguar Sovereign purred through the quintessential calendar photo village of Budleigh Hampton, sporadic shops and homes decorated for the fast approaching Halloween.

Stone barely registered the journey slumped drained in the comfortable tan leather back seat. He sat up as they slowed, turned down a short lane and paused while the driver murmured into a discretely placed monitor in front of massive black gold-tipped iron gates. Seconds later the gate swung quietly open and they murmured down the yellow gravel driveway through classic manicured grounds to a substantial mid-Victorian manor nestled amongst stately elms. Inside, a small sign discretely welcomed them to "The Grange. A place of solitude and healing". Unconsciously Stone gripped his jacket, holding the packet tight against his chest. A male nurse led them down a hall into a bright cheerful room slowly being flooded by the early morning sun.

"Bradstone! There's a sight you are boyo!"

He couldn't help it. A delighted grin quickly creased across his face as he saw the perky form of the professor in bandages but struggling to sit up.

"You don't look that great yourself, Huw."

A quick laugh boomed out from behind the door. Stone was delighted to see his old friend Chad coming up behind him. They grasped hands and hugged, Stone wincing as the bear hug pressed on his wounds. Chad nodded towards the professor.

"Man, he's one tough old bird. Sneaky too! Faked his injuries worse than they were once he found out Wyndham had him. Kept his eyes and ears open as well."

Stone quickly moved to the side of the bed. "I'm so glad to see you, old friend. How are you?"

"Doctor says I'll be right as rain in a short while. Not as much damage to the old frame as they thought. Plus, whatever I might think of the man, Wyndham provided the finest doctors and medical treatment even if it was done while traipsing all over the globe.

Maddox hovered near the door. Stone quickly introduced him. Huw nodded at him, and asked the nurse to leave while they had a private conversation. As soon as she left, Huw beckoned Stone, Dom and Maddox closer.

"We've got to get moving. I think Wyndham and his crowd are planning an attack on the Royal Family."

Stone and Maddox exchanged quick glances. Huw rapidly relayed as much as he knew.

"I made them think I was more out of it than they thought. I heard Wyndham demand assurances that the Frenchman would be ready when the attack occurred. He said once the 'Royals and the rest' are wiped out, the old ways and old gods could be resurrected.

"I've been wracking my brain trying to remember anything else, but at this point it's still a bit scrambled. I do remember a reference to crowning glories. Can't for the life of me think what it meant. Only that it was obviously something important.

Maddox jumped up and reached for his cell phone.

"Rest easy professor, we'll take it from here." He left the room speaking quietly into the phone asking for Sir Giles.

"Good God Huw, this is such a horrific mess."

Quickly, Stone told Huw and Chad about Mandy, Father Joe and Venice.

"We'll get her back safely, Huw, I promise. This is all my fault."

Huw looked at him deeply. "Well then, you said 'good God' and he is. We must pray."

"You think prayer is going to work at a time like this?" Stone sputtered. "We need to do something, anything!"

"One thing I've learned if you haven't, my boy, is that prayer is something for when you are helpless in your own strength."

Before Stone could respond, Huw held up his bandaged hand in admonition. "You may not believe in prayer or God, but I do! And that's where we're going to start!"

Chad was a silent observer as Huw closed his eyes and began. As he did, Stone's eyes began to tear up. He collapsed his face into his cupped hands. Pain, some physical, some emotional, gripped him. He ignored it as Huw's soft soothing voice filled the air.

When he was done, Huw looked silently at Stone. "You did the best you could, Bradstone. I firmly believe God will look after Mandy as he did me." Huw's soft voice coated soothing calm on Stone's troubled soul.

Suddenly, Stone snapped out of his reverie and excitedly pulled the package out. "I almost forgot. Father Joe passed this to us just before he was shot."

He ripped the package open, and laid the photocopies in front of Huw who struggled to put his half glasses on. He flipped through the pages, Byron's testament, Abbot Godfrey's brief letter and a large wad of paper.

"It's the rest of Thomas' story!" Huw excitedly scanned the pages. "Father Joe translated it for us. It tells what happened after Owain's death." His words poured like a waterfall, tripping over each other as he flung page after page down. As pages were thrown aside, Stone and Chad picked them up and read them just as avidly.

When he was finished Huw waited impatiently for the others, tapping his glasses on the sheets. As Stone put down the last page, Huw could hardly contain himself. "You know what this means, don't you?" Without waiting for a response he blurted out "it tells us where to find Excalibur!" He pushed the sheet and blanket aside and swung his legs slowly over the side of the bed. "Come on, don't just stand there. We've a sword to find."

Stone protested and held the eager professor down arguing the need to wait for medical clearance before they began a treasure hunt. As the debate bounced back and forth, Colin Maddox returned.

"Professor, do you know what Samhein means? Documents we got off those French computers, keep mentioning it as well as this crowning glory."

Huw lay back on the bed.

"Samhein is a Druid festival held around the beginning of November. It's the equivalent of our New Years Day. They believe it's a magical interval when the mundane laws of time and space are temporarily suspended, and the veil between us and the underworld is lifted." Huw had dropped into his professorial role once again. "It is one of the two 'spirit' nights, Beltane, the beginning of summer, is the other."

He paused and before he could continue, Maddox quickly interjected. "So this Samhein thing is November 1? Tomorrow?"

At Huw's affirmative, Maddox spun and rushed out of the room again. Before Huw could resume his struggles, Chad fetched the nurse, explaining that Huw wanted to leave. In short order the doctor appeared and rejected the idea.

Stone pleaded with Huw seeing the determination on his face. "Look Huw. You still have burns and other injuries to take care of. You stay here and be the brains while we become your arms and legs. We'll find that sword." Stone's words struck a chord and he could see the fight seep slowly out of Huw as reality sank in.

Grudgingly Huw conceded. "Mind you do what you're told and keep me fully informed." He turned to the documents once again and the disappointment of not going soon disappeared as he drilled deeper into Thomas's story.

"Give me a few moments peace to study these. Go talk to your friend Maddox." Huw dismissed them both, buried in the excitement of his paper treasure trove.

Outside the room, Maddox pulled the two aside. "Sir Giles is extremely worried. Huw mentioned a plot against the Royal Family. And Samhein keeps cropping up. Tomorrow is the State Opening of Parliament. Tomorrow is also November 1, Samhein. If anything is planned against the Queen…" his words trailed off.

Stone and Dom looked at him, horrified.

"Not only that, the guvnor wants you at the office immediately. Wyndham telephoned him and specifically asked for you. He's calling back in one hour. And no, we couldn't trace the call."

Hampshire, England

Wyndham paced the floor, his frustration palpable. A small twitch above his right eye moved almost in time with his footsteps. From the bar to the couch, to the desk and back to the bar he strode. Every once in a while he peered out the heavily curtained windows. The phone startled him when it rang even though he'd been waiting for it.

"Yes?" A frown creased his forehead. "Damn it. No delays. It must be delivered no later than tonight and I expect everything in place by early morning. No delays. No excuses." He hung up abruptly. Before he could move, the phone rang again.

Senator Murphy's voice trembled slightly with nerves. "Is Crowning Glory still on? Everything here hinges on it!" Wyndham drummed his fingers impatiently on the desktop while the worried American questioned him.

Wyndham's cultivated mid-Atlantic accent dissolved into native inflections as it always did in times of stress and excitement. "Look you, its better without Tonnerre anyway. The man was a loose cannon, always wanting to do things on his own. He created enough havoc in your country as it is. We're better off with a tighter team."

"I've got a lot riding on this Wyndham. You were to create chaos so we could jump in and fill the gap over here as well as there. Now all we have chaos with none of the benefit."

Wyndham listened impatiently and argued, his voice radiating more calmness and confidence than he felt.

"Keep calm, Liam. Tomorrow is still on. When this is over you will be perfectly placed. You will be a hero in America, strong consoling and Presidential. Your adoring public will lap it up and swarm to your support. It'll put you over the top. Just be ready."

He hung up. He would ask Murphy about leaks later. For now he had to make his way to the safe house in London.

Chantilly, Virginia

Within hours of his return from the White House Calvin Tyler quietly orchestrated the questioning and detention of key Homeland Security, FBI and congressional members and workers. Quietly and unobtrusively they were picked up either at home or their offices and driven to unassuming homes and apartments across the Northern Virginia and Maryland suburbs each not knowing others had also been taken. The lesser players were left. For now it was essential to slice off the head quickly.

The braggadocio and arrogance of many actually made the questioning easier. Presented with the evidence, most confirmed a three stage strategy to subvert the constitution under the guise of national security: Stage one, upheaval in Europe that would cause the United States to slam shut its borders in the name of security; Stage two, election of Liam Murphy as President and emergency control of Congress in reaction to the mess in Europe; Stage three, recognition of the new Europe including elimination of existing treaties including NATO and NORAD, and a new tighter bond between

Britain and the US. Elimination of religious belief would be stepped up as various religions, particularly Christianity, would be blamed for the chaos and painted as anti-social entities.

Most of those detained were considered 'true believers'. They'd bought in on the need to sweep away the existing system and replace it with something stronger. One detainee bluntly told them, "For more than two hundred years we've stumbled along with bad legislation, bad presidents, civil wars, depressions and recessions. All led by a Christian faith. We need a fresh start. The movement and Liam will give it to us."

The sad thing is, Tyler mused, the majority might just agree, accepting further restrictions on their freedoms in the name of 'security'. Look at the hassles imposed at airports, he thought, remembering shuffling through security beltless and shoeless even though the extra screening was little more than window dressing to soothe the masses.

He shook his head. When did we become a nation of wimps, insisting that we be kept safe from every harm that the world or mankind throws at us and when did we abdicate responsibility for our own decisions and safety?

He could see the twisted logic in the plotters' thinking. Thank God he thought, there are still some who believe in democracy with all its warts and are willing to move heaven and earth to safeguard it. He remembered a broadcaster's warning, in the middle of the Fifties McCarthy communism scare, that while we call ourselves defenders of freedom wherever it exists in the world, we cannot defend freedom abroad by deserting it at home!

It was also frightening how much hatred towards Christianity was evident in some interrogations. One Congressman spewed his bile about the failure of the Christian church and its influence on American society, arguing the church had to be destroyed so the old gods could be worshiped again. Tyler remembered the churches and bible college that had been attacked. Anger burned in him. He had to stop Liam Murphy if he could, and fast. The election was less than a week away and the polls were now predicting an election too close to call.

Llanmerddyn, Wales

The two women faced each other silently.

Mandy's mind was a jumble of thoughts. The academic world sometimes demanded that she compartmentalize her mind, concentrating only on the topic or problem at hand. She pushed her own fear and memories to a back file, forcing herself to focus on the Druids, Arthur and Excalibur. For now she would remain silent and uncooperative, she decided. When silence was no longer an option she was prepared to sow bogus information in the midst of real research in order to buy time. Time for what, she wasn't sure. But she had to buy it.

Finally Rhiannon shot up from her chair and flung her arms towards Mandy, arms flapping about in frustration.

"Your stubbornness is unbecoming a woman of your intelligence. Nothing will be gained for either of us by this stalemate." She smiled at Mandy, choosing honey instead of vinegar. "You of all people know and love Wales; the Wales that was, as much as the Wales that is. You're a historian. You know our history is linked inextricably with Arthur, Merddyn and the sword. You know that the legend is true; that the sword exists.

"Help me to find it," she purred. "You'll be rewarded beyond your comprehension. You will be honored above all others in your profession. Give me the information and it's all yours: any position in any Welsh university; publication of your papers; academic, financial, personal rewards; whatever you desire. Just give me Excalibur."

Mandy shivered at the look in Rhiannon's eyes. The glacial coldness in her gleaming black orbs were devoid of light and life and belied her coaxing tone and smile. Mandy said nothing.

Rhiannon's temper flashed.

"Speak to me, by Lleu. Show me there's some life in that scrawny body."

Exasperated she grabbed Mandy's hair fiercely with a hidden strength. Mandy winced and cried out in pain. "Make no mistake," Rhiannon hissed, "you will give me what I want. Cooperate and you leave wealthy and honored. Or...." The phrase was unfinished.

Mandy's blue eyes teared up with pain but she held Rhiannon's eyes stoically.

"I know nothing about Excalibur. I only know my father was engaged in research, injured in America and kidnapped by one of your brutes, Damien Wyndham. Other than that I know nothing."

The calm delivery was at odds with her inner turmoil. Rhiannon released her grip and stalked across the room, opened the door and signaled. A man, robed in grey, slithered over and firmly grasped Mandy's arm, lifting her out of the chair and out of the room.

Buckingham Palace Mews, London

A marked police car hurled the three men from the leafy village and into the urban confusion that was London. Blue lights and the mee-maw horn blasted through clogged traffic, spinning down bus lanes, the wrong way down one way streets and, at one point, mounting the pavement to get around a parked truck.

Breathless, they plunged into the office. Sir Giles sat calmly in his chair, a pot and several cups beside him. Stone flopped onto the sofa. "Tea while we wait?" A clock ticked quietly in the background as he poured and sipped.

"Why did he ask for me? How did he know I was here or even alive?"

"Assumptions probably. He obviously knows who I am. Assumed I would be aware of you. Once he asked for you and I asked why, it confirmed everything, dear boy." Sir Giles took another sip just as the phone rang again. Without a word, he picked it up and handed it to Stone.

"Wallace?" Wyndham's voice was harsh and sounded tired. "I do not want this traced. Go to Charing Cross railway station. There's a Boot's drug store with a bank of telephone boxes outside. Go to the one closest to the station entrance and wait for my call. You have fifteen minutes." The line went dead.

Twelve minutes later, Stone felt like a fool standing in the iconic red box waiting. He knew lots of eyes were on him; Maddox and his men, and probably some of Wyndham's—perhaps even Wyndham himself. The stillness inside the box dimmed the cacophony of noon traffic along the Strand. As soon as the phone rang, he picked it up, said his name and listened.

"I know Sir Giles has men watching you right now, but listen and make no signals. I must meet with you and talk about mutual needs"

"You kidnapped Huw and his daughter Mandy, killed a priest and God knows how many others and almost killed me. Why would I meet with you? Think I'm an idiot?"

"Collateral damage. Some necessary, some unfortunate." Wyndham's cold voice answered. "We both want something that the other has. You have no choice. Cooperate and we'll both be happy. Now do as I say." Wyndham did not wait for Stone's agreement. "Get on the Tube and take the Northern Line to Euston Station. In the main concourse there is a bookshop. Go in. You will be met there. Come alone. If you value the girl's life, do it."

The line went dead.

Stone hung up and began walking quickly toward the subway station. Chad and Maddox quickly swung up beside him and were briefed. They argued as they walked but Stone was adamant.

"I know. I don't trust him either. But what choice do we have. Even if they take me or kill me, we'll be no further ahead. On the other hand, I might find out something useful. There are no options really."

"Take this pen, it's a homing device, so we can track you," Maddox argued.

"And have them find it when they frisk me? Why not sign my death warrant now?"

"I'll go with you," Chad chimed in.

"No. Wyndham said alone."

The argument continued down the stairs to the ticket booth. Stone stopped and ended the discussion. "Listen. Huw is praying. If there is a God then now is a good time to show me."

Baffled by this argument Maddox finally gave in. He spun on his heel and stalked off, frustrated. He called the office to have a man in place at Euston.

Chad stood still. "I'm coming with you. They don't know me. They're looking for Brit agents, not me. I'll watch your back."

Without another word, he turned and walked off. As Stone purchased his ticket, he watched Chad stop at another booth on the opposite side. Comforted though worried, Stone proceeded through the barriers and down the escalators onto the platform. In the pack of urban travelers behind him, Chad did the same.

Euston is a plain, ugly, utilitarian monstrosity thoroughly lacking the Victorian/Edwardian charm of some of London's other mainline railway stations such as Kings Cross or St. Pancras. But Euston is busy, always busy.

Stone pushed through the crush of businesspeople, tourists and students scurrying through the terminus. A backpacker intent on what was before him, not around him, turned suddenly and the jammed pack swung heavily into Stone, causing him to grimace as pain from the wound shot through him. Backpackers! Why is it always backpackers?

"Sorry mate," the strapping young Londoner snapped and continued on.

As Stone stopped for the moment, he saw Chad tranquilly wandering along looking at the bakeries, fast food and flower shops lining the main concourse. Ahead he could see the bookshop. Without looking around, he entered. Unsure what to do next, he wandered over to the magazine rack and studied the myriad of titles available. He meandered slowly down the magazine stands and walked over to the latest fiction. Nobody approached him.

Discouraged, he wandered back past the cashier to the newsstand and picked up a copy of *The Times*. He scanned the headlines, noting calls for the government to address the wounded British economy. A hand reached out and touched him.

"You cannot read the paper here sir, it must be purchased."

A petite young woman, straight blonde bangs hanging down her forehead almost to her eyebrows looked at him. He nodded and put the paper down.

"Please follow me." She turned and headed toward the cashiers desk.

"I don't really want the paper" Stone stammered, "I'm just killing time until…er…my train."

"We both know that's not true Mr. Wallace. Please follow."

Stunned, Stone trotted after her, following behind the counter and through a small door into the stock room behind.

Outside the store, Chad watched Stone go after the girl until he disappeared. He muttered an oath under his breath and stepped in. He picked up a magazine as he passed and walked quickly to the cashier. After paying, he turned on the charm and asked who the pretty young staffer was. The cashier looked quizzically at him.

"What girl sir. There's only myself and Tom over there," she said, indicating a florid middle aged man restocking one of the bookshelves.

"The young girl who went through that door. She had a man with her."

"Nobody went back there sir. I was just over there restacking the non-fiction and I'm sure nobody went behind the counter."

As a line formed behind him, Chad insisted he'd seen two people enter the back room. Exasperated, the woman finally flung the door wide open and invited him to look for himself. It was devoid of people, filled only with stacks of books and magazines piled everywhere. To the left he saw another door. Ignoring the cashier, he rushed in and flung the second door open. He looked out onto a side concourse. Frantic he ran along the corridor searching for Stone and the woman.

They were gone. He tossed his copy of *Modern Woman's Health* in the garbage.

Chapter Twenty-Three

Mayfair, London

The woman ignored Stone's attempts at conversation. She hustled him out the back door into a corridor by the station's side entrance and then into a large car with darkened windows. Inside she thrust a blindfold at him and signaled him to put it on. For the next twenty minutes he sat back in the rear seat strangely calm.

He struggled to express his feelings in unfocused prayer, though why God would bother with one who'd abandoned faith years ago, he didn't know. But Huw assured him that God did care so this is one sure way to find out, he thought ruefully

Stone's blindfold was removed as the car pulled to a halt. He peered out at a non-descript though elegant crowded street of white Portland stone townhouses each with black wrought iron railings and pristine stone steps up to their various colored front doors.

Inside he entered a sumptuous living room with stylish furnishings and deep patterned floral carpet. Seated in a cavernous chair at the other end of the room was a distinguished looking man who waved Wallace to a seat opposite.

"I'm Damien Wyndham. Lovely house isn't it. Belongs to a friend of mine, the Duke of Brecon, who lets me borrow it discreetly from time to time." He poured a glass of whiskey, offering one to Stone who refused. Wyndham shrugged and took an appreciative sip.

"You've caused me great trouble, Mr. Wallace. You almost ruined a very necessary plan to get this country out of its mess."

As he spoke, Stone noticed a dragon tattoo on his right forearm. The servant also sported the same design just above his wrist and he remembered he'd seen one on the girl's arms as she handed him his blindfold.

Wyndham locked his eyes on Stone. Stone was up to the challenge, staring back and saying nothing. After a few moments Wyndham spoke. "You have something I want and I have something you want. It's a simple business proposition. We need to do a deal here. The professor's daughter is quite safe and well. I am not a violent man unless provoked."

"So why is Father Joe dead? Why was I shot and Huw almost killed?"

"As I said before, unfortunate byproducts of our needs. It is of no consequence. The priest represented a dead faith that stands in our way. As do you."

"Is that a threat?"

"No. Simply an observation. I cannot allow you to block my plans any longer." For the first time he smiled unemotionally at Stone. "Believe me, Mr. Wallace, I wish you were dead. I would love nothing more than to see you suffer and die in front of my eyes right now.

However, at this point you are no use to me dead. You have something I need and I want it."

He paused and took a long sip of his drink.

"My men in Venice were stupid. They are used to guns not brains. They succeeded in, shall we say, securing Miss Griffiths. However, they saw the priest pass you a package. Instead of grabbing you and the package, they shot. They claim they were hurried by another boat and men coming at them." He peered at Stone. "I presume they were British agents who saved you?"

At Stone's nod, he continued. "Be that as it may. I suspect that the package contained pertinent documents including the monk's letter." Again the cold smile crept across his face. He leaned forward, his voice silky but heavy with threat. "Oh yes, Mr. Wallace. We know about the monk Thomas. We know that a report was sent to the pope. Fortunately that pope and the many others who followed him were too interested in their own machinations and politics to pay too much attention to the drivel of a mad British monk."

Stone was startled by the venom in his voice.

"Actually, Mr. Wallace my colleague Rhiannon, and therefore I too, believe that Lleu and the gods protected that document from prying enemy eyes."

"I don't have them anymore. I turned them over." Stone hoped his white lie would pass muster.

"Oh, but I don't want the documents, Mr. Wallace. Oh dear me, no. In fact I don't even want the information they contain."

"What do you want then?" Stone said mystified.

"It's very simple. I believe those documents tell where Excalibur is. You find Excalibur and deliver it to me and Miss Griffiths will be free. She and you can then decide for yourselves whether you will be part of the new order or take the consequences. Personally, I hope you don't join us. I want you dead for all the grief you've given me," he snarled viciously.

He leaned forward in his chair and tapped Stone on the knee.

"However, I am a realistic man. I will sweeten the pot for you. A good journalist like you appreciates scoops, so I will give you an exclusive interview after the fact on the real meaning of the sword Excalibur and its place in our history."

"You're going to kill us anyway Wyndham. I'm not going to help you get the sword. Even if I knew where it was. And I don't."

Wyndham nodded, expecting Stone's response.

"I want you dead, Mr. Wallace. Oh yes, I want you dead. More than anything. But I want Excalibur more. So I propose a pragmatic bargain. The sword for your lives." He leaned forward, an icy smirk on his face. "But I promise you this. Even if you live you will wish you were dead."

He stood abruptly. "I want Excalibur and I will have it."

The girl stepped up and blindfolded Stone again.

"You will be dropped somewhere in London, Mr. Wallace. And by the way, tell Sir Giles not to bother searching this residence. We will leave nothing for him.

"Hwyl fawr, or goodbye until I see you again. Mr. Wallace. With the sword!"

Buckingham Palace Mews, London

Uncharacteristically, Sir Giles paced his office, back and forth the sixteen steps from the overflowing bookshelf across the room to the window overlooking their little backwater enclave within stone's throw of Buckingham Palace and the monarch he was sworn to protect.

A short, sharp knock on the door and Broderick and Maddox swept into the room closely tailed by Chad and Stone. Sir Giles plopped into his chair.

"Nothing guvnor." Maddox ran his fingers through his short dark hair.

"The house was clean as a surgeon's knife. We interviewed the Duke of Brecon. He admits knowing Wyndham—called him an acquaintance—and acknowledges lending the London house from time to time for business purposes. But swears he did not lend the house today and doesn't know where Wyndham is."

"We've got agents on the streets, and the police have staff at airports, ferry terminals and train stations looking for him. We alerted Charlie down in Wales and we've pulled in military intelligence. But without concrete information..." his voice trailed off.

Grimly, the security chief grunted acknowledgement and glanced at Stone.

"Nothing else you can remember? Something he or someone said? Some little item you noticed?" Stone shook his head. Sir Giles drummed his fingers on his desk, and then cupped his hands together.

"Gentlemen, in just over nine hours it will be Samhein. In twenty hours the Queen opens Parliament. Time is running out. Don't know what the Druids plan and don't know where. Calling it 'Crowning Glory' says it will be an attack on Her Majesty. I want answers. Now!"

"Who attends this opening of parliament?" Stone asked.

"Anyone who's anyone! Obviously the Queen. The entire government, Prime Minister, Opposition leaders, Members of Parliament, members of the House of Lords, the judiciary, plus foreign dignitaries."

So what happens at this opening, Chad casually asked. Sir Giles stood and walked to the window. He gestured towards the Palace and explained the centuries old tradition as briefly as he could. The Queen, in the horse-drawn state coach, left the Palace led by bands and the Household Cavalry down The Mall, through Horse Guards Parade and onto Whitehall, past Downing Street and Parliament Square, to the Sovereign's Entrance in the Victoria Tower at the south end of the Houses of Parliament.

"Once inside, there's a processional into the House of Lords. There's a bit more ceremonial where the House of Commons is called to attend the Queen as she reads the Speech from the Throne that outlines the government's plans and policies for the upcoming session. Then the whole thing, procession and all, reverses itself. Out of the Palace at eleven in the morning, back by one o'clock for late lunch. The whole thing is precisely timed"

It was the longest Maddox and Broderick had ever heard him speak in one go, certainly in full sentences.

Leaning against one of the bookshelves, Chad asked. "If they're going to try anything tomorrow, where would it be?"

"Been tumbling that one around m'self."

There had been solo attempts before he said, especially in 1981 when a man fired six shots at her during the Trooping of the Colour ceremony. The Queen, mounted on her horse, had remained cool while the man was arrested and taken away. "But Wyndham said 'the Royals and the rest' so they want to make a big splash. No. Has to be either the Palace or the Houses of Parliament."

He stared out of the window, ignoring the four, lost in thought and putting himself in the minds of the plotters, imagining their thought process step by step. Suddenly, he looked up intently.

"Parliament. Has to be there. Can't really get close to Buck House. Wyndham wants something big to make his mark. Attack on Parliament means he can take out the government and just about everyone of importance in this country." He slammed his fist into his hand, stunned by the audacity of the threat. Within minutes Freddy, Maddox and Broderick were bustling out of the office with fresh orders. Only Stone and Chad were left.

"Grateful to both of you for what you've done. Don't know what else you could do." Sir Giles said quietly as he pushed himself away from the desk. Stone saw for the first time how tired and grey-faced the old spymaster was and realized how great the strain had been and how much greater it was now. Chad noted it too.

"Sir Giles, we can help. Stone has seen some of Wyndham's people. Maybe we should be on the street with your men, close to Parliament. We might spot something your guys couldn't."

The guvnor acknowledged the offer with a nod and warned them to get some quick rest in view of the long night and day ahead of them.

Houses of Parliament, Westminster

Stone and Chad spent most of the night on the street meeting various police and security personnel. While London slept, a full-scale rehearsal with all the troops had taken place as was normal on state occasions. The only thing missing, Stone noted, was the music. Londoners, even those used to ceremonials, did not appreciate being woken by martial band music at four in the morning.

He checked his watch again. It was already nine thirty. Time was running out and they'd gotten nowhere. At precisely 11 a.m. the Queen's procession would trot out of the Palace and start its journey. Crowds already lined the streets but the cold wet winds interspersed with heavy drizzle did not dampen their spirits. Gloomy grey clouds scudded across the sky as members of the Guards and other regiments stationed themselves along the route. Inside the Palace forecourt, the band of the Coldstream Guards stood at ease, waiting. A troop of Household Cavalry trotted down Constitution Hill from their barracks at Knightsbridge, ready to take up station as the Queen's escort.

Behind the flanks of black bearskin and grey overcoated guards lining the route armed police wandered good naturedly amongst the crowd with vigilant eyes flicking everywhere. Unnoticed were hundreds of undercover police, security branch and military police swarming through the crowds. They too were scanning the crowds for anything suspicious, though Sir Giles had only been able to tell them to look for black dragon marks or tattoos, probably on an arm. That information generated caustic comments and sarcasm amongst the searchers, knowing that nobody in their right minds would bare their arms on this cold miserable day.

Stone and Chad met up with Maddox and Broderick. As they walked together, they wracked their brains trying to anticipate Wyndham's plan. The foul weather, tiredness and stress had done nothing for their dispositions. Stone didn't join in the discussion as they crossed Parliament Square for the third time that morning.

"It has to be a bomb of some kind. He wants to do lot of damage and kill or wound as many as possible."

Maddox shook his head. "He couldn't get close enough. It would take some kind of massive car bomb but this whole area is locked down to vehicles. A bomb on the periphery is no good to them."

Equally, a weapon inside was also dismissed. Exasperated Maddox reminded them that anyone allowed into the building, aristocracy, MP's or staff, had gone through the ultimate screening. They'd have to be some kind of suicidal extremist to commit the atrocity from inside, he finished.

"Your point?" Chad asked mildly. "We're not dealing with a bunch of boy scouts here. Suicidal extremists would seem to fit the description quite well. And we've seen that they can corrupt anyone in any office anywhere."

Maddox shut up. Chad's argument was tough to counter. His partner however argued Chad's point, noting that this time even more than prior occasions, security inside was air tight.

"Nobody could get a bomb in there. It doesn't matter if you're an earl, a duke, the prime minister or clergy, it's practically a strip search."

Maddox shook his head, rejecting their other idea of a bomb in a nearby building.

"It would have to be massive in order to have the impact we think the Druids want. And a bomb across the street might not impact those inside Parliament. More than a dozen bombs hit Parliament during the war, and it still stood up."

The four split into pairs again, patrolling the stretch between Westminster Abbey and the Houses of Parliament. Stone and Chad talked quietly as they walked, turning over each item they'd seen and heard both in France and Venice, looking for the missing clue.

Finally, plastic mugs of hot tea in hand, they stopped opposite the Victoria Tower as Big Ben tolled the quarter hour. In one hour the Queen's coach would pass this spot and make the turn towards the tower. They looked intently at each passing face and tried to look at the few bared arms in the crowd.

"Stone, it's got to be a bomb. It's the only way they can create the havoc they want. They obviously intend to kill the Queen and as many members of the government as possible. A bomb is the only way."

Stone swept his arm around the area. "How? No vehicles within two blocks. Boats kept off the river on the other side of Parliament. Like Maddox said, even if it is a bomb, it would be too far away."

Chad stared at the dark clouds sweeping across the skies as if they held the answer. Stone looked up too. So far he'd not seen answers to his frayed half prayers. Maybe the big answer was that this would be his final morning on earth. Perhaps this was God's plan; that Stone and many others would be killed in a Druid atrocity. He remembered Thomas's agonizing and self-doubts. He could relate.

Big Ben finished tolling 10:15. Chad continued to stare at the sky. Stone shrugged his shoulders and they began walking again. "Man, if nothing happens today, think of the fallout!"

Chad suddenly reached out and clamped a hand on Stone's good shoulder.

"Fallout! Stone, that's it. It's got to be some kind of nuclear or chemical weapon."

A clammy cold fear shuddered through Stone's body. Oh please God, let it not be that!

He grabbed his cell and reached Maddox with their theory. Minutes later Maddox and Broderick came running, breathless.

"The guvnor was one step ahead of us. He'd already considered that possibility and had feelers out." His grim facial expression warned there was worse to come. Maddox gulped another deep breath and beckoned them off to a quieter spot.

"Charlie confirmed it. The movement has a smart bomb capability."

"Wait a minute, who's Charlie?" Stone interjected.

"Charlie is our sleeper agent in Rhiannon's compound. Charlie says a small section of the place was turned into a lab three years ago. Maddox's phone rang. A finger in one ear to block out the increasing street noise and babble from those lining the route, he listened carefully. His face white, he hung up.

"We've tracked down reports of a nuclear theft in Russia earlier this year. Plutonium stolen by a Russian officer who died later of poisoning near Yekaterinburg. There's nothing to connect him, but Wyndham was in Russia at the time and we've got an airport log showing an Air Celtica charter at the local airport. So we have to assume the worst. He's got nuclear capability."

The implications turned Stone's stomach ice cold. Without another word, the four once again began scrutinizing people. As they sifted slowly through the crowd, a troop of dismounted Household Cavalry marched down the street white and red plumes dancing and swaying at each step. At the commanding officer's bark they wheeled left through the gothic entrance and into the building.

Big Ben pealed as the clock hit 10:45.

Llanmerddyn, Wales

She was being treated well considering, Mandy thought, but there was no doubt she was a prisoner. The door was locked and the room was spartan but clean with only one small window that looked out on the compound. All she could really see was that it was raining. But then, this was Wales, and it often was. If only she had a book, any book.

Three times in the past five hours she'd been paraded in front of Rhiannon to be alternately flattered, cajoled and threatened. Each time the result was the same, but Rhiannon's patience was wearing thin.

She heard the key turn in the lock. A gray robed man and woman entered carrying a tray with a sandwich and a small steaming pot. She hoped it was tea. Silently they placed the tray on the small wooden table. The man smiled slightly and beckoned her to pull up the room's single chair. As silently as they entered, they left.

Sighing, she walked over and sat down, picking up the rolled napkin that contained her cutlery. As she unfurled it, a small piece of paper fluttered out. Mandy picked it up, her heart racing.

She read the simple message. 'Be strong. Wallace alive and in London'. It was signed Charlie. Thank God, she thought, her pleading prayers had been answered. Stone is alive and must realize where she'd been taken. For the first time in forty eight hours she allowed herself a satisfied smile. God bless Charlie too, she thought. At least one man in here is a friend, remembering his brief smile moments ago. Maybe she could withstand Rhiannon after all. She attacked the sandwiches with gusto.

Westminster, London

Big Ben tolled eleven o'clock. In the far distance Stone could hear band music. The Queen had left the Palace. She was on her way.

The steady stream of cars dropping Lord This and Lady Such had stopped fifteen minutes ago. Those privileged to be inside were already in. The street was closed to traffic. On the River Thames, boat traffic died away. Crowds pushed and shoved to get a better glimpse of Her Majesty when she passed. The drizzle eased and hardy Londoners downed their umbrellas.

Perhaps it was the multitude of multi-colored umbrellas that had blocked his view, but as they came down, he saw her.

At first it was just a flashing glimpse through the crowds and the tall black bearskin headgear of the soldiers lining the route. Then he saw her again.

Stone pulled Chad's sleeve. "There. Over there. That girl." He pointed across the road.

"Where? I don't see anything."

Stone pushed through the crowd waving the temporary credential card Sir Giles had provided. Chad, Maddox and Broderick rushed after him, thrusting people aside as they closed on Stone. Two policemen in bright lime green safety jackets began running towards the commotion. Maddox shouted they were security and kept his ID card high. One bobby joined them as they crossed the street.

"I think it was her. Wyndham's assistant. The blonde from the bookstore. I recognized her. She's got dark hair now, probably a wig, but I'm sure it was her." Stone shouted.

They reached the opposite pavement, and began walking hurriedly along, policeman in tow, in front of the guards staring intently into the faces.

"Here. She was about here, walking behind the crowds." Stone led the way as they pushed through the crowd to the back. Practically running, his head swiveling constantly, he headed south away from Parliament, alongside the shrubs, trees and black wrought iron fence bordering the parliamentary gardens. In the background they could hear the bands coming ever closer. The cheering crowd was louder

"Going the wrong way isn't she? If she's the one, wouldn't she be going that way?" Maddox gasped, gesturing towards Parliament.

Stone stopped and took one more look down the street, frustrated. He stepped up and looked over the iron fence, pushing a small bush aside. A small crowd was gathering at the far end closest to the Tower. "She's got to be in there." Without waiting he vaulted the fence in front of the astonished bobby. Shrugging, Maddox and the others followed. Already the band and escorts were passing through Whitehall and Parliament Square.

Stone suddenly saw the girl again, pushing through the cheering throng. He barged into the crowd, pushing one man out of the way and bowling another over with his shoulder. The girl suddenly turned to see what was causing the uproar. She blanched as she recognized Stone, turned and began to push harder through the crowd.

Desperately, Stone lunged and pulled her by the arm. As Stone fell on top of her, an indignant, heavy set white haired senior began hitting him with her umbrella and handbag. Warding off the blows, Stone wrestled with the girl as the crowd gave way before them. As she swung at Stone, her overlarge shoulder tote bag flew off her arm. Chad vaulted over the struggling pair and grabbed the bag. Maddox and Broderick quickly asserted control as police and security flooded the area. The crowd cheering was louder now and they could hear the trotting horses of the escort as they neared the turn into the Houses of Parliament.

The girl snarled at Stone, her muddied face distorted by anger. "Fool. You can't stop it. It's too late. Nothing can save them. He has control. Ta muid anseo. The master has spoken.

Chad ripped open the bag. "It's a bomb of some kind," he sputtered.

Stone hesitated momentarily then grabbed it and raced across the rain slicked grass. As more police began to converge on him, Maddox jumped up yelling "let him go".

The crowd cheering intensified. The Queen's coach reached the turn. Big Ben tolled the quarter hour. It was 11:15 precisely.

Panting, Stone almost reached the walkway that ran alongside the river when he slipped in the wet grass. On his knees and with a mighty heave he launched the bag over the fence. Sound disappeared and time dropped into slow motion as he threw. His friends raced up as he scrambled to the stone wall. Together they watched the bag tumble over, finally disappearing in the water with a disappointing plop. Stone gripped the fence gasping, watching the spot where the purse had disappeared. Behind him the cheering began to dissipate as Her Majesty disappeared inside.

As he reached the fence and watched the purse disappear, Maddox turned to Stone.

"Whatever made you do that? Mind you, I'm bloody glad you did!"

Stone began brushing mud and grass bits off and watching as police hustled the girl away.

"Remember, she said 'he has control'. She could have meant her gods I suppose, but it flashed through my mind she meant Wyndham. The only way he could control it would be some kind of remote electronic device, like a cell phone. If it was a cell I figured the signal couldn't reach it underwater and there's no better dead zone than the bottom of the Thames, so I tossed it." He glanced up. "I think I was right."

"Jolly good luck that you were."

Smiling to himself, Stone began to slowly walk back towards the street still brushing himself off. Good luck? I don't think so, he thought. Maybe there was something to this God and prayer thing after all. Maybe Huw was right, God really does have a plan and I was part of it all along. But the plan was still incomplete. Mandy still had to be saved. And he had to find Excalibur to do it.

Chapter Twenty-Four

Hampshire, England

Damien Wyndham sped down the M3 motorway away from the mess that would be London. Everything was in place. Crowning Glory had arrived. It was set up so well, planned to the smallest detail despite the irritations and bumps caused by Griffiths, Wallace and Tonnerre.

Carys, the gods keep her, was their willing sacrifice. His weapon maker had designed a devious little nuclear device that perched inside Carys' bag. The blast would rip open part of the building well into the House of Lords where the explosion and radiation would wreak havoc.

This evening he would step in, aided and abetted by his underlings, to restore the Celtic-Druid form of government and religion. With the monarchy finished and the government non-existent his firm resolve to return home permanently and fix the nation would be welcome. With key supporters in the remainder of government to help him, his triumph would be complete. Murphy would then jump on the bandwagon and praise the new order in Britain. Liam's compassion, eloquence and persuasiveness would lead him to victory on election night.

He listened intently to the BBC's radio coverage of the Opening. At 11 a.m. he pulled into a service area and waited. At precisely 11: 15 he pushed a speed dial button on the specialized mobile phone prepared by his bomb maker. Avidly he listened to the BBC broadcast, expecting total chaos to break loose at that instant. Instead the announcer droned on, describing the centuries old ceremonial procession as the Queen entered the House of Lords.

He pressed the speed dial again, harder. The announcer still droned on. Sweat began to bead his forehead. He rubbed his eyebrow furiously. Suddenly his main mobile rang.

Wyndham turned redder and redder with anger as he listened to the reports of Carys' capture and Stone's race to the Thames before dumping the bomb in the river. The more he heard, the more he cursed and shouted as the details were revealed. He slammed his fist into the car dash. More curses flowed. He threw the phone into the back seat and cradled his head in one hand, the other fist beating against the dash.

He forced himself to regain calm and drove off remaining composed until he walked through the cottage door where the infamous Wyndham temper finally let loose. The hall lamp was the first to go, followed by other bric-a-brac and furniture. Glasses and bottles on the bar were next. Shards of glass and ceramic littered the floor.

Wyndham stormed into the den, forced himself to breathe deeply and called his agent again. He listened grimly at the report. The only glimmer of positive news was that in the confusion following Carys' arrest two of Wyndham's men followed Wallace first to an office near the Palace, then to a small but well-guarded manor house in the country.

"Keep watching. Lose him and your life is forfeit. If he does what I think, we may yet get a victory."

Cerunnos was playing with him, perhaps even angry. Sweat poured down his brow. Perhaps if he could return Excalibur to them, the gods would relent and approve him again. He promised Cerunnos he would sacrifice Wallace and the girl. Surely the gods would be pleased then. Wyndham began breathing deeply, willing himself to be calm muttering prayers to Cerunnos, Lleu and Taranis for endurance and calling on them to unleash their power.

Darkness was falling when his phone rang. Wallace and others were on the move speeding down the M4 motorway towards Wales. Wyndham slammed the table. At last, he thought. Wallace would only leave London if he knew where Excalibur was. Demanding constant updates on Wallace' whereabouts, he got in his car and headed west.

He would take pleasure in killing Wallace, he promised himself.

Budleigh Hampton, England

After a brief visit with a relieved and grateful Sir Giles, Stone, Chad and Maddox rested as they were driven through the heavy mid-day traffic of central London back to The Grange. Broderick pulled the short straw. He had the tougher task, coordinating the unenviable task of scouring London for traces of Wyndham.

All were sworn to secrecy. Nothing would be made public about the Druid attack on the Queen or Damien Wyndham's role in it. The sweeping powers of Britain's anti-terrorism laws would allow a discrete security pick-up of civil servants, peers and others who approved or supported the Druids.

"Nobody is safe and the job is not done until Wyndham is taken and this movement disemboweled," were Sir Giles' last words as they'd headed out the office door.

Huw glared as they entered, half glasses perched on the end of his nose annoyed at the interruption then smiled as he recognized the cause. Papers dropped off the bed as he moved and shifted a borrowed laptop to the side.

"Bradstone! Where have you been, boy? Flitting around sightseeing while I struggle to make sense of this pile of old papers?" Huw's smile took the sting out of his words. "Any progress on finding Mandy?" he asked plaintively.

"Good news and bad news. Mandy is alive, probably at Rhiannon's lair in Carmarthen. The bad news is they want Excalibur, not the papers, in order to free her. And Wyndham is still at large."

Huw grimaced then whispered that God would take care of her. A tear trickled down his face only to be swiftly wiped off. Suddenly he noticed the mud and grass stains on Stone's pants.

"What have you been up to boyo? Rolling in the mud with Wyndham?"

Stone laughed out loud. "Tell you about that later Huw. Right now, have you come up with anything?"

A twinkle popped into Huw's eyes and a smile creased across his face. "Ah, there you are, look you. While you were gallivanting around and playing in the mud I've been doing my homework."

He looked up at Maddox. "I must say your staff here is very coopera-tive. They got me anything I wanted, including a modern ordnance map of South Wales. Plus I used the laptop to download some absolutely fascinat-ing maps and documents of the area in the early 1300's out of the Bodleian Library in Oxford. Relatively good maps they are too, let me tell you."

The professor would have gone on, but Stone interjected. "Please Huw, no lectures. Not now. Just tell us what you've got."

Unrepentant, the perky professor pulled a map over. "It's very simple, bach. I think I know where Excalibur is!"

"You're kidding! Are you serious?" Stone could hardly contain himself

"Very serious. I have most of the documents from that ruined church. Then Father Joe provided Thomas' translation of Byron's original letter plus Abbot Godfrey's extensive letter to Pope Boniface. They all gave me clues and Thomas's journal confirmed it. I compared all that information with today's ordnance survey maps of the area. Yes, I know where it is. That is," he said worriedly, "if it still exists after more than 700 years underground."

They crowded around as he pulled the map over.

"It's down by here," he said, dropping into the colloquial speech of the Welsh valleys, "in a cave near the village of Llanffyron in a small valley west of Cardiff."

Maddox broke in as Stone began to move. "I know you want to get there as soon as possible, but it will take more than two hours. By the time we arrive it will be too dark to search. I'll get a helicopter for first thing in the morning."

"Sure! And why not take out ads on radio and TV at the same time, telling everyone we're coming and why. A helicopter landing in a small village with a bunch of us running around with all kinds of tools? No. It's not on, as you Brits would say. Mandy's safety is our priority now.

Maddox shook his head. "All of us need a good night's rest. You probably most of all."

"By then Wyndham or Rhiannon could have done anything. Don't forget we screwed up their plans. No, we go now and search by flashlight if we have to. We can take turns snoozing in the car."

Stone turned to Huw. "Give us everything you've got. What exactly are we looking for?"

It took more than half an hour before Huw had exhausted his knowledge and findings. While Stone and Chad pored over the maps and documents, Maddox was busy organizing equipment and a larger more utilitarian vehicle than the Jaguar. They wrapped up the session and headed out of Huw's room. Stone hung back as the others left.

"We'll get her out Huw. I promise. I've been praying and I think maybe God really is working some kind of plan in all this." He waved and walked out.

"Well, well," was all Huw said, settling back on his bed.

South Glamorgan, Wales

The light was fading rapidly. Chad leaned over and woke Stone from his restless sleep in the back of the Land Rover as Maddox slowed for the interchange.

"The village is about six miles from here," Maddox said, pointing north.

They'd made good time. The earlier drizzle and cloud still lingered however, he realized as he shook himself awake. That dashed their hopes for moonlight to aid their search. They drove down the narrow sleepy road and entered the village carefully. Maddox almost missed the turn off, hidden as it was by high dark hedges on either side of the road.

"The church is up here," he said as he climbed a narrow street, dodging around carelessly parked vehicles outside cozy hillside cottages. At the top the road leveled off and they made a sharp left turn. Ahead was a large stone wall and beyond, the unmistakable dark outline of a church.

"Llanffyron church, built and ministered to by Thomas" Stone murmured to himself, surprised by how much he had come to identify himself with the monk and the quest to save the sword. First Thomas; now it was his turn.

They gathered under a street light a map in hand. None paid attention as a car with two occupants drove by them and disappeared down a lane. Another car pulled into a driveway down the road.

Maddox looked up. "Time to go treasure hunting, gentlemen."

Darkness had fallen swiftly and the only light, other than streetlamps, shone out from the pub. Nobody passed them but they could hear the laughter and singing inside the pub as they edged around corner. Carefully they counted out 100 paces and turned, only to find a garden wall in their way. The garden trailed darkly down the hillside.

"Something tells me we should have alerted the local constabulary," Chad commented quietly as they scaled the wall. "Anyone looking out would think there was a trio of burglars on the loose."

A cat wailed in the gloom but the only other sound was their own breathing and careful steps. At the end of the garden they clambered over the wall again, finding now that the slope dropped dramatically. They scrambled down, grabbing a bush or shrub every so often to steady themselves in the uneven and rain-slickened ground cover.

"How far down," Chad murmured.

"Thomas said half way. He planted yew trees at the entrance so if they're still around we should find the cave entrance."

'We're about halfway now," Maddox declared coming to a halt. Below them a blackness of forest faced them.

"Are we sure there are caves around here," Chad asked?

"This whole part of Wales is riddled with caves. There's an eleven mile long chain of caverns not far from here. Big tourist attraction so it doesn't surprise me there might be one here."

Low misty clouds and drizzle obscured much of the hillside vegetation. Maddox laid down his back pack and lifted out a small apparatus. He switched it on and a dim red glow broke up the darkness.

"A new type of Ground Penetrating Radar. Thought it might be useful for cave sniffing."

He pointed it at the hillside and slowly edged his way along, stopping occasionally, following a grid pattern up and down every twenty feet. Fifteen minutes and ten grid searches later, Maddox stopped. "Nothing. Are you sure we're in the right area?"

Stone reread Huw's directions again. "It has to be here somewhere."

They moved further down the hill and began searching again hearing the occasional animals skittering around. Suddenly Maddox murmured with pleasure. Chad and Stone rushed to his side. In the pitch black they saw the shadows of massive black trees.

Maddox's GPR glowed green indicating open space in the hill face. He picked up a steel shaft, unfolded it so it doubled in length and began prodding where the equipment showed emptiness. Stone shone a light at the probe. After a few tries, the shaft disappeared into the hillside up to the British agent's hand.

"This is it. That monk knew what he was about."

In short order they hacked away the bushes and debris that covered the cave entrance. A stygian blackness faced them, blacker than the night.

"I'm going in," Stone whispered.

He lay on his belly, slithering slowly in, flashlight extended before him. It did not provide much light but he saw sharp rock edges, stones and animal bones in the ground as he pulled himself in. It sloped slightly uphill. He came to a slight bend and carefully crawled around it. His light suddenly showed a larger cavern. He warily got to his knees. If he bent over, he could duck walk forward. In the shadow against the cave wall he saw an unnatural lump perched on a shelf.

Gingerly he reached out. It was hard but long and handmade; a box of some kind. He had found it. He had found Excalibur! Carefully he began to back up, maneuvering himself around the bend and sliding slowly backwards to the cave entrance dragging the box as he did. As he eased himself out, the precious box gripped firmly, a large light suddenly flashed on.

"How very kind of you to find it for me, Mr. Wallace."

Stone whirled at Wyndham's voice. Maddox was lying on the ground groaning. Chad, his face white as a sheet had his back to a tree, eyes fixed firmly on the automatic in Wyndham's hand.

His heart sank. There was no bargaining for Mandy's life this time, he knew. The harsh sneer on Wyndham's face told him that.

"You won't be rash will you, Mr. Wallace. Your friend's lives depend on it. Not to mention your own. Now, open it!"

Stone hesitated and then chopped at it with the axe they'd used to clear brush. With each swing he silently pleaded for help.

Wyndham stood rigid, the gun aimed unswervingly at Chad. He could have executed both these men before Wallace crawled out of the cave. But part of the enjoyment of killing Wallace was going to be watching his face as he slaughtered his friends first.

Finally the axe splintered the iron-bound wooden chest. It split apart at the top, the rusted metal clasp falling free. Stone pried it open and gently took out a rigid package. Sweating even in the cold damp air, he chipped away at the rock hard bundle. Bit by bit larger and larger pieces eventually fell away. As he worked the clouds dissipated and a watery moonlight bathed them.

When the top layer of pitch covered oilskin was peeled off, he pulled out the still remarkably soft doeskin. A piece of parchment dropped to the ground along with some leather thongs. He pulled the skin back, then the remnants of the purple cloak. He pulled the sword smoothly from its scabbard. It gleamed in the dark, light from Wyndham's torch glinting off its still bright burnished shaft.

Enraptured by the sword and ignoring Wyndham momentarily, Stone held the sword by its hilt, his fingers reverently stroking the shaft as he read the engraving, "Christus supremus omnis; Christ above all" he murmured.

"What!? Gods no! It is ours, not the Christ's"

Wyndham screeched, stepping forward to snatch Excalibur from Stone's hands.

It was more a reaction than a planned move, but Stone rocked back on his heels as Wyndham lunged toward him. As he did, Excalibur's great shaft suddenly swung upwards. Before anyone could move, Wyndham impaled himself on the sword.

Chad jumped and grabbed Wyndham's gun before he could fire.

They watched horrified as Excalibur slipped easily through flesh and bone until its shimmering point emerged from Wyndham's back. Blood seeped from his mouth, his eyes staring uncomprehending. Not a sound passed his lips as he sank to the ground. Stone scrambled to his feet, pulling the sword free as he did.

Wyndham's body lay still, a dark fluid staining the ground.

Chapter Twenty-Five

"My God!" Stone and Chad turned at the voice, seeing a stumbling Maddox holding the back of his head struggling to gain his footing. Stone stared at the body at his feet.

"Quiet," Chad whispered. Wyndham may have backup."

He listened carefully, eyes straining to see in the dark, pistol at the ready, but saw and heard nothing. Chad slid over to Stone and leaned down.

"He came out of the dark, silent as a bat, slugged Colin before either of us was aware of him, then had the gun at my head and pushed me over by the tree. Said he'd kill both of us then you if I tried to warn you. Sorry buddy. We were so concentrated on you in the cave, listening in case you called out. We dropped our guard."

Even in the blackness Stone could see a grin crinkling Chad's face. "But I sure didn't know you were a swordsman on top of everything else. Thanks for saving our lives."

"You may not believe this Chad, but as I held the sword I felt a warmth come over me. It was as if the sword were alive. I did nothing. It swung up and seemed to aim itself."

"Bull! It just swung up as you moved. Wyndham wasn't expecting that. He was just trying to grab it."

"Whatever, Chad. I know what I know." Stone said wearily

They grimly pulled themselves together. Maddox rubbed the back of his head but assured them he was still capable. He began climbing upwards as Stone reached down with a handkerchief, quickly cleaned Wyndham's blood off the blade and picked up the tiny parchment and remnants of the king's robe. The Druid's body would stay where it was until Maddox could make arrangements.

Chad led them up, stopping every minute or so to peer into the darkness ahead, wondering where Wyndham's men were. They struggled over the garden walls again and made their way slowly towards the pub. As they neared it they heard an uproar in the street. Chad beckoned them against a wall and peeked around the corner. A crowd was gathered by the church gate, milling about and shouting. More were pouring out of the pub as a police car pulled to a halt. Two men were pushed against the stone wall as the police arrived.

"Bloody hooligans. You can't smash your way through our village church and get away with it!"

As the crowd angrily shouted approval. Maddox grinned at his companions. "I think we found Wyndham's backup. They must have caused a ruckus at the church while he followed us down the hill. Though how they tracked us is beyond me."

Motioning them to stay put, Maddox slipped across the street and made his way to the Land Rover. He drove down past the pub as the police waved him by authoritatively. He stopping briefly while his partners jumped in, then sedately drove off.

Outside the village, they pulled over. Maddox called Sir Giles and reported their success. He listened, then handed the phone to Stone.

"Well done my boy. Excellent. So the old sword really does exist. Had my doubts. Considered it all hogwash dreamt up by those Druids." Quickly he outlined plans for Excalibur's return to London and placement in the Tower of London with the crown jewels."

"No!" Stone's rejection of the proposal was flat and uncompromising. "I need Excalibur to free Mandy. Unless I take it to Rhiannon, she will die."

"My dear boy, we'll raid Rhiannon's compound and get Mandy out. Sword's a national treasure. Must be treated as such."

The debate, heated at times, continued with Stone unyielding, rejecting all arguments. Excalibur was his ace, his sole bargaining tool. He'd seen it through this far and would see it through to the end; besides a raid would cause more bloodshed like France, he counter argued.

Finally, Sir Giles reluctantly, and less than graciously, agreed. Stone returned the phone to Maddox and arrangements were quickly made to collect Wyndham's body before morning.

They would continue to Carmarthen.

Llanmerddyn, Wales

Maddox stopped the car beside a small copse of trees overlooking the valley, well hidden from the eyes of anyone not travelling the same road. Early morning sun began to light the valley. The rain and cold had dissipated and a warm sunny day was forecast.

"Llanmerddyn"

Maddox pointed across the small valley through the trees and hedgerows where they could make out buildings on top of the hill opposite. A plume of white smoke hung in the still air amongst the trees close to the structures. Chad shuddered. "Reminds me of Brittany. Hope they haven't sacrificed another poor devil." As soon as the words were out of his mouth he blanched and swore.

"Oh, God, I'm sorry Stone. I didn't mean they'd do it to Mandy."

"Rhiannon hasn't got her hands on Excalibur yet. Nor does she know about Wyndham. Mandy's safe for the moment I think."

Maddox broke the awkward silence.

"This is your game, Stone. How do you want to proceed?"

Stone got out of the car and knelt carefully, staring at the compound; willing himself inside. As they surveyed it Maddox reviewed Rhiannon's security measures, arguing again that they should wait for reinforcements then raid the place.

Stone thought hard as the three contemplated their objective. He picked up a blade of grass unconsciously and twirled it incessantly, his brain a swirl of thoughts. During the drive towards Llanmerddyn, he'd prayed again. It was a new experience. Before, he'd considered it a formalized ritual of words to an unseen and unresponsive being. Rereading Thomas' journal however, showed him it was simply a conversation with a caring God who accepted the one praying, warts and all. Using Maddox' binoculars he studied the road as it disappeared into the trees. He saw a brief movement and realized it was a robed man patrolling the grounds.

"We can't get in past Rhiannon's security. That much we know. No sneaking up on them like you did in France, Chad. They must have heard about that raid by now. So, since we can't get in by the back door, we'll go in the front." He brushed dried leaves off his pant legs.

"Colin, could you get me Rhiannon's phone number?"

"You're crazy. You're not going to call her are you?"

"Why not? I need to get in and she will see me because I have something she wants. Badly."

Chad coughed. "Colin's right. She's not going to just let us waltz in. As soon as we get near, she'll have her people grab us and the sword…" his voice trailed off, shrugging the remainder of his sentence.

"No. Rhiannon is not Wyndham. She may be a zealot, but I don't think she's as vicious or power mad." He looked at the two men. "But, I'm open to any other suggestions than a raid! And time is wasting!"

Maddox and Chad looked at each other, then Stone. Maddox spoke first. "Give me a second. We have Charlie in there. I can get word to look out for us once we're in."

Stone and Chad waited patiently while Maddox made his calls. Leaning against the car roof he jotted down a number, tore off the sheet of paper and hung up. He handed the cell and the paper to Stone who carefully punched the numbers. A groggy voice answered and argued with Stone when he asked for Rhiannon. Stone cut him off abruptly.

"Give her one word. Excalibur. And my name, Stone Wallace. Then give her this number." He hung up.

They stood waiting. In less than two minutes the phone rang. Stone answered and spoke abruptly. "You know who I am. I have Excalibur in my hands. I will trade it for Myfanwy Griffiths. I know she's there. Damien Wyndham told me that himself." He listened briefly.

"I have no idea where he is now," Stone answered truthfully. "His whereabouts are no longer my concern. I want Miss Griffiths alive and well and your assurances we will be allowed to leave your grounds peacefully. Keep your people well back. We'll meet alone. Then Excalibur is yours."

A grim smile crept over his face. He said a curt goodbye and turned to Chad and Maddox. "I'm expected in half an hour. I want the pair of you to wait here for me," Stone said, eyes still focused on Rhiannon's lair. As they began to argue with him, Stone turned and looked directly at Maddox. "I know you've got orders from Sir Giles to stick to me and get Excalibur back to London no matter what happens to me or Mandy." The flush on Maddox' face said he'd hit home.

"Frankly, I don't care what happens to Excalibur. It has been protected all along, whether by God or man doesn't really matter. I'm sure it will be protected now. But I need to do this alone." He headed for the car. Maddox finally spoke.

"You don't know Charlie. I have to go with you."

"Colin, I have to do this alone. Charlie will know me. He's expecting me, isn't he?"

Maddox opened his mouth and made a move towards Stone but Chad grabbed him. "If Stone wants us to stay, we stay." he declared, easing his tight grip somewhat.

Maddox smiled. He'd seen Stone, amateur though he was, battle through tough circumstances. Druids and magical swords were not topics on the curriculum of intelligence and security departments. This was way beyond him. Finally he relaxed and smiled at them.

"You'll tell Sir Giles I protested most vociferously?"

"Oh yes, you were most insistent, but Chad and I overpowered you. Chad held you while I grabbed your keys and drove off," Stone smiled.

Fifteen minutes later Maddox and Chad watched as the Land Rover made its way slowly down the hill and across the valley floor before disappearing into Llanmerddyn's entrance.

Rhiannon's office, Llanmerddyn

"You are Stone Wallace." The question was stated more as fact than query.

Stone was surprised at how short Rhiannon was. From her picture he'd somehow expected a taller woman. Instead, she was tubby and barely over five feet. Not the domineering Dragon Master he'd expected. Her black hair with the shock of white, he remembered from the photo, but could see now it was also streaked with grey. She pulled her black robe tighter around her. As she did, he noticed the black dragon tattoo on both forearms.

She'd swept into the room with another woman behind her. That woman took station behind Rhiannon close to the door and off to Stone's left side.

"I said alone."

Rhiannon spoke to the woman in Welsh. She glided out of the room, closing the door quietly behind her. Try as she might, Rhiannon could not take her eyes off the sword Stone held, blade down, in front of him.

It gleamed as he leaned slightly on the hilt, allowing the weapon to hold him steady. He needed its rigidity. His insides were churning and without the sword to hold him, his legs would be shaking betraying his fear. Nothing he had done before—not interviews with presidents not sky jumping, not even being shot at in Iraq—compared with the ominous feelings flooding his mind and body. He was in the presence of evil. He felt it. It was real. Remembering Wyndham's reaction, Stone deliberately kept the inscribed side of the shaft facing him.

"Give me Excalibur."

"You get nothing until I see Mandy."

"Ah, Mandy is it? Well, well. She has a protector does she?"

Rhiannon smiled frostily and called to the woman outside. The door opened. Stone heard a gasp.

"Stone! I knew you'd come".

He looked over. The woman held Mandy by the arm, preventing her from moving close to Stone. The door closed leaving the three women and Stone. Rhiannon anticipated his thoughts.

"I have men, armed men, just outside the door. One shout, one word from me and they will come in. They will not be gentle."

"We had a deal. None of your people around."

Rhiannon shrugged. "Give me Excalibur and you will go free."

She glided forward to stand in front of him. He was surprised by the steely black-grey of her eyes, devoid of warmth and color. He looked deep into her eyes, and sensed an overwhelming blackness. He felt himself being drawn in, floating towards her. He blinked to break eye contact and gripped the hilt tighter.

"Let Mandy go and it's yours." He knew it was naïve. He had no backup plan other than a dogged conviction that somehow God was in this.

Rhiannon reached out her hand, eyes still focused on him trying to draw him in again. He refused, turning his eyes down on her hand moving stealthily towards the sword. He stepped back and nodded towards Mandy.

"Let her go."

Rhiannon hissed, pulling her hand back. She stood momentarily then walked over to Mandy, seized her by the arm and pulled her towards Stone.

"Take the little slut then" she snarled shoving her brutally and suddenly towards him.

He reacted to catch her, loosening his grip on Excalibur. Screeching in triumph, Rhiannon snatched at it. As Mandy hit him the sword was yanked from his grasp. Stone stumbled with Mandy falling on top of him.

"Kill them!"

Rhiannon spun on her heels and ran to the opposite wall.

As Stone and Mandy struggled to their feet they saw her disappear through an unseen door that had suddenly opened in the wall and closed just as swiftly behind her. All the while Rhiannon's assistant stood silent. As the drama played out before her, she merely walked quietly to the main door and locked it. Stone looked around frantically for some kind of weapon he could use to protect them.

"Mr. Wallace, I'm Charlotte Thackery. You probably know me better as Charlie."

She laughed softly as he blinked in confusion. Before he could say anything, Mandy spoke up. "You're Charlie? You left the note when you brought the food!" Charlie nodded and reached down to help them up. "No chit chat. We've got to go after her."

They ran to where Rhiannon had disappeared. Charlie began feeling around on the bookshelf.

"I've only seen her use this door once, and that was by accident. She touched something up there, said something and the door opened." As she fumbled around, pulling books and rubbing their spines, Stone and Mandy joined her.

"I saw her touch this thing."

Stone pointed at an ugly miniature statue. He grabbed it and found it firmly fixed to the shelf. He pushed and pulled unable to budge it.

"That's a statue of Lleu, their god."

"She said something before it opened" Mandy reminded them.

Charlie stood in front of the effigy and repeated its name. Nothing happened. She repeated a number of Druidic chants and words but still the door refused to budge. Frustrated she thumped the wall.

Stone thought for a moment, and said "Open." Nothing happened. He leaned on the wall trying to physically force it open. "Quick," he said impulsively. "What's the Welsh word for open?"

"Agor" Charlie blurted.

Before Stone could repeat the word, the door slid smoothly open. They found themselves at the top of a curving set of stairs. Without waiting, Stone launched himself down with Mandy and Charlie in close pursuit.

At the bottom a line of lights outlined a tunnel. He charged along until he skidded to a halt, amazed at the sight before him. Mandy was so close behind she bumped into him as she too stopped awed at the cave stretching out before them.

"The Crystal Cave," Mandy breathed reverently.

"I always thought it was a legend. But it's real. The Crystal Cave exists. None of us in the compound knew about this," Charlie whispered.

Light bounced off crystals and quartz that lined the cavern's walls and roof. Sparkling stalactites poked down towards the ground. A multitude of colors splashed down, all the hues of the rainbow glinting and sparkling from unseen light sources. The cave's awesome beauty took their breath away.

Stone led as they edged gingerly out of the tunnel and into the open expanse. Where is she, he wondered. She's got to be here somewhere unless there's an exit. He quietly moved into the middle of the cave searching in all directions, when he heard a slight murmuring. Signing the others to be quiet, he stopped and listened intently. There it was again. A murmured chant, soft and wailing somewhere off to the right. Careful not to breathe too deeply, they slowly and softly moved towards the noise.

Above them, the cavern began to close in again as they neared the far end. The sound was louder, coming from a cleft in the side of the cavern wall. He looked at the split in the rocks feeling they could just make it through one at a time. His jaw dropped when he reached the end of the short crevice. An even larger crystal-filled cave opened before him. Against the far wall he saw Rhiannon's black outline, kneeling and facing a darkened corner of the cave. She held Excalibur above her head in both hands. Rhiannon was chanting quietly so absorbed in the chant he was sure she didn't realize they'd figured out the door and followed her. Mandy and Charlie silently pushed in behind him awestruck at the sight.

As he got closer, his shoe suddenly kicked a small pebble. The sound ricocheted around the walls. Rhiannon jumped up and spun in place. He face flashed with anger as she saw the intruders.

She waved Excalibur at them and shrieked. "Charlotte you have betrayed me, Lleu take your soul!" Rhiannon advanced toward them. "Nobody knows about this sanctuary. All of you must die."

Stone stopped in his track, the women bunched beside him.

"It's over, Rhiannon, Look at Excalibur's inscription. Wyndham is dead because of it. You are finished because of it. Your movement is destroyed. Give yourself up now."

Shocked, Rhiannon pulled the sword close to her, trying to read the engraved words. Stone stepped forward once again.

"It's Latin, Rhiannon. It says 'Christus Supremus Omnis'. That means Christ above all, Rhiannon. He has won. You have lost." He took another step forward.

Fury distorted her features. She shrieked curses upon all of them, calling upon her gods to destroy them where they stood. Other than the shrieks and cries reverberating around the cavern there was no other sound.

"Christ above all! That's what it says, Rhiannon!" Stone shouted above her curses. "He is supreme. Your old gods are finished. He has triumphed." He stepped closer hoping to grab Excalibur. As he did so, she began to back up still waving Excalibur.

"The Master created Excalibur. It is his sword. He who made it can undo the power your Christ has put over it," she barked, a cold intensity overtaking her. "Take no more steps towards me."

Stone estimated there were still ten yards before he'd even be close enough to grab her arm and the sword's hilt. "That sword was given to Arthur, Rhiannon. He dedicated it to Jesus Christ. That's what the inscription means. Your Master has no power over the sword anymore. It doesn't belong to him. Or you."

As he spoke light began to gleam off the sword's shaft. Whether it was light glinting off the crystal or something else, he could not say later. All he knew was that the sword began to shimmer with an iridescent golden hue. Rhiannon glanced up at the sword and spun suddenly. She sprang towards the dark corner of the cavern.

"Master Merddyn I bring Excalibur back to you" she screamed, "Imbue it with your power! Erase the Christ from this world." As she screeched, she flung Excalibur down onto what a shocked Stone now saw was a mummified corpse.

The golden glittering sword crashed and sparked on the crystals as it fell on the corpse. Suddenly, a rumbling noise began hammering through the cavern like a runaway train rushing through a station.

Stone began to back up as a piece of glittering rock dropped at his feet. He looked up and saw small fissures opening along the wall behind the Rhiannon who was now kneeling and wailing at the mummy's feet.

"Back up," he yelled at the two women behind him as they all began to scramble for the crack they'd come through. He glanced back at the moaning figure of Rhiannon. More rocks and crystal stalactites were dropping now.

He got to the gap where the women had slipped through. He turned to Rhiannon and shouted again.

"Rhiannon. You need to get out now!"

The last he saw Rhiannon she lay across the mummy weeping and wailing. Excalibur on the ground still gleaming beside her, lay too far for him to reach.

The flight through the smaller cave and tunnel and up the stairs was something Stone talked about very little in the days afterwards. All he really remembered was that appalling sight of the woman clutching the mummified corpse.

Charlie led them out of Rhiannon's office cautiously. The guards had disappeared. The buildings themselves were shaking and as they made their way along some back passages to a nearby exit they heard shouting as Rhiannon's followers fled what they thought was an earthquake.

Safe in a wooded area, Charlie stopped momentarily, took out a cell phone, made a quick call then led them down the hillside, towards the road. Minutes later Maddox and Chad pulled up. In the distance they could hear the mee-maw of police and emergency vehicles arriving from nearby Llandeilo. Stone and Mandy flopped to the ground shocked and exhausted by their nightmare experience.

As Charlie spoke to Maddox, Chad merely looked down at them.

"Good to have you back with us."

Epilogue

Stone stood alone at the edge of the small ornamental pond that graced the carefully manicured grounds of The Grange. It was five days since Llanmerddyn. Five days of warm reunion with Huw and Mandy. It was good to see her easy grin return and listen to her infectious giggle.

Politics disappeared off the front pages as journalists scampered to report a rare 4.5 earthquake in South Wales. Reporters breathlessly chased stories that the Druid compound Llanmerddyn was destroyed in the quake with only one known casualty, the leader Rhiannon whose body had not yet been recovered.

One of the more curious journalists chased down stories that the billionaire Sir Damien Wyndham, had also suddenly disappeared, reminding viewers that Rhiannon and the businessman were close confederates. After one airing, that report disappeared.

Much of the time Stone was involved in debriefing sessions, first with Sir Giles and Crown Security Branch, then later with Security Intelligence Directorate personnel. Calvin Tyler himself flew over from Washington to participate.

Sir Giles and Tyler considered themselves content that the Druid conspiracy had been smashed, though the Brit was still quietly miffed about Excalibur. At their first session, Tyler confirmed that with less than a week to the election, Murphy had withdrawn suddenly from the presidential race to deal with unspecified 'personal' issues requiring complete removal from public life.

"The President and the Director of the CIA confronted him with our evidence that he and his followers consorted with a foreign power and plotted to corrupt our system of government. We had him on everything right up to treason."

But, much as the British government kept a lid on the plot, the President had also demanded total silence. At a secret White House gathering of Congressional leaders whose loyalty could be counted on, the President had outlined the plot and its aftermath, persuading them that national unity was paramount. He called for support for Robert Greenaway, Murphy's opponent. Murphy's own Vice Presidential nominee was allowed to stay in the race even though he was known to be a minor cog in the conspiracy wheel. Murphy himself was moved to a carefully chosen safe house for further interrogation.

Tyler also told a relieved Stone that his name had been cleared. A brief release from the President's office noted that the search Stone for was a red herring while he was moved to safety.

"Networks and newspapers are lining up offering you work, though you cannot report the biggest story of your life," Tyler smiled apologetically. "You're a good man, Wallace. Smart, creative, determined, aggressive. We could use someone like you in the agency. Think about it."

The Queen continued her strenuous regimen of state duties and no word of the near disaster slipped out, though Her Majesty did recognize their heroism, Sir Giles told Stone and Chad. "She would like to meet you privately and express her great appreciation in the near future."

When the questioning was done and the briefings finished each day, Stone enjoyed spending time with Huw and Mandy.

"Disappointed I am that I never saw the sword, boy," Huw said ruefully one evening, his only comment on the fact that Excalibur had disappeared in the collapsing cave.

The five days also gave Stone time for reflection. He woke up several times the first two nights shaking with nightmares; the sword penetrating bodies all around him in the shadows of his mind. He shared his dreams with no one except God. By the third night, a peace descended on his sleep and he passed the night deep in slumber.

But he could not forget the great sword. From Huw's initial call right through to the reality, Excalibur had consumed him for the past weeks. It was probably only his imagination he knew, but it was uncanny that the weapon forged to destroy the new faith turned out to be the very thing that destroyed the old. He could not get out of his mind the warmth of the hilt when Wyndham lunged at him. Nor could he forget the sight of the gleaming sword almost throbbing on the ground as the cave disintegrated.

His musings were suddenly interrupted as he felt a presence beside him. He looked up and saw a smiling Mandy. She linked her arm in his.

"The doctors say that Da is a sturdy old specimen so we'll be going home tomorrow. There'll be a few scars yet, but he's mending. He's already planning a trip to Istanbul in a couple of months to study some new documents they've found. He'll be in his element."

He looked at her warm embracing grin, her large blue eyes sparkling with light and life, a book clutched in her hand. Each night those eyes and that smile had helped him forget the terrors of the past few weeks. He knew he was hopeless in the romantic field. Maybe this time it would be different.

"Mandy," he said, "we've got to talk."

"I know what you're going to say" she said softly, "but I'm not sure it would work." Before he could protest, she put her finger to his lips.

"Stone, I know how I feel for you right now and I know it wouldn't take much more for me to fall completely and utterly in love with you.

"But you have your career in broadcasting and writing in America. I have a career over here, teaching and researching." Hurriedly, she explained that the University of Wales had offered her a tenured position. "It's a great opportunity," she ended lamely.

"Who says we both have to continue our careers as they are laid out now," he countered. "I can write just as easily here as there. Or your teaching could be just as dynamic in an American university. Lots of schools would love to have someone like you on their faculty."

They began walking back to the main building. As they walked, she laid her head on his shoulder, their arms encircling each other.

"Stone, I just don't know. I have argued myself silly these past few days, knowing how I feel and yet knowing both of us have careers on opposite sides of an ocean. I just don't know." She faced him and kissed him softly.

Stone thought for a moment then grinned mischievously at her. "Well, maybe we could do what Thomas and Owain did. Pray!"

"Yes," Mandy grinned, "We can certainly do that."

Stone gently held her around the waist, pulled her to him and kissed her again.

From a second floor window, Huw looked down on the sight.

"Well, well," was all he said.

THE END

About The Author

Barrie Doyle is an award-winning storyteller. For much of his writing career, he has told stories as a journalist and public relations professional. He has taught PR at a major Canadian college and also trained corporate and non-profit leaders in how to utilize media to tell their own stories. His awards reflect his success in helping real people tell real stories.

Storytelling, whether fiction or non-fiction, is a reflection of the human condition in all its glory and depravity. Barrie has covered the triumphant moon landings and also told heart-wrenching stories of returned POWs who were tortured at the infamous Hanoi Hilton in Vietnam. He's also covered everything from tragic plane crashes to Royal visits.

As a PR consultant, his clients have ranged from General Motors to Kids Help Phone, from The Christian and Missionary Alliance in Canada to Huronia Cruise Lines. He has also founded successful magazines and taught writing at various conferences and workshops, including the famous Billy Graham Schools of Writing in both Canada and the United States.

Taking real-world experiences and people and putting them into different situations is part of the excitement and challenge for him in writing fiction.

Although he was born in Wales, Barrie has lived in various parts of the United States, including Washington D.C., where he was assistant news editor of Christianity Today. He now lives in Canada on the beautiful blue water shores of Georgian Bay just north of Toronto. An avid traveller, he brings his travel experience to his novels, providing exotic and sometimes unfamiliar locales.

He is married and has two daughters, two sons, and two wonderful grandsons.

Will the Druids recover from the loss of Excalibur? Will they continue their quest to force a return to the old gods? Here's a sneak preview of *The Lucifer Scroll*, Book Two of *The Oak Grove Conspiracies*.

Prologue
The shores of the Dead Sea, AD 34

It was the same every night. He dreaded the visitations. He wrapped his arms around his still-muscular knees, squatting in the dirt and rocking back and forth in his rocky cave high above the Salt Sea.

Marcus Lucinius Janus, former Centurion of the Tenth Fretensis Legion, howled his frustration. His ragged tunic was ripped and covered in filth—his own as well as that of the animals that'd inhabited the cave before him. Cominius Centra Bestia, his Optio, stood at the cave entrance, his shining helmet and armor contrasting with Janus' misery and filth.

"It begins again this night." Bestia's words were as much a comment as a question.

Janus mutely nodded. "I cannot fight any longer. This is my punishment for executing the Nazarene."

Spittle dripped down Janus' grizzled face, which had not seen a blade for days. The standards of cleanliness for Legionnaires didn't apply now, not since he'd left the garrison fourteen nights ago, renouncing his legion post and surviving as a beggar on his lonely trek from Jerusalem to the Salt Sea. He confided only in his Optio, his second-in-command Cominius, one of his few friends in the legion. Cominius didn't judge, but only nodded when Janus told him of the misery of the night demons.

When he could take it no longer, after months of fighting the visitations, Janus told Cominius of his plan to disappear from Jerusalem in the hopes that removing himself from the site where he had commanded the crucifixion of the Nazarene would stay the hauntings.

"You will be hunted down as a deserter and executed, Marcus," Cominius calmly told him when he heard the desperate plan.

"Better that than these horrible dreams."

"You obeyed Pilate's orders. You prevented revolt in the city."

"I did. And I have had the night demons each night since. They get stronger and more terrible until my mind feels like it must explode." Janus grabbed his tunic and ripped it open, exposing his scarred and bloody chest, the scrapes and scratches of his nails covering deeper, fresher scars.

It had been Cominius' plan to run to the Salt Sea. It was Cominius who had arranged for this lonely, hidden animal lair. Janus looked at his Optio standing coolly at the dusty cave entrance, his scarlet cape swirling in the hot winds that scoured the hillside.

"I cannot escape, not even when I try to kill myself," Janus said. "Look!"

Tears coursed down his face as he drew his short sword and dug it deeply across his body. Blood spurted out, staining his tunic yet again and dripping into the dirt at his feet.

He screamed towards the cave entrance. "Each night I slice my wrists, open my chest, or pierce my gut with my sword. And each day I wake up, scarred but healed. The Nazarene was a magician. He must be the one who heals me each night. They said he was a healer. It must be him. I cannot live in the city. I cannot carry out my duties. I am a madman driven from all I have known."

Janus dropped to his knees, tears and blood mixing and flowing to the ground.

"No relief. No relief, Cominius," he wept.

Unmoved, Cominius watched his senior officer. "There is relief, Marcus. Do as the night demons command." His voice seemed to deepen and change in the gloomy cave.

Janus turned and looked at his Optio. The face was the same, but there was a darkness about Cominius, a darkness that had little to do with the falling light and deepening shadows. The deeper, blacker darkness oozed out of Cominius' inner being.

"I have the materials. I have the tools. Do as the voices say, Marcus. Write the letter."

The man who had been Cominius stepped forward and pointed to Janus' mutilated body. As he did, the blood pouring out of the deep wound across Janus' chest stopped flowing. The sliced flesh began to scar before his eyes.

Janus fell on his back, staring at the soldier before him.

"Who are you?" Janus croaked. "You are not Cominius."

"What does it matter who I am? Do as the voice commands. Write the words you hear in your head. Write it in this scroll." The velvety voice seemed to come from depths beyond the human body.

The being inhabiting Cominius' body stepped forward, put a hand under Janus' elbow, and pulled him erect.

"Obey the voice, Janus. The torment will be over soon."